A chill darted through Blythe.
***Detective* Ryker Delaney.**

Had something bad happened, after all? She nixed that thought. Her husband's disappearance had to do with him screwing another woman, which unfortunately was not a crime.

So what was Delaney doing here?

Bristling, Blythe moved from behind her desk and folded her arms across her chest. If something was amiss, the department should have sent someone else.

Anyone but *him.*

Ryker Delaney was one man she'd hoped she would never encounter again. Reining in her runaway emotions, she asked, "So what brings you here today, Detective?"

He didn't mince words. "I'm afraid I have some bad news."

"What now?"

Though she appeared outwardly calm, Blythe's heart pounded wildly.

Ryker didn't flinch. "Your husband is dead."

"Mary Lynn Baxter has helped define the romance market."
—Affaire de Coeur

Also available from MIRA Books and
MARY LYNN BAXTER

A DAY IN APRIL
LONE STAR HEAT
AUTUMN AWAKENING

Watch for the newest blockbuster from
MARY LYNN BAXTER
August 1999

MARY LYNN BAXTER

HARD CANDY

ISBN 1-55166-440-2

HARD CANDY

Printed in U.S.A.

HARD CANDY

Prologue

An infinity of multicolored lights sparkled across the dark waters of the lake, creating a carnival effect on the teakwood deck of the cabin cruiser. Two men faced each other, unimpressed with the sight. One had seen it too often; the other was too angry to notice.

"I know what you're doing." The voice was low-pitched, the tone that of someone who preferred good bourbon to moderation. "Deny it all you want to, but I know better."

The other listened, then started to laugh, a cruel laugh with no pleasure in it. "Is that so? I suggest you wake up and smell the coffee. Even if I did have something going, what makes you think I'd give you a piece of the action?"

"The way I see it, you don't have any choice." The voice was crisp now, as the moonlight bled into the strands of the speaker's hair, lightening the dark color. "If the right people knew about you—and *you* know who I'm talking about—you'd be in deep shit."

Nothing in the other's face changed except the brown eyes; they narrowed and iced over. "And now you're threatening me, right?"

"I don't have to. I saw you two in Vegas—twice!" A pause hovered in the air just as the boat lurched in the wake of a small fishing craft. "Scotland Yard and all the cops in Europe want to talk to your partner about jewelry. Stolen jewelry.'' The voice rose. ''Hell, everybody knows he's a jewel thief.''

The brown eyes didn't waver. ''Listen carefully, you misguided asshole.'' The fury in the voice bit like acid into the humid breeze. ''You'd best forget what you saw in Vegas and keep your mouth shut, or you'll wish you had. I can bring you a lot more grief than you can bring me. So get the hell off my boat and stay away from me.''

Confident his point had been made, the figure spun, intending to go below.

''Oh, no, you don't.'' An arm jerked him back around. ''You don't scare me. You've got too much at stake now. You aren't willing to give up your floating cathouse, I know. So cut the crap and tell me what the two of you pulled off and where you've stashed the stuff!''

He bent his head and stared at the fingers around his arm. ''For starters, get your goddamn hand off me. And I won't tell you again. Get lost or get hurt.''

His companion released his hold, but the voice was strained, as though his throat were closing. ''We'll see who gets hurt.''

Blood flooded the other man's face. ''If you try anything, I'll put you in the emergency room. But you probably don't believe me, so I'll have to prove it.''

Their faces were so close, their breath mingled.

''Go ahead.'' Brown eyes flashed as the challenge was issued. ''Take your best shot!''

The blow to the side of his head packed a wallop. Air came out in a hoarse grunt as his feet slid out from under him. He landed hard on his back, but not before his head banged against the polished railing.

Suddenly the only sound was the soft lapping of wavelets against the expensive hull.

His companion knelt on one knee and eyed the figure sprawled full length on the deck. "Dammit, I told you, you didn't scare me."

His hand nudged the lifeless shoulder. Nothing. The body lay still. He turned the cumbersome frame ever so slightly. Blood, lots of it, pooled under his neck.

"Jesus!" Now panic further roughened the voice. He shook the man. No response, not even so much as a moan.

With stiff fingers he sought the pulse at the base of the other man's neck. "Don't you dare die on me, you bastard!" He latched his hands onto the front of the man's shirt, giving him a savage shake. "Don't you dare!"

One

Blythe Lambert walked to the window, where she was instantly drenched in the early morning sunlight. A flower garden filled with breathtaking pansies met her gaze. Their colorful, smiling faces should have commanded a return smile. They didn't.

While Blythe appreciated the beauty of the spring morning, she had no smile to spare. Instead, a deep frown marred her features.

Her husband hadn't been home in three days.

She had arrived at the office long before the growing city of Tyler awakened. The peace and quiet did little to revive her dejected spirits.

She wouldn't let him get away with this disappearing act, she vowed. Not this time. But first, she had to find him, and that wouldn't be easy.

Suddenly Blythe felt drained, but more than that, she felt angry. This time Mark's extracurricular activities were playing havoc with their business, their livelihood. She could no longer tolerate his behavior. Her patience had run out.

She turned and stared at the stack of design specifications on her desk. Her mind should be on those projects, because spring was the peak and busiest time of the year for Designs.

Designs by Lambert, the largest landscaping company

in the city, was her mainstay. And Mark's, she should add, but since he hadn't spent much time on the job lately, it was becoming increasingly difficult to credit him.

Tyler, known for its rose- and azalea-lined neighborhoods, was a landscaper's paradise, especially with all the new homes and businesses springing up. She would love to get those jobs. Her ideas for creating beauty out of the ground were free-flowing, all-consuming and never-ending.

But not this morning. Mark had managed to stifle her creativity, leaving her feeling empty and helpless, a feeling she detested.

Even the tranquil beauty of her office failed to soothe her dejected spirits. And a lovely office it was, too, with its melon-colored carpet, antique furniture and walls covered with photographs of the gardens and yards of satisfied customers.

Something akin to pride suddenly pricked Blythe's heavy heart. That pride was the main reason she was not about to let Mark undermine her work, which meant she had to get her act together, yank herself out of the doldrums and get busy.

First, though, she had to plan her strategy. When she came face-to-face with her husband, her emotional guns had to be loaded.

Perhaps another cup of coffee would jump-start her battery, Blythe told herself, entering the small anteroom where she kept her file cabinets, the sketching table with the tools of her trade and the coveted coffeemaker.

She had finished half a cup when she heard movement in the outer office. Craning her neck, she saw her assistant and friend, Curt Manning.

Shortly, he stepped up to the threshold and grinned. "Morning." His voice was low but upbeat.

Blythe reached for the glasses inside the pocket of her silk skirt and slipped them across the bridge of her nose. "I had to make sure I wasn't seeing things. I can't believe you beat Susan."

Susan, her secretary, was always the early bird, the only one to spend more hours at the office than Blythe.

"Cut me some slack, okay? The traffic seems to get worse by the day." Curt gave her a sheepish grin.

Blythe merely shook her head, then said, "Want some coffee?"

"Thought you'd never ask."

She poured him a cup and put it on the counter.

Curt picked at the tightly knotted tie around his neck before reaching for the mug and raising it to his lips.

Blythe watched him with a smile. He wasn't handsome. He was tall and thin, almost gaunt. Even though he was only in his late twenties, his receding hairline made him look older. Yet there was something about him that made one take a second look. She'd decided long ago it was his eyes. They were so gentle, so kind and so patient.

He had applied at Designs shortly after Blythe married Mark. He'd wanted the job as much for the opportunity to learn exterior design from Blythe as for the salary.

Blythe knew that Designs had worked its spell on Curt, too. It was the main interest in his life as surely as it was the *only* interest in hers. Not only was Curt an excellent assistant, but a deep respect and rapport had developed between them. She'd come to depend on him and his expertise as she once had Mark's.

Though Blythe's personality tended to be outgoing and vivacious, there was still a certain part of herself she kept isolated, which made it difficult to develop that extra degree of closeness that turns an acquaintance into a friend. With that in mind, she'd worked doubly hard to make her relationship with Curt smooth and amicable.

Because of that relationship, Curt was quick to pick up on Blythe's mood, which this morning was a subdued one.

"You seem preoccupied," he said, regarding her with his kind eyes.

"I am." In spite of her effort to control it, Blythe's voice was flat.

"More problems?"

"Yes, I'm sorry to say."

"It's Mark, isn't it?" Curt's voice reflected his disapproval.

Blythe tensed. "Yes."

"Still no word?"

"Nothing. No phone call, no message, no nothing. And I could cheerfully wring his neck."

Curt once again tinkered with his tie, while watching her closely.

Blythe knew what he was thinking. In fact, she was certain she could translate Curt's thoughts verbatim: why do you continue to put up with that unfaithful SOB?

Oftentimes, like *now,* she asked herself that same question. But she knew. She owed Mark a debt of gratitude for giving her a chance to rise above her past and make something of herself. Because of that debt, she was trapped in a loveless marriage.

"Is there anything I can do?" Curt asked, tapping into the silence.

Blythe shook her head. "Not a thing, but thanks all the same. This is something I have to work out on my own." She forced a smile. "Anyway, I was always under the impression that when a woman reached thirty, she should be able to handle her own problems."

Weak though it was, her attempt at humor did manage to ease the tension around her mouth.

Curt snorted. "Age has nothing to do with it, as you well know. We all have our moments. Besides, who says thirty's old?" He surveyed her with admiration. "You could pass for twenty any day."

And she could. Yet people's first impression of Blythe Lambert was not of youth but of elegance. With her glasses on, she looked as though she belonged on the cover of *Forbes* magazine, depicting the perfect executive. With them off, she looked like she belonged on the cover of *Cosmopolitan,* exemplifying the perfect model.

Blythe was blessed with the right stuff, starting with a mass of light brown hair that in the sun looked like spun gold. Her eyes were a deep brown and seemed filled with secrets. Though her figure was lean and willowy, there was a sensual voluptuousness about her that she continually downplayed.

She was brilliant, discerning and had a knack for getting things done efficiently and economically. Curt was one in a long line of many who admired and respected her. However, he never forgot Blythe was his boss and was careful not to push too hard.

"Flattery will get you anything," Blythe said, forcing another smile. "But while I might look twenty, I sure don't feel it. But, as we both know, I'm a survivor."

Without giving him a chance to respond, she turned and walked back into her office. Curt had no alternative but to follow.

"I still worry about you, though," he grumbled, jutting his chin.

Blythe sat behind her desk and reached for the Farmer

folder. "I'll be fine, especially when we get Mr. Farmer's name on the dotted line."

Curt pressed his lips together. "If Mark doesn't show, the deal with Farmer could be in jeopardy, right?"

Blythe drew in a breath. "It could nix it."

"You can't let that happen," Curt stressed, hooking his left leg over the corner of Blythe's desk and sitting down.

"Don't worry." Blythe's teeth touched her lower lip. "I don't intend to."

Not only was real estate magnate Cecil Farmer building a new office complex, he was building a two-million-dollar home on several acres outside the city.

Designs was in the running for both projects.

"But do you really think we have a chance of getting the contracts," Curt asked, "even if everything does fall into place?" His forehead bunched. "You must know that two big out-of-town companies are also at the top of the list."

"So? I'm still confident Designs will win the bidding war. I'm convinced we really know what's best for him."

Curt grinned. "I certainly like your style. All you have to do is convince old man Farmer."

Blythe picked up a pen and began toying with it. "I'm certain I have, even if he does want to take one more look at the plans. He just wants the extra attention. If you'll remember, the presentation I gave him was as detailed as I've ever done. And believe me, he scrutinized everything I did."

Blythe hadn't minded; in fact, she'd enjoyed the extra work, had seen it as a challenge. To obtain the degree of success she coveted, she had to add a personal touch;

in fact, most clients demanded it. Cecil Farmer was just one of many.

Curt's eyes twinkled. "I can just see him now, poking his face into that sketch, his breath actually blowing the paper."

Blythe laughed. "It was something to see." She turned serious. "I think his son wants to expand the business—Dallas, Houston, no telling where else."

"No shit?"

"No shit."

"Talk about a gravy train." Curt bounced off the desk. "I can just see your 'touch' all over Texas."

"I wouldn't get too carried away, if I were you. Not yet, anyway."

"Oh, well, it doesn't cost anything to dream."

"While you're dreaming, you might as well include the nursing home deal."

Curt straightened. "Yeah, right. How did that meeting go?"

"Good."

"That could be another feather in our cap."

"A huge feather." Blythe's eyes brimmed with excitement. "But first things first."

"Pleasing Mr. Farmer," Curt said, his mouth turned downward.

"That's why I don't want to take any unnecessary chances. If he wants Mark there, then Mark should be there. It's as simple as that."

"But you resent that, don't you?"

Blythe swiveled in her chair. "Does it show?"

Curt nodded. "Only because I know you better than most."

"Well, I'm not used to dealing with, quote, 'a male chauvinist.' But Cecil Farmer *is* the one in charge...."

Blythe gave an apologetic shrug when Curt's eyebrows shot up.

"He's done this before, has he? Disappeared, I mean," Curt asked, switching the conversation back to Mark. Before Blythe could answer, however, he averted his gaze, as if realizing he might have overstepped the boundaries.

Blythe saw the embarrassed flush creep into her assistant's face and gave a half smile. "It's okay. Maybe...maybe it would do me good to talk." She paused, lifting a hand to her forehead. "In answer to your question, yes, Mark's disappeared before. But he's never stayed away this long at one time."

Curt suddenly didn't seem to know what to say. "I'm...sorry."

"Don't be sorry," Blythe said, a hint of rebellion in her tone. "It's not Mark's absence that has me upset—it's the fact that he's endangering a major deal, the biggest to come along to date." Her mouth flattened into a bitter line. "You see, Mark lost interest in the ties that bind long ago. But so far, he's been a little more discreet with his affairs."

Curt let out his breath in an audible sigh. "At one time I thought you and Mark were the perfect couple."

"You and everyone else," Blythe said. "However, nothing could be further from the truth. Although, unlike Mark, I haven't been able to admit our marriage is a farce."

No longer, she thought. There were no more illusions to be shattered. Though she hated to fail at anything, much less admit that failure, she had finally come to terms with her status in life.

She was married. Yet she had no husband. She had no home life. She was on her own. But she hadn't come through it unscarred; there was an emptiness in her that nothing ever seemed to fill. Yet she hid that flaw like a secret, appalling illness.

Today, however, that gaping hole inside seemed to have widened, bringing with it an onslaught of despondency. Would there always be a part of her that remained arid? For all her success, she had been unsuccessful in filling that void.

"You deserve better, you know," Curt said, inclining his head forward.

"Unfortunately for me, there's no way out. Designs has Mark and me irrevocably linked."

"That's a goddamn shame."

Blythe smiled, and this time it was genuine. "I know that, too, but who said life was fair? But don't think I'm unappreciative of your support, because I'm not." She paused. "Meanwhile, life goes on, and I have a phone call to make."

Curt strode toward the door. "I'm hoping to put the finishing touches on the sketches for the Temple home. But until Suz gets here, I'll play receptionist, hold all incoming calls."

"All but Mark's."

"That goes without saying," Curt flung over his shoulder before closing the door behind him.

Blythe snatched up the phone, then stopped. Maybe it wasn't a good idea to call Cynthia, Mark's mother. Until now, she had refrained from even thinking about such a call. The head of the Lambert household had recently been diagnosed as having a weak heart. Since then, it seemed the entire family had been on edge so as not to do anything that would upset her.

Now, Blythe reasoned, she had no choice. Her mother-in-law might be able to help her locate Mark.

Hesitating no longer, Blythe punched out the number. On the third ring, Cynthia herself answered the phone.

"Why, hello, Blythe."

Her mother-in-law's tone was as cool as her appearance. Still, Blythe had a good rapport with her.

"I'm sorry to bother you, but—"

Cynthia cut her off. "Don't worry about it. What's wrong? You sound...oh, I don't know...tense."

"I'm tired, that's all," Blythe lied.

"You and Mark both work too hard." Cynthia's tone was mildly chastising.

Blythe rubbed the bridge of her nose. "Speaking of Mark, have you by any chance talked to him...today?" She held her breath and waited.

"No, no, I haven't. Actually, I haven't spoken to that son of mine in several days."

"I need to talk to him in connection with the deal we're working on," Blythe explained lamely.

"Sorry I can't be more help. Of course, if he calls or comes by, I'll give him your message."

"Thanks, Cynthia." Blythe tried to keep her dejection from showing. "Take care of yourself."

"You, too."

Once the connection was severed, Blythe began punching out the number of Mark's twin, Eleanor Brodrick, who was Designs' vice president and her sworn enemy. Midway, she halted. She wouldn't involve his sister or her husband. To do so would only add more trouble.

Following an audible sigh, Blythe leaned back in her chair and watched the sunlight shine on the carpet in a brilliant slant. But her mind was far away from the sights and sounds of the outside world. Her thoughts were on Mark.

Where the hell was he?

Two

Clouds were beginning to drift in from the west as Blythe steered her black Lexus into the parking lot at the Lake Tyler Yacht Basin. Although the air-conditioning was blasting, she was sticky and longed for a soothing bath. Even spring in the South could be a real bitch. She killed the engine but remained behind the wheel. Tension knotted her neck muscles, but it wasn't the weather that made her uncomfortable. It was the thought of confronting her husband. She had put off coming to Mark's hideaway for as long as she could. When she had left the office a short time ago, she'd had one thing on her mind, one thing only.

That hadn't changed. She was geared for battle. If Mark was on board the boat, he *would* be at the meeting tomorrow with Farmer.

Finally she got out of her car. The late March winds whipped around her, tossing her hair in every direction. She ignored both the humidity and the wind as she made her way to the boat slip that housed Mark's pride, the *Blythe II.*

After she mastered the length of the pier, she stepped onto the front deck. Only silence greeted her. She paused and looked around, searching for any signs of life. There were none, at least, not topside.

''Great,'' she muttered.

A flock of birds answered her, squawking, flapping through the air like small kites.

Blythe headed for the narrow passage that led to the cabin below. Once there, she slowly descended, ignoring the sinking feeling in the pit of her stomach. Would the sleeping quarters be as empty as the rest of the boat? Or would she find Mark in bed with his latest conquest?

Blythe hesitated at the door and stood like a fixture in the sultry stillness. The door wasn't closed all the way, and sunlight poured through the crack, spilling onto the stairs behind her. Still she hesitated.

It was the dread of being confronted with the second alternative that had kept her away from the boat these last three days. She hadn't wanted to walk in on him and another woman madly screwing, screwing on a boat named for her during happier days.

Reasons, Blythe thought. There were always so many reasons. Understanding what made a man unfaithful was impossible. There were too many variables.

The dryness in her mouth made it difficult to swallow. Her tongue felt swollen. Reason and anger warred inside her; she shook reason aside and pushed open the door.

"Mark?"

No response.

"Mark?" she said again, peeping inside. But the emptiness tossed her voice back at her. Then, as if her eyes had a will of their own, they drifted toward the bed and lingered.

Blythe's lips softened into a whimsical smile. Shortly after they were married, Mark had scooped her up in his arms and tossed her playfully onto that very bed. Full of himself, he'd pounced on top of her and pinned her arms above her head.

"Woman, let's christen the *Blythe II*," he'd said, the

light in his eyes as exciting as the hardness pressed against her stomach.

She had dug her fingernails into his back and whispered, "I can't imagine what we're waiting for."

Blythe gave her head a vicious shake, forcing herself back to reality. Those tender moments were gone, like a watercolor painting left out in the rain. Truthfully, she didn't want them back. What she'd once felt for Mark was dead, so it was fruitless to dredge up memories, for they were just that: memories and nothing more.

The sunlight met her, quickly bringing beads of perspiration to her face. But in it she found relief. She licked her lips, tasting the rapidly building humidity.

However, the contentment lasted only a matter of moments. To hell with you, Mark, she thought. Not only was she enraged that she couldn't confront him, but she couldn't help but feel a tiny bit of anxiety, as well. Had something happened to him? Maybe she should call the police.

With that thought growing, Blythe quickened her steps, only to feel the boat suddenly lurch. Her fingers curled around the rail for leverage.

It was while she was trying to regain her balance that she spied the gleaming object close to her right foot, wedged tightly in a corner. Bending over, Blythe reached for it. A brass button, probably off one of Mark's blazers. She eyed it carefully before stuffing it into her pocket.

Had one of his floozies yanked it off in her haste to undress him?

Who gave a damn? She didn't.

With a determined set to her shoulders, Blythe made her way off the boat and back to the car. Just as her hand touched the door, thunder grumbled in the distance.

She looked up. The weather seemed appropriate, somehow, as though her foul mood had penetrated the air and infected it.

If she could get her hands on her husband, she would wring his neck for putting her through this agony.

However, she refused to be overwhelmed by this latest and unexpected threat to her security. She could handle it; after all, she'd handled much worse. Though she sometimes came up bruised and battered, she never backed down.

And that was what counted.

Later, when Blythe entered the refurbished home she and Mark shared on Tyler's west side, she was almost giddy with relief. The large, bright rooms furnished in heavy wicker and splashed with bold but soothing colors offered a retreat from the hectic outside world.

Her feet sank into the plush mint carpet as she walked into the kitchen, where she paused and enjoyed another shot to her ego.

Her personal flair made the space her own, Mark having shown very little interest. Because of its casual charm, spiced with just the right amount of sophistication, the house had been written up in one of the lesser known design magazines. Of course, the gardens had been the drawing card. The article had spent much more time on the outside than the inside, which was just fine with her. It had given her some free and wonderful publicity.

Now, as she strode toward the refrigerator, Blythe acknowledged the pounding at her temples, followed by the growling of an empty stomach. She had forgotten to eat. But then, that wasn't out of the norm. Food was not that important to her, especially when she was upset.

Still, she made a salad, grilled a cheese sandwich and sliced some honeydew melon.

As she ate, her mind shifted back to her missing husband and his possible whereabouts.

"Leave it alone," Blythe muttered, jabbing her fork into the fruit.

Disgusted, she rose, cleaned up her mess, then went into the bedroom. The bathtub was her target; she was certain it would breathe new life back into her tired body. Before she made preparations for that indulgence, she reached into her pocket and removed the button, pitching it into the open jewelry box on her dresser.

Once she was out of the tub, she eyed the bed. May as well forget that, she told herself, returning downstairs and outside to the deck. Moonlight streamed onto the coarse wood under her bare feet, illuminating the dancing surface of the water that filled the small kidney-shaped pool. She could hear the melodious sound of the small, man-made waterfall. Somewhere close, a cricket chirped. The air smelled sweetly of flowering wisteria.

And of hope. She reveled in that smell. She needed it to stamp out the scent of Mark's duplicity.

Impossible. With a disgusted sigh, Blythe trudged back upstairs to her bedroom and fell into the bed. But as she'd suspected, sleep eluded her.

Instead, there were rare moments, like now, when the unsettling thoughts of the past stampeded through her mind, devouring everything in their path....

Her mother had died of complications shortly after her birth. Her father, because he was an alcoholic, couldn't handle the responsibility of rearing his daughter. That responsibility had been thrust into the hands of his mother-in-law, Hannah Thompson.

Blythe's young years had been far from easy. Poverty

was always just a step away from her grandmother's back door. Though she'd known she was different, the difference hadn't dawned on her until she reached junior high, where her peers began to poke fun at her homemade dresses and dime-store shoes, causing her to rush home and seek solace in her grandmother's arms. Words of love and encouragement had followed, while hands crippled with arthritis gently brushed away the tears.

In spite of the lack of material blessings, her grandmother, affectionately called Honey, who now resided in a nursing home, had instilled in her that if she wanted better out of life, she must work long and hard. Blythe took what her grandmother said literally. After finishing high school, she waited tables until she saved enough money to go to college and study commercial art.

It was during her college years that she met the charming Mark Lambert. She was working part-time for his mother as secretary and part-time in the family-owned landscaping business.

The head of the family, Tyson Lambert, had made the majority of his money in investments, so the family business did not have to thrive to provide the family with life's amenities.

When Tyson died, he left the business to Mark and cash to his twin, Eleanor. Cynthia also received cash in addition to the Lambert estate, which in itself was worth a sizable fortune.

Mark was enamored with Blythe and sought her out, flirting unmercifully, not only because her cool beauty intrigued him, but because he saw her as a potential asset. He had plans for the company, and he needed Blythe to help him.

However, Blythe hadn't known how much he needed

her help until she'd walked in on him that fateful day so long ago....

She had gotten out of class early and had gone to the Lambert house to catch up on some correspondence for Cynthia Lambert. Before she sat down at the desk, Cynthia sent her upstairs on an errand. It was only after she entered her employer's bedroom that she looked up and saw Mark. He was bent over his mother's jewelry box, clutching something in his hand. That something was a stunning diamond necklace.

Uncertain as to why he was in the room in the first place, Blythe came to a dead stop and blinked several times, hoping it would help clear her vision.

"Mark?"

"Dammit, Blythe!" He spun around and stared at her, the brilliance of the necklace rivaling the sunlight streaming through the blind. "Didn't anyone ever teach you it's rude to sneak up on someone?"

Blythe stiffened, taking umbrage at the slur against her upbringing. "In the first place," she snapped, "I didn't sneak up on you. If you didn't want to be disturbed, you should've closed the door. And in the second place, *your* mother sent me up here to get her glasses."

Blythe felt tears sting her eyes. Mark had never talked to her that way. Why, just last evening, he'd held her in his arms and, after kissing her deeply, told her how beautiful she was, how much she meant to him.

There was a long silence as Blythe's gaze held Mark's, and she found herself thinking that in spite of the pinched expression on his face, he was the best looking man she'd ever seen. Even with his unrelenting stance and his eyes anything but passionate, he made a striking figure. He wasn't much taller than her own five feet six inches, but what he lacked in height, he made up for in features. They were perfect, beginning with blond curly hair and ending with his square chin.

Even in her naiveté, she knew everyone possessed a flaw. Mark was no exception. His was the weak slant of his mouth. It damaged his bid for complete perfection.

"What...what are you doing?" Blythe asked, her raspy voice effectively shattering the silence. *With your mother's diamond necklace in your hand,* she added silently.

Resentment flared in Mark's eyes, then quickly disappeared. His lips eased into a grin, though his eyes remained cold. "Aw, shucks, it looks like you caught me red-handed, darlin'."

"That goes without saying." Not ready to let him off the hook, Blythe added in a dry tone, "You still haven't answered my question."

Mark closed the distance between them, having dropped all pretense of a smile. Holding the silence, he reached out and flicked a strand of hair off her cheek. "You trust me, don't you?"

Blythe swallowed hard, inhaling his expensive cologne. "You know I do, but..."

"There are no 'buts' about it. Either you trust me or you don't."

"But you're taking your mother's necklace, and I don't understand...." She was frowning.

"You're not supposed to, my love."

"Oh, Mark, one minute you treat me like a woman and the next like a child."

"Come here, love," he said, drawing her head against his chest. "Everything's going to be all right, I promise."

Blythe heard the despair in his voice and raised her

head. "Something's wrong, isn't it?" Not waiting for him to answer, she went on, "Please, tell me. If you're in some kind of trouble, I want to help."

"Then forget you saw me take Mother's necklace."

Blythe stiffened and moved out of his arms. "I can't...."

He grabbed her and pulled her close again. "Yes, you can. You have no choice. You have to help me."

"Only if you tell me why."

"All right, goddammit." After pushing her to arm's length once again, he turned his back and walked to the window, taking tense, jerky steps.

Blythe tapped her foot and waited.

Finally he faced her again and said, "I owe some money, a lot of money."

"To whom?"

"That's not important."

"I think it is," Blythe said softly.

"I'm taking the necklace for collateral, nothing more."

"Go on," Blythe said.

"A friend of mine's going to loan me money to pay off a gambling debt."

"You gamble?"

"I dabble here and there."

She was stunned, and it showed. "So how much do you owe?"

"More than I have." Mark snarled the answer.

"Oh, Mark," she cried, reaching for his hand and grasping it.

"I know, it's a bitch, isn't it?"

"Are you in any danger? I mean..." Blythe couldn't go on; fear paralyzed her throat. She had read and heard horror tales about people heavy into gambling who couldn't pay their debts. Bad things happened to them, things that her mind didn't want to conceive of.

"You're damn right I'm in danger. Otherwise I wouldn't be taking Mother's jewelry."

"Mark, will you promise me that once you get out of this mess, you won't gamble anymore?" Her tone was frantic, as was the squeeze on his hand. "Promise me."

"Of course, I promise, love," he said, folding her back into his arms. "But only if you'll promise *me* something."

She clutched at the front of his shirt. "Anything."

"Marry me."

"Marry you?" she mouthed, her eyes wide with amazement.

He bent down and whispered against her lips, "You heard me. If you'll marry me, I'll give up gambling, and together we'll concentrate on putting Designs on the map, so to speak." He kissed her long and hard. "What do you say?"

She'd said yes, of course.

For a poor young girl to be singled out by the charming son of one of Texas's most prominent families was the thing dreams were made of.

And Blythe was certainly not one to throw away a dream. She had lived on practically nothing but dreams for the majority of her life. She saw it as her chance to rise above the ghetto, bury the depressing memories of the cramped three-room house with its tattered wallpaper, dilapidated furniture and linoleum floor, so old and cracked that the pattern was obliterated. Not to mention the times she'd gone to bed with her stomach cramping because she was hungry.

So, confusing physical attraction and ambition with love, Blythe married Mark.

Once she helped him make Designs into a profitable and visible company, Mark made it quite clear that he did not plan to honor his marriage vows. Blythe, in turn, found solace in her work, making it the dominating force in her life. She needed the security, the feeling of belonging, of being connected, like a thread in a piece of fabric.

It also offered an overwhelming challenge. She told herself she was performing a service by turning something ordinary into something beautiful.

The end result had paid off handsomely. Her work brought her to new heights of power and respectability in the business world, but more than that, it kept the loneliness from closing in on her....

Hours later, Blythe still had not closed her eyes.

Three

"Another bad night, huh?"

"Terrible."

It was seven o'clock the following morning, and Susan Lindsay, Blythe's secretary, strode through the door that separated their offices. Blythe knew her sleepless night was mirrored in her eyes, as well as in the weary droop of her shoulders.

Susan, on the other hand, looked bright and perky. But then, her sharp green eyes, dark hair and petite features seemed to create that persona no matter her mood.

"Sorry," Susan said in a barely audible tone.

"Me, too." Blythe ran her fingers around the rim of her coffee cup until it hummed—an odd, jarring sound in the otherwise quiet room. "My eyes feel like someone threw grit in them."

Susan's voice held sympathy. "They look it, too. In fact, I've never seen you looking so..."

"Bedraggled?" Blythe finished for her.

Susan feigned a weak smile. "Well, not that bad."

They were both quiet for a long minute.

"I went to the boat to see if Mark was there," Blythe admitted at last, her face without expression.

"And was he?"

"No." Blythe's voice was flat, but with an edge.

Another silence.

"So what are you going to do?"

Blythe lifted her chin. "I'm moving forward without him. Like I told you, I don't intend to lose this contract. I'm determined to get Mr. Cecil Farmer's name on the dotted line."

Admiration shone in Susan's eyes. "I know that look. The old codger won't have a chance. Actually, he'll think a small hurricane hit him."

"Let us pray." Blythe shook her head as if to ward off an attack of insurmountable depression. "Let us pray," she repeated, more to herself than to Susan.

Susan leaned against the desk and stared pensively at her boss. "This latest round with Mark really has you going." It wasn't a question but a statement.

Blythe sighed. "Like Curt, you're much too perceptive for your own good."

"Is that a polite way of telling me you don't want to talk about it?"

Another brief silence ensued. A judgmental silence, Blythe thought, and wished she'd kept her mouth shut. "There's not anything I can say. I don't know where he is. End of story."

Oh, she could guess and would probably be dead-bang right, but she wasn't in the mood to air any more of her dirty laundry.

Susan held up her hand. "Oh, no, it's not. You can tell me to put a sock in my mouth, but I just can't seem to stop prying." Then, abruptly changing the subject, she said, "I put the final copies of the pending contracts on your desk for your last perusal. I hope they're okay."

Blythe reached for her glasses, a flush on her face. "To tell the truth, I haven't looked at them, but I will, especially the Farmer contract."

"I noticed the nursing home sketches. What a coup that would be."

"Curt and I talked about that very thing."

"Looks like we've got our work cut out for us."

"Which is good and bad. I want to be busy but not overwhelmed."

"I hear you. I'll do my best to see that you're not interrupted."

"By the way, Suz, thanks for coming in so early these last few weeks and for all your hard work. That new computer program you learned has been a lifesaver."

"You're welcome. Actually, I rather enjoyed the challenge, though at times I wanted to shove that piece of equipment off the desk."

Following those words with a grin, Susan left the office.

Blythe eyed the contracts, and even though her mind wanted to stray onto Mark, she refused. Lifting the top folder, she opened it and began reading, only to hear the door creak.

"I know I promised not to bug you, but—" Susan's tone was apologetic.

Blythe straightened and motioned for her secretary to cross the threshold. "It's okay. What is it?"

Susan leaned against the closed door. "It's a man, and he's determined to see you."

"What does that mean?"

Susan shrugged. "Says his name is Ryker Delaney."

A chill darted through Blythe. *Detective* Ryker Delaney.

Mark. Was this visit concerning Mark? Had something bad happened, after all? No. She nixed that thought. Her husband's disappearance had to do with him screwing another woman, which unfortunately was not a crime.

So what was Delaney doing here?

Bristling, Blythe moved from behind her desk and folded her arms across her chest. If something was amiss, the department should have sent someone else.

Anyone but *him.*

Ryker Delaney was one man she'd hoped she would never encounter again. From the moment she'd first met him, he'd been a royal pain in the butt.

His wealthy sister had hired Designs to landscape the grounds of her home. Blythe had stopped by one day to check on the job and to consult Mark, who was on the site, about another project. A man had been on the front porch in a big swing.

She had mistaken him for one of the company's laborers. After all, he was dressed in a pair of frayed denim cutoffs and a faded T-shirt. Both hugged his powerful body, showing off his muscles and his tan. And his tennis shoes were a sight to behold. They were without laces and dirty.

He'd inclined his head. "Morning, ma'am."

"Just what the hell do you think you're doing?" she'd lashed back.

He rose to a full six-foot-plus stance. "Taking in the view."

She realized what "view" he was talking about as his eyes began making a slow, assessing sweep of her figure, lingering a moment too long on the swell of her breasts, evident under the thin fabric of her blouse.

Her knees trembled. If she hadn't known better, she would have sworn she saw desire in his gaze.

Ridiculous!

Still, while he might be just a common laborer, he

was a damned attractive one—*if* you happened to like a macho mug with a clenched jaw and over-long hair—which she didn't. Of course she didn't.

To cover her embarrassment, she demanded, "Whatever you're doing, I suggest you get back to work. Now."

"Oh?"

"Yes, oh. We're not paying you to sit in our client's swing and waste time."

"Is that a fact, ma'am?"

While he maintained that lazy drawl, his eyes had changed. They bored into hers.

Unwittingly, Blythe stumbled backward. She had never been stared at with such icy coldness, such disdain. But he didn't stop there. His lips curled, and cold contempt radiated off him. But it was the sudden and chilling grin that could repel a snake that almost stopped her heart.

Before she could counterattack, her client, Marcy Stovall, walked out the front door.

"Ah, so you two have met," she said, her bright smile crisscrossing them.

The stranger's eyes never left Blythe. "Well, now, that's debatable."

She squirmed inside.

"I don't know what that means," Marcy quipped, "but I'll do the honors. Blythe Lambert, my brother, Detective Ryker Delaney."

Blythe's jaw went slack. "Your brother?"

"That's right," Delaney drawled, a smirk loosening that tight mouth.

Blythe felt like a fool, and the flush that invaded her face bore that out. She focused on Marcy. "I...er...owe your brother an apology."

"Why?" Marcy asked in a hesitant voice, as if she had finally picked up on the tension.

"She thought I worked for her," Delaney put in, his tone cutting.

Marcy's mouth fell open; then she grinned. "Well, brother dear, you do look like something the dogs dug up and the cats wouldn't have."

Shared hostility greeted her humorous comment.

"Hey, lighten up, you two," Marcy added. "No harm done."

Harm had been done, all right. Big time.

The case of mistaken identity had been bad enough, but it paled in comparison to what followed. A more serious confrontation had come later, when Ryker had investigated the murder of his niece, Stacey, a murder that had taken place while the Designs crew was working on his sister's estate.

Ryker had been convinced that because her crews had worked both outside and inside the house, having filled an atrium off the breakfast room with plants, someone associated with the business had been the guilty party.

Though he hadn't come up with a shred of evidence against her or Mark or anyone else, his harassment hadn't stopped until the chief of police ordered him to back off.

That murder had never been solved, and Blythe knew that a man like Ryker Delaney wouldn't give up, that he remained obsessed with finding his niece's killer. That made him an extremely dangerous man, a man Blythe wanted to avoid at all costs.

"Mrs. Lambert."

She regained her focus, thinking his voice was still as grating as sandpaper, though someone else might find that East Texas drawl sexy. Actually, most women would find *him* sexy. At one time she'd been guilty of the same thing, she thought, remembering the way he looked at her that day.

Unwittingly, color invaded her face. In the year and a half since she had seen him, he'd changed very little. Then again, he had one of those unforgettable faces. Now, however, his rough-and-tumble good looks couldn't disguise his seeming contempt for the human race. Or was it merely his contempt for *her?*

As he loomed over her, he appeared taller and more rawboned, and his abundance of unruly salt-and-pepper hair was still intact. She put his age in the forty-plus bracket.

But it was his stark blue eyes that affected her now as they had then, making her want to dodge. They were as hard and deadly as bullets, and aimed straight at her.

Dear Lord, what had she done to deserve this?

Seeing him again had definitely jarred her defenses. The awareness that he still had the ability to disturb her emotions was difficult to accept.

"Detective," she finally said, giving him a nod.

"Ah, so you do remember."

It didn't escape Blythe that he failed to shake her hand. "Remember?" Scorn turned her voice harsh. "You made it impossible to forget."

"Oh, I figured it'd be easy for a highfalutin' lady like you to dismiss the likes of me." His voice was as insulting as the badge he purposefully flashed at her before slipping it back inside his sport jacket.

Blythe took off her glasses and plunked them down on her desk. "You made it impossible for any of us to forget." Her tone was as curt as his was insulting.

Ryker's eyes narrowed at her barb. "I was merely doing my job."

"I'd say you went several steps further." Blythe's tone now bordered on total hostility.

Delaney shrugged. "You're entitled to your opinion."

"Have you come close to finding your niece's...?"

"Killer," he supplied. "No, but then, we both know why."

Though furious with the veiled accusation she heard in his voice, Blythe refused to extend this verbal slinging match. Reining in her runaway emotions, she asked, "So what brings you here today, Detective?"

He didn't mince words. "I'm afraid I have some bad news."

"What now?"

Though she appeared outwardly calm, Blythe's heart pounded wildly, as if it would burst from her chest.

Ryker didn't flinch. "Your husband is dead."

Four

Ryker watched every ounce of color drain from Blythe's face. She didn't move. She didn't speak. Everything about her seemed to have shut down.

"Are you all right?" he asked, stepping forward, as if ready to catch her should she topple over, though he knew she would never do that.

No matter how upset or devastated Blythe Lambert was, she would keep that devastation locked inside, away from his eyes. His past dealings with her had taught him that. That was the way these rich broads worked. And Blythe Lambert was sure as hell one classy broad.

While he despised her way of life, he couldn't help but admire the way she was handling this bombshell. However, when he looked closer, he noticed that she was now sitting hunched over on the couch near her desk, as though she were in pain, her face still ashen.

At least she wasn't crying and carrying on like most women would under the circumstances. Yet she still hadn't spoken.

The silence in the room became oppressive.

"Can I get you anything? Coffee, water?" *A shot of bourbon?* he was tempted to add, but didn't.

Blythe had straightened and now sat rigid on the edge

of the sofa. "No...I'm fine," she whispered. "Or at least I will be, if you'll give me a few minutes."

Delaney rubbed the back of his neck. For a cop, this scenario was usually one of the more unpleasant parts of the job, something he could gladly do without. There was no right or pleasant way to tell a family member that one of their loved ones was dead.

However, this was one time when he didn't mind. If that made him a sorry bastard, then he would own up to it. In his opinion, Mark Lambert had been a sonofabitch who got what was coming to him. Of course, he couldn't tell the man's widow that, even though he was tempted. His ass would be history with the department. He was already hanging on by a weak thread.

He stood over Blythe and, on closer observation, saw that fresh tears had gathered on her lashes, staining them a dark color, and that her bottom lip was trembling. If anything, those slight imperfections made her more hauntingly beautiful.

His jaw knotted. He couldn't afford to cut her any slack. She didn't deserve his admiration or his pity. If anything, she deserved his scorn for thinking she and her family were better than the average Joe walking around, when, in fact, he considered them to be capable of murder.

Suddenly Blythe stared up at him and asked, "How did—" She broke off, as if trying to figure a way to get the words past her lips. Finally she let them out, each one seemingly weighted with lead. "How did it...happen?"

"His body was found on the bank of Lake Tyler. A young boy riding his three-wheeler found him."

"Oh, God!" Blythe cried, reaching for the box of tissue that sat on the table next to her. She plucked one from the container and put it up to her nose. "I...I can't believe it." She shook her head as she once again lifted dazed eyes to Ryker. "Did...did he drown?"

"We don't know the exact cause of death. His body's been sent to Dallas for an autopsy. After it's completed, we'll have all the facts. Until then, I'd rather not speculate."

"Oh, God," Blythe said again, rising to her feet. "But I don't understand. Mark was an excellent swimmer. He wouldn't..."

Ryker was instantly on the alert. While he wouldn't speculate, the same didn't apply to her. Anything she had to say, he would listen to. "He wouldn't what?"

Blythe's breath came in quick spurts. "I guess what I'm trying to say is that Mark isn't...wasn't careless around water."

"Meaning?"

"When he was drinking, he never ventured far out into the lake, swimming or otherwise."

"And you assume he was drinking?"

"Yes...no. I mean...I don't know. He does...did drink a lot." Her voice played into nothingness as she twisted her head away.

"His blood alcohol level will certainly be checked."

She placed her hand to her lips, as though to stop herself from crying out. Then she started shaking, but not before she turned her back on him.

Delaney knew she wished he would go away and leave her alone, let her nurse her anger and pain in private. His gut experienced a sudden and unexpected kick of compassion. But, just as suddenly, his mind negated that. Neither Blythe Lambert nor anyone else in this family deserved his sympathy.

But that wasn't what had his ire up. Even in her shock

and pain, she had a pride and self-assurance that angered him. But more than that was the explosive kick of sexual awareness he felt.

"I'm going now," he muttered abruptly. "But I'll be in touch."

"I'm sure you will."

She didn't bother to hide the trembling sarcasm in her voice. Ryker stared at her for a moment longer, wanting to make a suitable comeback, anything to eliminate the frustration and heat that had him in a stranglehold.

Now, however, was not the time to show his hand. Soon. But not yet. Patience. That was the order of the moment.

Turning on his heel, he walked out the door.

Dead eyes.

Ryker couldn't describe his sister's odd-colored eyes any other way. On her best days, they were neither green nor brown, but somewhere in between. Today they were just plain dead.

Ryker felt a pinch in his heart and almost flinched visibly. For her sake, he held himself in check. She needed his strength, not his weakness.

Otherwise, she was one attractive lady. Her skin and hair were flawless, and so was her slender frame. Since that sorry piece of garbage who was her husband had walked out on her, she could have remarried several times over. She hadn't been interested and apparently still wasn't.

"This is a rare treat," Marcy said after he'd arrived unannounced at the back door.

Ryker forced a smile as he lowered his tired body into a straight-backed chair, only to grimace. "Man, these are killer chairs."

Marcy answered his smile with her lips only. Her eyes remained dead. He turned away, unable to look at her. Would the anguish ever lessen? he wondered.

She joined him across the table. "You're right, they aren't comfortable."

"So toss 'em."

"Sure. Four hundred dollars apiece."

Ryker almost choked. If he'd been drinking anything, he would have.

Marcy rolled her eyes behind a genuine smile. "You wouldn't understand, so there's no point in discussing it."

"Damn straight, I wouldn't. If my—" Ryker's features darkened.

"Want some coffee? Billie just made a fresh pot."

"Thanks, but I've had enough to sink a battleship as it is."

"How 'bout something to eat?"

"Nah."

"Bad day?"

"In my job, pretty much every day's bad. I deal with the scum of the earth."

"Why don't you quit?"

Ryker grimaced. "And live on what? My good looks? I don't think so."

"I still say you could do something else."

"Name it."

Marcy shrugged in obvious frustration. "I don't know, but surely there's something."

"Being a cop's my life. That's all I know, which at this point is nothing to brag about."

"Well, selfish as it might sound, I would like for you to stay on until..."

Her voice faded, but Ryker knew what she was about to say.

"Until Stacey's murderer is behind bars." Another pinch. Harder.

"It'll soon be two years, you know." Marcy's voice was now as broken as her eyes.

Ryker flexed his shoulders before rubbing the back of his neck. The knotted muscles rebelled. He removed his hand.

"Not for six more months." He quelled the urge to shake her, more out of love than anger.

"I know I shouldn't dwell on that, but I...I can't help it." A sob changed her voice. "I still can't believe my baby's gone." Her eyes pinned his. "Most mornings I don't even want to get out of bed."

Ryker reached over and took one of her small hands in his large one. "It'll get better." His tone was gruff.

"Will it?" she demanded bitterly. "When?"

"Whenever *you* let go."

"I can't!" she wailed. "The thought of what happened to Stacey makes me crazy. I dream about it over and over. If only someone was paying, dammit!"

"You've got to stop beating up on yourself."

"That's easy for you to say," she snapped.

"Is it?"

"Sorry." Her tone was contrite. "While wallowing in my own self-pity, I forgot about your loss."

"Two losses. My wife and my niece." His tone was harsh.

Marcy clung to his hand and stared at him out of tear-stained eyes. "We're certainly a pair, brother dear. To the outside world, we have our lives together. But inside, our hearts are shot full of holes."

Ryker removed his hand. "Life goes on, Marcy."

"Does it?"

He flushed.

"For everyone else, maybe. And I think that's what makes me the craziest of all."

"Hey, what triggered all this?" Ryker demanded. "I thought your shrink had gotten you through the worst."

"I read the paper."

"Ah, I see."

Like himself, Marcy had thought someone at Designs by Lambert was responsible for Stacey's murder. The setup had been too perfect. The Lamberts themselves, along with their crew, had had almost unlimited access to the house and grounds.

But his inability to find sufficient evidence against anyone at Designs—or anyone *period*—had driven Marcy to the edge. That was when he'd insisted she see a doctor. He couldn't have borne the loss of someone else he loved.

"I can't say I'm sorry Mark Lambert's dead, especially if..." Again Marcy couldn't go on.

"I'm the investigating officer."

Shock filled her face. "I can't believe it!"

"I was the first one on the scene, which means it's my case. Now I really have justification for digging into the Lamberts' affairs."

When she would have said something, Ryker stalled her. "Don't ask any more questions right now. You know I can't discuss the case. Besides, I don't have all the facts, not yet."

"Do you think Foley will let you handle it? After last time, I mean?"

Ryker's features turned to stone. "He damn well better."

"If I just knew Stacey's killer or killers were either dead or behind bars..."

"You *will* know. That's one promise I intend to keep."

Marcy didn't respond. But then, there was nothing to say, which made his gut burn. If he never accomplished anything else in his life, he would bring closure to his niece's murder. That way Marcy could go on with her life. It was too late for him. He had no life.

"You'll keep me posted?" she asked.

"As much as I can." He stood, bent over and kissed her on one cheek. "Gotta run."

She peered up at him, then looked down.

"Let's have it."

Marcy's head came back up. "What?"

"Something else is on your mind."

"Damn, how did you know?"

"You're my kid sister." Ryker tousled her hair.

"I went out."

"With a man?"

Her stare was cutting. "Cute."

Ryker grinned his approval.

"Don't get your hopes up." Marcy's tone was prim. "He's just a friend."

"For God's sake, you sound like you're doing something wrong."

"I feel like I am."

"You're having a good time. God forbid."

"How can I even think about myself when my daughter's dead?"

He stifled a curse. "Stacey would want you to have a life, which would logically include a man. She would be the first to say 'Go for it, Mom.'"

Marcy smiled a wobbly smile. "I know you're right."

Ryker flicked her on the chin, then, trying to hide his own unstable emotions, said in a brusque tone, "Of course I'm right. I'll call you later, okay?"

"It's about time you got back."

Clyde Raines, the coroner, jerked his bald head up and, in the process, almost swallowed the toothpick dangling from his lips. He glared at Ryker Delaney as the detective slouched against the doorjamb.

"Dammit, Delaney, I didn't hear you come in."

"You never do. In fact, the whole force plans on chipping in at Christmas and getting you a hearing aid."

"Over my dead body. And no pun intended."

Delaney shrugged as he moved deeper into the office. The room was like the man, small and sparse. But it was neat and orderly and depicted the coroner's personality, which was no muss, no fuss. Considered a relic around the department, being close to seventy, Clyde was almost always "difficult," even on his better days. While no one could get along with him for any length of time, no one could do without him, either. He was a whiz at his job.

"Get off your high horse, Raines," Delaney said. "What's the matter? You eat something that didn't agree with you?"

"As a matter of fact, I did," Raines spat, then proceeded to demonstrate by releasing a loud burp.

"Jesus, Clyde, sure you don't need to puke?"

"Don't tempt me, son. If the food in those friggin' machines gets any worse, somebody'll be doing an autopsy on me."

Delaney grinned. "Been tellin' you that for years, but you're either too stupid or hardheaded or both to listen."

"Your advice I don't need, Delaney," Clyde said,

shoving his glasses back against his nose, while a frown pinched his features. "Anyway, when's the last time you ate a decent meal?"

Delaney shrugged again. "That's beside the point. We're discussing your eating habits, not mine."

"Did anyone ever tell you that you're a pain in the ass, Delaney?"

"Daily. So why don't you tell this pain in the ass what you found?"

"It's the Lambert stiff," Raines said, spitting his toothpick into his hand, then tossing it into the nearest wastebasket.

Delaney's senses went on alert. "What about him?"

"The results of the autopsy are in."

"And?"

"He didn't drown. There was no water in his lungs."

Delaney whistled. "What do you know about that." It wasn't a question.

"Is that all you got to say?"

"Give me time. I'm warming up."

"A blow to the back of the head is what did him in," Raines added.

Delaney began pacing back and forth across the frayed carpet, only to stop and fire another question at Raines. "How 'bout the alcohol content?"

Raines scratched his head. "Legally drunk."

"So he could've slipped and whacked his head."

"It's possible, but not probable."

"What are you saying?"

"Do you recall that discoloration on the side of his face?"

"Yep."

"Well, he didn't get that by accident."

"He wasn't alone." Ryker succinctly stated the fact.

"Nope. I'm bettin' someone took a swing at him."

"And knocked him into the railing, then shoved him overboard."

"Right." Clyde eased his wiry frame down into his chair and looked through his horn-rimmed glasses at Delaney.

"So foul play's the name of this game."

"Most definitely."

Ryker slammed a fist into the palm of the other hand at the same time that his face lit up. "How 'bout them apples?"

Raines paused a moment, then asked, "Do I detect a hint of excitement?"

Delaney feigned surprise. "Me?"

"If I were you, son, I'd be careful about tangling with the Lamberts. Again."

Delaney snorted. "Why? Because they think their shit doesn't stink?"

"Good a reason as any, I guess."

"Well, it won't be the first time I've tangled with them, as you put it, and it won't be the last. *If* Mark Lambert was murdered, I'll find out why, even if it does mean airing all the Lamberts' dirty laundry."

Raines made a clucking sound with his tongue against his teeth. "Hope you don't lose your balls."

Ryker batted the air with a hand. "Trust me, that's not going to happen."

Five

The sun showed no mercy.

The mourners paying their last respects to Mark Clement Lambert squirmed under the sun's relentless rays. There were plenty of them on hand, too. And each was dressed to the utmost—both the men and the women determined to outdo one another, as if this were an important social event. For some, it was exactly that.

The death of the son of one of Texas's oldest and most prestigious families was news. The type of news that made for juicy gossip, especially since Mark Lambert's death had occurred under suspicious circumstances. So far, the wagging tongues were held to whispers among the elite behind closed doors.

The moment the body was laid to rest in the cold, damp earth, that would change. The whispers would burgeon into full-fledged voices, distorting the truth until no one recognized it, not even the ones who were spreading it.

Certainly Blythe was cognizant of that fact, and her best defense against the prying eyes and sharp tongues was to hide behind a polite but stony silence.

The funeral service had been held at the Davis Funeral Home, on the Loop. The parlor had been filled to capacity with friends of the Lamberts and satisfied patrons of Designs. There were hundreds of wreaths, bouquets and potted plants.

When the service ended, Blythe and the other members of the family had gotten into the long black limousines that led the funeral procession to the cemetery.

The Garden of Memories Cemetery was a huge park, the oldest in the city of roses. Many of the headstones were eroded by time and weather. At the request of the family, the ceremony was kept brief.

Now, as Blythe sat within touching distance of her husband's flower-decked coffin, her hands clasped tightly in her lap, it mattered to her not at all what anyone thought of Mark, of her, or of the rest of his family, not really.

All that mattered was getting through the remainder of the funeral.

After Ryker Delaney had walked out of her office, she had existed in a fog. Everything had been put on hold. Even the all-important meeting with Cecil Farmer had been canceled and all but forgotten.

Blythe's responses became automatic, almost robot-like, and had remained so since she'd told Cynthia her son was dead. However, when it came to telling Eleanor, her emotions had almost resurfaced. Eleanor had screamed like a banshee, and Blythe had wanted to throttle her.

She still did, even though it was Cynthia, and not Eleanor, who sat next to her in the folding chairs. It was all Blythe could do to concentrate on what the minister was saying.

"For I am persuaded that neither death, nor life, nor angels, nor principalities, nor powers, nor things present, nor things to come, nor height, nor depth, nor any other creature, shall be able to separate us from the love of God, which is in Christ Jesus, our Lord....''

Mark dead. It had not registered. But then, her time had not been her own since she'd gotten the news. Susan and Curt, as well as her other friends, had clung to her like shadows. And while she appreciated their love and concern, she needed to be alone to come to terms with Mark's death.

Peering sideways, she could see her mother-in-law, dressed in black, not a hair out of place on her regal head. But the lines were deeper around her dark eyes and the hollows in her cheeks more pronounced. She was suffering, all right, Blythe knew, but like herself, Cynthia would never let her friends or the curiosity-seekers see that. Blythe had to admire her.

Eleanor Brodrick had no such reservations. She wanted the entire crowd—or, better yet, the entire city—to know that she was devastated over the death of her brother. Her sobs were as fake as they were loud, Blythe thought with disgust as she stole a glance at her sister-in-law.

Eleanor's head was bent, but the profile of her strong-featured face was visible. She would never be considered attractive; her features were too harsh and too manly. But then, she did nothing to enhance her femininity, either—no makeup and no becoming hairstyle. It was almost as if she deliberately tried to be homely. Eleanor's voice was against her, as well. Not only was it low and roughly pitched, it carried like a man's, even when she was speaking in low tones, as she did now.

''Oh, Mother, how are we going to live without him?''

Without so much as looking in her daughter's direction, Cynthia Lambert whispered, "For heaven's sake, get hold of yourself."

Eleanor winced, then spat, "Sometimes I hate you, Mother."

Blythe longed to block out the harsh exchange between mother and daughter, an exchange she'd heard more often than she cared to over the years. But, short of putting her hands over her ears, she could not. Instead, she turned to the preacher, who was extending a hand toward her.

"May God be with you, Blythe, my dear," he said.

Then, mercifully, it was over.

Friends no longer crowded around her. And by choice Blythe found herself standing alone beside her husband's coffin, the rest of the family already on their way home. She had opted to ride alone, and, for once, none of the family had objected.

As Blythe leaned over and placed a single red rose at the head of the casket, her breathing was ragged.

A week ago, he was alive. Now he was in the ground. Dead.

It made no sense.

Ryker Delaney stood to one side in the shadows and watched as the subdued crowd slowly made its way toward the parked cars that lined the roads zigzagging through the cemetery.

He was in his element now, prodded by the certainty that something was about to be uncovered, a certainty that was alluring, almost sexual in its intensity.

His eyes missed nothing, least of all the widow, who stayed behind. While he still wasn't privy to exactly what made her tick, he aimed to fix that. If she was guilty of a crime, he'd find that out. If not, he'd find that out, too. She had become his business. Soon he would know her whims, her friends, her movements.

Her secrets.

Without taking his eyes off her, Ryker reached into his sport coat for a cigarette. Then, realizing that he'd quit smoking, he swallowed a blistering curse.

If he were the kind of man he ought to be, the kind his mother would have been proud of, he would feel sorry for the woman he was carefully scrutinizing. But he didn't. Far from it. The emotion that raged inside him was more akin to hatred.

Yet she was a woman men watched, for more reasons than one. Even now, she held herself with a grace that was impossible not to notice.

His gaze traveled unobtrusively from the sheer beauty of her bottomless brown eyes down to her breasts, where it remained. He guessed he'd been weaned too early, because women's breasts had always fascinated him. Blythe Lambert's were no exception. She was one well-endowed lady.

As before, when he was around her, his body stirred. Then, furious with his continued lack of control, Ryker let go of another stinging expletive. However, his eyes never wavered from his target, and details again claimed his attention.

She appeared fragile, the perfect grieving widow, tears flowing. But were they crocodile tears, or were they for real? Only time would tell.

Her navy silk dress fit to perfection. A tasteful string of pearls draped her neck, while a bracelet watch circled her wrist. Even in the muggy weather, her makeup was flawless, and her thick hair was mussed just enough to lend credence to her plight.

But he suspected there was another side to Blythe

Lambert. He saw her as a greedy bitch beneath all those airs of good breeding.

Until he had the proof he needed, he would do well to remember that.

Blythe knew she was being watched.

The moment the crowd began to thin, she'd noticed the detective propped against a huge oak tree. After that first quick glance, she had tried to ignore him. No longer.

She'd been sure he would disappear along with the crowd. He hadn't. The cemetery was virtually deserted now, and he hadn't budged an inch.

It would have been nice to shrug him off as she would a pesky varmint. Unfortunately, she couldn't. She likened him to a tenacious bulldog that grabbed its prey and never let go until…

Slamming the door shut on that unsettling thought, Blythe took a deep breath, then focused her eyes on her husband's casket. *Goodbye, Mark, goodbye,* she whispered silently.

Seconds later, as she made her way toward the funeral car that waited in the hot sun, she cast another furtive glance in the detective's direction. Nothing had changed. He had not moved.

Averting her gaze, Blythe tried to contain the instant's anxiousness, the niggling sensation, that cropped up in the pit of her stomach. Damn him. Damn his meddling.

Curiosity laced with outrage won. Blythe stole another look. Today he seemed bigger and more intimidating than ever. Older, too. His features bore scars of time and pain.

But nothing took away from those incredible eyes. It wasn't fair that a man with such a loathsome attitude should have eyes the color of morning glories.

It was then that she saw the gun.

Suddenly, with a thickening in her throat, Blythe turned away. She must not forget that he was a cop with an ax to grind. First puzzlement, then shock, filled her. Her mind tumbled into motion as possibilities slammed her from all sides, rendering her motionless.

He had no right to be there.

That hard fact goaded her into action. She looked up, then stopped. She was afraid that if she moved, even a fraction, the pent-up rage inside her would explode. She wouldn't let that happen. That would be playing into his hands.

He was in the wrong. He had the sensitivity of a bull in a china shop, which deepened her disgust and dislike of him.

In the past he might have been able to run roughshod over anyone he chose. No longer. He'd met his match. *She* wasn't about to be his next victim.

Blythe walked toward him, her breathing shallow. If he noticed her agitation, he gave no indication. His self-assured gaze never faltered, though he did ease himself out of a slouch into full height. For such a big man, his movements were fluid and agile.

Blythe stopped within touching distance of him, and their eyes connected.

She could hear the wind swishing through the stately oaks; she could smell the flowers that surrounded Mark's grave; she could even hear a bird's sweet chirp. Those sounds should have been reassuring, should have quelled the danger his presence brought. They did neither.

"We meet again." His voice was controlled.

Blythe blinked as that certain "something" stretched between them, taut, like wire.

"You shouldn't have come," she said evenly, her tone belying the stormy emotions inside her.

"It's part of my job."

His unwavering stare continued to send jolts of uneasiness through her. "And just which part is that?"

"Paying my respects to your husband, of course."

The wind tossed her hair. She smelled her own perfume. It seemed to fill the sudden stillness. His nostrils flared, as though he smelled it, too.

"We both know better than that. You had no respect for Mark." She spat the words. "And you didn't answer my question."

He shrugged, as if he didn't care whether she believed him or not.

"We have to talk."

There was a flare of silence.

"No."

"No?" Ryker's lips moved into what could be conceived as a smile, but Blythe knew better.

Her voice rose a little. "You have nothing else to say that could interest me."

"I wouldn't be too sure of that, if I were you." His smooth tone gave nothing away.

"I'm not sure I understand."

He looked at her through hard, narrowed eyes. "I think you do."

A sick premonition hummed inside Blythe, but she pushed it away, giving in to her raging fury. "I don't know anything except that you have no common decency! How dare you intrude on my privacy like this?"

Ryker pressed his lips together. "If I'm not mistaken, you approached me."

"And it was clearly a mistake," Blythe snapped. "Goodbye, Detective."

"Not goodbye, Mrs. Lambert. Merely good day."

Ryker's chilling comeback stopped her in her tracks. But she refused to acknowledge it. She wouldn't give him the satisfaction of seeing the concern etched in her face. He was an intrusion she hadn't counted on and certainly didn't want.

The moment the driver opened the car door and she was safely inside, Blythe sank against the cushion, but not before cutting her eyes sideways.

Ryker Delaney's eyes hadn't moved. She remained their only target. He had repositioned himself against the tree so that the sun stabbing its way through the leaves created a halo over his head.

What a comparison.

What a joke.

There was nothing angelic about him. In fact, he could be the devil himself.

Blythe shivered.

Six

The police department buzzed with activity.

Ryker was oblivious to the noise, or maybe he just didn't give a damn. As he paced his office, he was in his selfish mode, thinking only of his own misery.

But he wasn't oblivious to the fact that if his partner could see him now, he would be astounded at his behavior. Gone was the cool, collected cop who always remained unshakable no matter what the circumstances.

Whether in his office or on the streets, Ryker was known as a complicated man, a self-made man, a tough guy who rarely smiled. That was partly the result of having been reared in the slums of Houston and having to fend for himself.

His low-life daddy had finally walked out on his family, but not before he beat the living daylights out of Ryker time and again. His mother, now dead, had worked as a maid to feed and clothe him and Marcy. She, thank God, had somehow managed to dodge their daddy's fists and belt.

As far back as Ryker could remember, he'd fantasized about becoming a cop. Through hard work aided by a stint in the army as a weapons specialist, his dream had become a reality.

But then his life had taken a downward turn. It had gone from sugar to shit.

Ryker stopped his pacing and stared out the rather smudgy expanse of glass, watching as the sun sprinkled its rays over the city. But the beauty of the glorious spring morning did little to temper his fury factor. It was off the charts.

Suddenly he felt the old urge to kill in cold blood. The first time he'd experienced that feeling had been when his wife was killed by a car bomb meant for him.

After a slow and difficult healing process, he had gone back to work. And then tragedy struck a second time. His niece had been murdered. No one deserved that kind of luck, not even a sorry bastard like himself.

For his sister's sake, he had buried his own pain and set about the daunting task of finding Stacey's killer. Although his superior, Price Foley, had fought against his heading the investigation, he had won, having had pull in the D.A.'s office. But he'd been warned not to let his emotions override his good judgment or he would be jerked off the case in a heartbeat.

Ryker had held his emotions intact, but it had been hard, especially as he'd been unable to pin the murder or the accompanying burglary on his prime suspects. His gut instinct had told him that someone associated with the landscaping company was responsible, maybe even the Lamberts themselves.

To this day, he had not changed his mind. Following Mark Lambert's death and his encounters with Blythe Lambert, the smoldering fire in his gut had surged back to life, burning brighter than ever.

His hard eyes landed on the paper spread across his desk. The dark print once again leapt out at him: Lambert Family Scion Dead At Thirty-Eight. The article went on to say that an in-depth investigation was in the works.

Damn right an investigation was in the works, and even though one of his suspects in his niece's case was dead himself, Ryker didn't intend to back off. Mark Lambert's death had to be heaven-sent, because it re-opened the door into Stacey's unsolved murder.

Justice would be done, he assured himself, just as he'd assured his sister. No one screwed with him and got away with it. And he'd been screwed, all right, for well over a year.

"Ryker?"

At the unexpected sound of his name, he whirled, a scowl on his face. It partially cleared when he saw his partner, Mike Rushmore, standing in the doorway.

"Sorry, but I knocked several times." Rushmore's venture further into the room was followed by an apologetic shrug.

"No big deal. I didn't hear you, that's all."

Shorter than Ryker's six foot two by only a couple of inches, Mike Rushmore had brown, naturally curly hair and dark eyes. His features had a reddish flush, which somehow made the black mole on the left side of his nose stand out.

"Look, if it's a bad time..." Mike was saying. "I realize there's a lot happening."

Ryker sighed. "It involves you, too, so grab a cup of coffee and sit down."

Silence lingered over the room as Rushmore followed orders. Ryker drained the coffee from his own cup while his partner spotted the leather chair and eased gingerly down in it, as if he feared splattering the carpet with the coffee.

Although Mike Rushmore had worked with him for only six months, he was the most capable partner Ryker had ever had. And during those months, Ryker had come to think of him as a friend, as well.

"You don't seem in the frame of mind to hear more bad news."

Ryker's scowl returned. "Fire away. My day's already shot to hell, so it won't matter."

Mike was quick to react. "Are we talking a case or personal?"

"Both."

"I know you haven't known me long—"

"So?" Ryker interrupted.

Mike flushed, but went on, "I guess what I'm trying to say is that I've never pried into your personal life."

"Come on, Detective, spit it out." Ryker's tone was clipped.

"All right. What the hell's eating at you? I've seen that dark, brooding look on your face more times than I care to count."

Ryker grabbed the newspaper and shoved it at Rushmore. "This is what's eating at me!"

Mike reached for the crumpled paper and, after straightening it out, scanned the headlines. Then he gazed up at Ryker, a puzzled expression on his face.

"I don't get it. This guy's death is just another case that's turned out to be a homicide."

Ryker's breathing was harsh, but he remained silent.

"Right?" Mike prodded.

"Wrong. It's much more than that."

"If you're talking, I'm listening."

"Someone at Designs by Lambert was or *is* responsible for my niece's death." Ryker didn't bother with finesse. The words came out sounding dark and ugly.

"Are you serious?"

Ryker turned away from Rushmore's stunned expression and once again stared outside, his shoulders bunched in knots.

"How...I mean...?" Mike's words came out scratchy, as though his throat were sore.

When Ryker twisted around, his eyes were stark. "In her divorce settlement, my sister Marcy was awarded their new home. She commissioned Designs by Lambert to landscape the grounds as well as an inside atrium. During that time, someone broke into the house. My niece happened to walk in while that someone was helping himself to her mother's jewelry.

"The burglar shot my niece. She died a few hours later on the operating table." Ryker's tone had grown as stark as his eyes.

"Christ," Mike muttered. "Someone mentioned that you'd had some bad stuff happen to you, but he wasn't offering details, and I never asked. Figured it was your business."

Ryker curled his right hand into a fist and pounded it into his left palm. "Well, every day that goes by and Stacey's murder remains unsolved..." He paused, his mouth stretching into a grim line.

"You don't have to explain," Mike said. "I get the picture. I'd feel the exact same way. But what about your partner at the time? Did he suspect someone at Designs, too?"

Ryker smirked. "No, but then, it didn't matter what he thought. As far as I was concerned, he couldn't find his ass with a search party."

"That bad, huh?"

"That bad." Worse, but Ryker didn't say that out loud. His previous partner hadn't liked him, had thought of him as a trigger-happy lone ranger. In the end, the detective had asked the chief for a transfer and gotten it.

"So how much muscle did you use against the Lamberts?" Mike asked.

"As much as I could. We questioned Lambert and his wife and all of the employees, but nothing panned out. Their alibis checked out."

"But you still didn't buy it?"

"Sure as hell didn't. And still don't. Alibis are easy to come by. Someone at that company is guilty. At times, it seemed like the whole world was milling around the place. To make things worse, Marcy was one to flaunt her expensive jewelry."

"Did they get all of it?"

"Every piece. And if Stacey hadn't surprised the thief, it would've gone off without a hitch. It was a well-orchestrated burglary. That's why I don't think a common laborer planned it or pulled it off."

"Was any of the jewelry ever recovered?"

"Not a piece."

"But what makes you think it was Lambert or his wife?" Mike asked.

"Or both."

"Okay, both."

"For starters, pretty-boy Lambert was heavy into gambling and always needed money. And when I looked at the shifty-eyed sonofabitch, I knew he was guilty as sin of something.

"As for his wife—well, from what I was able to piece together, she was aggressively ambitious and wanted to expand the business."

"Am I hearing you right? Are you saying Lambert might've stolen the jewelry to pay off his gambling debts?"

"Anything's possible. Around that time, he was seen in Vegas with a known gambler and jewel thief, a Jacques Dawson."

"What about Mrs. Lambert? What's her role?"

"Who knows? Maybe just his partner in crime."

"But to accuse the Lamberts of robbery and murder is heavy, man. They're one of the oldest, most revered families in the state."

"That's what our 'fierceless' leader said. His exact words were 'You can't harass a man and his family with no concrete evidence to base it on.'"

"I can imagine what you said to that."

Ryker's laugh was bitter. "No, you can't."

"I can see both sides, yours and the chief's." There was a brief silence, then Rushmore asked, "How old was your niece?"

"Fifteen. She was a beautiful kid, and her death was so senseless, such a fluke."

"I guess no one really knows what happened but the perp himself."

Ryker's face was set in hard, impatient lines. "To some extent, it's obvious what happened. Stacey came home after school and begged Marcy to let her go to the movies with her boyfriend. Marcy refused. She didn't approve of the boy, thought he wasn't good enough for her daughter.

"Upset, Stacey ran to me and begged me to talk to her mother. Since her scumbag dad was too busy for her, after he married a younger woman, she depended on me. Lord only knows why. Anyway, I took Stacey's side. Marcy and I had a few words, but in the end I got my way.

"Then Marcy and I went to dinner with plans to get her back home before Stacey returned, only Stacey and her boyfriend had an argument. Stacey arrived home earlier than expected."

"Hell, Ryker, I'm sorry."

"Not as sorry as that bastard who actually murdered my niece is going to be. I live to see the day he gets the needle. And that day *is* coming. He'll make a mistake, and when he does, I'll be waiting."

He meant that, too. Outside of his work, his quest for vengeance was his reason for living; it was home, hearth, wife and child to him. He had adored her; she was the child he and Karen would never have. When Stacey died, it had been as if a part of him, the best part, had died, as well.

"Since you think Lambert was definitely involved, do you think he actually did it?"

Ryker shook his head. "Lambert might've planned the burglary, but he wouldn't have gotten his hands dirty. No fuckin' way. That wasn't his style."

"Now Lambert's death allows you to home back on the family, the business—and Stacey."

"Bingo."

"So who's your main target now? Mrs. Blythe Lambert?"

"Double bingo." Ryker paused. "By the way, Clyde finished the autopsy report on the Lambert stiff earlier today."

"So, let's have the rest of the story."

"He was murdered." Ryker gave him the details.

Mike whistled. "Whoa. Think his old lady knocked him off?"

"It's possible."

Mike whistled again. "Man, things could get ugly and complicated."

"I expect they will."

"Have you told Mrs. Lambert that her husband was murdered?"

"I went to the cemetery, but I didn't tell her."

"Why not?"

"I wanted to observe her in action, see just how brokenhearted she was."

"That's cold."

"That's gathering evidence."

"So how did she perform?"

"Oh, there were tears, all right. But I'm not sure how genuine, especially since she knew I was watching."

"This gets more like a soap opera by the minute."

"It's just getting started."

Mike fingered the mole on his nose. "What about Foley? Think he'll put the shackles on you again?"

"He'll try, I'm sure. But I've become an expert at getting around him."

"He hates your guts, you know."

Ryker almost smiled. "He knows I want his job."

Mike looked incredulous. "Are you joking?"

"Not hardly."

"Think that'll ever happen?"

"Nope." Ryker's tone was bitter. "But I'm not giving up."

"So what's my move?"

"Let's see if we can find Dawson. That's a long shot, I know, but worth the effort. Also, find out everything you can about Mark Lambert's recent comings and goings. I want to know every time he wiped his butt."

"You got it." Mike stood, then changed the subject. "The autopsy came back on that homeless man in the park."

"And?"

"Someone bludgeoned him to death."

"Shit."

"Ditto."

"We'll get on that as soon as I knock out some of this paperwork."

Once the door closed behind his partner, Ryker made another trip to the coffeepot in the corner of his austere room, refilled his cup, then sat back down at his desk.

He was exhausted; he felt the exhaustion in every bone of his body. Yet he was also keyed up, so keyed up that he couldn't do any paperwork.

As if of their own volition, Ryker's eyes strayed once again to the newspaper. Blood pounded through his veins while he scrutinized the part of the article that dealt with Blythe Lambert and her role in the business.

According to the staff writer, there was turmoil and dissension in the family ranks. Couldn't happen to a better bunch, he thought, reaching out and wadding the paper into a tiny ball.

"Shit," he muttered again, and tossed it across the room. Then, leaning his head back against the worn cushion, he forced aside the feeling of helplessness. He would not give in to it, not now, not ever. That emotion would only serve to slow him down, impair his wits.

As long as there was breath inside him, he would hold firmly to his conviction that the Lamberts or someone in their company was responsible. Call his evidence circumstantial. Call it gut instinct. Whatever. To his way of thinking, neither was to be ridiculed nor taken lightly.

Gut instinct had served him well in the past. He'd made ranking detective on it. He'd also survived two wars on it—the Gulf and Grenada. He considered it his secret weapon. Hopefully, it would continue to serve him well.

Ryker sighed and was struck by a sudden and terrible

pang of loneliness that refused to pass, like the constant throb of the wound inside him. But out of that pain surfaced an almost blinding revelation. He knew what he had to do.

Even though his plan might prove a long shot, it would at least anesthetize the pain for another day.

Seven

Blythe had always been enthralled with the Lambert family home. From both Mark and his mother, she had learned that it was built around the turn of the century, along with many of the other elegant mansions in this neighborhood.

Sitting in the midst of a spacious lawn and towering shade trees in an old but affluent section of the city, the redbrick structure had over the years faded to a dull rose color. Still, it was a thing of beauty, especially the grounds, which she had relandscaped. Every time Blythe looked at it, Keats' poetic verse jumped to mind: *A thing of beauty is a joy forever.*

The house itself was two-story, with grilled porches spanning the front of each level. Tall, floor-to-ceiling windows trimmed with tan shutters symmetrically flanked the front.

She knew it to be equally impressive on the inside, as she'd had a hand in refurbishing the interior shortly after she'd married Mark. A whimsical smile reshaped Blythe's lips as she remembered the first time Cynthia Lambert had brought her here. She'd never before had the opportunity to enter the home of a member of the elite, much less be taken on a guided tour.

Vases of flowers filled each of the large and airy

rooms. Yet at times it seemed crowded, with Eleanor and Frank living there with Cynthia.

Blythe stood poised, her gaze resting on the gorgeous wisteria trees that were in full bloom. The smell of the sweet blossoms was intoxicating. The grounds were dead quiet. For once there was no wind sighing through the treetops. The only sound was her heart thudding in her chest.

She dreaded going inside. She would much rather have gone straight home, climbed into bed and pulled the covers over her head. She ached to be alone. But after the funeral, she knew her mother-in-law expected her to be with the family, and she could not disappoint her.

Blythe squared her shoulders and walked up the wide stone steps to the front door. After tapping on it several times, she pushed it open and stepped into a large entry hall.

The housekeeper was coming down the winding stairs. At the sight of Blythe, she stopped and smiled, though her lower lip trembled. Daisy Elrod had been with the Lambert family for years, and Mark had been her favorite. Blythe noted that her sallow complexion appeared more washed-out than usual and the bags under her eyes more pronounced. It was obvious that she was upset.

"Hello, Daisy," Blythe said.

Daisy cleared the bottom stair and grabbed Blythe's extended hand. "Oh, Ms. Blythe, I'm so sorry. We all loved him so."

Blythe patted Daisy's clinging fingers and said gently, "I know."

"The other members of the family are in the living room waiting for you." Daisy withdrew her hand and used the back of it to swipe at a tear rolling down her cheek. "Will you be wanting anything to drink?"

"Iced tea will be fine. And thank you, Daisy."

The housekeeper nodded and then disappeared, leaving Blythe standing in the hall, which smelled highly of beeswax. Again she made the most of the silence, thinking of it as the quiet before the storm.

"Blythe?"

Caught off guard by the unexpected voice, Blythe wheeled around. Her brother-in-law, Frank Brodrick, was making his way toward her.

She had never liked Frank. It wasn't just his cocksure manner that made him offensive to her. In the beginning she hadn't been able to pinpoint the reason. But when he'd tried to entice her into his bed, the reasons became clear and her guilty feelings completely disappeared. She had since patted herself on the back more than once, telling herself what a good judge of character she was.

By then she'd also learned that his favorite pastime was twofold: gambling and spending money he hadn't earned, which made him even sorrier in her eyes.

He was stockily built, with amber-colored eyes and thinning brown hair that served as a backdrop for a nose a shade too long and a chin that was too square. But it was the wolfish quality of his features that disturbed Blythe, especially when he looked at her as he did now.

Blythe hid her dislike behind a cold but polite smile.

"Blythe," he said again, "if there's anything you need—"

She cut him short. "Thank you, but there isn't. Not from you, anyway."

Her insult seemed not to affect him in the least. He didn't even pause until he was within touching distance of her, his strong-smelling cologne setting her teeth on edge. "Are you sure?" he asked, his gaze simmering.

"Yes, I'm sure." Blythe bristled under his scrutiny.

Frank displayed his evenly matched teeth in a suggestive smile and wrapped his fingers around her arm. "Well, if I were you, I wouldn't be too quick to say no. Remember, you're all alone. You just might need Frankie."

"Never."

His face turned nasty, and his voice lowered. "'Never' is a long time, sweetheart."

She sighed. "Get out of my way, Frank."

"You're a cold bitch, you know that?" he responded, increasing the pressure on her arm.

Blythe's expression tightened, and the bite returned to her voice. "Take your hand off me."

He did, but only after he leaned closer and whispered, "No wonder Mark chased pussy."

"You're disgusting!" Blythe swept past him then, her purse hitting her on the hip as she moved down the hall toward the living room.

Blythe paused outside the arched doorway and drew a deep breath. The players were all in their places. Even Frank had slipped in behind her and was stalking toward his favorite leather chair. Only Mark was missing.

Cynthia was sitting in her high-backed velvet chair adjacent to the huge fireplace. Eleanor was perched on the edge of the hearth close to her mother, one long, cumbersome leg crossed over the other.

All eyes were focused on Blythe. She swallowed hard, positive she knew exactly how Daniel must have felt when he entered the lions' den. As long as Eleanor and Frank lived here, she would never feel welcome. She would rather die than let them know the uncertainty that smoldered inside her. To the outside world looking in, and especially to her in-laws, she was in control.

"Well, Her Highness has arrived," Eleanor said, sarcasm curling around each syllable she spoke.

Blythe dreaded being around her sister-in-law for any length of time. Since Mark's death, Blythe had made it a point to stay out of Eleanor's way. Today, however, there was no avoiding her. As usual, Eleanor was determined to cause trouble.

Blythe ignored her and turned her attention to Cynthia, asking, "Are you all right?" Blythe feared the strain of losing Mark might cause her mother-in-law's heart trouble to flare up again.

The lines on her mother-in-law's face, deep and longstanding, eased a bit. "I'll make it, but what…what about you?"

Although Blythe's exhaustion was complete, she forced herself to say, "I'm making it."

Cynthia sat transfixed, like someone who'd been drugged. "Hopefully time will help us both."

"Is there anything you need?" Blythe asked, her brow furrowing.

Cynthia's chin trembled.

Blythe's alarm renewed itself; this was the first time she had seen Mark's mother lose her composure. Tears flooded Cynthia's pale blue eyes, so like her son's, Blythe thought, with a pang in the vicinity of her own heart.

Cynthia shook her head and groped for the tissue in her pocket, then dabbed at her eyes.

"Now that this touching scene is over, can we get down to business?" Eleanor had risen and was glaring at Blythe, her gruff voice more offensive than ever. "While there may not be anything you can do for

Mother, there's something you damn well can do for me.''

Blythe didn't flinch. ''Oh, and what might that be?'' The moment the words slipped out, she knew she had made a mistake.

''Not now, Eleanor, please,'' Cynthia demanded in a weak but authoritative tone.

''Yes, now, Mother.''

Blythe felt rather than saw Daisy as she shuffled into the room. Thankful for the reprieve, she twisted around and found the housekeeper at her elbow, holding a tray filled not only with glasses of tea but finger sandwiches and pastries.

''Thanks,'' Blythe murmured, reaching for a glass. ''But nothing else for me.''

Once Daisy had made the rounds and served everyone, she exited as quietly as she'd entered.

The silence in the room was intense.

Then Frank ambled over to his wife and held out a pack of cigarettes. ''Here, why don't you smoke one of these?'' he suggested. ''Maybe it'll calm you down.''

''Don't you dare patronize me,'' Eleanor said, and swatted his hand away as if he were an errant child.

''One of these days,'' Frank began, flinging a beefy hand to the back of his neck. ''Oh, what the hell. I don't know why I try to reason with you, anyway.'' He then lit his own cigarette and took an angry puff on it.

Blythe crossed to the settee adjacent to Cynthia's chair and sat down. It was her mother-in-law whom she was concerned about. The others could fend for themselves. She had learned from past experience that it was best simply to overlook Eleanor's childish outbursts.

Blythe reached across, placed her hand over Cynthia's and squeezed it.

"Why don't you go upstairs and rest? I plan to do the same thing the minute I leave here." Blythe eyed the older woman closely. "We're all too tired even to think," she added, concerned that there was no color left beneath Cynthia's skin.

Suddenly Eleanor jumped up and stood in front of Blythe, looming over her. "You're not going anyplace until you hear what I have to say. Is that clear?" Her entire body was shaking, almost as if she were shivering.

Before Blythe could defend herself, Frank made himself heard. "Jesus, Eleanor, knock it off!" His voice sounded like a cannon going off.

"And sit down!" Cynthia snapped.

Blythe's eyes never left Eleanor's face, though for the moment Eleanor's gaze was concentrated on her mother. If there had been any truth to the old adage that looks could kill, Cynthia would have been dead.

Blythe did not want to feel sorry for Eleanor, but for some absurd reason she did. It was no secret that Mark had been his mother's fair-haired boy, literally and figuratively.

Blythe had picked up on that shortly after she joined the family. Eleanor's jealousy of her twin had no doubt stemmed from their parents' blatant show of partiality. Blythe had been told that Eleanor had been a sickly, whiny child who got on her mother's nerves, while her father had simply avoided her.

Still, Blythe could not afford to let Eleanor get the upper hand. Not now. Not ever.

When Blythe spoke, her tone was steel. "I'll be glad to hear what you have to say tomorrow."

"No!" The word came out of Eleanor's mouth in a vicious, intense whisper. "We'll settle this right now."

A flicker of distaste crossed Cynthia's face. "Don't, Eleanor."

"Stay out of this, Mother. This is between Blythe and me."

Blythe remained still, her eyes moving between mother and daughter. Never had she heard Eleanor speak to her mother in quite that tone.

Suddenly Eleanor seemed to come alive, to take on a new personality. It was as if Mark's death had given her new life. Crazy as it sounded, Blythe believed it. Eleanor's cheeks bloomed with color, and her eyes were almost feverish.

"As for you, Blythe," Eleanor was saying, "I want you to clean out your desk and get out!"

If Eleanor hadn't been so serious, Blythe would have laughed, so preposterous was her demand. Instead she stared at Mark's twin as if she'd taken leave of her senses.

But Eleanor was on a roll. "You're not wanted here, Blythe Lambert. You never have been." She paused and drew in a huge gulp of air. "You've never belonged. I warned Mark about you. Told him he shouldn't have married you, that you were nothing but poor white trash."

There was a shocked silence.

Then Cynthia cried, "Eleanor! Have you lost your mind?"

"Dammit, Eleanor," Frank put in. "I swear you've got diarrhea of the mouth and constipation of the brain."

"And you can go to hell, Frank!" Eleanor spat. "Surely she doesn't need you to defend her."

Blythe held up her hand. "That's right, I don't. Besides, I'm glad her feelings are finally out in the open.

Eleanor is only saying to my face what she's been saying behind my back for years.''

''And that's not all I have to say, either!'' As if hearing how close she sounded to hysteria, Eleanor lowered her voice and added, ''I'm going to take over Designs.''

Eight

This time the silence was even longer.

Cynthia fanned herself with her hand, and stared at her daughter.

Frank laughed, a hollow sound.

Blythe purposely stared at a point beyond Eleanor's shoulder, watching as the sunlight, muted from passing through the tinted glass, softened the room's insubstantial shadows, while a ball of fury stuck in her throat.

Taking advantage of Blythe's silence, Eleanor hammered on, her voice more grating with every word she uttered. "I've never been given any responsibility."

"Oh, come on, Eleanor," Blythe said, her contempt clear in the set of her mouth. "You got what you wanted when your daddy died—hard cash. Besides that, you're the vice president. And from what I see, you're as busy as you want to be."

"That's just my point," Eleanor countered. "I'm only given petty chores to keep me busy and out of the way. I'm tired of that. I want to implement some of *my* ideas. I want to be in charge."

"That's apparently *not* what your daddy intended, or he wouldn't have left the company to Mark."

Blythe knew her unvarnished words were like rubbing salt into an already nasty wound. But she didn't care. If Eleanor wanted a fight, then she would get one. Someone needed to put a stopper in her mouth once and for all.

"Wrong," Eleanor declared in her harsh, raspy tone. "He was coerced into doing what he did."

"Oh, spare us," Frank muttered, rolling his eyes toward the ceiling.

Cynthia clutched at her breast, looking as if she might collapse at any second, though her posture was regal as ever. Blythe knew better; Cynthia's eyes mirrored her exhaustion.

This fiasco should end. Yet Blythe couldn't seem to control her own tongue. Eleanor had pushed her too far. She dug her nails into her palms and put ice into her voice.

"No. What's wrong is that you've never forgiven your father for not leaving you the business. Instead you got cash, which your husband has already depleted."

"Now, just wait one goddamn minute," Frank began, glaring at Blythe.

"Shut up, Frank," Eleanor snapped without looking at him, her eyes still on Blythe. "That's not true. All I've ever wanted is a chance to prove myself. And now that Mark's gone, I'm going to get that chance."

"God, Eleanor," Frank said, "your brother's not even cold in the grave."

"Enough!" Cynthia cried, lunging off the couch.

Blythe followed suit. "I couldn't agree more." Eleanor was beyond anyone's power of endurance. "I'm going home."

"I meant what I said, Blythe." While Eleanor's voice was calm now, it held an ominous ring.

The hold Blythe had on her patience suddenly snapped. "And I mean this. I have no intention of going anywhere. *Is that clear?* Designs belongs to me. I'll make the decisions as to what's best for the company."

"Grow up, Blythe." Eleanor's smile was brittle. "You're nothing but a dreamer. Mark's will leaves the company to me."

"We'll see who's dreaming. Shortly after we were married, Mark made out a will leaving the majority of the shares in Designs to *me,* with the others going to your mother."

"Prove it."

Blythe swallowed her hot reply and once again tried a reasonable approach. "Trust me, I intend to."

Eleanor merely shrugged. "We'll see."

Blythe felt her insides draw themselves into a small, tight coil. "If I were you, I wouldn't push my luck. You just might find yourself on the outside looking in."

Without another word, Blythe turned and walked out of the room. Moments later, when she reached her car, which she'd left here when she took the limo, she could still hear Eleanor's laughter ringing in her ears.

She sagged against the door of the Lexus, filled with another kind of rage. It wasn't as if she didn't have enough to cope with as it was. She hadn't even come to terms with Mark's death. Now it seemed as if she was going to have to duke it out with Eleanor over the business.

Somehow she would manage. She always had. After all, there was tomorrow. She must not forget that.

The instant Blythe opened her eyes the following morning, Mark's death hit her with a renewed vengeance. She had to dispose of his personal belongings, both here and on the *Blythe II.*

Massaging her temples, Blythe gave in to the ache in

her head from hunger, from exhaustion, from loss. Maybe if she had tried harder to make their marriage work, Mark wouldn't have turned to fast cars, fast money and fast women. If that had been the case, would he be alive today?

Was she in some way responsible for his death?

How and why had Mark died? What were the circumstances surrounding his plunge into the water? She knew the results of the autopsy would be forthcoming soon. She wanted to know those results, yet she didn't.

When Ryker Delaney had intruded at the gravesite, she'd been tempted to ask him.

Blythe was glad she had refrained. Somehow, she figured that was exactly what he'd wanted her to ask. She also figured he'd been hinting at something when he'd said they needed to talk. What did he know that she didn't?

Or was he just using Mark's death as an excuse to waltz back into her life and taunt her because of his inability to solve his niece's murder?

The questions continued to nag her. She hated herself for that. Mark's body was barely in the grave, and she should be grieving. And she was, in her own way. Even if she had no longer loved Mark as a wife should love her husband, she would never have wanted him dead, no matter how despicable he'd been to her.

Blythe stared up at the ceiling and felt tears trickle down her face, realizing in horror that the tears and the core of sadness inside her were for herself and for what might have been.

Feeling as if she were strangling, Blythe pitched back the top sheet and got out of bed. Her first stop was the bathroom, then, shortly after, she padded down the stairs to the kitchen.

She didn't pause until she reached the coffeemaker sitting on the counter. Her movements were unsteady, and after a minute, coffee grounds littered the countertop like an army of ants.

"Way to go," she muttered, and brushed them into the sink.

Once the coffeemaker was gurgling, Blythe made the most of the warm sunlight sifting though the window. *I'm alive. I can feel,* she reminded herself, watching the way the light danced across her skin.

But the problem was, she didn't feel alive, though she had to admit the despair she had experienced last night was somewhat lessened by the sun's warmth. Still, she felt hollow, as if there were nothing at all inside her.

She cupped her hands under her chin and stared outside. Either her own misery was tarnishing her vision, or the pink hibiscus bushes and the Chinese tallow trees in her terraced yard were also drooping, as if in sympathy with her. Even the water in her pool and fountain seemed minus its sparkle.

She had to face reality. Her life must go on. She turned her back on the sunlight and undertook the task of fixing a bowl of cereal.

She forced the food down, along with a cup of coffee, trying not to think of everything facing her, most of all how she had to handle the chaos left by Mark's death.

As if of its own volition, her spoon clattered to the table. The room suddenly seemed too small, closed. She knew she could not stay here any longer. She also knew she could not go through Mark's things. Not today. Maybe not for a long time.

When the thought struck her that nothing was going to be all right again, she went into the bedroom, showered, then dressed for work.

Surely there, as always, she could find relief for her troubled mind.

It was early when Blythe twisted the key in the lock of her office. After stashing her purse in her desk drawer, she went immediately to Mark's domain. For a moment she pulled up short, an eerie feeling washing through her.

Then, shaking it off, she went straight to the wall safe behind his desk. Before she tackled anything else, she was determined to put her hands on the will, then present it to Eleanor.

Blythe opened the safe and reached for the document, only to find that it wasn't there. Her eyes widened, and her heart plummeted.

"Oh, no," she whimpered, beginning to rummage through the neatly piled stacks of papers.

It has to be here, she told herself. By now she was hurling the envelopes onto the floor. The will was nowhere to be found. Dammit, she had watched Mark put it there. Why would he have removed it?

"Don't panic." Speaking aloud seemed to somehow calm her frayed nerves. "Just keep your cool." There had to be a reasonable explanation for the missing document. Yet she couldn't stop shivering. What was going on? Had Eleanor taken it?

No way, she thought, pushing the idea aside as ludicrous. Stealing the will, even for Eleanor, would be a bit ballsy. Yet there was something going on.

Blythe didn't know how to explain it, and it was only a feeling, a kind of worrisome tickle in her brain, and not anything she could find words for, but there was something about the way Eleanor had looked at her when the will had been mentioned.

Suddenly Blythe went giddy with relief. The attorney. He would have a copy, negating any stunt Eleanor might have pulled.

Her head drooped, and she felt it nudge the cold safe door. She remained in that position for a moment longer, making the most of the relief coursing through her.

The urge to immediately put her hands on a copy of the will propelled her into action. Slamming the door to the safe, she scurried back to her office and, after reaching for her glasses, punched out a number on the phone, then waited.

"Marion, this is Blythe Lambert. May I please speak to Mr. Miller?"

"I'm sorry, Ms. Lambert, he's already in conference. You know how early he gets to the office."

Blythe gnawed at her lower lip. "Well, you should be able to handle it, anyway. What I need is a copy of our—Mark's will."

"Does Mr. Miller have it?"

"I'm sure he does."

"Then I'll take care of it right away. And let me express my deepest sympathy for your loss."

Blythe's tone softened. "Thanks, Marion."

"When do you need the copy?"

"Now, if you can get it for me."

"No problem."

"I'll see you shortly, then."

Blythe lost no time in scribbling her whereabouts in a note to Susan. The second she had exchanged her reading glasses for her sunglasses and slung her purse strap over her shoulder, she was out the door.

When her heels connected with the brick sidewalk, the sweet spring air caressed her face. Even her dark glasses offered no shelter from the morning brightness.

Maybe she should have opted to drive, she thought, feeling a fine line of perspiration dot her upper lip. But that would have been ridiculous, since the attorney's office was only two blocks over from Designs.

Blythe upped her pace to a brisk walk, while her eyes soaked up her surroundings. No matter how often she walked this restored section of downtown, she never failed to notice something new, especially now, when the azaleas were at their grandest.

She looked on as tourists ambled around the square, oohing and aahing at the beauty surrounding them. But then, the downtown area was nothing compared to the seven-mile Azalea Trail, which, during this time of year, turned into a sea of red, pink and white. The azaleas, along with the Rose Festival, put Tyler, Texas, on the map.

Blythe was proud she had been astute enough to insist that Designs relocate here as it grew, instead of in Dallas, even though some of her biggest accounts were located there.

Within minutes Blythe had climbed the stairs of the building labeled Miller and Tate, Attorneys at Law, and was standing in front of the secretary's desk.

Marion Bishop pushed a strand of red hair out of her eyes and frowned. "My, but that was fast."

"Too fast?"

"Did you walk?"

"As a matter of fact, I did."

"But it's so muggy."

Blythe smiled. "Crazy, aren't I?"

"Let's just say I wouldn't do it."

Changing the subject, Blythe asked, "Do you have the will?"

Marion looked away. "Actually, Mr. Miller told me not to bother, that he'd take care of it."

Blythe raised her eyebrows. "Oh?"

"He said for you to go right on in."

Blythe nodded and lost no time in tapping on the door to the right of Marion's desk. In answer to the crisp command, she opened the door.

Perry Miller, the Lamberts' family attorney and, consequently, the company's, was sitting behind the desk in his ostentatious office, fiddling with a fountain pen.

However, the moment he saw Blythe, he stood, then threaded his way across the room.

He was a tall, silver-haired man, very distinguished, with a reputation for ruthlessness. Maybe that was why she had never trusted him, in spite of Mark's insistence that he was one of the best lawyers in the business.

Blythe wasn't so sure about the latter; she thought Perry was actually lazy and was still sponging off the clients his daddy had brought to the firm before his death. Too, there was that urbane charm Perry used with calculated effectiveness, which was off-putting to her.

But this morning the smile that was one of his polished trademarks was not in place. His features were as somber as his tone was formal.

"I'm sorry about Mark, Blythe."

She drew a deep breath and took the seat in front of his desk, which he indicated with a wave of his hand. "I know, Perry."

He cleared his throat and went back to his own chair. "Marion tells me you called about a copy of Mark's will."

"Right. Somehow his copy's gotten misplaced."

Perry Miller met Blythe's direct gaze and asked, "What makes you think I can help you?"

Blythe gave him a blank stare, too flabbergasted for a moment to speak. Then, recovering, she said, "I think that's rather obvious since you—" she stressed the *you* "—made out the will."

"But I don't have a copy."

His calmly spoken words struck her like a thunderbolt.

"What do you mean, you don't have a copy?"

"I mean exactly that."

Again speech deserted her. Then her voice burned across the desk. "You should have the original, actually."

"Sorry, Mark asked for the original, and I gave it to him."

"Now, why would he do that?"

"That's something you'll have to ask—" He broke off, red-faced, as if it had just dawned on him what he'd been about to say.

"You're lying, Perry. But what I'd like to know is, why?"

Miller's eyes slid over her. "Why would I lie to you, Blythe, dear?"

"Don't you dare use that patronizing tone with me."

He merely smiled. "Come, come, let's not argue."

Blythe stood up. "I know how to settle this." Without another word, she stamped to the door and flung it open. "Marion, would you come in here, please?"

Blythe's grip tightened on the doorknob as she watched the flustered-looking secretary rush into the room.

Marion's gaze slid past Blythe to her boss. "Have I done something wrong, sir?"

"No, you haven't," Blythe chimed in. "Did you file a copy of Mark's will?"

Marion opened her mouth as if to speak, then closed

it, confusion entering into her face. "I'm...I'm afraid I know nothing about that," she stammered. "You see, I've only been working here a couple of years...."

Blythe's head began spinning as she grappled to come to terms with what was happening. She hardly even registered Marion's exit.

Perry Miller was looking at her with sympathy, as if she were a child who needed mollycoddling. "I'm sure you're just upset over nothing, worrying about a will I'm not at all sure ever existed, due to your condition."

"And just what condition is that?"

"Grief. I'm assuming you're consumed with it."

There was such a violent mixture of emotions churning inside her that Blythe could barely get the words out. "Just what kind of game are you playing, anyway?" Her voice was deadly calm.

Miller stood up. "I suggest you go home and get some rest. You're blowing this way out of proportion." He paused. "Of course, if you *don't* find the will you think Mark made, then the one leaving everything to Eleanor is good."

"I've always thought you were a bastard, now I know it. If you and Eleanor think I'm going to take this sabotage sitting down, think again."

"You're blowing this all out of proportion."

"We'll see who's blowing what when I slap an injunction on you!"

Blythe watched as the cords stood out on Perry's neck, but she didn't give him a chance to say anything. She took a deep, shuddering breath, then bolted to the door.

Once there, she swung around. "Designs belongs to me. I'll see you or anyone else in hell before I give up what is rightfully mine."

* * *

Miller watched her close the door, and though he was still smarting from the insult she'd hurled at him, there was a triumphant expression on his face. She was not nearly as smart as she thought she was; she would soon find that out the hard way.

Let her file her injunction. He didn't care. He would beat it. He had the kind of arsenal he needed for the fight—Eleanor Brodrick. Blythe had been right about their alliance. If things worked out the way he planned, he and Eleanor would soon be married, just as soon as she got rid of that asshole, Frank.

But he was a patient man, and he was willing to wait.

He was tired of working, of kissing ass in order to make ends meet. And with the money Eleanor stood to inherit from her old lady, he wouldn't have to do that anymore. He would have it made.

With that thought in mind, Perry lifted the phone at his elbow and punched out a number.

Moments later, he said into the receiver, "She's gone, and everything went off without a hitch."

Nine

"I'm too old for this crap."

"Hanging around with you is gettin' me there real fast, too."

Ryker glanced over at his partner. "Hell, you got a long way to go. You're just now getting your feet wet."

"Maybe so, but still I hate like hell dodging bullets first thing in the morning, especially when my breakfast isn't even settled."

"That's what you get for eating. This job is better handled on an empty stomach."

Mike Rushmore snorted. "Who you kiddin'? Your stomach's never empty. It's so full of coffee you actually slosh when you walk."

"I can't argue with that."

Silence fell between them as Ryker maneuvered the unmarked car toward the hospital.

"Think I'll ever get used to it?"

"You talking about death?"

"Yeah."

"Nope, not when it's related to violence," Ryker said.

"So how do you deal with it?"

"Get through the situation as best you can, then go home and puke your guts up."

"Great."

"Man, if you're going to stay in this business, you got to get past that."

"Even if it means getting dead?"

"Getting dead is part of the job, my friend." Ryker's tone was flat and devoid of emotion.

Mike slumped further down in the seat. "I know you're right. We could've waited for backup before we charged in like the goddamn cavalry. I'd like to live to see my thirty-fifth birthday, you know."

"You will."

"I'm not too sure about that."

"I am."

Mike didn't respond. But then he was otherwise occupied. He was busy tightening a handkerchief around his middle finger. If the situation hadn't had the potential to be lethal, Ryker would have been tempted to laugh. However, getting your finger bitten by a drug addict was no laughing matter.

"Hold on. We're about there, and you *are* going to be fine." Ryker cut him another quick glance before he focused his attention back on his driving.

"We'll see," Rushmore muttered glumly, his usually red face now an ashen color.

Shortly after Ryker had arrived at the station, a domestic violence call had come in. A hysterical neighbor reported hearing gunshots from the trailer park across the street. Ryker had hollered for Rushmore, and they had taken off.

Just as they arrived on the scene and got out of the car, shots were fired at them. They immediately hit the ground. By the time they had managed to sneak around the back of the dilapidated wooden house and get inside, it was too late. The damage was done.

A young woman who had been used as a punching

bag had already shot the man who had punched her. They had been high on drugs.

When Rushmore tried to cuff her, she'd hollered, but not before sinking her teeth into his finger.

"Think that bitch gave me something alcohol can't kill?" Mike asked, breaking into the silence.

"Nah. Just keep the faith."

"Yeah, right. That's easy for you to say. Your finger's still intact."

It *wasn't* easy for Ryker to say. He was worried himself, but he wasn't about to let on. Instead he concentrated on wheeling up to the emergency room entrance. After shoving the car into park, he faced his partner. "Want me to come in with you?"

Mike threw him a dark look.

Ryker grinned. "Figured as much."

"Where're you going?"

Ryker's grin disappeared. "To see Blythe Lambert."

Mike cursed. "I wanted to be in on that fireworks show."

"This is just the beginning, so get your ass out and take care of yourself."

Once Mike disappeared inside, Ryker set the vehicle in motion, Blythe Lambert front and center in his mind.

"She can't get by with it, can she?"

"Not according to the attorney I just hired."

"Who did you decide on?"

"Tony Upshaw."

Curt Manning rubbed his head where hair should have been. The gesture left a red mark that held Blythe's attention.

"You chose wisely," he said. "From what I hear,

Upshaw has one of the best legal minds in town—in the state, for that matter.''

''I hope you're right,'' Blythe responded, staring at him from across her desk. ''Before this war with Eleanor's over, I'm going to need all the ammunition I can get.''

Blythe had arrived at the office at around five o'clock that morning. She might as well not have bothered going to bed; she hadn't slept a wink, especially since she hadn't been able to talk with Upshaw until now.

After she had left Perry's office, she had returned to Designs, where she'd tried to call the attorney. He'd been out of town, which had increased her frustration. At Susan's insistence she'd left the office and returned home, where she'd worked in the yard, even though she had a service that came on a weekly basis.

The truth was, she loved digging in the dirt. It proved to be the stress-buster she needed.

Now, back at work, Blythe overlooked the fact that every muscle in her body was screaming for relief.

''So what did Upshaw say?''

''He's going to file a temporary injunction.''

''Which will bring Eleanor's plans to a screeching halt, right?''

''For now.'' Blythe lunged out of the chair behind her desk and walked to the window, where her gaze soaked up the beauty of a huge dogwood tree. Unfortunately, that beauty failed to soothe her troubled thoughts. ''But I've got to find that will.'' She didn't bother to hide the anxiety in her voice.

''Where have you looked?''

''Everywhere. The document started out in that safe. I saw Mark put it there.''

''Did anyone else know about it or see it, someone who can testify that there was a second will?''

''Not after it was completed,'' Blythe said in a bleak tone.

''So what the hell happened?''

''Somehow Eleanor must've gotten her hands on it. At first I didn't think she had the balls, but I guess I was wrong.''

''But you can't prove it.''

''No, dammit, I can't.''

''I still can't believe Eleanor would stoop so low as to do something like this.''

Blythe's eyebrows rose. ''Yes, you can. Think about it.''

''You're right,'' Curt mused. ''She's an egomaniac. And the thought of her having anything to do with Designs—'' He broke off, shaking his head.

''That's not going to happen, I can assure you, although one should never underestimate hate. It's a great motivator, and Eleanor hates me. She always has and always will.''

''Bitch,'' Curt muttered.

''Don't worry. I have to think that Upshaw will whip her back into place. Meanwhile, things around here will go on.'' Blythe paused, then added on a weak note, ''As best they can...under the circumstances.''

Curt cleared his throat. ''God, what a mess. Mark's death, now the will's missing. It's not fair.''

''We both know life's not fair.''

''Still, you've had more than your share of grief.''

''I refuse to become a martyr.''

''Atta girl. In time, you'll be fine. I have no doubt about that.''

''Me, either.'' Blythe smiled through tears at Curt,

who had gotten up and was now standing within touching distance. "Thanks for being here for me."

"That goes without saying." Curt gave her a brief bear hug. "That's what friends are for."

"Sorry if I'm interrupting."

Curt jumped back as if he'd been shot.

Blythe stiffened.

Ryker Delaney. Again. Blythe whipped around and stared at the detective, whose unexpected and menacing presence filled the doorway. His gaze was hard and fixed on her. Despite that, something electric seemed to flare between them.

She turned away, but not before noticing how lean and tough and inflexible he looked.

Undercurrents moved through the quiet room. Something was up.

"How did you get in here?" Blythe demanded.

A contrite-looking Susan appeared at his side. "I told him you were tied up."

"It's all right, Susan."

"What's going on, Blythe?" Curt asked, frowning, his eyes darting between her and Ryker.

After Blythe introduced the two men, Curt looked back at her, a question hanging in his gaze.

"It's okay. We'll talk later."

Silence continued its hold on the room long after they were alone. Finally Blythe asked, "Okay, Detective, what now?"

"I warned you at the cemetery that it wasn't goodbye."

"I'm assuming you're here about the autopsy."

"Sure am."

"Then say what you have to say and leave."

He raised an eyebrow, but when he spoke, his voice

was cool and controlled. "All right, we'll do it your way."

For the second time their eyes connected. Blythe was the first to look away, chilled to the bone.

"Your husband didn't drown."

"Then what did cause his death?" Blythe had difficulty getting the words past the huge lump that appeared in her throat as a feeling of dread washed through her.

"Ultimately, a blow to the back of the head." Ryker paused deliberately, as if to make sure his words hit their mark.

"Ultimately?"

"Someone actually knocked him into the railing, where he hit his head."

Blythe opened her mouth, but nothing came out.

"Then that someone apparently tossed him overboard, probably to make it looked like he drowned."

"Oh, no," Blythe whispered, staggering back, her eyes wide. "So what you're saying is that he was...murdered?" She almost choked on the last word.

"For now, that's how we're treating it. Manslaughter, if you want to get technical."

"I—" This time Blythe's voice withered to nothing.

"So, you see we have a lot to talk about, Mrs. Lambert."

Murder. Mark murdered? That couldn't be. Blythe's head reeled. Now was not the time to fall apart. She had to keep her emotions under rigid guard. But she knew she hadn't fooled the detective. He was staring at her, tapping into her deepest and darkest misery.

"You've told me. Now will you please go?"

"It's not quite that simple."

"I don't see why not."

"I have to ask you some questions."

Blythe gasped. "You surely don't think *I* killed him?"

"At this point, everyone's a suspect, including you."

"Well, I didn't kill my husband."

"Then you won't mind answering my questions."

"I have nothing to hide, but I'm *not* going to answer your questions. Not without my attorney present, that is."

She walked to the door and opened it. "So unless you've come to arrest me, get the hell out of my face."

Ten

He walked into the bedroom grasping his penis with his right hand.

Eleanor looked down at the burgeoning flesh; then, with a smirk on her face, she raised her eyes to her husband's face. ''Surely you're not serious?''

Frank's already flushed face turned even redder. ''One of these days I'm—''

''What?'' Eleanor interrupted.

''Going to leave your empty ass, that's what.''

Eleanor laughed, her large frame shaking all over. ''That's a joke, and you know it. You're all talk and no action, except when it comes to bonking other women.''

With his flush still in place, Frank stuffed his penis back into his pants and zipped them. ''Have you ever asked yourself why I bonk other women?''

Eleanor tried to disregard his taunting tone, but she couldn't. ''No, because I don't care about your sluts,'' she finally said. ''As long as Mother doesn't find out, then you can dally all you want to.''

She hated sex and always had. The thought of any part of a man entering her body was repulsive, especially any part that belonged to her husband. Frank hadn't touched her in months, and she didn't intend to change that.

Still, when it was necessary and it got her what she

wanted, she would spread her legs with other men, go through the motions of enjoyment. Despite the fact that her gyrations were all put on, she got by with it. Much to her unhappiness, she'd had to perform a lot lately. Hopefully the sacrifice, both mentally and physically, would be worth it.

Eleanor smiled inwardly, thinking about the coup she'd pulled off.

"Even if I fuck Blythe?"

His taunting words jarred her back to reality.

"Leave her be, you bastard."

Frank laughed, a bitter, controlled laugh. "You can't have your cake and eat it, too, you know."

"Oh, I think I can. If I were you, I'd be careful just how far I pushed. Even though Mother doesn't believe in divorce, I do."

"I'm not worried."

Eleanor quelled the urge to claw his face, asking herself again why she put up with him. He spent money that he didn't have on gambling. He slept with any woman who would climb into his bed.

She knew why she tolerated him. The ugly duckling in the family had snagged a man, something her parents thought would never happen.

All her life, she'd played second fiddle to her brother. He was big and handsome, while she was big and homely. Even if Frank was a sorry piece of shit, she was lucky to have a husband. But now that her brother was dead, the situation would be different. She would be the fair-haired one who called the shots.

Forcing her thoughts back to the issue at hand, she said, "At the moment, we have more important things to worry about than where you stick your dick."

Frank stopped coating his face with cologne and stared at her through the mirror.

They were in their bedroom at the mansion, dressing for dinner. Rarely did Frank dine at the family table. When he wasn't throwing away money at Vegas or the Louisiana casinos, he dabbled in selling insurance, which was a joke. He often used his clients as a reason for not showing up in the evenings.

Eleanor saw through that lie, knowing that his clientele were few and far between.

"I'm assuming one important thing is your brother's murder."

Eleanor kept her cool. "Ah, so you know?"

"Yep. Had a visit from that asshole detective. He caught up with me at the office."

"He came here, as well."

"Is that why Cynthia's in bed?"

"Yes. The shock was too much for her."

"What about you?"

"What about me?"

"Were you shocked?" Frank asked, his eyes boring into hers.

She refused to be pinned. "Were you?"

"Not really," he said in a nonchalant tone. "Your brother did his own thing. No telling what he was up to."

"What did Delaney ask you?" Eleanor chose her words carefully.

"The usual. Where I was when pretty-boy was killed."

"So where were you?"

"At the office."

"Did Delaney believe you?"

"Probably not, since I was alone."

"That's a first," Eleanor said snidely.

He ignored her. "But, as you well know, I didn't kill your brother, because I don't go near the goddamn water."

"That's right, you're afraid."

"So fucking what? Everyone's afraid of something, including you." He paused. "So where were you?"

"Here."

"Can you prove that?"

"I don't have to. I didn't kill him."

Frank gave her one of those "knowing" looks that galled her. "I bet that detective doesn't see it that way. He's still got his stinger out for the Lambert family."

"Don't forget that includes you, Frankie. So I'd watch my step, if I were you."

"Go to hell."

Eleanor laughed without humor. "Not quite yet. I still have too much to do. Take over the company, for starters."

Frank seemed amused. "Good luck."

"As soon as I get that temporary injunction lifted, I'll be in business, then we'll see who's amused."

Frank's brows shot up. "Injunction? What the hell are you talking about?"

"Blythe dear has slapped me with a temporary injunction."

Frank laughed. "Well, I'll be damned."

"It's not funny," Eleanor lashed out.

Frank's features sobered. "You're right, it's not. What it boils down to is that you can't do jack-shit with the business or the money."

"You just watch. The bitch thinks she's smart, but I've got news for her. I'm smarter. Injunction or not, she'll be out on her butt in no time."

"I wouldn't underestimate her, if I were you."

"She shouldn't underestimate *me!*"

"You stole Mark's will, didn't you?"

"I don't know what you're talking about."

"Sure you do."

"How do you know he even made another will?"

"Come on, Eleanor, get real."

Her temperature rose. "No, you get real. Don't forget, I've got your number, too, Frankie dear."

Frank's curse failed to drown out the knock on the door.

"Ms. Eleanor," Daisy said, "Ms. Blythe is downstairs wanting to see Ms. Cynthia."

"Speak of the devil and she shows up," Eleanor muttered. "Tell her I'll be right down."

"Yes, ma'am."

Eleanor looked at Frank. "You coming?"

"Shortly."

Blythe was in the library, perched on the edge of the couch. Eleanor paused outside the door and watched from the shadows. There were dark circles under Blythe's eyes, accentuating her distress. It was a given that Detective Ryker Delaney had also paid her a visit.

Still, those circles did nothing to detract from her beauty. If possible, Blythe was more fragile-looking and hauntingly beautiful than ever. Jealousy stampeded through Eleanor, holding her in its grip. For the longest time, she couldn't move.

As if she sensed she was being watched, Blythe stood and walked toward the foyer. "Cynthia?"

"No, it's me."

Blythe pulled up short. "Where's your mother?"

"In bed."

"Is it her heart?"

"Yes. News of Mark's murder was too much."

Blythe's face lost its remaining color. "Then she knows?"

"Delaney beat you to the draw," Eleanor said with a nonchalant shrug.

Blythe's eyes flashed. "How can you sound so cavalier? Someone killed your brother, for God's sake."

Eleanor strolled up to Blythe and didn't stop until she was within touching distance. Blythe backed up. Eleanor smiled. "We both know who that someone is."

"You mean you know who murdered Mark?"

"Don't play the innocent with me," Eleanor spat. "*You* did, and we both know why."

Blythe thought her heart would explode. The tears wouldn't come but they wanted to. They were bottled inside her with nowhere to go.

Reaching for her grandmother's hand, she lifted it to one cheek and held it there. After she'd left the Lambert mansion, Eleanor's accusation ringing in her ears, she had headed straight for the nursing facility.

Hannah Thompson was Blythe's mainstay. When troubles mounted, she could always count on her grandmother's wisdom and sage advice, even though there were times when Honey was not as sharp as she used to be.

Several strokes had seen to that. Still, even in her seventies and bedridden, she remained a pretty woman. She was blessed with a small nose, a firm chin and a high forehead, topped by a thick spray of blue-white hair. Her eyes were deep black, and when she was at her best, they blazed with a zest for life.

Hopefully, today would be one of those "best" days. Blythe stood quietly and stared at her grandmother, thinking how much she loved her and how much she owed her.

Honey had never failed her. It didn't matter what Blythe did—good or bad—her grandmother had always been there for her. Now that she could no longer count on that stability, Blythe had a hard time adjusting, especially today.

Blythe needed someone to confide in, someone who understood her deepest and innermost fears. That someone was Honey.

Murder.

She still had trouble coming to grips with something so ugly, so vile.

After Ryker had delivered his bombshell, Curt had stormed back into the office in a huff, demanding to know what that detective had wanted. Blythe had told him, only to watch his face turn white with shock.

But it had been Susan who had offered the most comfort. "Mark was murdered," she had echoed in a dazed voice.

Tears had streamed down Blythe's face, and she couldn't even answer, not when a lump of pain had crawled up into her throat, choking her.

Susan drew her into her arms, and Blythe let her. Death alone was a hit to the emotional gut. But murder... That raised death to a level so terrifying that the mind couldn't deal with it. People fought to remain healthy, to live no matter what.

Then, to have your life taken from you without warning... That was something so foreign, so overwhelmingly frightening, that she felt totally disoriented.

"God, Blythe," Susan said, pulling back. "Who...who would do such a thing?"

"I don't know." Tears began to flow again.

"What now?"

"I don't know that, either."

"Do they have a suspect?"

"Me...possibly."

Susan gasped, then stared at her as if she'd lost her mind. Perhaps she had. At that moment, she felt like it.

"Why, that's absurd! You couldn't possibly take someone else's life."

"Please, I can't talk about it anymore right now. I need some time alone."

Susan had given her that time alone, but it hadn't helped. The painful questions kept on coming, questions to which there would sooner or later be painful answers.

People were murdered every day, only not in her life. How could this be? Murder was something that happened to someone else, not in a prestigious family like the Lamberts.

And worse, not only did Ryker Delaney think she was capable of such a heinous thing, though he hadn't come right out and accused her, so did Eleanor—who *had* slapped her in the face with the accusation. If the two of them teamed up against her, she wouldn't have a chance.

She must have cried out, because Hannah's eyes popped open.

Blythe squeezed the old woman's hand and prayed to be recognized. "Honey, it's me."

"Blythe, darling," the old lady whispered, her tone weak. "So glad to see you."

Although Blythe was delighted that her grandmother was alert, she also heard the weakness in Honey's voice and knew this was not one of her better days. No way could she burden this fragile soul with her problems. Maybe she never could again.

That thought was the catalyst that burst the dam inside her. The tears flowed unhampered down her cheeks.

"Oh, sweetheart, what's the matter?"

Blythe forced herself to smile while she smoothed the hair off Honey's forehead, noticing that the skin was hot. "Nothing," she lied. "Just a bad day at work."

"You work much too hard. I worry about you."

"I know you do. But I'm all right."

"Will you stay with me for a while?" Honey asked, even as her eyes drifted shut again.

"Of course." Blythe's response came out a croak as she reached once again for her grandmother's hand.

She didn't know how long she sat there, trying to sort through the maze that was her mind. Only when her foot went to sleep did she move. Wincing, Blythe rose, leaned over and kissed her grandmother on the cheek.

"I love you," she whispered before turning and walking out of the room.

Twenty minutes later, Blythe pulled into the parking lot of Designs. Although she turned off the engine, she didn't get out of the car. Instead, she stared at the beauty in front of her.

Her handiwork. Beds of azaleas flanked the sides of the building, as well as the front and back. The mixture of colors—red, orange and fuchsia—was so vivid, the flowers were almost blinding.

Now that blinding beauty suddenly filled her with a peace that had eluded her since Mark had turned up missing. Holding on to that sense of peace for dear life, Blythe got out.

It was then that she saw him. His vehicle was beside hers, the passenger door open.

"Get in," he said.

"And if I don't?"

"We can make this official. It's your call."

With her lips stretched into a thin line, Blythe climbed in beside him.

Eleven

The air inside the closed vehicle turned heavy.

Though neither one spoke, Ryker's thoughts were spreading in different directions, like a California wildfire out of control. At first he had decided to leave Blythe alone, not to crowd her, to let her think about their encounter at the cemetery, let her stew in the juices he'd stirred.

He had also wanted to wait for the information he'd asked Mike to gather on Mark.

Then he'd changed his mind, deciding that another unexpected visit would throw her further off guard, giving him additional insight into what simmered underneath that cool facade.

Now that she was sitting with him in the confines of his car, he suddenly felt at a loss for words, which was bullshit.

He knew what he had to do. And he would damn well do it. Yet he didn't break the growing silence. Instead he used that silence to study her, sharpening his gaze on her profile.

She was not happy. More to the point, she was pissed. That emotion registered in the set of her cheekbones and the jut of her chin. But it was her body that was the tell-all. Her neck was stiff, and her slender shoulders were bowed, which in turn enhanced the rich thrust of those incredible breasts. Large, but not too large. Full, but soft. *Perfect.*

Swallowing an expletive, Ryker tore his gaze away. So she was a walking sexual fantasy. So fucking what? He'd run into her kind before, and he would again. But if he ever married again, he didn't want a woman who put herself and her career before everything else, something Blythe apparently did.

As if realizing where his thoughts had taken him, he almost bit a hole in his tongue. God, had he lost his mind completely? Blythe Lambert was high on his suspect list, involved in not one but *two* murders. She was his job, nothing more, nothing less.

Any thoughts to the contrary were pure garbage and off-limits. Still, he had one helluva time getting his mind back on track, especially with her perfume filling the interior and tantalizing his senses unmercifully.

Her husky voice pulled him up short. "I want you to stay away from me."

"Until your husband's killer's in custody, that's not going to happen."

"Even you have limits." Blythe's tone was taunting. "We both already know that, don't we?"

He refused to acknowledge the jab or let it get to him, even if it meant stretching the truth a tad. "Not this time. I have carte blanche to do my job."

"Your *job* is to find out who killed my husband." She spoke through clenched teeth.

"And that's exactly what I'm doing." His tone was deliberately lazy and nonconfrontational.

She faced him then. The sudden move sent her hair swinging into her face. Nonetheless, he could see her eyes—dark and tortured, like those of someone trapped in a cage.

Don't be fooled, he warned himself. Don't be taken in by her show of innocence. Don't let her con you just because she gives you a walking hard-on. He could find all the nookie he wanted, only for some insane reason he wanted *her*.

"If that's the case, you shouldn't be here."

Thank God her words had jerked his mind back to the real world. But he didn't have a clue about what she'd said. "Come again?"

She sighed. "You should be out looking for whoever…hurt…Mark, not spending your time on me." She paused. "But then, we've already had this conversation."

"And will again until you realize you're part of the investigation."

"Not if I get an attorney."

"You can hire ten attorneys, and that won't change."

She glared at him, then said in a mocking tone, "In that case, may I go now, Detective?"

He fought the urge to grab her and shake her, wanting to dent that armor she had wrapped around herself. But that was exactly what *she* wanted. Then she could slap all kinds of lawsuits on him, and he wouldn't be allowed near her again.

He couldn't chance that. Neither could he let her get the upper hand. If this was a battle of wills, then he would win.

"No. You'll go when I say you can."

She tensed, but she held her silence.

"Now, about the family—"

"Leave my mother-in-law alone."

Ah, so there was a thermostat under that cool facade. He'd just upped it a bit. Score one for him. "She had to be questioned."

"No, she didn't. You know damn good and well that she didn't kill her son."

"I'll decide who should be questioned and who shouldn't."

"You cops just love playing God." Her tone was a sneer.

That almost brought a smile. "What about Eleanor and Frank?"

"What about them?"

Pay dirt. Her tone was definitely different, far less on the defensive. He decided to milk that for all it was worth.

"Think they could've done him in?"

She flinched at his crudeness but didn't call him on it. "I have no idea."

"Tell me about them."

"I don't gossip about my—Mark's family."

That one brought a laugh, but one with no humor. "That's good, especially when the same doesn't apply to your sister-in-law."

He watched her face redden.

"What did she say?"

"She thinks you're capable of killing him, but then, you know that, don't you?"

Blythe lifted her shoulders in a shrug. "Okay, so there's no love lost between us. I'll admit it."

"Why is that?"

"She wants the company."

"Ah, so now that brother's out of the way, she's made her play."

"Only that's not going to happen, even though she stole Mark's—"

Blythe stopped abruptly and clamped down on her lower lip, as though she knew she'd spoken out of turn.

"Stole Mark's what?"

"Will."

"Care to elaborate?"

"No, it's personal."

He let that go for now, determined to find out what the stolen will business was all about later.

"What about your sleazebag brother-in-law?"

"He's weak and lazy, but he wouldn't...kill anyone. He doesn't have what it takes."

"But you don't like him?"

"No," she said tightly. "I don't."

Ryker smirked. "I bet I know why. He'd like to get in your pants, right?"

"Damn you!" she snapped.

"That was a cheap shot," Ryker said, which was as close to an apology as she was going to get. He should have watched his big mouth, though. He shouldn't give a shit who she spread her legs for. But he did, and that was what made him see red.

"That goes without saying," she fired back, before taking a deep breath and regrouping. "While the family has its problems, none of us killed Mark. So you're wasting your time and the taxpayers' money, especially when it comes to *me*."

Her sudden and calm declaration in the face of the storm irritated him. "That remains to be proved."

"Is that why you came to the cemetery, to watch the widow in action?" Her tone reeked of sarcasm. "To see if I was grieving sufficiently?"

"Look, I'm the one asking the questions."

"That's your way of saying yes," she said flatly. "I bet you were hoping for crocodile tears, so your conscience would be clear in your lust for vengeance."

"And if it is?"

"God, you're a piece of work."

"What I am is a detective investigating a murder."

"Well, I'm not your murderer." Her tone was more mutinous than ever.

He ignored that. Besides, her declaration of innocence was just another verse to the same old song. When the time came, he would make that call, not her, despite her confidence and arrogance.

"You don't...didn't seem brokenhearted over his death."

"How would you know?" she flared. "You don't know me."

"I know you better than you think."

"Leave me alone, you hear?"

"Answer my questions and maybe I will."

"All right, dammit."

"When did you see your husband last?"

"Three days before he died."

"Did you want him dead?"

That one raised her ire to another level. She sucked in her breath, and her eyes sparked. "How dare you ask such a thing? How dare you even *think* it?"

"Cut the dramatics, okay?" Ryker said in bored tone. "Just answer the question."

"Of course I didn't want him dead."

"Did you love him?"

"Yes...no."

"Explain."

"No. I told you before, if you're accusing me of murder, then why not just spit it out?"

"All in due time, Mrs. Lambert," he said in a lazy drawl.

"I'd advise you to stop playing games with me, Detective."

"Believe me, you're in no position to advise anyone, and this is no game."

"Oh, yes, it is, and you're loving every minute of tormenting Mark's family and me."

"You're entitled to your opinion."

"It's your niece, isn't it? That's what this is all about."

His eyes frosted over.

Before he could say anything, she went on. "I'm going to tell you one more time. Neither I nor Mark nor anyone else at Designs had anything to do with her death. You couldn't prove it before, and you can't prove it now."

"For the moment, let's leave my niece out of this." Ryker's voice was harsh.

Another hard silence fell between them, which gave him time to regroup. He hadn't wanted Stacey mentioned. When it came to her, he was much too vulnerable. He had to keep the upper hand with this woman. Talking about his niece and Blythe's possible involvement was not the way to do that.

"How does Curt Manning fit into the scheme of things?"

Blythe blinked. "Excuse me?"

"You heard me," Ryker responded in a scoffing tone.

"He's my assistant."

"Don't you mean lover?"

That remark also hit its target. She flinched, then opened her mouth, only to shut it just as quickly. It was obvious she was furious and grasping for a suitable counterattack.

He'd rattled her, exactly what he had set out to do. He was certain her simmer was slowly climbing to the boiling point. In the heat of the moment, a person's hidden thoughts were often revealed.

"No comeback, Mrs. Lambert?"

"I told you," she said through gritted teeth, "he's not my lover. He's my assistant."

"Come, come. When I walked into your office, you were in his arms."

"Damn you, he was showing me sympathy, something you wouldn't understand."

"Looked like more than sympathy to me. Did the two of you conspire to knock Mark off for personal reasons?"

She gasped out loud, but not before lifting her hand as if to strike him. He grabbed her hand and was in her face before he realized it, so close that he could smell her breath, see the fear in her eyes, even *lick* the moisture that had collected on her parted lips.

For a split second his gaze lingered on that full bottom lip, stained red like ripe cherries, luscious and beckoning....

He jerked away from her, then turned his back, swearing silently. God, he'd almost kissed her. He couldn't believe he'd lost control to that extent.

Almost. That was the key word.

He went weak with relief, thankful he'd managed to rein in his emotions in the nick of time. Still, the fact that he'd nearly crossed the line scared him shitless. It wouldn't happen again.

"Get out," he said, violence coloring his voice.

She stared at him wide-eyed, then lashed back, "With pleasure."

Her parting shot was to slam the door so hard that it actually shook the car.

Ryker struck the steering wheel with the palm of one

hand and cursed. Loud and profusely. He didn't know how long he remained slumped behind the wheel, but it was long after she'd disappeared into the building.

There was no doubt in Ryker's mind that Blythe Lambert was a liar. What he still didn't know was whether or not she was a murderer.

Twelve

"I'm so sorry about your husband."

Blythe stared at the petite, blue-haired woman walking beside her and tried not to show the anxiety those words brought.

"Me, too," she finally responded, then forced a smile for Mrs. Applegate, who had just purchased a home in the country club subdivision and had hired Designs to do the landscaping. "Thanks for caring."

"It's just so awful. I mean—"

"I know."

Although people meant well, both friends and clients, Blythe cringed on more occasions than not at the mention of Mark's death. Yet she had to expect comments, both sympathetic and otherwise. What she needed was to become thick-skinned and not care what people thought or said.

Only she did. She despised being the talk of the town, taking verbal hits from the gossipmongers. The looks, the innuendos were hard to take.

Thank heavens Mrs. Applegate's curiosity didn't appear to stem from meanness. She was a kind lady, and while her project was not all that large or lucrative, it was nonetheless appreciated. Too, it had given Blythe the chance to spread her creative wings.

The silence continued to hover as they strolled toward

the edge of the front yard, where a huge flower garden was to be built.

"Do the police have any clues?" Mrs. Applegate asked, much to Blythe's irritation. "I don't mean to pry, but I'm sure you're worried out of your mind."

Worried.

Blythe wanted to laugh at such a limp word when it came to the emotions charging through her. Ryker Delaney alone had given her enough nightmares to last a lifetime. So far, she had gotten away with dodging direct questions about Mark, about their traumatic personal life. But for how much longer?

Blythe shook herself mentally. Now was not the time to let thoughts of Ryker intrude.

"I have every confidence that Mark's killer will be brought to justice," Blythe finally replied, then switched the subject back to the project. "I love this location."

Taking the hint, Mrs Applegate asked, "So have you put together anything definite?"

Blythe focused her attention on the contemporary house for a moment, then turned back to her client. "I think the design here should be simple and clean, to reflect the structure of your home."

Hazel Applegate pursed her mouth. "Think so? I kind of had something more natural in mind, more—"

"Casual?" Blythe said with a smile.

Mrs. Applegate answered Blythe's smile. "Exactly. *Fussy* was the actual word that came to my mind."

"Including the trees?"

"If that's possible."

Blythe was quiet, her mind working overtime. "Oh, anything's possible, but we do have to be careful. Some types of tree—these cypresses, for example—aren't really suitable this close to the driveway because of their invasive root systems."

"Should we go back to the drawing board, then?"

"Not necessarily."

Mrs. Applegate's features brightened. "Ah, so you have something in mind?"

"If I didn't, I wouldn't be here." A warm smile followed her words.

"Oh, you'd be here, all right. I wouldn't let anyone else do my work. Designs is the best."

Blythe warmed to those words and fought the urge to hug the woman. Of course she refrained, knowing how unprofessional such a gesture would be. Still, it did her battered heart good to know that, regardless of the dark cloud hanging over her personal life, there were still people willing to trust her.

"You're a treasure, Mrs. Applegate. And I appreciate you more than you'll ever know." Blythe paused, shifting her thoughts back to the garden site. "Here's what I propose. How about we build four-inch-deep concrete bends around the trees to keep the roots from spreading under the driveway."

Blythe paused again, gauging her client's reaction. "Will that work?"

"Absolutely."

"That sounds fine to me. When can you get started?"

"That's the kicker," Blythe said. "Right now, we have several projects ahead of yours, but it won't be long."

"You promise?"

"Well," Blythe hedged with a smile, "I promise to do the best I can."

"That's good enough."

"Once I incorporate these ideas into the plans, I'll return them for your and your husband's final approval."

Ten minutes later, Blythe had said her goodbyes and was on her way back to the office, the feeling of accomplishment having vanished.

Welcome back to the real world, the world of *murder.*

Gripping the steering wheel for all it was worth, she managed to keep the car on the road, though tears welled in her eyes, tears of fear and anger.

The thought of Ryker Delaney once again intruded, pushing everything else aside. She wished she knew the details of what had turned that man into such a bastard. Suddenly it was as if a light bulb popped on inside Blythe's head. Maybe it was time she found out. Maybe it was time she pried into his life just as he had pried into hers.

Blythe wasn't sure what she was going to do until she swerved her car into a parking place in front of the public library. Ten minutes later, she was seated in the reference section, her head buried in old newspapers, one article in particular catching her attention.

Car Bomb Kills Cop's Wife

Following that brutal headline was a detailed account of how that bomb had taken the life of Ryker Delaney's wife, Karen. A photograph accompanied the article, showing the face of a smiling young woman in the prime of her life.

Another photograph was of Ryker after the fact. His face was that of a broken man, his features twisted with rage and pain.

Blythe's breath caught, and for an instant she had to look away. Even though his wife was lost to him forever, at least the culprit had been apprehended and was on death row. Not a happy ending, but closure, at least. Still, Blythe sensed that Ryker had never dropped that baggage, that he would carry the guilt of his wife's death to the grave.

The subsequent death of his niece hadn't helped. The tragic incidents combined, Blythe decided, were what had made him into such a hard-ass, so inflexible in his actions and his opinions.

But that knowledge brought her little comfort. She still had to deal with the multifaceted man who both intrigued her and repelled her.

Maybe if his niece's murder had been solved, maybe… Blythe paused in her thoughts, kicking herself. Maybe what? Maybe he wouldn't be giving her such a hard time?

Who could tell about a man like him? He seemed an entity unto himself, a man who made the rules as he went along, but who didn't mind breaking them to suit his whims.

He scared her, murder insanely linking her life to his. Those laser beam eyes seemed to see far too much. And to think he had nearly kissed her. Her heart bucked at that thought. Or had that been her imagination?

Absolutely not.

Her heart had literally stopped beating for a moment when his anger had sent him flying across the seat, not stopping until his face was so close that she could see the gleam of sweat on his forehead, see the beginning stubble of a beard.

Most of all, she had inhaled his animal scent.

That was when her eyes had dipped to his lips. If she had so much as moved a fraction, those lips would have ground into hers; she would bet her life on that.

What would she have done if he *had* kissed her?

She didn't want to think about that. She didn't want to think about him and the animal heat she could still smell. Most of all, she didn't want to think about the desire that had stabbed her deep down in her belly.

Shame.

That was the emotion she should have felt. She had just buried her husband, for God's sake. What kind of woman did that make her?

Someone who faced the cruel truth, she thought, defending herself. She had stopped loving Mark a long time ago. And while he hadn't deserved to die that way, she wasn't responsible. And she didn't deserve the wrath that Ryker was heaping on her.

Perhaps she should undermine Ryker and hire a private detective, have him trace Mark's last days. Doing something would be preferable to doing nothing. But then, that was what Ryker was supposed to do.

He should be looking for the real killer instead of dogging her.

But her troubles didn't stop with the detective. The missing will loomed large. Just this morning she had once again torn the house apart looking for it. No luck. It wasn't at the house or at the office.

Eleanor.

Nothing had changed her mind as to her sister-in-law's culpability. For now, though, she'd done all she could. Upshaw had slapped that injunction on Eleanor. So far, it had worked. However, she knew her sister-in-law would fight back. She was merely lying in wait, Blythe suspected, sharpening her claws.

Blythe rubbed her fingers across her aching forehead.

Suddenly, it seemed as though the world was closing in on her, squeezing the very life out of her. Then she thought about Designs, her one remaining source of pleasure, which allowed her to create beauty from the earth, and a weird sort of peace came over her.

At least she had her work. For now.

Susan grimaced as she pushed the door all the way open. "You're going to kill me, but it's Moody. He says he's got to talk to you now, that it can't wait."

"Story of my life," Blythe muttered beneath her breath.

After leaving the library, she had returned to the office with the determination to put everything aside and concentrate on her work. So far, she'd done exactly that.

"You're damn right it can't wait!" a voice boomed from behind Susan.

"You have my pity," Susan mouthed, raising her brows.

Blythe hid a smile.

The interruption was Moody Bowers, Designs' business manager. The instant he swept past Susan, the size of Blythe's office seemed to shrink. Moody was six five and as fleshy as he was tall. His brown hair was short, blown dry, then sprayed so heavily into place that he looked as if he was wearing a wig.

His manner was as abrasive as his appearance.

"Need to speak to you alone," he said rudely, his gaze on Susan.

"No problem," Susan said. "I had no intention of staying." Before she pulled the door shut, she grinned and shot Blythe another "pity you" look.

For a moment afterward the room was silent.

"What's wrong?" Blythe asked before standing and facing the huge man. Moody had eased down on one corner of her desk and was chewing on the stem of an ever-present pipe, a scowl lining his face.

"We got troubles," he said between chomps, knowing better than to light the thing on the premises.

Blythe tried not to show her disgust at such a nasty habit, but she couldn't hide it. Frowning, she turned away, then said, "I'm listening." She often asked herself why she and Mark put up with Moody's provocative manner, but then she would think of the times he'd saved the company thousands of dollars and the answer was clear.

"Designs is in trouble, financial trouble," Moody said into the silence. "And I'm talking big dollars."

Blythe gasped as she swung back around. "You can't be serious!"

Moody gave his pipe stem another savage chomp. "More serious than a heart attack, actually."

Feeling as if the wind had been knocked out of her, Blythe grabbed the edge of the desk and stood in shocked disbelief.

"Blast it all, Blythe, don't look like that." Moody lurched off the desk.

"It's Mark's fault, isn't it?" The floor seemed to shift under her feet.

"You want it straight?"

"Of course I want it straight," Blythe snapped, experiencing a resurgence of strength. "Anyway, I didn't think you knew how to soft-pedal anything."

"Mark was dipping into company funds."

No way could Blythe have prepared or protected herself from this blow.

"You didn't know?" Moody's tone was incredulous.

"I knew he was living above his—our means." But

she'd never let herself think too closely about where the money had come from.

"But did you know where he was getting the money? Or what he was doing with it?"

Blythe shook her head. "I asked, but he wouldn't tell me."

"Surely you put two and two together?"

Women and gambling, she thought, barely able to breathe. Yet she was unwilling to voice those thoughts, at least, not to Moody. There was a limit to how much she would reveal about her private life. Too, she had to come to terms with this latest gun blast, then make sense out of it all.

When she didn't respond, Moody continued, taking advantage of Blythe's silence. "My gut says he pissed the money away in some casino. Anyway, where he blew it and on what doesn't matter now. What does matter is that I caught him at it and I told him to put it back."

"He didn't replace any of it?" Although Blythe asked the question, the answer was obvious, or they wouldn't be having this conversation.

"Not one nickel of it."

Slowly finding her voice, Blythe said, "That sorry...bastard...!"

Realizing Moody was staring at her with his mouth gaping open, never having seen her lose her temper, much less speak ill of the dead, Blythe swallowed another retort. But it wasn't so easy to stop her mind from racing. She still found it inconceivable that Mark could have done this to the company that at one time had meant everything to him.

Moody smiled, but it was a small, grim smile that vanished almost immediately. "I couldn't agree more."

"Anything else?" Blythe asked in a voice she no longer recognized as her own. She should have seen something like this coming. More than that, she should have kept closer tabs on her husband.

Moody scrutinized Blythe, as if to test her mental state, before continuing. "'Fraid so."

"Let's have it."

He ran a slow hand over his lacquered hair, as though to prolong the agony.

"Moody!"

"If something's not done, and soon, Designs will go under."

Thirteen

Blythe looked at Moody in muted horror. *Lose Designs by Lambert?* Impossible. She couldn't imagine such a thing, especially when she had put her soul into building the business into the success it was today.

When Blythe had married Mark, she'd pledged to work diligently to upgrade Designs. The business meant more to her than it did her husband, because he'd been born with everything while she had been born with nothing. Because the company was small and had never worried about being competitive, Blythe had had to work that much harder.

She more than met the challenge; her fierce loyalty to her husband, combined with her innate talent as a landscape artist, had made it easy. Designs burgeoned into a highly competitive and successful business.

However, Blythe was not satisfied. She wanted the company to reach an even higher pinnacle. Her goal was the same today as had been then: expand Designs, make it competitive.

She would be damned if she would let anyone stop her.

"Blythe?" There was a question in Moody's brusque tone.

"Don't worry, I'm not going to fall apart." Her voice was hoarse but steady.

Moody let out a sigh, removed his pipe, then stared at it with longing.

"Don't even think it."

He gave Blythe a quarrelsome look. "Pipe tobacco actually smells good, you know."

"Not to me it doesn't."

"Suit yourself," he said peevishly, jamming the stem back between his teeth. Then he leaned his head to one side and narrowed his eyes on her. "You sure you're all right? You look like I hit you in the head with a hammer."

Blythe fiddled with her glasses. "Trust me, I'm fine."

He shrugged. "Whatever you say."

"But I do wish you'd told me what Mark was up to."

For the first time, Moody seemed to hedge, as if weighing the consequences of what he was about to say. "I kept thinking Mark would fork over some of the money he'd taken, but when I cornered him the other day, he told me in no uncertain terms to back off, that his business was *none* of mine."

Another surge of fury almost choked Blythe, but her face betrayed nothing. "I see."

"Yeah, I'm sure you do, just like I did." Sweat beaded on Moody's forehead. "Hell, he acted so goddamn strange that—" His voice came to a halt.

"It's not your fault."

Moody rocked forward on the balls of his feet while repacking his pipe, as if to give him something to do with his hands. "I know, but..."

His voice played out, but this time Blythe encouraged him to go on. "But what?"

"It's something I should've jumped on much sooner, especially under the circumstances."

"What circumstances?"

"The sonofabitch actually threatened me." Moody flushed. "Sorry, don't mean to talk about the dead like that."

Blythe was dumbstruck. "Threatened you? Mark?"

"Yeah, Mark."

"How?"

"Told me he'd fire me if I said anything to you." Moody pawed the carpet. "I couldn't afford to be without a job, not with two kids in college," he added lamely.

A tiny shudder rippled through Blythe. "Who can? Still, it's hard for me to believe Mark stooped to that level."

"So where do we go from here?" Moody asked.

"I'll take care of it."

"I sure as hell hope so," Moody said with more punch to his bluntness. "I'd hate for Designs to bite the proverbial dust."

Tears appeared in Blythe's eyes, but she was determined not to shed them. Instead she gave him a weak smile and said, "I'll keep you posted, and thanks."

A strange sound erupted from Moody's throat. "For what, ruining your day?"

"For being honest."

"Hope it's not too little, too late."

"I'll take care of things."

Aware that he was being dismissed, the bull-size man strode to the door and, without looking back, closed it firmly behind him.

"Well?"

Mike Rushmore stared at Ryker, whose eyebrows were raised in question. "Well, what?"

"Don't play dumb with me."

Mike grinned. "I'm going to live, at least for the time being."

"So the blood test for AIDS was negative?"

"They won't get my results back for a while, but she was checked recently, and she was negative, so the docs think I'll be fine."

"You're one lucky sonofabitch."

"And this is one sonofabitch who, from now on, is going to keep his distance from needle lovers."

Ryker grinned. "Just stay away from the ones who bite."

"Funny," Mike responded darkly.

Ryker changed the subject, his own features sobering. "So what've you got?"

Mike tossed a folder on Ryker's desk. "Plenty."

"Give it to me in a nutshell," Ryker said, even as he opened the folder.

Mike sat down and crossed one leg over the other. "Dear beloved Mark loved women, but he loved gambling more."

"That's old news. He was heavy into that when my niece was killed."

"Well, it hadn't changed. In fact, the stakes jumped considerably."

"In debt up to his eyeballs, huh?"

"How'd you know?"

"Unless you've got millions," Ryker declared, "which the Lamberts don't anymore, you can't feed that habit indefinitely. Sooner or later, it's bound to bite you on the ass."

"Apparently it had already taken a big chunk out of Lambert's. It's all there in the bank records."

"Good work."

"The company's accounts were down to the bare bones."

"I wonder if the family knows that, especially the widow."

"I'm bettin' she does," Mike said.

Ryker shifted his holster, then stood. "I'm bettin' she does, too."

"Which gives her a good motive for getting rid of him."

Ryker was reluctant to share his thoughts on Blythe Lambert's innocence or guilt. After that last encounter, his insides were still too raw. "She's just one in a long line," he finally volunteered.

"In step with Lambert's sister and brother-in-law."

"And any number of gambling thugs."

"Speaking of gambling thugs," Mike said in a dejected tone, "so far, we've got zip on that Canadian, Jacques Dawson. It's like looking for a needle in a haystack. I'm hoping Lambert's murderer is closer to home."

"I suspect he or she is."

"Well, neither Eleanor nor Frank Brodrick has come up with a firm alibi yet. And Frankie boy likes to roll the dice, too." Mike rubbed his jaw. "Could be a connection there."

"If there is, we'll find it." Ryker glanced out the window, then back at his partner. "I just found out that Eleanor's playing games with her brother's will."

"Ah, now, that's an interesting tidbit."

"And worth pursuing," Ryker said.

"How'd you find that out?"

"Blythe Lambert let it slip, then clammed up."

"So I guess you want me to get on it?"

"I want you to get on it and *them* ASAP."

"Gotcha," Mike said. "Is there anyone in that family who isn't a suspect?"

"Maybe the mother, Cynthia Lambert."

"And you're not one hundred percent sure about her?"

"Right." Ryker sighed.

"Mark chased pussy."

"That's old news, too."

"He must've had shit for brains."

"What makes you say that?"

"If I had a wife that looked like Blythe Lambert, it'd never occur to me to dip my wick somewhere else."

Ryker ignored the reference to Blythe, along with the last remark. "You got a name?"

"Sure do."

"Man, you're making my day."

"I even got an address."

Ryker came from behind his desk. "I ought to kiss you."

"Not if you wanna continue breathing."

Ryker smirked, looking Mike up and down. "Well, now that you mention it, you're not my type."

"Go to hell."

"I'm sure I'm headed that way, only right now, we're going fishing."

Mike followed him to the door. "Hope we catch something."

"Trust me, we will."

Tears stained her lashes.

"Ms. Britton?"

"Yes?" Her voice was hesitant.

Ryker hated to see a woman cry. And this one had definitely been crying a lot. He flashed his badge. "I'm

Detective Delaney, and this is Detective Rushmore. May we come in?''

Her pale face turned even paler. ''Now's not a good time. Could you...come back another time?''

''Sorry, but we have to ask you some questions. Now.''

''About...Mark?''

''Yes.'' Ryker glanced at Mike, whose eyebrows were raised.

Still the young woman hesitated.

''Are you here alone, Ms. Britton?'' Mike asked.

''Yes.''

''Then let us in.'' Ryker's tone brooked no argument.

She moved aside and let them in. Ryker's eyes scanned the premises, noticing that her garden home was well furnished but ill-kept. But then, so was she. While attractive enough, she was definitely no Blythe Lambert.

Shaking that thought aside, Ryker cleared his throat and asked, ''Were you and Mark Lambert having an affair?''

Amy Britton stiffened. ''It was more than an affair. We were in love.''

''Where were you at the time he was killed?''

''At my parents' house. You can check that out.''

''I will.''

Mike scribbled the information in his notebook.

''He was going to marry me.''

Weren't they all? Ryker thought. ''What made you think that?''

''Wait here. I have something I want to show you.''

Turning her back, she walked to an antique secretary and reached for an envelope. When she faced the two men again, her tears were free-flowing.

''Read that.''

Fourteen

Blythe slammed the front page of the newspaper face-down on her desk, then watched in horror as her cup toppled over and hot coffee ran everywhere.

"Damn!" she muttered out loud.

Ryker Delaney. This was all his fault, she told herself as she cleaned up the mess.

She blamed him, and his snooping into her family's affairs, for her shot nerves and the continuing blasts from the local papers.

To add insult to injury, she couldn't shake the urge to peer over her shoulder every time she moved, convinced the detective was nipping at her heels, literally and figuratively.

She knew that he and his partner had been checking on her family. Friends and even mere acquaintances had called with that information, sounding both offended and curious as to why they had been singled out.

Although Blythe hadn't had the nerve to ask them the gist of those interviews, she could imagine. Before this investigation was over, the Tyler police would know everything there was to know about her family.

She shuddered at the thought, hating what was happening to her and the company. Still, she wanted the bastard who'd killed her husband brought to justice. She was torn in two. She hated having her privacy invaded, but she had no choice if Mark's death was going to be avenged.

After her conversation with the president of the bank, Alfred Jacobs, she knew he had been among those who had been grilled by one of Delaney's men.

Blythe didn't have to be told that. It was apparent in Jacobs' posture, in his speech, in his entire attitude. Once Moody had left her office, she had studied Designs' financial records in detail; then, more sick at heart than furious, she had lost no time in setting up an appointment with the banker, certain he would loan her the much needed cash to keep the company afloat until one of the big jobs came through.

That confidence had been the driving force behind her visit to the bank first thing that morning.

After polite greetings had been exchanged, Blythe hadn't minced words. "I...the company needs your help, Al."

He was a small man with thick glasses and dark hair combed straight back from a high forehead. "First, let me express my condolences concerning Mark."

"Thank you."

"How's Cynthia?"

"Not good, I'm afraid, especially since—" Blythe let the words trail off. *Murder* was still a difficult word to get past her lips.

Al fiddled with his glasses, almost as an excuse for not looking directly at her, which was not a good sign, Blythe thought. But for someone who should have been a "people person," this little man was shy. He seemed to relate to figures better than people.

"His death has rocked this town," Al was saying.

"That's an understatement."

His response to that was to run a finger under his

collar as if it were suddenly too tight. Blythe decided to put him out of his misery. "Since we're both so busy, I don't want to take up any more of your time than necessary."

"When you said 'help,' you're talking about a loan."

"Yes."

He frowned. "I thought the company was doing well."

"It was...it is, only Mark—" Blythe stopped short of blurting out the brutal truth, while unsure if she could get by without doing so.

"Mark what?" Al pressed.

"Borrowed money from the company," she admitted on a sigh.

Al rubbed his chin and averted his gaze. "That's too bad."

Yes, wasn't it? she thought. And degrading, to boot, leaving her feeling like a beggar on a street corner with a tin cup. "I was just made aware of that fact yesterday, and it was definitely a shock. Anyway, Designs has several big deals pending, two of which we're certain to get." She paused and took a breath. "Meanwhile, I need a loan."

"I wish I could help you."

Blythe gave him an incredulous stare. "You mean you can't?"

"I'm sorry."

"But why? I mean, the company's track record is impeccable."

"That's true."

"Well, then what's the problem?" Blythe heard hysteria in its early stages creeping into her voice, though she tried hard to disguise it.

Al squirmed at the same time that his face turned red.

"My dear, you know how much we respect the Lambert clan, how much—"

"Get to the point, Al."

The color in his pinched face deepened. "It's Mark."

"What about Mark?"

"He already owes the bank a large sum."

"You mean he borrowed money in his own name?"

"That's exactly what I mean, money that we were hoping you could repay though the company."

"Oh, my God," Blythe said, her head reeling.

"From the look on your face, you didn't know."

Blythe swallowed. "No, I didn't." During the silence that followed, she collected herself enough to ask, "Do the police know?"

Al nodded. "They asked for Mark's financial records."

"Don't worry, Al," Blythe said, straightening, forcing him to meet her eyes. "You won't take a hit on this, I assure you. The debt will be paid."

"I appreciate that. I almost called Cynthia."

"No, don't do that. Mark's debts are my responsibility."

"But you do understand why I can't loan you anything on the company? The board—"

Blythe held up her hand. "No further explanation necessary. I'll be in touch."

Now, back in her office, Blythe couldn't get that humiliating conversation out of her mind. Once she'd walked out into the sunlight, she'd cursed Mark, then felt terrible, thinking God was going to strike her dead. Under the circumstances, she wasn't sure she would care.

Yes, she would. She was made of stronger stuff than that. Besides, she had the certainty—well, almost certainty—of those lucrative contracts. In fact, she was waiting for a call from the nursing home president.

Curt had just dropped off the plans they had put together, and they were sensational. She couldn't wait to set up a meeting and go over them.

"Any news yet?"

She looked up as Curt sauntered into the room, looking like he'd been digging ditches. Dirt covered his face and arms. And his clothes—well, they were stained, especially his shirt. It looked as though he'd used it for a napkin.

He had just come from the nursery, where he'd obviously done some hands-on work, which was all right. Since Mark was no longer alive to oversee the hard labor, Curt had assumed that responsibility until they could find someone capable and trustworthy.

"Not yet," she said, trying to keep her tone upbeat.

"Pennington won't turn us down."

"I hope you're right."

"Do I detect a desperate note in your voice?"

Blythe didn't hesitate. "Mark's got us in a bind."

Despite his soiled clothes, Curt slouched down into the chair nearest her desk. "How so?"

Blythe didn't hold anything back, starting with Moody's visit, then her trek to the bank.

"Why, that sorry bastard!" Curt spat; then, as if he realized what he'd said and who he'd said it to, his face lost its color.

"It's okay. I feel the same way."

The phone rang. They both froze. Then, with less than steady hands, Blythe lifted the receiver.

"Put him on, Susan."

"Mrs. Lambert, Tom Pennington."

"Ah, Mr. Pennington..."

A few minutes later Blythe replaced the receiver in the hushed room. She didn't have to verbalize a deal gone sour. Curt had heard the conversation, and so had Susan, who was hovering on the threshold, her eyes wide with unshed tears.

"Why?" Curt finally managed to ask through white, thin lips.

Blythe's mind felt crippled, yet she whispered, "Mark's death."

"What does that have to do with the quality of our work?" Susan demanded, walking deeper into the room.

"Apparently a lot," Blythe responded, dread filling her. "He'd rather not be associated with our tainted image."

"That sucks," Curt said with a gruff snort.

"Whatever it is, it's not going to happen." Blythe's tone was flat.

"Well, we still have Mr. Farmer," Susan said in a light tone, helping to breathe life back into an otherwise dead room. "And the Temple home. Both are big moneymakers."

"What if they've been bitten by the same bug as Pennington?" Blythe asked, shock mingled with an almost unbearable pain. She was going to lose Designs. As sure as the sun was shining, that was going to happen.

No. She couldn't lose hope. As Susan had said, they had other deals in the offing. She had to cling to that, she told herself, glancing first at Curt, then Susan.

"Thanks again for being here for me. But if you don't mind, I'd like to be alone."

They nodded soberly and left the room. Blythe's eyes focused back on the phone. She could call her mother-in-law. She was loaded with money and could certainly fix Designs' financial woes.

But if she called Cynthia, she would have to tell her mother-in-law how low Mark had stooped, how rotten he'd become, which could cause her to have a fatal heart attack.

Could she take that chance? Blythe didn't know how long she stared at the phone before she got up and walked to window. She saw him right off. He was sitting in his unmarked car, her office the target of his eyes.

Blythe stood in grim silence before turning and marching out of the room, armed for battle. However, by the time she stepped outside, Ryker's car was gone.

"Damn!"

She'd been charged up for a full-blown confrontation. Now she stood on the pavement feeling limp, like an overinflated balloon that had just been popped. Her only consolation was that there would be another time.

Ryker didn't intend to leave her alone.

"When am I going to see you again?"

Eleanor frowned into the receiver, recognizing Perry's voice. "How did you know to call here?" she demanded.

"Since you weren't at home, I took a wild guess."

"What do you want?"

"You. I'm horny."

"Go find a whore and screw her," Eleanor said in a bored tone.

She heard his sharp intake of breath through the line. "Listen, you owe me for what I did. Besides, we struck a deal. I'll see you tonight. Same time, same place. Be there."

The dial tone assaulted Eleanor's ears before she had a chance to slam down the receiver. No way was she going to keep her end of the bargain.

Eleanor was not in the mood to fuck any man—her husband or her attorney. Right now, she had a much more important agenda, bigger fish to fry. She smiled and looked around her office, heretofore known as Mark's domain.

While she had been expecting trouble when she had let herself into the building an hour ago, surprisingly, no one had been at the front desk. She'd walked past Blythe's door, which had been shut, and into Mark's office unnoticed.

Standing, Eleanor smiled, then hugged herself. Now that she was no longer in the shadow of her twin, she felt free, like a prisoner must feel when he walked out of the pen following years of incarceration.

If her brother had to die, it couldn't have come at a better time.

When she had received the cash bequest from her father, she'd been glad to have the money. But once her worthless husband had gambled it away, she'd been sorry she'd been given the cash, not the business.

Since then she'd been floundering, living life without purpose. No longer. The "lost will" gambit—she paused in her thoughts and grinned—was working out just perfectly.

Injunction or not, Blythe wouldn't win. Without the document, her claim on the company remained dead in the water.

The only fly in Eleanor's ointment, so to speak, was the fact that that loathsome detective hadn't arrested Blythe for Mark's murder. She couldn't imagine what was taking him so long. Maybe she would have to use... No. She would just cool her heels and enjoy watching Blythe squirm.

Eleanor's grin grew as she walked to the door and flung it open.

Blythe was coming down the hall. Good. Just the person she wanted to see.

"Hello, sister-in-law," Eleanor said, stepping out into the hallway, directly in Blythe's path.

Blythe stopped. "What on earth are you doing here?"

"Working." Eleanor put forth her most triumphant smile.

"In Mark's office?" Blythe's laugh was humorless. "You've got to be kidding."

"We'll see who's kidding," Eleanor countered in an ugly tone. "I'm taking over my brother's office along with his responsibilities. And don't think you can do anything about it."

Fifteen

"Oh yes, baby, oh yes."

Frank's eyes bulged as he stared down at the young woman whose mouth was doing wondrous things to his dick. Moaning, his eyes rolled shut, he relaxed back against the couch, knowing it was only a matter of seconds before she rocked his body with another hard climax.

Suddenly his body jerked, and he moaned out loud as he dug his hands into her dirty blond hair, holding her mouth on him. Once it was over, she got up and ran to the bathroom. His eyes trailed her over-endowed buttocks, watching her jellied thighs quiver. So what if she was no Miss America? She could give head better than anyone he'd ever been with.

He scrambled to a sitting position on the couch, that thought bringing a twist to his lips. He remembered the time he'd tried to get Eleanor to taste him *there;* he'd even gone so far as to shove her mouth down onto his penis. She'd instantly gagged, then backhanded him across the face.

"That's too disgusting for words!"

"For you, maybe, but not for me," he'd spat back, rubbing the welt on his cheek.

"Don't ever force me to do anything like that again, or you'll be sorry."

Frank had let her get by with her threat, only to regret it later. Early on, he'd humped her plenty of times, but she didn't know how to please a man and didn't care to learn. He'd often thought Eleanor was on the cusp of homosexuality.

Still, on occasion, it had been easier to fuck his own wife than look for someone else. With all the diseases out there these days, you couldn't be too careful.

However, it wasn't the threat of a sexually transmitted disease that brought him to his feet, sweat popping onto his forehead and oozing from his hairy armpits, but the ugly picture that rose to the forefront of his mind.

"Wanna come take a shower with me?" the blonde asked, peeping her head around the bathroom door, a grin spread across her face.

"No," Frank said. "And I don't want you to take one, either."

"Now, Frankie, don't be like that," she whined. "The evening's just getting started."

"Wrong, baby. It just finished. *You* just finished."

"But—" She broke off into a pout.

Frank waved a hand at her. "Get dressed and get out."

She seemed to know better than to argue, though her flouncing around spoke volumes. "You will call me again?" she finally asked.

"Yeah, real soon," Frank responded absently.

He wasn't even sure when she left. He'd slipped into his underwear and was standing by the window, his mind back on more important things—such as how to stay alive.

A stinging expletive rent the air as he swatted at a pesky mosquito buzzing around his head. But what could he expect, when he'd chosen this sleazy motel to have his little tryst?

He'd thought a good fuck would make him feel better, make him forget the pressure he was under. It had, but only for the moment. Once the woman had drained his energy, the fear and desperation that were his constant companions reared their ugly heads.

What was he going to do?

He had to find the money. He didn't know for sure, but he suspected his time was running out. How the hell had things gotten so screwed up? Why did…?

No, he wouldn't wander down that forbidden path. What was done was done. Now he had to get his mind on target and figure a way out of this latest jam.

What if he went to his mother-in-law? Just that thought soured his stomach and forced out a belch. That old woman, with a smile on her face and sugar in her voice, would most likely rip his hide off cleaner than a flayed rabbit without so much as raising her voice.

Definitely a bad idea.

His wife was out, as well. If she knew how much he owed, she'd boot him out. He suspected that since Mark had gotten his just due, Eleanor would indeed rule the roost. The thought that she just might shit-can him almost sent him running to the bathroom to retch.

How had things gone downhill so fast?

Deciding he might as well get dressed, he slipped on his pants. Only problem, he didn't really have anywhere to go. His office was a joke; hell, he could barely scrape together the money to pay rent on that cubbyhole.

It was then that he heard the noise. He paused and listened, thinking his nerves were playing tricks on him. Then he heard it again. Although he couldn't identify the sound, Frank sensed he was no longer alone, that someone was outside the door.

He stood transfixed. And listened.

Silence greeted him. His insides sagged in relief. Maybe he'd imagined things. Or maybe the noise had come from somewhere else. After all, he wasn't the only one here who was cheating on his wife, banging a whore.

Finally Frank buttoned his pants, then reached for his shirt, noticing that his hands were shaking as if he had the old-age tremors. If he was going to die in some sleazy motel room, the least he could do was have his clothes on.

He had the top button fastened when the door burst open.

Terror froze his body in place.

One of his worst nightmares had come true. His time had run out.

"Well, well," a tall man with an acne-scarred face said. "Look what we have here."

Frank couldn't have moved a muscle even if he'd wanted to. Terror had a stranglehold on his body.

His companion, shorter and rounder, but just as mean-looking, chuckled. "We got us a rat who's messing in his britches." He faced the man with the holes in his face. "Don't you smell the stench, Larry?"

"Sure do, Barney."

Both sets of eyes pinned Frank. "Look guys, I—"

"Shh," Larry said in a soft voice. "All you have to do is give us the money like you promised."

Frank's gaze pinged from one to the other while he tightened his thigh muscles, hoping that would prevent him from wetting his pants. It didn't. He felt the hot liquid run down his leg. He stifled a groan.

"I...don't have the money," he said in a quivering voice. "But...but I can get it."

The two men punched each other, then snickered, having noticed the stain on his khakis. "Seems like we've heard that story before. In fact, Frankie, you're beginning to sound like a broken record."

"I have someone who's going to give me the cash," Frank lied, backing up.

They took a step forward.

"Our boss says we have to get the money now," Larry said.

Frank's body banged against the wall. Trapped, like a rat, he thought, feeling very much as if he was going to upchuck, which would be the final humiliation.

"Please," Frank begged. "Give me another chance. I promise I'll come through."

"I don't think so, Frankie. Your promises don't mean shit."

"Yes, yes, they do. I told you, man, someone—"

The slap to the face came out of the blue, but hard and fast, bursting Frank's lip. He whimpered, then cringed further back against the wall. "Please, don't hurt me."

"Hurt you?" Larry whispered close to his face. "What makes you think we're gonna do that?"

"You're...going to kill me, aren't you?"

The two men looked at each other, then back at Frank. "Now, that's an idea," Larry said, grinning.

The punch to the belly knocked Frank to his knees.

"I appreciate you seeing me, Mrs. Lambert."

Cynthia's in-place expression didn't change, though her nod was pleasant enough. But then, Ryker couldn't look a gift horse in the mouth. He hadn't thought he would even get inside the front door of the Lambert compound, much less talk to the lady of the house herself.

He knew she had suffered a setback with her heart on hearing that Mark had been murdered. Understandable, Ryker thought, having been down a similar path himself. Shaking off that thought, he sat on the sofa across from her, noticing the fine lines around her still-beautiful blue eyes. No doubt about it, Cynthia was a striking woman, but a cold one, he would bet.

"Would you care for some coffee, Detective?"

"No thanks, ma'am."

"Then we'll get straight to business."

"The sooner the better."

"So what do you want to know?"

"Where were you at the time of your son's death?"

She seemed taken aback by his question, or maybe it was his bluntness. "Surely you don't think—"

"No, I don't, but I have to ask."

"Very well. I was here, hosting a small dinner party for one of my favorite charities."

"Good enough," Ryker said.

"The other members of my family aren't that lucky." Her words were a flat statement of fact.

Her heart might be failing, but there was nothing wrong with the old lady's mind. "You're right, ma'am, they're not."

"Is there anything else?" she asked in a tired voice.

"Do you know of anyone who might have wanted your son dead?"

Her features turned pasty white, and she clutched at her chest. Ryker rose off the couch just as she seemed to get hold of herself.

"Please, sit back down. I'll be fine."

"We can do this another day."

"No." Her tone was emphatic. "I want to get this over with. Back to your question, I have no clue who would have wanted to take my son's life."

"Did you know about his gambling problems?"

"No."

She was lying, but there wasn't one thing he could do about that. If he called her hand on it, she would just phone her attorney. He would let that lie slide for now.

"What about his wife?"

Again Cynthia Lambert clutched at her chest. "On second thought, maybe this isn't a good day. I'm not feeling all that well."

Ryker stood. "Another time, then?"

Her eyes turned hostile. "I'm sure that won't be necessary, Detective."

That conversation had taken place two hours ago. Now Ryker was back in his office at the station, mulling it over in his mind. He hadn't learned a thing except that Cynthia Lambert was going to protect her clan, no matter what. No one was going to uncover the skeletons buried in that family closet without a fight from her.

Well, she might not know it, but he was up to the fight.

"Foley wants you in his office ASAP."

Scowling, Ryker looked up at Mike, who was standing just inside his office. "What about you?"

"It's your ass he wants, not mine."

"Lucky me."

Mike grinned. "Sarcasm doesn't become you."

"Get lost."

"Actually, I was just about to do that. Got a call on that missing teen. They found a girl's body in the woods off Highway 59, inside the city limits."

"Damn," Ryker muttered. "When Foley gets though chewing on me, I'll meet you there."

Seconds later, Ryker knocked on the chief's door and was told in a brusque tone to come in.

Price Foley, a tall, robust man in his early sixties, was in charge of a police force that was riddled with problems. To Ryker's thinking, Foley was the main problem. He was a cold, taciturn man who wouldn't give an inch.

Maybe that was why the two of them butted heads; they were too much alike.

"Give me an update on the Lambert case," Foley said without preamble.

Ryker didn't bother to sit down, standing eyeball to eyeball with his superior. "I'm hard and fast on it."

"Doing what?"

"Checking out and watching the family members."

"I'm expecting you to make a collar, and quick, too."

That rankled. "As soon as I have a suspect, you'll be the first to know."

"What do you have so far?" Foley pressed. "As in specifics."

Ryker forced a hold on his temper. "We're concentrating on the family, as well as his gambling contacts. I think it was a member of his family, though."

"We're not going to have the problem we had before, right?"

Ryker wanted to knock that sanctimonious sneer off Foley's face. He didn't. That would be playing into the chief's hand. Instead, Ryker lifted his shoulders in a careless shrug. However, his tone was deadly. "I'll do whatever's necessary to bring Lambert's killer in."

Foley's face turned red, but he didn't offer a biting comeback. Yet he didn't back off, either. "Anyone heading the list?"

"Blythe Lambert, of course. But we're also tailing his brother-in-law and his sister. They each have something to gain from Mark's death."

"And Lambert's penchant for gambling?"

"As I said, we're on that angle, as well. He was in debt up to his eyeballs, which means some goon might've gotten tired of waiting for his money and whacked him."

"Anything else?" Foley pressed.

"He had a mistress."

"Does she have a motive?"

"Yes and no."

The phone chose that moment to ring. Foley answered it. After a moment of listening, he said in a clipped tone, "I'll be right there."

"You're off the hook for now." Foley paused. "I'd be inclined to look real close at the widow. From what I've heard, there was no love lost between them."

"You're right about that, especially since he'd milked all the money out of the business."

"Well, if you have to lean on someone in the family, then lean on her."

Ryker's expression showed his irritation. "Is that an order?"

"Yeah, that's an order."

Sixteen

"How'd your session with Foley go?"

Ryker stepped into the cordoned-off area and stood beside Mike before he answered, "Better than expected."

"Turn around."

Ryker grimaced. "What the hell for?"

"Wanna see if your ass is intact. You said Foley was going to chew on it."

"Actually, he gave me his blessings."

"You shittin' me?"

"Well, up to a point," Ryker admitted. "He told me to put pressure on the widow."

"Man, I can't believe that," Mike said, placing a hand over his forehead as if to shade his eyes from the glaring sun. "It's a known fact that he's afraid of crossing the Lamberts, especially the old lady."

"Remember, Blythe isn't really a Lambert."

"Ah, right. Compared to them, she's poor white trash."

"Something like that," Ryker said, smiling ironically.

"Before that investigation's over, I figure there's going to be some mighty big turds in the punch bowl."

"Speaking of turds, do we have any suspects here?"

Mike sobered. "Nary a one."

"Is this kid the missing teen?"

"Looks that way."

"I was hoping we'd get lucky and find her alive."

"Not this time."

"So what *do* we have?" Ryker asked, shifting his holster so as to retrieve his sunglasses and slip them onto his nose.

"Not much, I'm afraid."

"How 'bout tire tracks?"

"The boys are working on that, but the perp obviously killed her someplace else, then dumped her here."

"Molested, I take it?" Ryker's voice was terse, but matter of fact.

"Yep, then strangled her."

Ryker cursed, then said, "I'm heading back to the office. Keep me informed."

Nail Blythe Lambert for murder.

Long after Ryker had left the crime scene and returned to his office, his marching orders continued to rattle around in his head like marbles hitting together. Now that he'd had the time to think about it, it was incredible that Foley had actually sanctioned such a move.

Was the chief suddenly getting some balls? Or was something going on that Ryker wasn't privy to? Either way, he should be ecstatic. Blythe Lambert was, after all, his main target. Because of her, he had a constant hard-on, both mentally and physically.

That latter thought etched a deeper scowl in his face. No matter how he felt about Blythe Lambert personally, she *wasn't* his only suspect, and he would do well to keep that in mind. Because he prided himself on being a good cop, he intended to keep an eye on the other turds in the punch bowl, as Mike had so aptly phrased it.

Unwittingly, a smile relaxed Ryker's lips. Leave it to his partner to think of such an appropriate analogy. Idly tapping his pen on his desk, Ryker thought again about all those unknowns who were his other suspects, those who lived in the gambling world.

That well-known jewel thief and fence, Jacques Dawson, remained part of that world. He also ranked high on Ryker's mental list. Only problem was, they hadn't been able to find the guy.

But he wanted Blythe Lambert to be guilty, didn't he? Of course he did. Just as Blythe had accused him, the burning inside went back to his niece's death.

He had no idea how the two murders—Stacey's and Mark's—would connect, but he knew that they would. The Lamberts *were* involved. Until he could prove that, he would continue to feel as if he'd been zapped with a terminal illness. The catch was that he couldn't die until his mission was fulfilled, which was to bring the sonofabitch who killed Stacey to justice.

That illness had also been his salvation. It gave him a reason for getting up every morning and returning to the sewer where he worked.

Now he was being given a second chance to even the score with the Lamberts. So why was he tiptoeing around the mulberry bush? Why was his gut roiling? For starters, he would just as soon not be around Mark's widow, which wasn't possible, of course. But dammit, she disturbed him.

Although Ryker hated to admit that weakness in himself, it was nonetheless a factor that he had to face and come to terms with. Then maybe he could move on, do his job with the tenacity and grit that he would use to pursue any other homicide.

She had gotten under his skin in a way that he hadn't

expected. She had turned into a walking wet dream. When he'd shown up at her office unannounced and she'd been in her assistant's arms, jealousy had kicked him in the gut.

While unexpected and irrational, that emotion had been something he hadn't been able to ignore.

Ryker swore silently, his face white and grim. Sex without love was a cold and insensitive thing. Yet he didn't give a damn how ugly it appeared under a harsh light, he had wanted to kiss her so badly that day in the car, he'd actually ached. If the tip of her pink tongue had appeared one more time, he swore he would have...

"Shit!" he moaned, then shook his head.

Since his wife's death, there had been plenty of women in his life; they came through the door, then went quickly out again. None had meant anything to him. They had just been faces, bodies, women who filled a physical need at the time, who made him forget his guilt over Karen's death and that he lived life in the toilet.

None, however, had been in the same class as Blythe Lambert. Hell, his wife hadn't been, either. So why was he attracted to her? When she'd mistaken him for a common laborer, he had reveled in jerking her off the pedestal she existed on. Still, there had been something about her that had fascinated him and repelled him all at the same time.

And he'd sure as hell never forgotten her.

Beyond the fact that he thought her capable of murder, she shouldn't have the ability to tap into his emotional reservoir. He detested the type of woman Blythe was, convinced she ran in the fast lane and didn't care who she crushed to remain there.

From his background check on her, he knew she'd been reared without life's amenities, just like him. Unlike him, she had achieved fame and fortune, while he continued to struggle on a detective's salary with little chance for advancement.

"You're sick, Ryker," he muttered. "Certifiably sick."

Knowing his limitations didn't change them. He didn't need another headache, another crisis. At this point in his life, he wished that either Blythe Lambert wasn't quite so alluring or that she wasn't the target of his vengeance.

That last thought brought him out of the chair with such force that the back banged against the wall. The ringing of the phone rivaled that noise.

He reached for the receiver and snapped into it, "Delaney here." Moments later, color surged into his cheeks. "Hold what you got. I'll be right there."

Curt paced the floor.

"Please, will you just stop? You're making me crazy."

Curt did as Blythe asked, though the expression on his face remained highly charged. "If she thinks she's going to tell me what to do—"

Blythe raised her hand and cut him off. "Settle down, will you? The best way to handle Eleanor is to ignore her."

"Ignore her!"

Blythe flinched; his vocal cords sounded strained to the maximum. "For the moment, you have no choice."

"Oh, yes, I do. I don't work for that bitch."

"You're blowing Eleanor's presence all out of proportion."

Blythe hoped he couldn't see through her posturing, but she feared he could. Curt was too bright not to. Still, she didn't have any recourse but to try to reason with him, because her hands were tied.

At this juncture, it would take a bulldozer to remove Eleanor from the premises.

"Then tell her to get off my back." He took a deep breath. "How the hell did this happen? I mean—" Curt was clearly spluttering. "You own the company, don't you?"

"Yes."

"Then why can't you boot her out?"

Other than Susan, Blythe had had no intention of telling anyone at Designs about the debacle concerning the will. Now she had no alternative. She couldn't afford for Curt to walk out. He could go anywhere and get a job today. The thought of him doing that made her frantic.

Damn Eleanor.

"What's going on, Blythe? You owe me the truth."

"You're right, I do."

She told him about the will. Once she was finished, he seemed to wilt in front of her, which made her that much more nervous. "So you see my predicament?"

"Yeah, she's got you right where she wants you."

"No, she doesn't. I'm just treating her like a child who's pitching a temper tantrum. You should do the same thing. This power trip she's on is nothing but a sham."

"Does *she* know that?" Curt's tone was petulant.

"Apparently not yet, which is my mistake. But I'll take care of that."

"If she summons me into her sanctum again, I'm going to tell her to go to hell."

"You have my permission." Blythe made herself smile. "Along with my blessings."

"Good. Now that that's settled, I'm on my way to the

nursery. Two truckloads of plants are waiting to be unloaded.''

''Thanks, Curt. I honestly don't know what I'd do without you.''

He gave her a pointed look. ''Honestly, I don't either.''

Once the door had closed, leaving her alone, Blythe sank into her chair and released her pent-up breath. What else was going to happen?

She still hadn't found the financial backing or gotten the big job that would keep Designs afloat. Thank God she'd had a sizable certificate of deposit of her own. Despite taking a penalty, she'd cashed it in, and that was what the company was using to operate.

The ongoing murder investigation weighed on her. The question of who had murdered Mark, and why, hammered at her day and night. And Ryker Delaney—he hung over her life like a threatening storm cloud.

Now Eleanor.

Although Blythe hadn't been able to prove that Eleanor and Perry had conspired against her, she still didn't think of her sister-in-law as a threat. Her attorney, Tony Upshaw, would take care of that problem. Meanwhile, she would heed her own advice to Curt and treat Eleanor as a pesky but nonpoisonous varmint.

''You have a call on line one.''

Blythe jerked her head up and around. Susan stood in the doorway.

''It's not that detective, is it?''

''No. It's some guy I've never heard before.''

Blythe frowned, then said in a lighter vein, ''I'm sure it's a million dollar client.''

''Works for me,'' Susan responded with a grin as she backed out of the room and closed the door.

Blythe picked up the phone. "Hello."

"Where is it?"

It wasn't so much what he said, though his words made no immediate sense, but rather the way he said it. His voice sent a chill feathering down Blythe's spine.

"Who is this?"

"It doesn't matter."

"It does to me," she said, noticing his deep accent, which teased at the edges of her mind with its familiarity.

"Listen, lady, shut up and listen."

"Look, you obviously have the wrong number."

"You're Blythe Lambert, right?"

"Yes." Blythe's tone was hesitant, while her blood ran cold.

"Your husband had the hard candy, and I want it."

Hard candy? What did that mean? "I don't have a clue what you're talking about."

"Stop jacking me off, lady. Your old man had the goods—the candy, the list and the key. Now I want them."

"I told you, I don't know what you're talking about."

"Liar."

This time that strange-sounding voice was low but deadly. Before Blythe could reply, he went on. "You'll be hearing back from me. Soon." A sudden click indicated the caller had hung up.

Blythe didn't know how long she stood holding the receiver, fear coiling through her, bombarded by more questions. Who was that man? Was he one of Mark's gambling buddies? Were gambling debts what this was all about?

That was her best guess. Yet she had no idea what all that gibberish meant. Hard candy? List? Key? What did any of that have to do with gambling? Was the man who just called her somehow connected to Mark's murder?

Was he the murderer?

The only saving grace about that call was that, if she could get Ryker to believe her about it, it went a long way toward proving she hadn't killed her husband. With that thought uppermost in her mind, she picked up the receiver, though she couldn't dial right off; her hands were too unsteady and her stomach too queasy.

Finally, overlooking her personal reasons for wanting to steer clear of Ryker Delaney, she punched out his number.

Seventeen

She shouldn't have called him. Insidious waves of panic washed through Blythe. What had she been thinking? Apparently she hadn't been thinking at all. Trying to explain *anything* to Ryker Delaney would be a colossal mistake.

The way his mind worked, he would misconstrue the information so as to use it against her. She forced her brain into action. When he arrived, she would tell him that she'd changed her mind, that she didn't want to talk about the stranger who had called.

Blythe's surge of energy suddenly abated. Ryker wouldn't buy that for a second. Okay, so she would leave. That was her only other viable alternative. When she saw him again, she would be more rational.

"Susan, I'm going to the Temples'."

"Don't forget the cellular, so I can call if I need you."

Blythe nodded, then walked out of the office into the blinding sunlight. She paused and dug into her purse for her shades.

When she looked up, a shadow blocked her vision. Ryker Delaney was standing in front of her.

"Now, why am I not surprised?"

Blythe's mouth went taut and dry with tension, and she couldn't move. Yet she found her eyes locking with his. Her stomach flip-flopped. She recovered only with an effort.

His gaze seemed to bore into her, as both the silence and tension lengthened. Finally Ryker cleared his throat, and she could breathe.

"What are you not surprised about?" Blythe asked inanely.

"You running out on me like a scalded dog."

She took umbrage to that analogy. "That's not what I was doing."

"Oh, really, then what do you call it?"

She glared at him.

"You were leaving, right?"

He wasn't about to let her off the hook. Uneasily aware of his attractiveness and his danger, Blythe averted her gaze, taking no more chances on their eyes meeting again. "Yes, I was."

"I rest my case."

"How dare you creep up on me?"

His mouth split into a mocking grin. "I hardly call walking across a parking lot in broad daylight creeping up on anyone."

She wanted to respond with a stinging retort, but she knew it would make her look more foolish than she already did. Besides, he had a point. Now that he was close enough for her to smell his minty breath, she couldn't believe she hadn't seen him coming.

Apparently she was more fractured than she'd thought.

"What do you want?" she demanded in a huffy tone.

"More than you're prepared to give, that's for sure."

She wasn't about to touch that statement with a ten-foot pole, though she felt a surge of heat invade her, which was exactly what he'd intended.

"I have work to do," she said tersely.

"So do I."

"Look, I never should have called you."

"Why?"

"I don't have to answer that."

"Yes, you do."

Her uneasiness deepened. "Can't you just forget I called you?"

"Nope."

Blythe shivered inwardly, wondering how she was going to get out of this predicament, all the while lambasting herself for creating the situation in the first place.

"Are you hungry?"

She blinked. "Excuse me?"

"I said, are you hungry?"

"What does that have to do with anything?"

"We *are* going to talk, Mrs. Lambert." Ryker peered at his watch. "And since it's lunchtime, we might as well grab a bite."

"I don't think that's a good idea."

"I do." Ryker opened his car door and motioned for her to get in.

She could have made a scene and was tempted to do just that, but in the end, it would only hurt her. Already this man had the intuitiveness to see through her. Aggravating him further wouldn't be wise. Too, she was reaping what she had sown.

"All right, you win."

Although he didn't say another word to her until they were seated inside an out-of-the-way deli, Blythe was conscious of his every move. Conscious of *him,* period. His cologne teased her senses, as did his big hands when they had surrounded the steering wheel a few moments ago, and now as he lifted the water glass to his lips.

Her heart was thudding like an old, ungreased engine. She forced her gaze off the hairs that colored his knuckles.

"The turkey sandwiches on wheat are great."

Her astonishment must have shown, because he came close to smiling. "Surprised, huh?"

"Yes."

"Well, I do eat."

"But only out of machines. At least, that's what cops do on TV."

"Surely you don't believe everything you see on TV?"

His drawling voice sounded lazy, which added another dimension to his attractiveness.

"Not really."

"Good."

Blythe couldn't believe they were actually having a normal conversation, which in itself was dangerous. She wished she were anywhere but here with a man who not only made her feel strange and vulnerable, but who wanted her to be guilty of murdering her husband.

God, something was wrong with her and this whole scenario.

However, until Mark's killer was in custody, she wouldn't be rid of him. Somehow she had to make him understand that he was wasting his time with her.

The waitress appeared, forcing her back to the moment of reckoning. Ryker was looking at her with a question in his eyes. "Uh, I'll have whatever you're having."

He ordered the sandwiches, then faced her. A frown scored the lines deeper on his face. "So who called you?"

"Probably just a pervert."

"Let me be the judge of that."

"Look, I'm sure I'm overreacting," she added in a pinched tone, her gaze roaming, settling for a time on the garden of azaleas in the yard across the street.

Ryker leaned across the table and pinned her with his eyes. "So give me all the details."

"He had what sounded like a French Canadian accent."

"Go on."

Although his tone didn't change, *he* did. Every muscle seemed to tighten. She felt that reaction, rather than saw it. She had definitely struck a nerve.

"Do you know this man?" she asked.

"I'm asking the questions, remember?"

"He told me Mark had the hard candy and that he wanted it."

"Did...does that mean anything to you?"

"No."

"What else?"

"He accused me of having a list and a key."

"Neither of which you have."

"That's right, Detective. But then, you don't believe me, do you?"

"I didn't say that."

"You don't have to. I can see it in your eyes."

The waitress appeared with their food. Blythe took one look at hers and feared she would choke if she took a bite. Ryker certainly didn't have that problem. He wolfed his down like a man without a care in the world.

She fought the urge to get up and walk off.

"Aren't you going to eat?"

"I've lost my appetite."

He sighed. "Do you think this man had something to do with your husband's murder?"

"Of course," she snapped. "Why else would I have called you?"

Ryker wiped his mouth with his napkin, never taking his eyes off her. She squirmed under their directness. "Your husband had lots of enemies. However, considering what that guy said to you, he could easily jump to the top of the suspect list."

"Right behind me, is that it?"

Seemingly unfazed by her snippy tone, he countered, "There you go, putting words in my mouth."

"You're holding back. You know who this creep is, don't you?"

"Maybe."

"Tell me."

"No can do."

"Then I 'no can do' this anymore. So please take me back to my office."

"When I'm ready," Ryker said in a tone underlined with steel.

Blythe stood. "You can't dictate to—"

He touched her bare arm. She swallowed a tortured breath, the unexpected contact sending an electrical jolt along the surface of her skin.

Ryker's only visible reaction was to keep those incredibly blue eyes latched on her.

But she knew he wasn't as unaffected as he pretended. A hint of annoyance tightened his features. And there was something in his eyes that she didn't care to put a name to.

"Yes, I can," he muttered harshly. "Now sit down."

She sat back down, and for another long moment, silence reined supreme.

"I'll put a tracer on your line."

"I'd rather you hold off on that. My invasion of privacy has already reached the abusive stage."

Her obstinacy pissed him off. The glare he threw at her told her that. But when he spoke, his voice was low and under control. "I'm sure the call's related to your husband's gambling."

"So you know?"

"Oh, I know, all right." Ryker gave her a strange look. "Are you saying you didn't?"

"Not the extent, until—" She broke off.

"Until what?"

"Nothing."

"I'll be the judge of that."

"Designs' business manager dropped the bombshell in my lap that the company is nearly broke. Mark was milking it to pay what I'm assuming were gambling debts."

"So the company's in trouble, too?"

"Too?"

"I know about his debt to the bank."

Blythe's eyes flashed. "Is there anything you *don't* know about us?"

"Hopefully not."

"Well, I only found out about that when I tried to borrow money to get the business out of hock."

"Mark was a busy man."

"Spending money he didn't have." Blythe's tone was sour.

"Does the family know?"

"*I* haven't told them."

"Me, either."

"Then don't. Please."

"I'm making no promises about anything."

She pursed her lips but remained silent.

"Let's talk about Frank."

She raised her eyebrows. "Again?"

"Did you know that he gambles with the same lack of control as your husband?"

"Yes, but what does that have to do with Mark's death?"

"They might have kept company with the same people."

"Like that guy who called me?"

"Yeah, like him."

"Well, if Frank and Mark were a team, I didn't know about it."

"Has the will turned up?"

She recognized his ploy in that out-of-the-blue question, but it wasn't going to work. "No, and I'm not going to discuss that, even if we sit here all day."

"Just doing my job."

"And loving every dirty minute of it, too."

"You're right, I am."

He looked suddenly angry, the same kind of anger he'd shown the first time he questioned her about his niece. She wished she understood why he was hellbent on taking that anger out on her, why she brought out the worst in him.

One thing she *did* understand was that she reacted to him as strongly as he reacted to her, like the lethal combination of fire and gasoline.

"So go ahead and have your fun," Blythe finally said. "But I'll have the last laugh."

His response was to pin her with an unflinching stare. "Does the name Amy Britton mean anything to you?"

Another poke with the needle? If so, he would once again be disappointed. She wasn't about to rise to that bait, either. Besides, that name didn't mean diddly-squat to her. "No, should it?" she asked in a bored tone.

"She was having an affair with your husband."

Suddenly Blythe's lungs seemed unwilling to perform their function. How dare he say such a thing to her? But she wouldn't give him the satisfaction of knowing that he'd hit a raw nerve. "Another in a long line of many," she retorted.

"She said he was going to marry her."

Even though she had stopped loving Mark long ago, Blythe didn't want to know the name of the person he was sleeping with nor the particulars of their relationship. Only the thought that she had to remain strong for her own sake kept her from breaking into little fragments.

Blythe rolled her eyes with a nonchalance she was far from feeling. "Don't they all?"

A moment of silence followed.

"He left a life insurance policy."

Blythe should have seen this slam dunk coming, only she hadn't. And God, those words had cut deep. She stared at him in stunned disbelief. "Payable to…her?"

"To her," he echoed.

"How…much?"

"Half a mil."

Eighteen

Further speech eluded her for a moment. The staggering implication of what Ryker had just said finally shoved its way down her throat and loosened up her vocal cords.

"That...can't be," she whispered at last.

"It can and is," Ryker muttered, turning away as if he couldn't bear to look at the shock mirrored on her face.

But did he believe her reaction was sincere?

"Drink some water. You need it."

Blythe blinked again, then followed his advice, grabbing her glass and taking a sip. The cold liquid seemed to have the desired effect. Having collected herself she asked, "Is it legit? The policy, I mean?"

"We're checking it out. But from the way it's looking, it's airtight."

"Can...she collect on it?"

"Yep."

Blythe thought a moment. "I see."

"I'm not so sure you do."

Oh, she saw, all right. Mark had taken another cheap shot at her, another of his ways to knock her down another peg. She could picture the triumphant look his face would have worn when he'd gotten around to telling her about this Britton woman. Only he hadn't gotten the chance.

Suddenly Blythe wanted to sink into the floor. The humiliation was almost too much to bear, especially in front of Ryker. Somehow, though, she managed to hold herself together one more time and hide her true feelings from his all-seeing eyes.

Or did she?

The way Delaney was staring at her made her think otherwise.

"You really had no idea, did you?"

"I told you I didn't," she snapped. "And I don't lie."

He didn't respond to that, which made her angrier than ever. She knew what was going through his mind. He thought she was both a liar and a cheat. He thought she was a murderer, too, only he didn't have the guts to come right out and say that.

Yet.

He would, if and when he put together enough evidence against her. She wouldn't think about that now. She couldn't and remain sane. Still, there was one more question she had to ask. "Is she—"

"No," Ryker interrupted.

"You don't know what I was about to ask."

"Want to bet? Is she pregnant? Wasn't that your question?"

"Okay, is she?" Blythe's humiliation reached a new low point.

"No. Or at least she didn't say so, nor did she look it."

Blythe blew air out of her lungs. "Thank God for small favors."

A silence followed.

"This doesn't look good for me, does it?"

"'Fraid not."

"You think I'm lying about her?"

"Are you?"

"Dammit, I told you I had no idea Mark was that involved with anyone. Oh, I knew about his stable of women, but I had no clue he was involved with just one to that extent."

"What else *didn't* you know about your husband?"

"I'm beginning to ask myself that same question."

Silence surrounded them.

She broke it by asking, "What about this Amy Britton? Why isn't she at the top of your suspect list? A half million dollars is a great motive for murder."

"I agree, only she said she didn't know she was getting the money."

"I find that hard to believe." Blythe's tone was snide.

"We've checked that out, too. A few days before I arrived on her doorstep, she received a registered letter from an out-of-state attorney informing her that Mark had left her the money. The attorney has confirmed that Mark didn't want her to know about it."

"Lucky her."

"Unlucky you."

Blythe's eyes were filled with hostility. "I never expected or wanted a dime of life insurance from my husband. The business was all the insurance I needed."

He shrugged, then said, "Tell me something, okay? Off the record."

"That depends on what it is."

Ryker rubbed his chin, but his gaze never wavered. His eyes remained brooding and unreadable. "Why did you stay with the bastard, knowing he screwed around?"

Once his bluntness would have taken her aback. No longer. She was used to it. Still, her face was suffused with color. Shock, she knew, was a tactic the police often used in grilling suspects. Was that what had motivated him to ask that particular question?

"He must've been blind," Ryker muttered, throwing her a look that was easy to read. His eyes were filled with heat, sexual heat.

Her breath caught, and her skin turned clammy. Yet she couldn't pull her eyes away. That tangible heat drew them together, its power so potent she couldn't resist.

But she *had* to resist that pull. He was a cop with a mission. When that mission was done, he'd move on to another murder, another suspect. And she might be in jail, convicted of a crime she hadn't committed.

It was that brutal truth that broke the spell and forced her back into a combative mode, much safer ground.

Deliberately, she took another drink of water. "That's none of your business."

"That's where you're wrong," he countered, now stone-faced. "Right now, everything you do is my goddamn business." He paused. "You might say I own you."

Blythe fought down the urge to slap that smug stone face. If she did, he would probably slap handcuffs on her and haul her to jail for assaulting a police officer. That was his style.

"For the record, official or otherwise, I didn't kill my husband because of that woman or an insurance policy."

He seemed to ponder her harshly spoken declaration of innocence before changing the subject. "Let's talk about Eleanor."

"Because she's...?"

"A suspect."

Blythe should have been glad he was homing in on someone else for a change, and she was. Still, she didn't trust him, even to talk about Eleanor.

"Tell me about her relationship with Mark."

"There was no love lost between them, that's for sure. It goes back a long way."

"Could she have hated him enough to kill him?"

"No, but she was certainly jealous of him. It's me she hates."

"That's obvious."

"She'd be in her glory if you'd arrest me."

He raised uneven brows before turning away and staring at the couple next to their table. When he faced her again, that cold shutter was once more in place. "Any more trouble with your scumbag brother-in-law?"

"No, why?"

"Just checking."

There was a long silence, during which they both pushed their plates aside and sipped the coffee that the waitress served them after clearing the table.

"You know what I think?" Blythe asked into the silence, knowing she was treading on dangerous ground, but he couldn't have it all his way.

"I have a feeling you're going to tell me, anyway, right?"

"My guess is that you're meandering down a road that's leading nowhere, Detective."

"Oh, really now?" he asked darkly.

"Yes, really."

Their eyes tangled again, each holding their own secrets.

Blythe took a breath. "Like I've already told you, while my brother-in-law's a pain in the rear, he's too chicken to murder anyone. Besides, he's got it made. He doesn't work, he plays. Why would he mess that up?"

"If that's the case, then we're back to square one."

"Which is me."

Ryker looked at her, his face devoid of emotion.

"Well I'm not the only one!" Blythe lashed out. "That man who called me is a suspect, but you're not taking me or him seriously."

"It's a mistake to assume you know what I'm thinking."

Blythe heard the deadly note in his voice, but she ignored it. She'd had enough of him and his veiled accusations for one day. "I don't have—"

Her cell phone rang, chopping off her words, which was probably a good thing. With each passing moment, this "talk session" was going from bad to worse.

After taking the call, she flipped her phone closed, then stood. "I have to go."

"Where?"

Later, she couldn't say why she'd answered him. Maybe it was because she'd been livid. "To a job site."

"I'll take you."

Blythe shook her head. "That's not necessary."

"That's beside the point."

"No, that *is* the point. Just take me to get my car."

He plopped some bills down on the table. "Come on, let's get out of here."

"You're the most hardheaded man I know."

He laughed, but without any humor.

After muttering directions, Blythe hadn't said another word on the way to the job site. She had sat with her chin jutted.

Now Ryker stood to the side and watched the scene play out in front of him.

"What did Mrs. Brodrick tell you?"

A worker stepped forward to answer. "That from now on she'd be giving the orders."

"And did she give you orders?"

"Yes, ma'am."

"Exactly what did she tell you, Eli?"

The man removed his cap and wiped his sweat-stained brow, leaving a trail of dirt. "That if we finished this project by tomorrow, we'd all get bonuses."

"What?"

"Those were her exact words, ma'am."

"Surely you misunderstood—"

"I heard her say it, too," a big burly man cut in, stepping up to Blythe, his belly poking out as if he were a pregnant woman about to deliver.

Blythe stared at him in complete disbelief, looking as if she'd been punched in the stomach.

That was exactly what *had* happened. She'd been sucker-punched by her own sister-in-law, Ryker thought, which merely added even more spice to the gumbo, thickening it considerably.

"And who are you?" Blythe demanded of the big man.

"Jeb Mahon."

"Well Jeb Mahon, Mrs. Brodrick spoke out of turn," Blythe told him. "I'm still in charge."

Mahon stepped closer. Ryker straightened and also stepped closer.

"Whatcha saying, lady?"

"I'm saying there will be no bonuses. Understood?"

"No, bitch," he said, "that ain't understood."

Ryker moved to Blythe's side with every intention of kicking the living daylights out of this man before feeding him his balls.

As though Blythe read his mind, she waved her hand at him. He pulled up short.

"I'll handle this, Detective."

The way she used his title rankled, but he kept his mouth shut. If that bastard opened his mouth and said one more derogatory thing, he would bust him in the chops, regardless of what Blythe said.

"You're fired."

The man's mouth gaped.

"You heard me. Get your stuff and get off the premises. I won't have a troublemaker working for me."

The man muttered several expletives under his breath before turning to his fellow workers. "You guys gonna stand there and let this broad rob us of our money?"

No one said a word.

"Get back to work, all of you," Blythe ordered. "Now!"

"Well, I ain't budging," the potbellied man said. "I don't have to take orders from you."

"That's where you're wrong."

Despite the difference in size and height, Blythe stood toe-to-toe with him, her eyes challenging, as if daring him to say anything else.

He didn't. Muttering beneath his breath, Mahon whipped around and stalked off.

A few minutes later, in the car, Blythe sat still, then released a long sigh. Though he hated to admit it, Ryker admired her fire and spunk, a side he was sure she would prefer to keep buried. It showed signs of her rough-and-tumble background. Too bad she hadn't used some of that spunk when it came to her sleazebag husband.

When he would have said something, she raised her hand. "Please, just take me back to the office."

"Fine."

Twenty minutes later, Ryker headed the car into the parking lot of Designs, then looked at her. "I like your style."

"I didn't ask for your opinion."

His mouth stretched into a grim line. "No, you didn't."

"Look, Detective, I think we've had about enough of each other for today. For a lifetime, actually."

He ignored the brush-off. "It's a good thing you knew how to get down to their level."

Her features hardened. "What's that supposed to mean?"

"I was complimenting you, actually. Again."

"Some compliment."

"Dammit, it was."

"I hardly think making reference to my background qualifies as a compliment."

"Then you're too sensitive."

"You're too insulting."

"Give it a rest." He'd tried to keep the derision out of his tone but had obviously failed. "You rose above it," he added in a bored tone. "In a flurry of fame and power, no less."

"But you haven't."

That smarted. "We're not talking about me."

"Oh, yes, we are. That's what this conversation's all about. You're bitter, Detective. It's written all over you. We're both poor white trash, but I've made it, and you haven't."

"That's bullshit!"

"Sure it is," she said in a mocking tone. "But just because you're still wallowing in the gutter doesn't give you the right to ridicule me because I'm *not.*"

"Dammit, you just don't know when to shut your mouth, do you."

Exasperated, and without thinking, he reached for her and jerked her hard against his chest. She cried out, not only from the unexpected contact but from the fact that his gun poked her in the belly.

Realizing what he'd done and where this was heading, he muttered, "Sorry." It was when he went to release her that he made his second mistake.

He looked at her.

Her eyes were wide and her breathing had suspended. But it was her mouth that was his undoing. Moist and parted, it caused something to twist in his gut.

He groaned inwardly even as he leaned toward those bee-stung lips that begged to be kissed.

"Please," she whispered in a husky voice.

"Please what? Please don't do something we've both wanted from the start?"

Several expressions darted across her features. "Detective, you—"

"Don't you think it's time you called me Ryker?" he asked in a guttural tone.

"What—"

He sank his mouth against hers, accurately and deeply. She tasted like cinnamon, tart and sweet, as if she'd just eaten a ripe apple.

He delved for more, giving in to the same hot current that passed through him earlier when he'd touched her on the arm.

It rocked him, and he wanted more of that fire he sensed was still untapped. It was a realization that forced him to pull back.

For the longest time, neither one of them said a word, though Ryker cursed silently. This time he'd really fucked up; he'd crossed the line.

In light of the mistress, Blythe Lambert still topped his suspect list.

And because his dick had overruled his brain, he was in a world of hurt—physically and mentally.

"Don't ever touch me again, Detective Delaney," Blythe said through clenched teeth. "Or I'll report you."

Nineteen

Blythe seethed inwardly as she drove. She had called herself every name in the book, ranging from stupid to just plain foolish. However, her self-flagellation hadn't worked. She simply had to face the fact that she'd let her emotions get the better of her sane judgment.

Never again. She had meant what she'd said to Ryker Delaney. If he laid a hand on her again, she would report him in a heartbeat.

Suddenly Blythe's conscience pricked her, forcing her to admit that she had kissed him back. She had felt the stimulation from his hot lips deep in her breasts, her tummy, *her toes,* for God's sake.

No man, not even Mark, had ever kissed her quite like that, as if she'd been the only woman in the world. The problem was, she was having difficulty dealing with this off-the-wall situation. Despite the way he felt about her, what he believed about her, she was attracted to him. She was terrified for herself, terrified it would be fatally easy to succumb to her physical need.

Insane.

And dangerous.

Feeling as though her blood pressure was off the charts, Blythe considered pulling off the road for several minutes to collect herself. But she didn't have far to go to the office. Once there, she had so much to do that maybe she could erase Ryker Delaney from her mind.

Fat chance—as in *no* chance.

Still, she had to try. Ryker's nagging presence was playing havoc with her confidence, undermining everything she did and said, something she couldn't allow to go on happening. She had to believe in her own strength of mind and common sense.

She had to believe that kiss had been just a fluke, a one time thing. She wouldn't be caught off guard again.

Breathing deeply to counteract the queasiness, Blythe wheeled into her parking place at Designs and walked into the building. She didn't stop at her office. Instead, she headed to Mark's, knowing that Eleanor was there. Her car had been parked in the slot next to Blythe's.

Maybe because she herself was in such a cantankerous mood, she would have to try harder to keep a lid on her temper. If not, she would play right into Eleanor's hands. Already, Ryker and Eleanor together were dreadful crosses to bear, but not for much longer. She intended to purge them both from her life.

Now.

Blythe didn't bother knocking. She thrust open the door and walked in. Eleanor was sitting behind Mark's huge desk, about to raise a glass to her lips. Booze was in it, Blythe suspected.

"I don't recall hearing you knock," Eleanor said in a surly but slurred voice, followed by a loud hiccough.

"I didn't."

"Whadda you want?"

"To talk."

"Speak your piece, then get the hell out of my face."

Eleanor's drunkenness didn't soften the belligerence in her tone. Blythe knew that the hostile attitude was part of her sister-in-law's defenses. Behind that blustering mask lurked deep insecurities, insecurities that had been there from birth. Even Mark's death couldn't change that.

Blythe intended to play on those insecurities. In order to beat Eleanor at her own game, she had to play dirty. She hated that, but she was fighting for the business and maybe... No. She wouldn't let Ryker and what he was up to clutter her mind for one more minute.

"Are you *able* to talk?" Blythe asked.

"Hell, can't you see I'm busy?" Eleanor asked, taking another healthy swallow of her drink.

Blythe frowned. She'd known her sister-in-law drank, though not to this extent. When you indulged in whiskey this early in the day, you were in deep trouble. However, Eleanor didn't look any different, except maybe for the circles under her blue eyes. They seemed darker and more pronounced. On closer observation, her features were a bit more gaunt, making her look older and even more unattractive.

"You're about to be un-busy," Blythe said. "Don't ever usurp my authority again."

Eleanor slammed her drink down on the desk, sending it splashing in several directions. Then she stood to her full height, her eyes glaring. "I'll do whatever I damn well please."

Blythe didn't raise her voice. "No, you won't, Eleanor."

"You don't scare me," Eleanor spat.

"I'm not trying to. But you'd best keep in mind that until the issue of the will is settled, you're bound by the terms of the injunction."

"Fuck the injunction." She took another gulp, then laughed a harsh laugh. "On second thought, *fuck you!*"

Blythe heard the slur in the words and knew that Eleanor was falling-down drunk. Realizing that, she also knew that she was wasting her time and effort trying to reason with the woman.

Still, Blythe couldn't stop herself from saying, "You're disgusting, Eleanor, more so than I ever knew."

"Why, you sanctimonious bitch, get outta my office."

"Your office? I don't think so, but I don't intend to stand here and talk to someone who's so drunk she doesn't know what she's saying. It's a waste of my time."

"I may be tipsy, but I know exactly what I'm saying."

"No, you don't. We'll continue this discussion at another time."

"There may not be another time." Eleanor winked and smiled a knowing smile.

"What does that mean?" Blythe wanted to chop her tongue off for letting Eleanor goad her into continuing this absurd conversation.

"I figure you'll soon be in a goon outfit looking through bars."

Blythe saw stars. Did Eleanor know something she didn't? No. Eleanor was simply jerking her chain, and she had fallen for her crap, hook, line and sinker.

"Sorry if I busted your bubble, but you're definitely at the top of Delaney's hit list."

"That's nothing new to me."

"Good, then you won't be surprised when your ass is arrested."

Blythe drew deeply for her next breath, knowing that Eleanor was yanking her chain harder than ever. Somewhere she had lost control of the situation. She had to get it back.

"Okay, so you've had your fun," Blythe said. "Now I'm going to have mine. So drunk or not, you'd best take note. If you ever undermine my orders on any job, I'll have *you* arrested."

Blythe walked to the door, where she turned and stared back at Eleanor, who continued to glare at her, a snarl on her lips. "Oh, by the way, even if Designs wanted to give bonuses, they couldn't." She looked Eleanor up and down. "Your leech of a brother sucked every drop of cash out of the business."

"I don't believe that," Eleanor said, her voice surlier than ever.

"Believe it. Ask Moody. He'll tell you."

Eleanor launched herself from behind the desk, her eyes wild. "You're all liars! Designs is worth millions."

"Sorry to burst *your* bubble. Designs is about to crash and burn. But I intend to save it. So don't get in my way, or you'll be sorry."

"You stay out of mine, or *you'll* be the one that's sorry!" Eleanor shouted just as Blythe closed the door.

Leaning against it for support, Blythe fought back her fury.

"Jesus! What was that all about?"

Blythe pushed herself away from the door and fell in step with Moody, who was in the process of moving his pipe from one side of his mouth to the other.

"You won't believe it."

"Try me."

Blythe gave him the gist of the verbal slinging match that had just taken place.

"Are you serious?"

Blythe cut him a look that spoke volumes.

"I hope you put that crazy bitch in her place. Why, she doesn't know shit from shinola about running this company."

"We both know that, but she doesn't."

"You think she knocked her brother off just so she could—" Moody broke off with a curse and a red face. "Sorry, I didn't mean any disrespect...." This time his voice played out before the sentence was complete.

Blythe touched his arm briefly. "Take it easy on yourself. I know what you meant. To answer your question, I certainly don't think she'd go that far." She shivered. "It takes an amoral animal to take someone else's life."

"Well, she's the consummate bitch," he mumbled in his deep, gruff voice. "And up to no good."

"I agree she definitely bears watching."

"So what if she comes to me and asks to see the records?"

"Show them to her. She doesn't believe me. Maybe you'll have better luck."

Moody stopped and looked down at Blythe once they reached the door to her office. "Any luck finding some cash?"

"Not yet," Blythe said in a forlorn voice, then brightened, refusing to give in to the depression that wanted to drag her down. "But I refuse to throw in the towel. Something will happen. It just has to."

"Well, keep me posted."

"Oh, Moody, no one on the payroll, including you, has to worry about not getting paid. I had some money of my own. I—"

"We're not worried," Moody interrupted. "We trust you."

You seem to be the only ones, Blythe thought, slipping into the second door, which bypassed Susan's office, and going straight into hers.

She shut the door behind her, only to pull up short.

"What the hell do you think you're doing?" she snapped, marching across the room, her eyes fixed on her brother-in-law.

From his position behind her desk, he jerked upright and dropped his hands to his sides.

Blythe sucked in her breath and held it. Lord, he looked like he'd been in a fight with a mad dog and lost. Someone had taken their wrath out on him. Even though she winced just looking at his black-and-blue face, she had trouble conjuring up any sympathy. Some dark part of her rejoiced that he'd finally gotten what he deserved.

"What are you staring at?" he asked, his tone snarling.

"What happened? Did you finally say the wrong thing to the wrong person?"

"Shut up."

She knew she'd hit the nail on the head, which gave her courage to continue. "Did one of your gambling buddies rough you up?"

"I told you to shut up."

"How about Mark? Were the two of you involved?" She paused on purpose. "Detective Delaney thinks that might be the case."

"He's full of it."

"Then what are you doing in my office?"

He smiled even as he shut the drawer he'd been rummaging through. "Looking for something."

Bastard!

"Well now, did you find that something?" she asked, clamping down on the fury threatening to erupt.

Frank smiled his pat smile, thinking it could charm the birds out of the trees. "As a matter of fact, I didn't."

"Since you're in *my* office and snooping through *my* desk, I think I have the right to know why." Sarcasm thickened her voice.

His smile merely broadened. "When you cleaned out Mark's desk, I thought you might've found something that belonged to me."

Blythe almost laughed, but she was too angry. She was trembling inside. "What is that something?"

Frank shrugged, then walked from behind the desk, stopping within touching distance of Blythe. "Nothing important."

Repulsed by his nearness, she backed up. "Oh, really? Then why did you sneak in like a thief and riffle through my drawers?"

Instead of answering her, Frank reached out and trailed a finger down one cheek. "God, you're beautiful."

Blythe slapped his hand away and spat, "Keep your filthy hands to yourself."

"Or what?" he taunted. "I have your number. You're all bark and no bite, sweetheart."

Blythe reached out and poked a finger in his chest. "If I ever catch you in my office again, or if you ever put your hands on me again, we'll see who bites."

"Ah, sweetheart, you're more beautiful than ever when you're mad. I'll let you bite me anywhere, anytime."

"You're a pig and a pervert!"

"You've got a nasty mouth."

"Not nearly as nasty as your wife's. I swear I'll tell Eleanor that you're still trying to get me in your bed." She poked him hard in the chest again. "You think you've been worked over, just wait till she gets through with you. She'll be the one who bites you where it hurts the most."

"Tell her. I don't give a damn."

"You will. Trust me, you will."

Frank ambled to the door, where he turned around. Instead of smiling, he gave her an odd look, then winked. "Have a nice day, sweetheart."

Blythe wanted to scream obscenities at him, then head for the shower. His slimy presence never failed to make her feel dirty. However, her personal vendetta wasn't the issue, at least not right now. Her own ineptitude was what had her in an uproar.

She'd caught him red-handed but had failed to find out from the weasel what he'd been after.

What had Mark had that Frank wanted?

Twenty

Blythe stared into her rearview mirror. Nothing, at least for the moment. She didn't know what had made her think she was being followed. Nonetheless, she'd felt that way, and it not only made her uneasy, it made her madder than hell.

Her first inclination was to blame Ryker. Sneaky. That was his modus operandi. He would show up when least expected, which kept her unnerved. One day she envisioned herself being charged with murder, the next she'd tell herself how ridiculous that was.

She hadn't killed Mark. The idea that Ryker thought she could have was beyond her. And to think she had let him kiss her. Worse, she couldn't stop thinking about that kiss. It seemed as though his lips had turned her inside out, leaving her aching for more.

Feeling her heart go into overdrive, Blythe veered off that mental path and once again fixed her gaze on the rearview mirror. There it was again—that same car, cruising behind her. Her heart upped its rhythm. Suddenly the vehicle whizzed past her, and she felt like a fool.

Damn. Her imagination had run wild yet again. Still, that niggling in her gut remained. Her husband was dead. Murdered. Someone, either family or stranger, had killed him. As long as that killer was on the loose, then she couldn't let down her physical or emotional guard.

The strange voice on the phone jumped to mind. *Hard candy,* he'd said. She had racked her brain and still had no idea what he was talking about.

And Frank. She couldn't forget about finding him beaten up and snooping in her desk drawer. Were those strange happenings related? If so, how much danger was she in?

Then there was the matter of Mark's mistress and the insurance policy. What role, if any, had she played in this? Could she have killed Mark for the insurance money?

The questions had no answers.

Before she blew everything out of proportion, Blythe concentrated on what was ahead of her. She hadn't planned to visit the Lambert compound. But when she got into her car to return home after a frustrating day of following up on jobs, none of which had materialized, it seemed she had no other alternative.

Mark's murder was crippling the company. She had to have help. Now, as she pulled up in front of the lovely home, Blythe took several deep breaths. If she had to beg, she would, though she prayed it wouldn't came to that.

But with this family, one never knew.

She rang the doorbell, and to her surprise, Cynthia herself answered it. Blythe was stunned. "Surely you're not alone?"

Cynthia actually smiled, though her lovely eyes carried a shadow of sadness. Blythe knew she would never get over losing a child, no matter how old that child happened to be.

"No, Daisy's just busy doing something else." Cynthia moved aside for Blythe to enter. "It's so good to see you."

"Same here." Blythe leaned over and kissed her mother-in-law's pale but still unlined cheek.

"Is this a social or business call?"

Blythe was once again taken aback by this woman's resilience and intuitiveness. "Both," she admitted honestly, though she wished it were only the former.

Despite the strained undercurrents in this family, she and Cynthia had managed to keep a good rapport. Unfortunately, Blythe told herself, this visit might put an end to that.

"Have a seat in the library, and I'll have Daisy bring us some iced mint tea."

"That sounds good."

The sofa felt as though she'd sunk into satin, but Blythe couldn't relax. If Cynthia... She wouldn't think about that. She would think positive. After all, it would behoove Cynthia to keep Designs afloat. The family had already been hit with enough scandal.

"Let's get the business out of the way first," Cynthia said, sitting, then smiling at Daisy, who set a platter on the coffee table before disappearing from the room.

Blythe reached for the tea but declined the goodies. Her digestive system was already on the warpath. "First, tell me how you're feeling."

"The old ticker's better, at least for the time being."

"Thank God."

"So, how've you been?"

"Tired," Blythe blurted out before she thought.

"I can tell. You're much too thin." Cynthia's tone expressed her disapproval.

"Look, Cynthia, I need to ask a favor, and you have no idea how hard it is."

"Is it money?"

Blythe nodded.

"For you personally?"

"Heavens, no."

"Then why—"

Oh, Lord, she doesn't know. "Designs. It's...in financial trouble."

"Why, that's impossible."

"That was my reaction, but we're both wrong."

"How much do you need?"

"Quite a lot, actually."

Cynthia picked up her glass and took several sips. "Whose fault is it? Eleanor's?"

Blythe heard the dread and pain in her mother-in-law's voice, and wished she hadn't had to initiate this conversation. But she'd been left with no other alternative.

"She's certainly partly at fault, undermining me at every turn. In fact, I had to put out a fire she started on one of the jobs. She interfered where she shouldn't have."

"You're still convinced she's behind Mark's missing will, too, aren't you?"

"Absolutely."

"Oh dear."

Blythe would certainly have used stronger words, but she didn't reveal her thoughts. No use pouring more gas on that already raging fire, when Eleanor wasn't the one ultimately responsible for the financial catastrophe.

"How does Mark fit into the problems at Designs?"

"He's actually the one responsible."

Cynthia's hand shook so hard that she had to set the glass back down.

"I'm sorry to be so blunt, but it's the truth. He gambled, and he borrowed against the company to pay off his gambling debts.''

"You stopped loving him a long time ago, didn't you?"

Blythe winced. "Yes, I did, but that doesn't have anything to do with what we're talking about."

"I think it does."

"Well, I don't. Anyway, Mark's to blame for killing my love for him."

"Are you sure?"

"Are you saying I should have condoned his affairs?"

Cynthia stiffened, but her tone was still pleasant. "There's never been a divorce in our family."

What if Cynthia knew about the Britton woman and the policy he'd left her? Would she think differently about her son? Probably not, Blythe told herself. Anyway, she wasn't going to be the one who broke the news to her. What would it matter now, anyway?

"Don't you think this conversation is moot? I mean, Mark's dead, after all."

Cynthia's lower lip quivered; then she seemed to collect herself. "I'm sorry about the business."

"Your sympathy's not what I need."

"What you need is cash," Cynthia responded in a far-off tone.

"Exactly. So will you help?" Blythe pressed, her frustration building. "It will only be a loan, I promise you that."

Cynthia stood, her eyes veiled. "We'll talk later, all right?"

Blythe couldn't believe her own ears. Cynthia, in her quiet, standoffish way, was brushing her off like some pesky fly, which was both shocking and frightening. Without her mother-in-law's help, she was in deep trouble. Unless a miracle happened and Designs landed one of those big contracts, *it* was in deep trouble.

"Cynthia, what's the bottom line here?" Blythe demanded, standing and scrutinizing her, trying to read what lurked behind her eyes.

"I'm not feeling well, that's all."

She was hedging. Big time. And there wasn't one thing Blythe could do about it. But something was wrong. She could guess, though, and the thought not only upset her, but it made her sick.

"Eleanor's been to see you." Her words were a flat statement of fact.

"Look, Blythe—"

Blythe held up her hand. "It's okay. I get the picture."

"I'm not sure you do."

Blythe smiled a grim smile. "Oh, I get it, all right. Eleanor's poisoned you against me."

"No, that's—"

"You think I might have killed Mark."

The old woman's lips snapped shut, and her eyes filled with tears. But she didn't deny the charge.

"I didn't kill your son, Cynthia. I didn't love him, but I would never have taken his life. If you think I did, then God help us both."

With that, Blythe turned and walked out of the house.

Did everyone in Tyler think she was guilty of murder?

Who cared? Blythe asked herself, pulling into her drive, where she paused and leaned her head against the steering wheel. She cared, and for that reason, the gossip stung.

Once she had left the Lambert mansion, she'd gone straight to the office, but she hadn't stayed. She couldn't bear to be surrounded by walls. The outdoors had beckoned.

However, the cloudless day couldn't dispel the shadow that lingered from her conversation with Cynthia and the ugly insinuation that Blythe might have killed Mark.

It had followed her all day, at work, at the nursery, on the job, and now, as she finally got out of the car. It had nipped at her heels like a vicious, barking dog.

Feeling the tears smart behind her eyes, Blythe unlocked the door and went inside. It wasn't quite dark yet, but still she switched on the light.

Spooked.

That was how she felt most of the time, and she hated it. She just wished Ryker Delaney would veer his investigation in another direction. Maybe she wouldn't feel so threatened by him.

Wishful thinking.

Later, she knew why she hadn't realized something was wrong. Ryker. He'd consumed her thoughts. Only after she had slipped off her shoes and plopped her purse down on the bar did she freeze, her blood literally turning to ice.

Cigar smoke.

The foul odor hit her with all the force of a brick upside her head. She stood rooted to the spot. Someone had been in her house. What if he was still there? With her heart stuck in her throat, Blythe tiptoed to the den.

He was sitting in *her* chair as if he belonged there.

Blythe's first thought was to bolt. But she couldn't. Her legs were too rubbery. "Who...are you?"

"That's not important."

She gasped. That voice. The French Canadian who had called her on the phone now sat in her house.

"Get out!"

"Not until I get what I came for."

Fear joined her heart in her throat. If she made a run for it, would he try to stop her? Shoot her? She hadn't seen a gun, but that didn't mean he didn't have one.

"We can do this the easy way or the hard way," he said. "It's your call."

Although he remained seated, she knew he wasn't a tall man—short, in fact. Still, he came off as a big man. His biceps and thighs were those of someone who lifted weights daily and with affection.

However, it wasn't his strength that frightened her the most, but rather his face. He was swarthy, with black hair, black eyes and a black mustache that draped fat red lips.

And that cigar. She couldn't get past that. It reminded her of a lizard hanging out of one side of that repulsive mouth.

"Well, what's it going to be?"

"I don't know what you're talking about."

"Then I'll refresh your memory. I'm in no hurry. I got all night, as long as it takes, actually."

Her fear turned into panic. "If I had whatever it is you wanted, I'd give it to you."

"I was your husband's partner."

Blythe blinked her shock. "Partner? In what?"

"Oh, in a side venture we had going." He paused, flipping ashes on the floor. "But then, I'm sure you know what I'm talking about."

"No, I don't, dammit."

The man lunged off the chair. Blythe's eyes widened, and she backed up.

"So you were Mark's gambling partner?" she forced out.

He sneered. "Of sorts."

"Are you saying Mark owes you money?"

"As in millions."

"Millions?" Blythe croaked. She took another step back as her heart banged against her rib cage.

"That's right, Mrs. Lambert, millions. But then, you know that, so quit playing dumb."

"I'm not playing dumb! None of this makes sense to me."

"Well, it had better start, because I intend to get what's coming to me, hard candy and all."

"I still don't know what 'hard candy' is." Her voice had risen far above its normal range, but she couldn't seem to control it. It was almost as though she were on stage, acting out a play. But this ugly man in front of her was no actor, nor was she on stage.

"Stop lying, lady!"

He had invaded her home, damn him. But as long as he thought she had something of value that he wanted, she was safe, which meant she could call his bluff. "I don't have what you want. I sure don't have any millions. So get out of my house and don't come back. If you don't, I'll call the police."

"Lady," he sneered, edging toward her, "I'm calling the shots."

"Stay away from me."

"If you do anything stupid, you'll be sorry—and so will your grandmother!"

Twenty-one

Honey was sleeping. Blythe stood in the doorway, fear lodged in her throat. She took a deep breath. The air she inhaled was fresh; no repugnant cigar odor filled her lungs. Thank God, Blythe thought, easing into the chair beside her grandmother's bed.

Immediately after her surprise visitor had left, she headed to the nursing facility. By the time she arrived, her mind had become a chamber of horrors. If that bastard had hurt her grandmother because of her, she would never get over it.

The frail figure on the bed seemed mercifully unaware that anything was amiss. Blythe, however, was too weak to move so she sat there for the longest time, trying to calm her fractured nerves.

What to do?

She had asked herself that question over and over. She couldn't afford to let that man harm Honey. Yet if she reported him to the cops, he just might make good on his threat. Since she didn't know him or what he was capable of doing, she wasn't about to take that chance. She would just have to keep her mouth shut and make sure Honey was protected.

Of course, reporting the incident to Ryker would be the smart thing, at least from a personal standpoint, as it would go a long way toward proving her innocence.

But when she measured that against her concern for Honey... No, she had to keep her mouth shut.

Besides, she had no idea how Ryker would react. All she knew was that she had to stay away from him. After that kiss, he was dangerous in more ways than one. But she wouldn't think about him now. She couldn't.

Moments later, Blythe tiptoed out of Honey's room, then went straight to the office, where she told the administrator that no one other than the staff members was to enter her grandmother's room.

If she had to, she would hire someone to sit with Honey. She would find the extra money somewhere. That lack of money was still very much on her mind a short time later when she walked into Designs.

"Something's wrong," Susan said with concern.

"That's an understatement."

Susan didn't ask. She merely followed Blythe to her office and sat down. "I'm listening." The concern was now laced with determination.

"You know me too well."

"That's another of friendship's little quirks."

"I don't know where to start," Blythe responded, walking to the window, then turning back around.

"Preferably at the beginning."

Blythe hesitated. While she wanted to dump her fears and troubles in Susan's lap, she couldn't. Pride kept her from sharing the news about Mark's mistress and the insurance policy. She didn't want to talk about Frank, either, whom she considered more of a pest than anything. And she *couldn't* tell her about the French Canadian and his threat to her grandmother, which was seared on her brain.

"How 'bout I go first?" Susan said, cutting into her thoughts.

Blythe's stomach lurched. "Uh-oh, I don't like the sound of that."

"That detective was here."

Susan spat out the words as if she was trying to get rid of something terrible in her mouth.

Blythe tried to hide her agitation. "I'm not surprised."

"He wouldn't tell me what he wanted, of course."

"Of course. He only wants to torment me." Blythe didn't bother hiding the bitterness in her tone.

Susan raised her eyebrows. "What's with that guy, anyway? He just keeps showing up like the proverbial bad penny."

Blythe didn't say anything.

"Surely he doesn't think you could kill anyone?"

Blythe crossed her arms over her breasts. "Who knows what he thinks? And therein lies the problem."

"Hell's bells, if I didn't know better, I'd think he has the hots for you."

"Don't be ridiculous," Blythe muttered, swinging back around to face the window to hide the hot flush that crept up her face.

If only Susan knew how close she'd come to the truth, she would be appalled. But then, so was Blythe. Appalled at herself for letting her emotions get completely out of hand.

Susan chuckled. "Hey, I was just kidding. He's good-looking, all right. But I prefer someone who doesn't eat nails for breakfast."

"I second that. Besides, that man's fast becoming my worst nightmare come true."

"I hear you."

They were both quiet for a minute; then Susan said,

"I've been trying to reschedule your appointment with Cecil Farmer."

"Any luck?"

"Not so far. He's always out of town."

"Keep trying. We can't let that job slip through our fingers."

"So how are things financially? Not good, I take it."

"'Not good' is an understatement. We're more or less operating on the small jobs in progress, plus a certificate of deposit I cashed in." Blythe walked to her desk and sat down.

"What about Cynthia?"

"I swallowed my pride and went to her, but she didn't offer to bail us out, which is a good thing, really." Blythe gritted her teeth. "I've made up my mind that I'm going to pull Designs out of the hole on my own. Taking money from Cynthia would only complicate things more."

"But what if you can't?"

"I can," Blythe told her with more confidence than she was feeling.

"Good girl, but I don't know how you're going to do it—what with Eleanor stepping on one foot and that damn detective on the other."

"Designs' success or failure pretty much hinges on getting that Farmer contract."

"What about Eleanor? Do you think she'll undermine that?"

"No, because she wants the company to survive so she can run it."

Susan rolled her eyes. "That's the joke of the century. As it stands, she can't find her rear with a compass."

Blythe laughed outright, which felt good. "Trust me, after our battle royal yesterday, she's pulled in her claws.

Or rather, I clipped them down to the quick. She had no idea Designs is close to bankruptcy.''

''I'd like to have seen her face.''

''No, you wouldn't. It wasn't a pretty sight.''

''Still—''

''Can I join the party?''

They both swung around and stared at Curt as he stepped into the room.

''Sure,'' Susan said drolly. ''We're having a ball.''

Curt snorted, plopping his bony body down in the chair next to Susan.

''How are things at the nursery?'' Blythe asked.

''Holding their own,'' Curt said, his mouth curved down. ''I delivered the trees to Hazel Applegate and got the crew started.''

''That's good. I don't know what we'd do without all those small jobs.''

Curt rubbed his exposed forehead though his eyes were fastened on Blythe. ''Those might soon be in short supply, too.''

''What makes you say that?'' Blythe demanded, while Susan stared at him, panic written on her face.

''For starters, your sister-in-law's big mouth.''

''Oh, brother,'' Blythe muttered. ''What's she done now? I was just bragging about having clipped her claws.''

''She's got a smear campaign going against you that you wouldn't believe.''

''Oh, I'd believe it, all right.''

''Rumor has it she's telling everyone that you killed Mark,'' Curt said.

''That bitch!'' Susan exclaimed, lunging out of her chair.

''Anything else?'' Blythe asked.

"Yeah, she's also spreading word that the cops think you're guilty, too," Curt added. "And the fact that Delaney keeps showing up doesn't help."

"I just got through telling her the same thing," Susan said. "He's bad news."

"I couldn't agree more," Blythe said, staring into space.

"So what are you going to do?" Curt asked.

Blythe's hard gaze went from one to the other. "Something, that's for sure."

Ryker eased back in his chair, but he was far from relaxed. It had been a bitch of a day, and it wasn't over yet. Part of his ill humor stemmed from the knot in his gut.

He couldn't get over the nut-ball stunt he'd pulled.

Not only had his kissed his main suspect in a murder case, he wanted to fuck her, as well. Just thinking about how she felt against him, how sweet her mouth tasted, made him hard.

Jesus! What a mess, a mess like none he'd ever gotten into before. He knew how to solve this dilemma—stay the hell away from her. Unfortunately, that wasn't an option. Not if he wanted to keep his job.

If Blythe hadn't killed her husband, then she might lead him to who did. And then there was his niece. Until her killer was found, Blythe would have his up-close-and-personal attention.

During that time, he would have to keep his dick in his pants and bear his pain like a big boy. After all, this debacle was his own doing. What worried him, though, was his inability to do his job. Hell, when he'd gone to her office to see her and she hadn't been there, he'd been relieved.

What a chickenshit.

Even a visit from his sister a few minutes ago hadn't improved his mood, though he'd covered it well.

"Think your sister would go out with me?"

Ryker gave his partner, who was walking into his office, a scathing look. "Don't even think about it."

"Why the hell not? I'm okay-looking. I'm—"

"Full of it."

"That, too," Mike said with a good-natured grin.

"Most of all, you're a cop."

"So?"

"So Marcy needs someone in her life who's not likely to get his ass shot off."

"Makes sense."

Ryker threw Mike another look, then said, "Bring me up to speed on the girl's murder and the trailer park shooting."

When Mike finished, he got up and stretched. "Now it's your turn. What's happening on the Lambert case?"

"I still don't have enough to arrest Blythe Lambert, if that's what you're asking."

The room fell silent while Mike rubbed his jaw and Ryker moved out from behind his desk.

"You think she knocked him off?"

Ryker stopped in his tracks and frowned. "It doesn't matter what I think."

"Since when?"

"Since now."

"What's chewin' on you?"

Ryker threw him another scathing glance.

Mike shrugged. "Okay, whatever it is, it can keep chewin' while I go check on the mistress, see if she actually loved his dick more than his money."

"Go for it."

"What about you?"

"I have a lead."

"I'm listening."

"Not yet. It'll probably turn out to be nothing. I'll keep you posted."

"Let's go, then."

They walked outside into the harsh humidity. Ryker stopped and looked in his pocket for his shades.

"Uh-oh."

Although Mike spoke in a hushed mutter, Ryker heard him. "What's wrong?" he asked, slipping his glasses on the bridge of his nose."

"Look who's driving up."

Ryker stared in the direction of Mike's nod. His heart skipped an unexpected beat; then he cursed.

Mike whistled, then cut a glance at Ryker. "Man alive, it looks to me like her piss factor's off the charts."

"Shut up, Rushmore."

"I'll do better than that." Mike winked. "I'll leave you to face the music alone."

Rushmore swaggered toward his car while Ryker headed toward Blythe's. Just as he got there, she slammed on the brakes, reached across the seat and flung open the door.

He leaned down and peered inside. "What's up?"

"Turnabout's fair play, Detective."

"Meaning?" he asked, feeling suddenly amused. Unfortunately, she wasn't.

"Get in!"

Twenty-two

"Chalk one up for you."

Blythe didn't answer Ryker, even after he slammed the door, binding them together once again in the close confines of a car.

He cut her a glance and saw that she wasn't composed, as he'd first thought, although she *was* mad. The jut of her delicate chin told him that.

She turned and looked at him then. His insides twisted. She was furious, no doubt about that. But she also appeared extremely vulnerable, which insanely pricked his conscience.

Then his own anger set in. Hell, he didn't want to feel sorry for her. He didn't want to feel anything for her. He wanted more than anything to forget he'd shown his own vulnerability and kissed her.

"Leave me alone," she snapped coldly.

"Is that what you came to tell me?"

"Yes."

"I can't, and you know why."

"It looks like I'm going to have to make good on my threat and go to Foley."

"Go ahead."

"You're harassing me, dammit, for no good reason. And that's hurting my business."

"I have a murder to solve."

"And an ax to grind along with it."

"Look, we've gone over this territory before, so you're wasting my time. Unless you've got some reason for taking up my time, I'm out of here." He gripped the door handle. He wanted out of there for a much more selfish reason. Her closeness was eating at him. God, he wanted to touch her.

"No, wait."

She reached out as if to touch *him,* but her hand froze as though it had just dawned on her what she'd been about to do. She snatched her hand back like a child who'd had it slapped.

"I have to go," he ground out, once again grabbing the handle.

"Please."

"Please what?" He should have been proud to hear that pleading note in her voice. But he wasn't. Suddenly he felt like the one in the wrong, a feeling he didn't like.

"I have something to tell you."

That sexy, husky voice drew his eyes to her face. A mistake.

Her lips were parted and wet.

The memory of that kiss hung between them, something tempting yet forbidden. He could sympathize with Adam in the Garden of Eden. Groaning inwardly, Ryker fought the urge to jerk her into his arms again and repeat that hot kiss they had exchanged. His body responded to the erotic memory, forcing him to shift both his position and his gaze.

"Ryker?"

Again that voice kicked him where it hurt the worst. "So tell me."

"Someone beat up Frank."

"I know," he said with disinterest, chancing another look at her.

"You know?" She sounded surprised. "How?"

"The 'how' is part of my job."

"So doesn't that mean something to you?"

"Such as?" He knew he was goading her, but he couldn't seem to stop himself. God, but this was a dangerous game he was playing.

"Dammit, that's your job, not mine."

"Then let me do it."

Her eyes flashed. "You're not prepared to give an inch, are you."

"If that's all you have to say, then I'm outta here."

"It isn't," she said, her voice once again on an even keel. "I also caught him in my office, snooping through my desk."

"Did he find anything?"

"No—not that I know of, anyway."

"So what's your point?"

"You know what my point is." Again, he heard the irritation in her voice, though he knew she was trying hard to control it.

"That Frank killed your husband?"

"Yes."

"I thought you said he didn't have the guts."

"I know, but—" she floundered "—something's going on."

"Maybe. Or maybe you're making something out of nothing. Maybe you're just using Frankie boy as a ploy to take the heat off you."

"That's not true, and you know it. You said yourself that they both gambled, and now, with Frank looking for something Mark had..."

Her voice dwindled to nothing, but her chest was heaving, out of anger at him, Ryker knew.

"You've told me, now can I go?"

"So are you going to check him out?" Blythe pressed in a tight voice.

"I'm already checking him out along with everyone else."

He felt her hot gaze stab him.

"No, you're not," she said. "You're only checking *me* out."

"You kissed me back, you know."

For a second her eyes widened, and she sucked in her breath.

"And *that's* what this is all about."

"You really are a bastard."

"And if you think that kiss changes anything, then you're wrong." He just couldn't let it go. He didn't know what the hell had made him mention that kiss in the first place. But to keep belaboring the point showed what kind of emotional mess he was in.

"Get out," she said, focusing straight ahead.

He looked at her profile for a long moment, feeling the tension in the car crackle.

"With pleasure," he finally said.

Ryker stood in the hot sun long after she'd driven off, wanting her more than he'd ever wanted a woman in his life. He might as well wish for a million dollars.

He could never have her.

"I know why you're back here."

The laugh came out a snort. "No, you don't. Anyway, it's none of your goddamn business."

"What if I make it my business?"

"Then you're a bigger fool than I thought."

"Your being here has to do with Mark, right?"

"Not necessarily."

"Hey, man, you know better than to shit a shitter."

"Back off."

"I know you two worked together."

"How?"

"That's not important."

"Get lost."

"Simmer down, okay? You and Mark had something big going."

"Even if we did, what's it to you?"

"I want in on the action."

"People in hell want ice water, too."

"Meaning?"

"They don't get it."

"I could make things real tough for you."

"Yeah, right."

"I suggest you take me seriously."

"I suggest you fuck off, or you'll be sorry."

"That works both ways, you know? Old Mark knew how to make the goose lay that golden egg, and I'm determined to get my hands on some of those eggs."

"I don't know what you're talking about." The voice had a bored edge to it.

"Jewelry and money. That's what I'm talking about."

"Get out of my face and my business. As it is, you're already up to your eyeballs in trouble."

"Look, there's enough to go around. There's no reason to be greedy."

"Not on your life."

"What if we work together? I can help you."

Black brows rose. "Like how?"

"Mark's old lady. She has the info you want."

The man tensed. "Do you know that for sure?"

"Ah, now I've got your interest."

"Stop playing games."

"Okay, okay. Of course she has it."

"If you're jacking me around, I'll kill you."

"I swear I'm not. I can help you put the screws to her, help you get the goods."

"I doubt that."

"It's true. In fact I—"

"You what?"

"Nothing."

"Did you kill him?"

Eyes narrowed. "No. Did you?"

"No."

They both stared at each other, all the while trying to gauge who was lying and who was not.

"I have to warn you about someone."

"That detective?"

"How'd you know?"

"I make it my business to know."

"Well, he's trouble on more than one front. He's on a mission, and he'll stop at nothing until he makes his point, which makes him more dangerous than ever. Plus, the SOB has ice water in his veins."

"How would you know?"

"Trust me on that. He bites without even growling."

Silence fell between them.

"So what's it going to be? Are you and me in this together?"

"No."

Eyes turned ugly. "No? But I just told you—"

"And I'm telling you there's no deal. So fucking back off!"

"Is that a threat?"

"If you want to take it as one."

"There's enough to go around."

"For chrissake, stop begging. It's my money. I'm the one who did all the work."

"Mark promised to cut me in."

"That's a damn lie, and you know it."

With those words, he turned and walked off, leaving his companion squealing inside like a stuck pig.

The vase slammed into a section of the mirrored wall, shattering the reflective surface.

"What the hell?" Frank screamed as he ran into the bedroom.

Eleanor swung around. "Get out of here!"

"You crazy bitch! What are you doing?"

"What does it look like I'm doing?"

"Pitching a hissy fit."

"That's right, and I'm not finished yet."

"Oh, yes, you are."

"You can't tell me what to do."

"You're right, but your mother can. I'm sure she heard that godawful noise."

Eleanor's free hand curled into a tight fist before letting the vase in the other hand go. It made a thudding sound when it hit the carpet.

"What's the matter with you, anyway?"

"That bitch!"

"Blythe?"

"Yes, Blythe. Your main whore. Or maybe just in your dreams, Frankie love."

He flushed even as his voice turned nasty. "I suggest you give that a rest."

"When I'm ready and not one minute sooner."

"Then I'm leaving."

"No, you're not. You're going to hear what I have to say."

"And what is that?"

"The company's about to go belly up."

She watched his flushed face turn an ashen color; then she laughed an ugly laugh.

"As in broke?"

"Flat broke. So no more gravy train."

Frank crossed the room and stood within touching distance of her. He snapped his fingers in her face. "You can't cut me off just like that."

Eleanor wouldn't have budged if her life depended on it. She stood rock steady. "I can do anything I please. It's my money, always has been, always will be."

"I'll go to your mother and tell her I'm going to leave you."

"So what?"

"You know how she feels about divorce."

"You're bluffing. You don't have enough nerve to go to Cynthia, especially since you've had the shit beat out of you."

"I want what's coming to me."

"Well, you can just go on wanting, you gutless wonder. Giving you money is the same as pissing down a rat hole."

His nostrils flared, but she didn't care. She still couldn't believe that her brother and Blythe had drained the business bone dry. The way Eleanor saw it, both were at fault—Mark for gambling and Blythe for being a lousy businesswoman.

"So you're on your own," she finished triumphantly.

Having the nerve finally to put her husband in his place felt damn good. In fact, that victory beat the hell out of an orgasm any day. Actually, an orgasm had never felt this good. More than that, she knew she had Frank where she wanted him. Without money, he would be at her mercy. She planned to make the most of that situation, too.

Eleanor rejoiced in her newfound confidence. When she got through with Frank, he would be begging for mercy.

"You won't get away with any of this shit."

"Who's to stop me?"

"Blythe, for one. Ryker Delaney, for another."

She blinked, breaking her reverie, certain she'd misunderstood him. "Excuse me?"

This time he threw back his head and laughed. Not a pretty sight, she thought, especially since one side of his face was still discolored from the beating he'd taken.

"You've got a sweet motive for buzzing off your brother." He reached out and tweaked a nipple. "Don't think Delaney doesn't know that. And when you're arrested, your ugly ass will be history."

"You wormy sonofabitch!"

He pivoted on his heel and stomped to the door. A third vase crashed against the door frame, barely missing his head. Eleanor watched Frank jump.

When he turned around, there was murder in his eyes. "Don't ever do that again!"

"Or what?"

"I've already told you, so don't say you weren't warned."

"We'll see whose ass is history!" she screamed to a closed door.

Twenty-three

Ted Armstrong stood in front of the mirror and shook his long hair. Ignoring the dandruff that rained onto his shoulders, he secured the curly mass with a rubber band, then walked to the commode.

"Teddy, whatcha doing?"

"Taking a leak."

His wife's laugh caressed his ears, and he smiled, but only fleetingly. He didn't have a whole lot to smile about these days, except maybe Irma. An airhead she might be, but she cared about him. As far as he knew, she was the only living soul who did.

"Hurry, okay?"

When he was finished, he didn't bother stuffing his dick back into his underwear. He knew she'd be naked, waiting. He was right. She was in the middle of the bed, flat on her back, with her legs spread.

"We have to talk," Ted said, even as he tossed his boxers and crawled atop her.

"Let's do it first, then we'll talk."

Without any foreplay, Ted aimed his hardness into her and rode her until he couldn't move anymore. That made the third time he'd fucked her since midnight, and he was damn tired.

"I hope you remembered to take your pill."

Irma propped her head in the palm of one hand and stared into his face. "I don't have none."

That was what he was afraid of. But he couldn't get mad at her. She couldn't help that her light bulb was dim. He loved her, anyway, despite the fact that Irma wasn't pretty, nowhere near it. But she had a great body, full in all the right places.

It was their mutually insatiable appetite for sex that had landed them in financial trouble. They had four children, ranging from one to five years. Without the pill, another one could very well be in the oven.

He'd thought about getting fixed himself, but he couldn't. He knew he wouldn't actually lose his balls, or anything like that. Still, one of his fellow laborers had told him it wasn't no cakewalk and don't have it done. He hadn't.

So what if she was pregnant? If the deal he had on the front burner caught fire, they would be in great shape. Hell, they could fuck their brains out and have ten kids. It wouldn't matter.

"Aren't you s'posed to be at work?"

He didn't have a job, but he hadn't bothered to tell her that yet. Since he'd left Designs, he hadn't even looked for anything else.

"Yeah," he lied, "but I have something I gotta do first."

"Won't you git fired?"

He pushed Irma's stringy hair out of one eye. "You let me worry about that."

"Are y'all still working at the park?"

"No, we've moved on," he lied again.

"So whatcha gonna do?" Irma pressed, grinning, the space between her front teeth seeming to have widened. He wondered why he'd never noticed that.

"Take care of some business."

"I wish you didn't have to work at all."

"I won't for long, I hope."

"I thought you said we were gonna be rich."

"Things didn't work out like I planned. The bastard had to go and git himself bumped off."

Irma's empty blue eyes held confusion. "Bumped off?"

"Dead. Someone turned out his lights permanently."

"Oh, goodness. You didn't kill 'im, did you?"

"You're not thinking straight, honey. Why would I knock off our gravy train?"

She snuggled up to him. "So whatcha gonna do now?"

"I have plans to git on someone else's gravy train."

"Good, 'cause we need money."

"And I'm gonna git it, too."

He hated having to work; in fact, he'd hated every job he'd ever had. With no education, he'd done manual labor all of his twenty-five years, and he was tired of it. He wanted to live like the people whose yards and gardens he manicured. He'd been close, so very damn close. The smell of that first check had been in his nostrils, and then the unthinkable had happened. But all was not lost. He was too close now to stop.

Ted rolled off the bed and reached for his torn jeans and muscle shirt.

"Tell me again where you're goin'."

"To meet a goddamn foreigner."

She frowned. "What—"

"Never you mind about anything. I'll be home at my usual time."

Twenty minutes later, he knocked on the door of an out-of-the-way motel. The man who was on the other side wouldn't know him from Adam, which was in his favor.

"Who is it?" a gruff, foreign-sounding voice demanded from the other side.

Ted snickered inwardly. "A friend."

"I don't have any friends."

"You do now."

"Go the hell away."

"The words *hard candy* ring any bells?"

A pause, then, "Get out of here before I ring your bell. You don't know nothing."

"I guess I'll have to go to the cops, then."

The door was flung open, and a dark-faced man glared at him, but not before his eyes moved up and down Ted's body. "Why, you little fly on a pile of shit, you'd best get yourself back where you came from or—"

"I want what your partner promised me."

"I don't know what you're talking about."

"Yes, you do."

Jacques Dawson leaned against the door, a smirk on his face, making his mustache droop like a horse's tail. "Enlighten me."

Thinking he would see a gun aimed at his forehead any minute now, sweat turned into a salty film over Ted's body. But he'd come this far and wasn't about to back down now. "Money. I'm talking about money."

Dawson snorted gruffly. "Aren't we all."

"I know what you and Lambert were doing," Ted said, swallowing hard.

"Doing?"

"Yeah, doing. I overheard you two talking on one of the jobs."

Jacques Dawson's swarthy features turned darker;

then he leaned forward and warned, ''I suggest you keep that to yourself.''

''And if I don't?''

''You're stupid, but you're not that stupid. I'm sure of it.''

Before Ted could reply, he slammed the door in his face.

The lady squealed again. Louder.

While Ryker didn't blame her, under the circumstances, he couldn't let her keep hollering. ''Ma'am, please, we're doing what we can.''

The overly thin lady with milky eyes moaned. ''He shot him, and...and blood spewed everywhere.''

''I know.''

Ryker patted her awkwardly on the shoulder, then crossed to Mike. The convenience store was inundated with cops. That afternoon, in broad daylight, another store had taken a hit, a total of five in the past month.

Till now, this rash of break-ins had claimed no casualties. Today, with the death of the store manager, that had changed. Robbery had turned into murder.

''Forensics about through?'' Ryker asked Mike, whose features were grim.

''Yeah.''

''I bet they won't find a damn thing we can use.''

''You're probably right. These bastards are professionals.''

''Until now,'' Ryker said.

''No one was supposed to get dead?''

''You got it. Now they're in deep dung and more dangerous to boot.''

Ryker's cell phone jangled. He punched the button,

then put it to his ear. After listening a moment, he said, "Call her and tell her I'm on my way."

"Where?" Mike asked.

"To check on that lead I told you about the other day."

"You didn't do more than mention its existence. I'm still in the dark, but I'm assuming it has to do with the Lambert case."

"Righto."

"Want me to come along?"

"Nope. You stay here and make sure forensics doesn't screw up."

Mike made a face. "Thanks, partner."

Ryker grinned, then patted Mike on the arm. "I knew you'd be grateful."

"Hey, call me."

"I will, assuming I have something to call you about."

"You mean this may not be your smoking gun, after all?"

"The way we've been chasing our tails on this case, who the hell knows?"

By the time he reached his car, Ryker's face was taut. He hadn't been bullshitting Mike when he'd admitted they were chasing their own tails, which made him want to gnash his teeth.

He also knew that Mike was probably gnashing his own over Ryker's continued obsession with the Lamberts.

What if Mike was right and he was barking up the wrong tree?

What if none of the family was guilty of either of the murders—Stacey's or Mark's? He wouldn't think about that, not now, not when his gut was telling him otherwise.

Yet he didn't believe for a second that Frank was a murderer, despite what Blythe had told him. Still, he was curious as to what Frank had been looking for in Blythe's desk.

As to who had given Frank a butt-whipping, Ryker knew it was a loan shark. When you ran with a pack of dogs, you were bound to get fleas, though pretty-boy Frank got more than fleas. That misfortune couldn't have happened to anyone who deserved it more. Ryker smiled.

That smile didn't last when his thoughts landed on Blythe, something he didn't want to do. *She* wasn't worth thinking about, he reminded himself, except as a primary suspect in a murder investigation.

So why am I thinking more about fucking her than arresting her?

That damn kiss. While he couldn't undo it, he had to compartmentalize it and move on—for no other reason than that she could be a murderer. Cold sweat oozed from his palms as he clung to the steering wheel, fighting off a feeling of queasiness, which infuriated him.

Queasy? Hell!

While he was in the service, and since he'd been a cop, he'd seen untold horrors, horrors that would send most normal people over the edge. But then, he wasn't normal. He'd figured that out long ago, when he'd taken the beatings his daddy had given him without so much as a wince.

Maybe the people who knew him were right. Maybe he did have ice water in his veins instead of blood. Not when it came to Blythe Lambert, though.

When he'd tasted that berry-stained mouth, his blood had heated to the boiling point....

"Shit!"

Even muttering the obscenity out loud couldn't stop his stampeding thoughts. What the hell had he done to deserve this unexpected fixation?

His goal had been and still was to do his job and in accomplishing that, find out who had killed his niece. He was determined to ease the pain of his sister's life. Hell, he wanted to ease the pain of his own. But he'd wallowed in the muck and mire for so long now, he wasn't sure he'd know how to be normal.

Disillusionment and disappointment had become a way of life for him. Right now, he didn't see that changing. His obsession with a woman he could never have just added insult to injury.

Enough of this mental torture, he told himself. He'd already had enough of that to last a lifetime. Besides, he'd reached his destination.

Whipping into the driveway of a modest brick home, he flung open the door, got out, then bounded up the steps, feeling his heart race.

With luck he was about to turn over a boulder and under it would be the key to this case.

He rang the doorbell and waited. Finally the door opened, and he stared into the face of a plump but attractive woman.

"Mrs. Tanner?" he asked, removing his badge and showing it to her.

She nodded, staring up at him through apprehensive gray eyes. "I'm not sure I'm doing the right thing. My husband—"

"Trust me, you're doing exactly the right thing." Ryker paused. "May I come in?"

She let out a heavy sigh. "This won't take long, will it? I have to pick up my kids from school."

"You have my word."

"All right, you can come in."

Ryker walked into the sunlit room and closed the door behind him.

Twenty-four

"I see."

Of course, Blythe didn't see at all. Her disappointment was so acute that she actually felt nauseous.

"I'll give you a call after I return from the Far East," Mr. Farmer said. "We'll talk then."

When she was certain he was no longer on the line, Blythe slammed the receiver down. She hadn't just fallen off a turnip truck. She knew a brush-off when she heard one.

Well, it would be a cold day in hell before she called him again. *Liar.* By the time Cecil Farmer got back to the States—if he was even going out of the country—she would be more desperate than ever. In her mind's eye, she could picture dropping to her knees in front of him and begging.

Never.

But she *would* call him. She wouldn't give up. Because if she could pull off a miracle and get the contract, Designs would be out of the red. Meanwhile, she would have to keep her fingers crossed that the small jobs kept on coming. Without them, the company couldn't remain afloat.

Too, she had to keep those same fingers crossed that Eleanor wouldn't pull another stunt like she had with that bonus thing.

Eleanor's vindictiveness, Blythe knew, was directed not at Designs but at her personally. Jealousy festered inside Eleanor like a boil ready to rupture, spewing its poison on everyone around.

However, at the moment, her sister-in-law wasn't stirring up trouble, not that Blythe found that reassuring. She figured Eleanor was biding her time and would strike when least expected. The calm before the storm.

What more could she do? Blythe asked herself, moving from behind her desk and over to the window, only to find more gloom and doom. The sky looked threatening, as if the bottom were about to fall out—her grandmother's favorite expression.

Honey. Suddenly, Blythe's heart lurched. She checked in with the nursing home every day to make sure the precious old lady was all right. To date, Mark's so-called partner hadn't made good on his threat. Nor had Ryker.

Along with her in-laws, she'd had a respite from him. However, she knew he hadn't changed his mind about her guilt in Mark's murder.

Mark murdered.

At times she still couldn't grasp the fact that someone had deliberately taken Mark's life. She shivered, wondering what had flashed through her husband's mind at that moment when he faced death. She prayed it had been quick and painless.

And that hers would be, too, if she were convicted of his murder. Blythe placed her hand over her mouth to keep from crying out. While that thought might be well beyond comprehension, she knew that a conviction based on circumstantial evidence could be in the offing.

Thanks to Detective Ryker Delaney.

Had he loved his wife? Staggering against such an inane question, she grabbed the windowsill, fearing her legs might betray her. What on earth had made her ask a thing like that? What had made her even think such a thing? Hell, he wasn't capable of liking anyone, much less loving them.

But then that kiss jumped back to the forefront of her mind. His moist lips had taken hers with a passion and lust she'd never experienced. She had felt the fire down to her toes, and she wanted to feel it again, God help her.

She would have moaned aloud, except that the door opened. Swinging around, Blythe faced a smiling Susan.

"You okay?" her secretary asked.

"I'm fine."

"I wish that were true, but I'm not going to argue."

"Good."

"Speaking of good, I have good news and bad news."

"Give me the good news first."

"We got another job, not a big one, mind you, but a job."

Blythe brightened. "I'm listening."

"A Mrs. Mary Boyd called, said she wanted to talk to you about relandscaping her yard. She wants a pond and gazebo added."

"All right!"

"I thought so. I set the appointment for tomorrow."

"What's the bad news?"

Susan hesitated, squeezing her forehead into a frown. "That detective's here to see you."

"Oh, great."

"Honest to Pete, that man scares me half out of my wits. If anyone was suited for his job, it's him. You'd think he'd never have to pull his gun." Susan paused to catch a breath. "What with that stone-faced expression and those frosted-over eyes, most bad guys probably surrender on the spot."

"He's one of a kind, I'll admit."

"Well that 'one of a kind' is waiting—and not patiently, either."

"Send him in." Blythe hid a sigh. "The sooner the better."

Moments later, Ryker strode through the door. Tension followed him. His mouth was slashed in a thin line, and his big body was taut. Blythe steeled herself against what was to come, keeping her eyes averted. She had to get her emotions under control.

"To what do I owe this visit?" she asked in a cold tone, and without so much as asking him to sit down.

"It's official, that's for sure."

She turned her head, and their eyes met. Her pulse rate elevated. Not a good sign. She whipped her gaze away from him, grabbing a pen off her desk and fiddling with it.

"Why didn't you tell me about your knock-down-drag-out with Mark?"

Blythe gave him an incredulous stare. "I didn't think it was any of your business."

He closed the short distance between them. "When are you going to get it?"

"Get what?" she asked before stepping back.

"That everything you do and have ever done is my business."

"Don't you mean police business?"

Was that a flush she saw invade his face, or had she imagined it? Nothing ruffled him, or nearly nothing, she corrected herself, thinking again of his reaction to kissing her. Shaking herself mentally, she tilted her chin.

''You know what I mean,'' he finally said in a tight, clipped voice.

''Look, Mark and I, like most married couples, had our differences.''

''What I'm referring to is more than a difference.''

''Then you'll have to refresh my memory.''

''My pleasure.''

''No doubt.''

A strained silence followed that sarcastic exchange while they stared at each other again, neither prepared to give an inch.

''Just say what you have to say,'' she finally said in a resigned tone.

''Do you know a lady by the name of Mary Tanner?''

Blythe pitted her forehead, ''No.''

''Are you sure?''

''Yes, dammit, I'm sure. Why won't you believe anything I say? I don't make a habit of lying.''

He scoffed but wisely held his tongue. She had just about reached her saturation point, and he seemed to have picked up on that. Soon she wouldn't be responsible for her actions. She would like nothing better than to knock that chip off his shoulder.

''She and her husband rent the boat stall next to yours.''

''What does that have to do with anything?''

''A few days before your husband was killed, she heard the two of you arguing aboard the boat.''

Blythe tried to hide her shock, but she knew she hadn't. ''So we had an argument and she heard it. So what?''

Ryker's eyes drilled her. ''It was more than an argument, and you damn well know it.''

"How does she know?" Blythe's voice stopped short of hysteria.

"I told you, her boat was docked next to yours. Not only could she hear what was being said, but she could see it, as well."

Blythe gasped.

"That's right. Now you get the picture."

"It wasn't what you think."

He gave a harsh laugh. "Oh, really? Suppose you tell me how it really was?" Irony had taken the place of his harsh laughter.

"All right. He shoved me against the wall," Blythe lashed out, "and he would have done more if I hadn't threatened him with the wine bottle."

"Great," Ryker muttered.

"What I was doing was defending myself. Furthermore, I didn't strike him. He backed off, and I left." Blythe paused, struggling for breath, so she could continue. "Did Mrs. Tanner tell you that?"

"No, she said she got interrupted."

"Well, I'm telling you what happened."

"It's your word against hers."

"Well then, you've got a problem, Detective."

"I've had a problem since the day I first met you."

Somehow his face was suddenly close to hers. She could not only smell him but see every ripple of muscle in his body. Feeling her senses spin, she moved out of harm's way.

"Look, somebody else killed Mark. Not me." She hated it that her voice shook. But for a moment, she'd thought he was going to kiss her again. He had wanted to. That flare of fire in his eyes hadn't escaped her.

"The sooner you face that," she forced herself to say into the silence, "the sooner you'll get the killer."

Ryker honored that with a grim half smile. "Don't leave town, Mrs. Lambert."

"Where would I go?"

"Nowhere that I couldn't find you, that's for sure."

She didn't bother to respond. Instead, she turned her back and waited for him to leave.

Another bad day.

As long as Ryker lurked around every corner, there would be no such thing as a good day.

Every bone, every nerve, in her body still cried out for relief, although she'd taken a long soak in the bath. Now, as she sat on the sofa and stirred her soup, she wanted to cry. But she refused to give in to her maudlin feelings, knowing that would only make her feel worse.

After tasting the soup, she leaned her head against the cushion. That was when the phone rang. She jumped, then spat an expletive. God, but she was on edge, she thought, scrambling for the receiver.

"Hello," she said.

Nothing.

Her heart slammed against her chest. The French Canadian. Was it him on the other end of the line?

"Hello," she said again, this time in a more forceful tone. She didn't intend to let him know she was afraid. That would just give him more leverage.

Still nothing.

She had the receiver halfway back to its cradle when a man said, "Mrs. Lambert?"

"Yes," she answered tentatively, not recognizing the voice.

"You don't know me, but I used to work for your company."

"So?"

"So I know something about your husband."

Blythe's heart raced. "What?"

"I can't tell you over the phone."

"Why not?"

"Because it's going to cost you. Big bucks."

"Look—"

"No, you look. If you want to know about your husband's extracurricular activities, then you'll do things my way."

"Okay, I'm listening."

"Meet me."

"Now?"

"Yes, now."

He told her where.

"Are you sure we can't talk on the phone?"

"Lady, you wanna hear what I have to say?"

"Yes, if you're on the up-and-up."

"Then haul ass."

"I'm on my way," Blythe said in a breathless voice.

"Come alone."

His terse words and his voice sent a chill through Blythe. He sounded almost as frightened as she was. Who the hell was this man?

She didn't know. But she had to find out for her own sake, if nothing else. So, stupid or not, she was going to meet him. At least she would be doing something toward finding out who had killed Mark.

After slamming down the phone and dashing into her bedroom, Blythe shed her nightgown, then slipped on some clothes. Just before she turned out the light, it hit her.

The gun.

To be on the safe side, she'd better take her pistol with her.

* * *

Uh-oh.

The figure slouched behind the wheel across the street straightened, then he blinked several times. Where the hell was she going at this time of night?

Following her was the only way to find out. On the first turn of the key, the vehicle came to life.

Twenty-five

"You're nutty as a pecan tree," Blythe muttered.

But did she turn around and head back to the house? Hell, no. She was determined to see this through, even though the end result could be disastrous. Might even cost her her life.

Get real, she told herself, shaking off the feeling of impending doom. What could possibly happen to her? Her caller was probably some kook who was out to make a dime without doing an honest day's work. Chances were he wouldn't know anything.

On the other hand, what if he was on the up-and-up? What if he did have valuable information that would shift the suspicion off her and put it on the killer, where it belonged?

Ryker Delaney certainly hadn't been diligent in his search for the culprit. He wanted to hang the crime on her. Vengeance against her, Designs and Mark's family was what pushed his buttons. If this clandestine venture did nothing but take him down a notch or two, then the danger she might encounter would be worth it.

She was tired of her life being turned topsy-turvy. If someone else was implicated in Mark's murder, then that news would travel like wildfire on a dry hill, and she would be vindicated, which would translate into jobs for Designs.

Her work, such as it was, was all she had left. She hadn't known just how widespread or vindictive the gossip was until yesterday. She'd stopped by her favorite place to buy a few pounds of gourmet coffee.

The shop had been filled with people, laughing and talking, and she had been stealing a moment's pleasure by perusing the shelves when she heard her name mentioned.

She stood by and listened.

"Can you believe it?" a lady said in a low but carrying voice.

"No, I can't," her companion responded. "Of course, I don't know Blythe Lambert personally, but I know the family."

"What a shame to have your nasty little secrets out in the open."

"Poor Cynthia. I feel so sorry for her, having a daughter-in-law who's suspected of killing your son. Think how *you* would feel."

Blythe could almost feel the shudder that surely must have gone through them.

"Do you think she's guilty?"

Blythe waited with bated breath instead of charging over and facing her accusers outright. What would that accomplish? she asked herself. Nothing. Until she was legally exonerated, the gossipmongers would continue to have a field day. Besides, talking about one of the town's most prestigious families seemed to be a favorite sport.

Well, let the old biddies talk. She didn't give a damn, she told herself. But she did. She gave a big-time damn.

"Who knows?" the first lady continued. "What I do know is that Mark, uh, you know...messed around on her. Maybe she got tired and—"

Blythe couldn't take any more. She whipped around and stalked out of the store, her purchase forgotten.

Now, as she turned into the parking lot of the seedy motel, darkness had prevailed over dusk. Thank goodness, she thought. She would rather not be seen here. Talk about the rumor mill. They would have her indulging in an affair of her own.

Trembling, she killed the motor but didn't move. The flashing neon sign, so typical of a place like this, almost made her smile. As poor as she'd been growing up, she had never been in a roach-motel that she could remember, and she hadn't planned on going into one.

Things changed. *Lives* changed. Refusing to get back in a maudlin mode, she got out of the car, only to stop again and look around. No other cars were in sight, unless they were parked in the back.

The caller had told her to go to room fifteen, which was along the front. She could see the number from where she stood, even though she was a ways down from it.

Instead of moving her car, she decided to walk the short distance. She was halfway there when she stopped again and peered over her shoulder. No one was behind her or around her.

Strange.

It was as though she had the place to herself. She knew better; nonetheless, an eerie feeling passed through her.

What the hell did she think she was doing? After all, she wasn't one of those female detectives on TV who could do anything a male cop could do, only better. In fact, she almost smiled at that comparison.

Still, she was determined and reassured. She had her

gun, though she had never fired it outside a firing range and wasn't sure she could.

She finally reached the room with its dimly lit lantern hanging askew over the facing. Her heart was banging against her chest when she tapped on the door.

No response.

She knocked this time. Again, no response.

"It's Mrs. Lambert," she said in a whispery voice, then wondered why she was talking so low.

The place. It gave her the creeps, and for a moment she considered tossing the whole idea and dashing back to her car. Curiosity won. She stayed put and knocked one more time. Louder. When she got no answer the third time, she instinctively tried the knob.

Surprisingly, the door was unlocked. What now? she asked herself, clutching the metal knob in her clammy hand. Should she walk in?

"It's Mrs. Lambert," she said again, her voice sounding like a croaking bullfrog. She cleared her throat as she peeped through the slight opening she'd created. A crooked lamp met her gaze. Beyond that, she couldn't see anything.

Without weighing the consequences, Blythe shoved the door open and stepped across the threshold. Her eyes rested on an empty bed covered in a godawful tattered pink bedspread.

Her feathers wilted. The room was empty. She'd been had. But why? Had the man chickened out? Lost his nerve? Questions with no answers hammered at her. Finally admitting she'd been a fool on a fool's errand, she swung around with every intention of leaving.

That was when she saw him.

Oh, God, no!

She knew she hadn't spoken the words out loud. Undiluted terror had seized her by the throat and wouldn't let go. She couldn't have said a word even if her life had depended on it, and under the circumstances, it just might.

Even realizing that, she stood still. It was as though all the bones in her body had liquefied, rendering her helpless. She wanted to scream, to turn her eyes away, but there was no way. The scene seemed to hold her in its terrifying grip.

A strange man sat in a chair, his head lowered so that his chin rested on his chest.

But it wasn't the man himself that had her feet nailed to the dirty floor and her heart in her throat, but rather the knife that protruded from his belly.

Blood. Blood was all over him. She could even smell its stench. It turned her stomach, and she fought off the urge to upchuck.

She took several deep gulps, which helped combat the growing queasiness and building terror. Was he dead? If he wasn't, it would be a miracle.

He moaned. Or did he? Had she imagined the sound? He looked dead. He had to be dead. There was too much blood. This time she lifted a quivering hand to her mouth, smothering her cry. As if sensing he wasn't alone, he raised his head and stared at her from pain-glazed eyes.

"Please, help me," he rasped.

Later Blythe couldn't understand what made her do what she did next, which ranked among the most asinine things she'd ever done in her life. Instead of calling 911, she crossed to his side and knelt beside him.

"Help me," he begged.

"Shh. Don't talk. I'll go get someone to—"

"No, don't leave me!" He grabbed her with a bloody hand.

Blythe cringed but didn't pull away. Oh God, what to do?

"Get up. Need…need your…help."

"I…can't." Blythe felt her head spin and her stomach churn.

"Yes…you can," he rasped again. Then, holding on to her, he rose to his feet and he swayed against her.

Blythe cried out, the smell of blood shooting up her nostrils. The room spun again. Still, she managed to stay on her feet. More than that, she managed to loosen herself from his grasp.

"I…I have to get…help."

Before he could say or do anything else, Blythe lunged upright, lowered her head and ran out the door, only to bump into something hard.

"Oh!" she cried, bouncing off that hardness like a rubber ball off a wall. She looked up then, into the grim face of Ryker Delaney.

"Going somewhere, Mrs. Lambert?" he drawled.

Twenty-six

The police station gave her the creeps. What was even more creepy was that she was there as a *suspect,* for God's sake, in the possible death of a man other than her husband.

From start to finish, the entire incident reminded Blythe of a dark comedy of errors that was certain to have no happy ending. She had called her attorney, but he was out. Curt was on his way.

She stared at the austere walls of the interrogation room and shivered visibly, despite the cup of coffee Ryker had given her before heading toward the door.

"Where are you going?" she had asked, unable to contain the trepidation in her voice.

He had swung around, his expression unreadable. He might as well have been a big block of wood standing there. "Out."

"Out where?"

"To take care of business."

"But...but you can't just leave me here."

"Oh, yes, I can."

"Dammit, I didn't do anything."

He threw back his head and laughed. "I'd say you zigged when you should've zagged, darlin'."

"I'm not your darling."

His features hardened. "That's right, you're not.

You're a goddamn suspect.'' He paused, then added, ''In two murders.''

''You're crazy! *That's* crazy!''

''Maybe so. Still, I'm not the one who's sitting in this room about to be interrogated.''

Blythe dug her long nails into her palms, unmindful of the pain. ''You know I didn't—''

''Save it for when your attorney gets here.''

''He's…not coming.''

An expletive singed the air. ''Why the hell not?''

''He wasn't at home.''

''Did you leave a message?''

''Of course.'' Blythe's head was pounding. If she didn't know better, she would think Ryker cared. This man was truly an enigma.

''Call someone else,'' he was saying. ''With your family's pull, you can hire any top crook in the country.''

So much for his caring. ''You're despicable.''

''So I've been told.''

Blythe's lips tightened. Their heated exchange had sounded like two children bickering over a toy or something just as ridiculous. If only something as simple as a toy was at stake here.

''So?''

''So what?'' she snapped.

''Did you call anyone else?''

''Curt.''

Ryker cursed again. ''Ah, so lover boy's coming to the rescue.''

''He's not my lover. How many times do I have to tell you that?''

''As many times as it takes to convince me otherwise.''

She turned away from his probing eyes and tried to control the tears that were imminent. But she wouldn't shed one tear, not in front of this man who had no heart or soul, but whose hot and intoxicating lips had the power to set her insides on fire and keep them burning.

She guessed that what puzzled her the most—and, yes, infuriated her—was his attitude, as if no personal contact had ever taken place between them. How could he shut his emotions on and off like a water faucet? She couldn't, and she didn't know how he could. It galled her that he was treating her now as if she had a contagious disease.

"Blythe."

The unexpected and husky use of her name almost proved her undoing. She raised shocked eyes to his face. Even though he tried to disguise it, she saw the hint of struggle in his own eyes, as though he had read her mind.

His expression softened, yet his tone was brusque. "I won't be gone long."

She wasn't sure how comforting those words were supposed to be, she thought now as she sat waiting for the next torturous phase of this debacle. What if she couldn't cope? What if she fell apart?

God, she still had blood on her. A stranger's blood. If she let herself think about that, she could easily go off the deep end. She couldn't think about the seriousness of her situation or she wouldn't be able to contain her tears.

The door opened, and Ryker and another man walked in. "My partner, Mike Rushmore," Ryker said without preamble.

Blythe nodded, licked her dry lips, then asked, "Where's Curt?"

''Outside.''

''Can he come in?''

''No,'' Ryker said, his old hard self once again, moving sinuously and silently around the room, as if to purposely unnerve her.

''Please,'' she whispered.

The two men looked at each other, then Mike concentrated on her. ''Sorry, Mrs. Lambert, but since you don't want another lawyer, you're on your own in here.''

''But I didn't do anything,'' she wailed, then hated herself for showing them how upset she was.

''He died,'' Ryker said, his eyes cold and remote.

Blythe sucked in her breath. ''Oh, no.''

''Oh, yes.''

''But you have to know I didn't kill him.''

''What were you doing there?'' Mike asked in a softer tone, for which Blythe was grateful.

''He...that man called and said he knew something about my...about Mark.''

''What?'' Ryker demanded.

Blythe flashed him a look. ''If you'll give me a chance, I'll tell you.''

Although Ryker kept his silence, he wasn't happy. He looked as if he was about ready to pounce. She shuddered inwardly. Would this night ever end?

''He told me that Mark was involved in something, but it would cost me big bucks to find out.''

''Go on,'' Mike encouraged, glaring at Ryker as if daring him to say anything.

''When I got to the motel and opened the door, he...he was sitting in the chair—'' Blythe's voice broke, and she couldn't go on.

''With a knife buried in his gut,'' Ryker finished for her.

"That's right." She jutted her chin. "But I didn't put it there, and you damn well know it."

"If I knew that, you wouldn't be here."

"Well, you're wasting your time. I don't even know the man's name."

"Look, Mrs. Lambert," Mike said, obviously trying to keep the peace between Ryker and Blythe, "we just want to get to the truth here."

"That's the problem, I don't know the truth." Her voice had risen again.

"Let us be the judge of that."

"I've already told you all I know."

"Dammit," Ryker put in, his voice harsh once again, "two men have been murdered, your husband and someone apparently connected to him in some way."

Blythe stared at him with her mouth open. "What do you take me for? Don't you think I'm aware of that?"

"Of course you are," Mike continued in a mild tone, shooting Ryker a scathing look that told him to butt out. "But by the same token, Mrs. Lambert, you have to know you're in a tough spot."

"I know you can't hold me without—"

The door opened suddenly, and Tony Upshaw strode in, his eyes going straight to Blythe. "Don't say another word, you hear?"

She squelched the urge to jump up and hug the dapper little man. "But I thought you—"

"Forget what you thought," the attorney said, his sharp eyes circling the room, touching on each person.

Ryker, Blythe noticed, didn't so much as blink. He kept his stone face, looking at Upshaw with unvarnished contempt.

"I'm here now, and that's all that counts," Upshaw added.

"Thank God," Blythe wheezed, knowing that she'd won this first round.

"Have you got enough evidence to arrest my client?"

"Not yet," Ryker said roughly.

"Then she's out of here." He held his hand out to Blythe.

"It's only a matter of time before she's back."

"Delaney, you'd best watch it." Upshaw's tone was curt but even. "You're treading on thin ice. Be careful you don't fall through."

Ryker shrugged. "I'm not worried."

"You should be," the lawyer spat, then turned to Blythe. "Curt's waiting to follow you home."

"Now, why am I not surprised about that?" Ryker muttered.

Blythe dared not look at Ryker, but she didn't have to in order to read his thoughts. Who cared? She didn't. If he thought she could do something so heinous as plunge a knife into someone's body, then to hell with him.

Holding herself erect, she walked out the door and took pleasure in slamming it behind her.

"I love your idea."

Blythe smiled at the young pregnant woman, Mary Boyd, as twilight settled over the huge yard. She hoped her smile came off as genuine. But smiles were especially hard these days. In fact, she was in a funk and couldn't seem to jerk herself out of it.

"I'm glad," Blythe finally said, on realizing her client was giving her a strange look. "I'm also sorry I was so late getting here."

Mary flapped her hand. "Don't worry about it. You

came, and there was plenty of daylight left to go over everything."

"You have a lovely place."

Mary rubbed her stomach. "Ralph, my husband, wanted lots of land for our boys to play on."

"Boys?"

Mary giggled. "Didn't I tell you? We're having twins."

"That's great," Blythe said, fighting off feelings of jealousy. When she had first married Mark, she'd had the same starry-eyed look in her eyes as she'd held fast to the same dream of a lovely home filled with children's laughter.

Ashes. Those dreams were nothing but a pile of ashes. Mark's indiscretions, followed by his untimely death, had seen to that.

"Are you okay?"

Blythe gave her another lame smile. "Just wool-gathering."

"Look, I know about your husband..." Mary's voice trailed off, and she looked away.

Uh-oh, here it comes, Blythe warned herself. The proverbial brush-off. She fought to hide her acute disappointment. Just because the Boyds liked her ideas didn't mean they were going to commission Designs to do their work, not with the gossipmongers continuing to do a number on her.

"Can you make our acreage look like the Azalea Trail?"

Blythe was so immersed in her misery that she wasn't sure she'd heard right. "Excuse me?"

Mary gave her a strange look but repeated what she'd said.

"Of course we can." Blythe paused, still afraid to get her hopes up. "Does that mean Designs has the job?"

"Of course." Mary sounded shocked. "Why would you think otherwise? So when can you get started?"

"Is tomorrow too soon?"

A short time later, Blythe hugged herself all the way to the car. However, once inside and headed toward home, her happiness waned. If she only had several more jobs like this one, she could breathe easier. But she didn't, so she would have to keep treading water on more than one front.

The dead man soaked with blood haunted her.

Nor could she get past that mind-boggling horror at the police station. It had been three days since she'd been hauled in and grilled like some common criminal straight off the streets.

The man who'd died in the motel room had at one time worked for Mark at Designs, which gave the police suppositions a ring of truth, which didn't bode well for her. As a result, her nerves were riding on the outside of her skin. She couldn't eat; she couldn't sleep. She couldn't *think.*

Since that grueling and humiliating question-and-answer session, Blythe hadn't seen or heard from Ryker, which was all right with her. That relief would be short-lived, though, she knew.

At every moment, she expected to look up and see him, that smirk in place, that cold look in his eyes, informing her that he finally had enough evidence to arrest her.

Her mind rebelled, but she couldn't keep those thoughts away.

How anyone could think that she could take another human's life was beyond her. But then, Ryker Delaney didn't know her, didn't know her soul. *He'd just sampled a part of her body.*

At last Blythe stumbled into the house, berating herself again for playing detective. If she had stayed home where she belonged, she wouldn't be a player in this newest circus of horrors.

Everything around her was crumbling. Maybe that was why she didn't notice the smell right off, the faint but nonetheless pungent odor. Then it reached her. Sniffing several times, she walked through the house, ending up in her bedroom, where the odor was stronger. She stopped dead in her tracks.

Cigar smoke.

She wanted to scream. How could she not have recognized that stench right off? She hadn't been expecting it, that was why. Fear bubbled inside her. What did this second break-in mean? A fear tactic? Or more?

Keeping her on edge seemed to have become the French Canadian's weapon of choice. The fact that he was still around, and could come and go at will, added to his arsenal.

Blythe's blood curdled.

What about Honey? Had he been to the nursing home? With quivering fingers, Blythe dashed to the bedside table, clicked on the light, then punched out the number.

Minutes later, relief made her weak, though she didn't bother to sit. What to do now was utmost on her mind. Call Curt? That was certainly an option. He'd stayed with her for a short time after she'd come home from the station, despite her protest. He was a trusted and faithful friend, but she'd encroached on his friendship enough.

There was Susan. She could call her, and she would come and spend the night. That wasn't the answer, either. She had to get hold of both herself and the situation. Both Curt and Susan would demand she call the police—Ryker, to be specific.

No. At this point, that was still unacceptable. She couldn't tell Ryker about her intruder; it would put Honey's life in greater jeopardy.

After searching the premises and ensuring that she was alone, Blythe took a quick shower and dressed for bed. She had to admit she was frightened. If she weren't, she would be nuts. But she wasn't going to let his scare tactics force her into doing anything against her sound judgment. Besides, she still didn't have what he wanted. Sooner or later he was bound to figure that out and leave her alone.

Meanwhile, if he hurt Honey...

She wouldn't think about that. Not now, anyway. She was much too tired and overwrought to add insult to injury. Sleep was what she needed. In the morning light, things always looked better.

She tossed back the covers and suddenly screamed.

"Ohmy-ohmy-ohmy," she whispered, her hands over her face. At first she thought she might be hallucinating. But when she opened her eyes again and peeped through her fingers, she wasn't.

A huge snake lay coiled on her pillow.

Twenty-seven

"You really don't belong here, you know."

Eleanor wished she had locked the door to *her* office, though no one else thought of it as that. It was as if the room were haunted by Mark.

It was after hours, and as far as Eleanor had known, she was the only one in the building, at least until now.

She stared at her husband in disgust. "You're drunk."

"Not as drunk as I'd like to be," Frank slurred.

"How did you find me?"

"Easy. You weren't home." He shrugged. "Where else would you be?"

Making whoopie with my attorney, Perry Miller, she was tempted to add, but didn't. Adding to his agitation wouldn't be smart. When Frank was drinking, he could be mean.

"I'm sure you've heard?"

"About Blythe?"

"Yup." He belched.

"When Mother read about it in the paper, she nearly had a cow."

"What's going on?"

"Beats the hell out of me."

He cocked an eyebrow at the same time that he belched again. "Are you sure you don't know what's going on?" Another belch.

Eleanor was repulsed, and it showed. "I could ask *you* the same thing, but I won't waste my time. You're nothing but a brain-dead, drunken slob."

"Name callin', honey, will getcha nowhere."

"Get out of here, Frank." Eleanor's tone was tired.

"Do you think she really stabbed that man?"

Eleanor sighed. "When it comes to Blythe getting what she wants, I think she's capable of anything. But, then you know her better than I do." Her words sounded snide, even to her own ears.

Frank's eyes narrowed. "If I didn't know better, I'd say you were actually jealous."

"In your dreams."

His flushed face turned even redder. "I can't believe they haven't arrested her yet."

"It's coming. I'm just sitting back and waiting to enjoy the fireworks, actually."

"What if she doesn't get arrested?"

"I'm confident she will." One way or the other, Eleanor thought with a silent smile.

"I wouldn't be too confident, if I were you."

"But then, you're *not* me."

"The tables could turn," Frank pointed out.

Eleanor's mouth curved downward. "That's not likely. Without that second will, she's out of here for sure."

"Speaking of that will, how'd you pull off that coup?"

"I don't know what you're talking about."

"Right." He belched again, then fell into the nearest chair. "If I didn't know your legs were welded together, I'd say you gave old Miller a little." Frank's belch was mingled with a harsh laugh.

Eleanor turned away, feeling her own face turn scarlet.

Frank seemed more perceptive drunk than sober; she would have to remember that.

"The will's no big deal," she said at last. "What with Mark's death and now this man who was stabbed, Blythe's in a deep hole."

"Since she hasn't been officially arrested, seems to me we're all in that hole with her."

"Speak for yourself," Eleanor responded coldly. "Look, what do you want?" When he would have spoken, she held up her hand. "Don't bother to answer. I know. Money."

"Right, wife dear."

Ignoring that second insult, she said, "Well, you made a trip for nothing. I thought I made it clear that the well's dried up."

"I know we've had our differences, but—"

"Groveling doesn't become you, Frank. Anyway, it won't work."

He grimaced as if she'd slapped him. "I'm still your husband."

She laughed. "In name only. The answer is no. That's all I'm going to say."

"No?"

"You have a lot of problems, Frank, but hearing loss is not one of them."

He lurched at her, grabbed her by the arm and jerked her against his chest. She tried to avert her head, so as not to see the spittle gathered at both sides of his mouth, knowing that it would spew on her. She was right.

"I have to have money."

"Turn me loose." Her voice shook with anger. "And don't ever touch me like that again or you'll be sorry."

He sneered. "Whatcha gonna do?"

"Kill you."

That hit the mark. He let go and stood back, a dumbfounded look on his booze-riddled features. Then he said, "Like you killed your brother?"

"Get the hell out of here."

"Not until I get some money."

"Go crawl into one of your bimbettes' beds and sleep it off. Afterward, you'll feel better."

His face turned ugly. "It's not going to look good for the family when I get the crap beat of out me again and land in the hospital."

"After what we've been through with Mark, what's one more scandal? Anyway, maybe it would finally teach you a lesson. You should be more careful who you hang out with."

"She's playing you for a fool, you know."

His abrupt change of tone and subject matter pulled Eleanor up short. "I don't follow you."

"Yes, you do."

"My patience is gone, Frank."

He looked her up and down. "You're such a smart businesswoman, you figure it out."

"You get out."

"I'm going, but don't say I didn't warn you." He paused. "And don't think you won't pay for leaving me in the lurch, because you will."

Still fuming, even minutes after he'd left, Eleanor walked out of her office and down the hall to Blythe's domain. Only after she peered both right and left, making certain she was indeed alone, did she use the master key to let herself into the dimly lit room.

Once inside, she leaned against the door and waited for her heart to stop pounding.

* * *

A door down the hall quietly clicked shut. What to do? Spy on the *spy?* Or stay the hell out of it?

"Why don't you take a load off?"

Jacques Dawson ignored the strident note in her voice and continued to pace. If the carpet hadn't been the best money could buy, he could easily have worn a hole in it.

"Why don't you go do what women do?" he asked absently.

His companion, a young woman named Maxine Avery who he'd been screwing on and off between jobs, shot him a look. "What's eating you, anyway?"

"Nothing that concerns you."

"I thought we were a team."

"Even if we were, this isn't teamwork."

Her long but pretty face bunched into a frown, making her look older than her twenty-odd years. "It should be, since every time you come to the States, you run to me."

"Are you complaining?"

"No, but there must be something you like about me."

Dawson stopped walking and stared at her. "I like the way you fuck me."

His blunt words didn't seem to be the least offensive to her. Maxine merely smiled, spread her naked legs and beckoned with the crook of one finger. "The feeling's mutual, so what are we waiting for?"

"Not now. I have to think."

She made a face, her lips turning pouty. "That's no fun."

He couldn't agree more, especially since his mind was hopping all over the charts.

"Honey?" she cooed.

"What?"

"You know what." She was staring at his crotch. "How 'bout I put some starch back in your jeans?"

Unwittingly, Dawson's eyes dropped. He was indeed limp. But then, sex was the last thing on his mind right now. In fact, he was teetering on the edge mentally.

He had to get hold of himself. But how, when he'd done something really stupid?

Fear of losing what he'd worked so hard for was what had driven him to do what he'd done on both accounts. If only he hadn't lost his temper, then…

Hell, he wouldn't think about that now. He'd never been one to cry over spilled milk, and he wasn't about to start now. He'd never been in this position before. But then, his monetary security had never been threatened before, either.

Megabucks had always been at his disposal. No longer. As a result, his grand life-style was in serious jeopardy.

The thought of having to give up this luxurious condo, not to mention either of his two Mercedes, almost sent him dashing to the toilet. Then he looked at Maxine, who was gazing at him with such unsuppressed longing that for a moment he forget everything except his penis, which rose to the occasion, then fell.

"Can I help?" Maxine asked, shifting on the bed just enough to make her big breasts move.

"No," he said tersely.

"Is it money?"

"How did you know?"

"Just because I have fire in my belly doesn't mean I have air in my head."

"Good point."

"Is money all it is?"

"No. It's much more complicated and serious."

"I'll listen if you want to talk."

"There's nothing to talk about. Besides, I don't want to involve you in my problems."

He meant that, too. He was a loner, always had been, with no intention of changing. Then he'd met Maxine, something he wished hadn't happened. Now was the worst possible time to get involved. He had to admit she was more than just a good lay; he genuinely looked forward to being with her, and they had a lot in common.

Now, though, instead of fucking her, he'd fucked up.

Sound business sense and a sensitive gut instinct had kept him out of a cell so far. He'd never trusted anyone in his entire life, either. So why had he trusted Mark Lambert? He should have been calling the shots, not Lambert.

Sweat lathered Dawson's forehead and his armpits. He had to keep his cool. Just because he'd made a stupid mistake, done something he shouldn't have done, didn't mean the party was over.

After all, he had Blythe Lambert. She was the key to his holding on to his material blessings. With any luck, he'd just put the fear of hell into her. She *had* to give him what he wanted. That was nonnegotiable.

Oh, he had other jobs pending, but Lambert owed him, and he needed what was coming to him now in order to meet his debts. He didn't have time to wait for the other jobs to materialize.

Hell, it was a thousand wonders the cops weren't already on his tail. If that Lambert bitch were ever to rat...

"I'm already involved."

Jacques shook his head, Maxine's words seeming to come out of nowhere. "What did you say?" His tone was distracted and impatient. Why didn't she leave?

"You just said you didn't want to involve me."

"I meant it, too."

"Well, it's too late."

"What the hell does that mean?"

The room fell silent while she plucked at the covers on the bed.

"If you're playing games," he growled, "I'm not in the mood."

Their eyes met, his angry, hers wary.

"And I'm not in the mood to be pregnant with your child, but I am."

The day had been a bitch.

Nothing had gone right, and Ryker was stewing in juices of his own making. Now that he was at his sister's, stretched out on her long sofa, waiting for her to call him to the dinner table, his mood was bound to improve.

Before he went home to his dismal abode, he hoped to chill out.

If Blythe Lambert would let him, that is. Thoughts of her and that session at the station haunted him. He knew she hadn't stuck that knife into that man's gut, that she'd just been in the wrong place at the wrong time. Still, people had been convicted on much less evidence.

And as far as her husband's death, he couldn't discount that episode on board their boat. If only that dim-witted Tanner woman hadn't gotten distracted at the wrong time, Blythe might already have been behind bars.

What had him uptight was whether or not Blythe had told the truth. Had Lambert attacked her first? If so, then he better be glad he was already dead. Ryker would have killed the sonofabitch himself.

Thoughts like that were dangerous and better left untapped, he warned himself. Sticking to his job and gathering sound evidence was all he need be concerned with.

He just needed that one *ah-ha* that tied up the evidence into a neat package; then he would be home free.

Of course, Ryker knew Upshaw would argue otherwise. But then, he didn't give a damn what that little turd thought. When the evidence presented itself—and it would—then he would cuff Blythe Lambert, big-dick attorney or not.

"Ryker?"

He roused and squinted out of one eye at his sister, who walked into the room, holding a cordless phone. He groaned inwardly, cursed, then fell back on the sofa.

He was off duty, for chrissake. He'd even left his cell phone at home on purpose. Only Mike knew where he was, and he'd given him strict orders not to bug him.

"Wait'll I get my hands on Mike," he grumbled, turning over.

"It's not Mike."

He flipped onto his back, his eyes all the way open. "Who the hell is it, then?"

"A woman."

"A woman?"

"Yes, and she's hysterical."

Twenty-eight

He was shaking like a fool and sick with terror to boot. What could have happened to her? Blythe had been so incoherent, he hadn't been able to make heads or tails out of what she was saying.

Snake.

Between sobs, she'd kept saying that over and over. "I'm on my way!" had been his only comeback.

Now, as he turned onto her street, he continued to grip the steering wheel with white-knuckled hands. Had the snake bitten her? He'd tried to get her to tell him, only to realize that he was wasting precious moments trying to reason with her.

At the same time, he was reeling from the fact that she'd called *him.* Why? He didn't know the answer, might never know the answer. Right now, he didn't give a damn. All he cared about was getting there.

Finally rolling the car to a stop, he jumped out and dashed up the front steps. Since she was expecting him, he figured the door would be open. It was.

He bounded inside and called "Blythe?"

"In…here."

Following the sound of her choked whisper, Ryker ended up in the living room. She was sitting on the sofa, but when he walked in, she stood, though on wobbly legs.

Her eyes were wide and tear-stained, and her lower lip was trembling. And even though her mass of honey-colored hair was in total disarray, she was so lovely that his breath caught in his throat.

"What happened?" he managed to ask, though fear still had a stranglehold on his guts. She didn't look as though she was in pain. Traumatized, yes. Pain, no. His insides went limp with relief. Thank heavens, the snake hadn't bitten her.

She licked her lips, then tightened her arms across her chest. "It's...in there. Or at least it was."

"The snake?"

"Yes."

"I'm assuming it didn't bite you."

"It...didn't."

"Where is it?"

"In...my bedroom."

Ryker was stunned. "Bedroom? How—" His voice dried up again when he saw a resurgence of terror in her eyes. It was all he could do not to jerk her into his arms and hold her until that fear was gone.

"I've never been so..." This time her frail voice faded to nothing.

But she didn't have to say anything further. He knew what she was thinking and how she felt. Snakes, dead or alive, weren't one of his favorite play toys, either. And women seemed especially afraid of them.

"It's okay to be scared. I would be, too."

"It...it might still be there."

"Where exactly?"

"On my...pillow."

"Jesus!"

Blythe could only shudder.

"Is it real?"

She gave him an incredulous look before shaking her head. "Do you think it might not be?"

"Could be fake. Who the hell knows? But I'm about to find out. You stay put. And sit down before you fall down."

"I'm all right."

"You're far from all right, but we'll let that slide for now." Ryker paused, shoved his hand through his disheveled hair, then strode out of the room.

Ten minutes later, he walked back into her living room. She was still standing, her back to him. For a moment he couldn't help but admire her slender body, her tight ass and the seemingly endless flow of her slender legs.

If she would only turn a tiny bit, he would be able to see the swell of her breasts....

Ryker coughed to alert her that he was back in the room. She'd had enough fright for one night.

"Did you take care of it?"

"It's gone. Dead and disposed of."

"Was it alive?"

"Yes, but sedated."

Her already big eyes seemed to grow bigger. "Sedated?"

"The bastard who put it there didn't want it to kill you, just scare you."

"Are you sure it's dead?"

"I popped it, then put the body in a garbage bag I got out of your bathroom."

"Where...is it now?"

"In the trunk of my car."

"I didn't even hear you go out."

"That's because you're in shock."

She didn't respond.

"I found out how the bastard got in."

"How?"

"He jimmied the lock in the kitchen."

When he'd gone to the car and discarded the snake, he'd taken the time to look around. Although the job was professional, it was obvious, nonetheless, how her tormentor had gotten in.

"Why would..." Again her voice simply faded away.

"That's what I'd like to know. Suppose you tell me who'd do such a thing and why? Could it have been that French Canadian?"

Blythe smothered a gasp.

"Dammit, now's not the time to clam up. Talk to me."

"I can't."

"Can't! Don't you mean *won't?*"

"Look, I shouldn't have called you."

"But you did."

A loaded silence followed.

"Look, please don't ask me any questions."

He blew out his breath. "That's crazy. I *have* to ask you questions. Even if I weren't a cop, I'd want to know why some nutball put a snake on your pillow, for chrissake!"

"I don't want to talk about it."

"Well, I do."

Another silence.

"I think you should leave."

"You can forget that, especially since cops will be crawling all over the place as soon as I call this in."

"I can handle it."

"Sure."

"I can."

While there was still a hint of stubbornness in her tone, it wasn't as strong. He played on that weakness.

"I don't think you should even stay here, period."

"I don't have a choice."

"That's bullshit."

"I'm not letting that pervert chase me out of my own home."

"You're about the most hardheaded woman I've ever known."

"And I'm sure you've known a lot."

Their eyes met, and for ten seconds neither one said a word.

"Sorry, I shouldn't have said that," she muttered, turning away.

"Dammit, Blythe—"

"Please, don't say anything else. I—"

He should have let it go, should have let sleeping dogs lie. But he didn't. When she started trembling all over, he couldn't handle it.

"If you won't leave, then I won't, either."

She swung around. "That's ridiculous. You can't stay here."

"Wanna bet?"

"I don't need a baby-sitter."

"Well, you need something!"

"Don't holler at me."

"I'm not hollering at you."

"Yes, you are," she whispered, a big tear rolling down her cheek.

"Don't," he said, more brusquely than he intended.

"I can't help it."

"Ah, hell, cry if you want to. You deserve it." He clenched and unclenched his fingers, trying to keep from hauling her into his arms. So far so good.

"I keep seeing that...that thing on my pillow."

"Shh, don't think about it."

"I can't stop."

She stared up at him with those big teary eyes, her teeth chattering together. That was the catalyst that made him do something he knew he would regret. He reached for her and pulled her into his arms.

Right off she stiffened, then murmured incoherent words of protest. Still, he didn't let her go. "It's okay," he whispered into her sweet-smelling hair.

Pulling back, she peered into his face. If it hadn't been for that single tear stuck on her top lip, he might have been able to maintain control.

But the tear *was* there, and his control disappeared.

His lips adhered to hers. The kiss was hot and deep, and it seemed to last forever. Cupping her buttocks, he lifted her against him. He heard her moan as his hard penis rammed into her stomach.

Later he couldn't remember how, but they made it to the bed, where clothes came off piece by piece. Ignoring Blythe's wide-eyed gaze, his eyes soaked up every inch of her body before he lowered his head, cupped a breast and lifted it to his mouth.

She gasped as he sucked. The feel of her nipple between his lips sent a throb of desire so intense shooting through him that he almost blacked out.

Before moving to the other breast, he paused and looked at her. She opened her mouth.

"No," he ground out. "This is insane, I know, but it's got to happen."

She didn't argue. Instead, she reached for his flesh, almost causing him to explode in her hand. Only the greater need to be inside her kept him from doing so.

Too, he needed to bring her the same pleasure she was bringing him. With that in mind, he parted her legs.

His fingers sank deeply into her. She was more than ready.

Hot and wet.

In fact, he was sure she'd already come. Unable to hold back another moment, he stood at the foot of the bed, leaned in a bit, then thrust into her. But still wanting to prolong the sweet agony, he pulled out ever so slowly.

That sensuous movement sent an electric shock through him, especially when she reached down and circled his penis, using it to coax him to her. She didn't turn loose until he was beside her on the bed.

"Blythe?"

"Be quiet," she ordered thickly.

Before he could respond to that order, she bent over him and took him in her mouth. His cry was bestial in nature, knowing that she could taste herself on him. That thought drove him out of his mind.

Lifting her mouth from him, he rolled back up and off the bed. Then, standing again, he plunged into her. Nothing could have prepared him for the sensations that licked like an out-of-control flame through him.

His climax was instant and hard. When it was over, his eyes once again perused her quivering, moist body as she lay facing the wall.

Careful not to touch her, he lay down beside her, stretched his arms above his head and stared up at the ceiling. He wanted to say something, but he didn't know what. For one thing, he was too exhausted. More to the point, what was there to say?

Instead of thinking, he closed his eyes.

He was in the mood to kick something. *Himself.* He had no idea how long he'd slept, but too long, he would bet. He peered at his watch.

Five o'clock in the damn morning.

Ryker muttered a silent expletive even as he turned his head to check the place beside him. Blythe was still there, lying in fetal position, which called attention to the enticing curve of her buttocks.

The temptation to trail his finger between those moist cheeks, making her come again, was so tempting that he held himself rigid for the longest time. What had he done? The answer to that was obvious and easy.

He'd crossed the line. Again. He was already emotionally and mentally involved with a suspect—his number one suspect. Now he was physically involved, as well.

Shit for brains.

That described him to a tee. But what was done was done, and he sure as hell couldn't undo it. Furthermore, he wouldn't, even if he could. That frantic coupling of their bodies, that trial-by-fire closeness, would be with him for as long as he lived.

Still, he had to deal with the here and now, something he didn't know how to do. If only she had answered his question, then maybe this fiasco wouldn't have happened.

She knew who was responsible for that snake. He would bet his life on that, for what it was worth, he thought with cynical honesty. So why had she withheld the information? He couldn't begin to understand her reasoning, especially when it would cast the blame elsewhere.

Or maybe he was barking up the wrong tree. Maybe she was in cahoots with the pervert and something had gone wrong between them. Was she just cunning as hell and holding out on whoever had murdered her husband?

Or was she indeed the innocent pawn she claimed to be?

He didn't know the answers to those questions, but he was damn sure going to find out.

Without looking in her direction again, he got up and put on his clothes.

"Ryker?"

For a moment her soft voice behind him forced him to stop. Yet he didn't dare turn around. If he did, he wouldn't be responsible for his actions.

Without so much as a word or a backward glance, he walked out.

Twenty-nine

No use crying after the fact, Blythe told herself as she smoothed lotion over her body following a long, hot shower. But she was, inside, where the tears didn't show.

She had one thing to be thankful for: her grandmother was all right. After Ryker had left, she hadn't thought she could function. But she had, calling the nursing home and checking on her grandmother. Honey had had no visitors, which meant the cigar man hadn't been there.

The thought of his doing to Honey what he'd done to her filled her with mind-numbing terror. Trying to soothe her troubled mind by stroking her body, Blythe continued enriching her skin with the scented cream, concentrating on her breasts, where Ryker's five o'clock shadow had left whisker burns.

Ryker.

She suppressed a groan and, ignoring her pounding heart, slammed down the bottle and tore out of the bathroom. Her casual linen suit was already on the bed. With jerky motions she dressed, grabbed her purse and walked out.

Fifteen minutes later, she was at the office. But she couldn't work. Her mind reverted into a cyclone of images: death, knives, blood, snakes… Her nerves screamed with such pain that she was useless.

Blythe placed her hands over her temples and rubbed, hoping to head off a dizzy spell. After she'd taken several deep breaths, the room righted. Her staff must not catch her in this condition. Fear and hopelessness already prevailed in this office; she couldn't afford to crumble now.

If only she could work, could figure out a way to snare some big contract. What a blessing that would be, but that couldn't happen, not until she came to terms with what had happened between her and Ryker.

It was as if Ryker were still inside her. Even now, she could feel his powerful arms surrounding her, the high heat of his body pressed against hers.

She whimpered out loud, then clamped her lips together. She had no defense. She had no excuses. Not only had she let him make love to her, she had encouraged it.

She had wanted him.

His mouth, his fingers, his hands, had created sensations in her that she'd never experienced or ever imagined she could experience. Incredible things. Her body had never known such delights. Still, physical gratification was all it was and all it would ever be.

And it carried a high and disastrous price. The man thought she was a murderer, for heaven's sake. Where was her pride? Where was her self-control? Where was her common sense? Last night, all three had deserted her. No matter, the act was a done deal, and she couldn't undo it. She could only take her licks on the chin and move on.

To what? *To where?* That was the main question. To jail? Fear lodged in her belly like a cold stone, as it had when she had thrown back the cover on her bed and seen the snake. Was it fear that had made her so vulnerable, that had made her seek comfort in Ryker's arms?

No. A certain chemistry had hovered between them since they had first met, a chemistry that had finally come together and created an internal explosion. Now she was left to deal with the external cleanup.

When Ryker had walked out without looking at her, she had known the score. That *did* matter. She'd been a one-night lay and that was all. He'd gotten his jollies, and now, for him, it was back to business as usual.

"If I didn't know better, I'd say you were hungover."

At the sound of Curt's voice, Blythe quickly averted her red face and pretended to study a bluebird perched on the brick wall outside the window. At any other time she would have been delighted to watch that special creature.

"Yo?"

She faced Curt, who was frowning. "Sorry," she muttered.

"About what? If this is a bad time, just tell me to get lost."

His actions spoke louder than his words. He stood rooted to the spot, obviously counting on her asking him to stay. Blythe knew he was curious as to what was going on, why she looked as if she been ridden hard and put up wet. But good manners kept him from expressing that, and she was grateful. Susan would not have hesitated.

"Are you hungry?" Curt asked.

Blythe gave a start. "I hadn't even thought about it."

"Come on, I'll buy you breakfast."

"I don't—"

"I won't take no for an answer. Besides, we have to talk."

"All right. I'm not accomplishing anything here."

A few minutes later they were seated across from each other at an outside café in the Azalea district, her favorite coffee shop, in fact. This morning, however, Blythe failed to take pleasure in her surroundings. Still, she ordered a bagel and coffee, more to appease Curt than anything else.

"What's up?" he finally asked.

"I know I look awful," Blythe said, prolonging the inevitable.

"Never awful, just exhausted, actually."

"I am that."

"Want to talk about it?"

"No, but I have to. It's driving me crazy."

"I'm all ears."

She told him about the cigar man and the snake. But nothing else. She would cut out her tongue before she would admit she'd had sex with Ryker Delaney. Shame kept her silent.

Curt visibly cringed. "Christ! What the hell's going on? First someone lures you to a motel, where you find a knife buried in his belly, then there's a snake on your pillow and a cigar-smoking stranger in your home."

"It's unbelievable, isn't it?"

Curt harrumphed. "That's a gross understatement. I'd say you've really pissed someone off."

"I wish I knew what all this meant, what Mark was involved in."

"I assume you've told all this to that obnoxious detective."

Blythe's breathing turned labored. "No."

"Why not?"

"Because that creep also turned up in my home a

while back and threatened to hurt my grandmother if I didn't cooperate with him.''

''Christ,'' Curt muttered again. ''What are you going to do?''

''I haven't decided yet. But I'm not going to sit by and let him hurt Honey or me. Somehow I've got to convince him that I don't have the things he wants.''

''Does this fruitcake have a name?''

''Not that I know.''

Curt ran his hands through his hair. ''What a mess.''

''It's worse than that.''

''You're right, it is,'' he said in a pointed tone.

Blythe's heart sank another notch. ''Eleanor?''

''How'd you know?''

''My intuition's on a roll.''

''So is the bitch. She's on the warpath.''

''What now?''

''I caught her going into your office.''

Blythe gasped. ''But she doesn't have a key.''

''Need I say more?''

''Did she see you?''

''Nope.''

''Damn.''

''I debated whether or not to even tell you,'' Curt said.

''Why wouldn't you?''

''As it is, your boat's already loaded.''

''When it comes to Eleanor's shenanigans, it can always hold more.''

''What are you going to do about her?''

''I thought I'd already done enough, along with my attorney.''

''Well, her wings haven't been clipped as far as I can tell.''

Blythe pushed aside the plate that the waitress had

just brought. Food was the last thing she wanted. "Well, we can't lock her out, that's for sure. But on the other hand, she can't force me out, either."

"She's also still flapping her tongue, undermining you at every turn."

"She thinks I killed Mark."

"Hell, I wouldn't put that past her." He paused. "Anyway, what she thinks is her problem. Ours is to shut her mouth," he went on when Blythe didn't respond.

"What do you think she was looking for?"

"My guess would be the Farmer file."

"Mine, too, and I have to confess I haven't checked it recently. But then, I'm not sure I'd know if she'd fooled with it or not."

"We can't forget about Frank pulling the same stunt," Curt said, after taking a sip of his coffee. He hadn't touched his food, either. "Think they're in cahoots?"

"It's possible, but I doubt it. They certainly don't have a marriage made in heaven. Besides, they each have their own agenda."

"Well, whatever," Curt said, "Eleanor needs to have a muzzle put on her."

"As long as she just undermines me and not Designs—"

"No," Curt interrupted. "You *are* Designs. When she hurts you, she hurts the company, only she's too full of herself to understand that."

"You're right. And I can't have her pilfering through my office."

"So nail her ass for sure this time."

Blythe's lips thinned. "I promise."

"Since we've both lost our appetites, you ready to go?"

Without saying anything, Blythe stood, then walked out ahead of him, feeling as if she'd been tossed into a pool of quicksand and was sinking.

Ryker put the gun to the man's temple. "On your belly, buddy!"

The short, bony man began shaking all over. "Hey, man, don't...don't shoot."

"Shut up and do like you're told."

The man hit the floor. Ryker immediately placed a knee on the small of his back and clamped the cuffs on him. Then, standing, he faced Mike, who was striding toward him, herding his own handcuffed perp.

The fleabag motel was surrounded by cops. Earlier they had gotten a tip on the convenience store suspects, that they were holed up here. Sure enough, they had gotten lucky, and now the killers were in custody.

"Good work," Ryker said to his partner whose hand was on his prisoner's head as he ushered him into the police car.

"You, too," Mike responded, grinning. "Hell, though, this was an easy arrest. I expected more of a fight."

"After looking at them, I don't know how they had the brains to load a gun, much less use it."

"You're right. Dumb and dumber."

Ryker was silent for a moment, watching as the suspects were driven from the scene. Then he turned to Mike and asked, "Did you find out anything?"

"Sure enough."

Ryker tensed. "Was I right?"

"Yep. Dead on."

"That info's bound to give Price a hard-on," Ryker said, grim-faced.

"What about you?"

"What about me?"

"It's another nail in Blythe Lambert's coffin."

"So?"

Mike flushed before shifting his gaze. "So I know how you feel about...her."

"And just how is that?"

Mike looked down and pawed a cigarette butt on the cement, as if he knew he'd opened his mouth and inserted his foot. "I've, er, seen how you look at her."

"You haven't seen jack-shit!" Ryker's tone was bitingly harsh. "If she's guilty, I'll throw her in jail just like I did those two we just arrested."

Mike held up his hands and backed up. "Hey, I didn't mean anything by—"

"Then shut the fuck up and get back to the station."

Mike's flush deepened. "Where are you going?"

Ryker walked off without bothering to answer.

"You're just the person I wanted to see."

"Oh, really?" Eleanor's tone was hostile.

Blythe's tone was equally hostile. "Yes, really."

Ever since she'd returned to the office from her outing with Curt, she'd had every intention of confronting Eleanor. Now the opportunity had arrived.

"I'm on my way out," Eleanor said.

"We're going to talk first. Mark's office will be as good a place as any."

Without waiting for a comeback from her sister-in-law, Blythe crossed the threshold into Mark's office. For a moment, a sadness settled over her, more for the what-might-have-been than anything else.

Mark had betrayed her on more than one front. Even though he was dead, she still hadn't forgiven him.

Eleanor slammed the door, forcing her back to the ugly reality of the moment.

"Say your piece, then get out."

Blythe swung around, her eyes as cold as her tone. "Don't ever sneak into my office again."

"So you know?"

"What did you steal?"

Eleanor moved away from the door. "I don't have to answer that."

Blythe bore down on her. "You damn sure do. Until the judge says otherwise, you're *not* in charge of this company. The sooner you come to terms with that, the better off you'll be."

Before Eleanor could reply, Blythe whipped around and walked back to the door. Once there, she added, "Meanwhile, stay out of my way."

"You can't give *me* orders!" Eleanor screamed. "You'll be sorry you ever crossed me."

Blythe froze, then slowly turned back around. "Don't you ever threaten me again," she spat. "Or *you'll* be the one who's sorry." Seconds later, she was still shaking when she reached her own office. Susan was away from her desk, which was a relief. She didn't want to see anyone. She was halfway to her desk before she realized she wasn't alone.

She pulled up short and stared. Ryker Delaney was leaning against her desk with his arms crossed over his chest.

Thirty

"How'd you get in here?" she asked, her voice thick with emotion.

"Walked."

Their gazes tangled, and her stomach took a dive. Quickly she looked away and muttered, "Funny."

Of course, neither the situation nor his presence was funny, far from it. She wished she could whip around and flee like a scalded cat. However, she wouldn't budge, not only because that would give him power over her, but for her own self-preservation.

What had happened between them couldn't be undone, and she didn't intend to insult her intelligence by pretending otherwise. Nor did she intend to keep beating that same dead horse. She had to move on. Too much in her life depended on her having all her faculties about her.

Dealing with this man, for starters.

Ryker cocked his head to one side. The movement drew her gaze back to those penetrating eyes. Blythe felt as though he could see through to her skull, that he was privy to every thought she'd ever had or ever hoped to have.

Laser eyes. Was that why he was perfect for his job? Blythe tightened her lips into a thin line, but she still couldn't look away.

That certain something continued to connect them, though neither was eager even to acknowledge it, much less share it verbally.

Blythe was the first to shift her gaze, but that didn't stop her thoughts from veering in his direction. Seeing him brought vivid memories of their shared intimacies, intimacies that she'd never shared with Mark, moans of pleasure that her husband had never pulled from her.

"I shouldn't be surprised," she said, invading the incriminating silence.

"That I'm here?"

"Yes." Her voice sounded brittle. She took a steadying breath.

"That's right, you shouldn't be."

"Are you on official business?"

"I'm sure as hell not here to talk about last night."

Inwardly, Blythe flinched, then gritted her teeth. Holding her tongue was hard when she wanted to lash back at him, to verbalize her anger and hurt at his callousness, to give him tit for tat.

But she wouldn't give him the satisfaction of knowing how deeply his words cut. So she kept a stiff upper lip, feeling her mood turn suddenly reckless.

"All right, state your business and get out."

"I'm calling the shots here. Not you."

"So call them."

"You think this is a joke, don't you." Ryker's eyes were hooded, but she could still see the coldness beneath those thick eyelashes.

How could his mouth, his fingers, his hands, have done such incredible things to her body one time, then be so cold and cruel the next?

Suddenly she had to fight back the urge to cry, which made her furious at herself. She knew what he was doing, appeasing his own conscience. He'd slept with her, knowing that he was breaking every rule in his book of ethics, and that fact was eating at him.

"I'm not going to get into a verbal slinging match with you," she said coldly.

"That's not why I'm here."

"Yes, it is. You're pissed about last night, and you're blaming me. And it's not my fault."

"You could've said no."

"You could've stopped on your own."

Another silence, longer and heavier than before.

Blythe could hear the hammering of her heart in her chest. How she had gotten herself into this mess was beyond her. He was everything she didn't want in a man, including a heart-stopping one-night stand.

He was arrogant, bitter, opinionated.... The list could go on. Actually, she hated him, yet she wanted him. If he were to shove her against the desk, spread her legs...

She chopped off those dangerous thoughts and averted her gaze, though she felt the heat in her face.

"Did you come to arrest me?"

"Not yet."

"Then leave."

"No."

"Fine."

"Prior to his death, did your husband give you any rare or expensive pieces of jewelry?"

Blythe's head popped back. "What kind of question is that?"

"One you need to answer."

"Then the answer is no."

"Does the name Jacques Dawson mean anything to you?"

"No."

"Are you sure?" His tone was thick with impatience.

Her eyes flared. "Yes, dammit, I'm sure. Who is he?"

"A jewel thief, a highly skilled one at that."

"What does that have to do with Mark and me?"

"That's what I'm trying to find out."

"You already know something or else we wouldn't be having this conversation. So what's the punch line?"

"Your husband was seen in his company more than once."

"Meaning?"

"Meaning there's a real possibility that Lambert had something going on the side with this guy."

"Such as?"

"Theft on a large scale, using the company as a front."

Blythe's air of false bravado crumbled. "You're joking."

"Hardly."

"Why, that's the craziest thing I've ever heard."

His gaze trapped hers. "Are you saying you don't know anything about it?"

"Of course I don't," she snapped. "The idea that Mark would have used the business as a front for criminal activities is ludicrous."

"I disagree."

"I would have known about it!"

"My point."

"Damn you. I don't know what you're talking about nor do I know who Dawson is."

The instant the words were out of her mouth, it hit her. She should have put two and two together before now. But then, she hadn't been thinking straight lately—about anything.

The creep with the cigar. He'd said he was Mark's

partner, that Mark had something that belonged to him. Suddenly the man and the threats fell into place with sickening clarity.

The man in the motel with the knife in his belly rose again to haunt her. Somehow he'd been involved in this rotten mess. He had told her that he had information about Mark's extracurricular activities, which, at the time, she had linked with his gambling. Now she wasn't so sure. What if...?

"Let's have it."

"There's...nothing to have," Blythe hedged, knowing she wasn't making sense and that he could see through her bluster.

"Dammit, Blythe, don't make me do something I don't want to do."

His fierce expression forced her to step backward. Perhaps she should confide in Ryker about the visits from the French Canadian. Then she remembered the snake on her pillow and the threat to her grandmother.

She couldn't forget Ryker's distrust of *her,* either. What if he didn't believe her? What if her blabbing put Honey and herself in grave danger? And for nothing? It didn't matter so much about herself, but she couldn't afford to take a chance with her grandmother's life.

Besides, she would stake her life on the fact that Ryker remained convinced that she had been involved with Mark in his criminal dealings, which meant that at any time she could be charged with her husband's murder.

"I've run out of patience."

His voice, thick with rage, returned her to her senses. "I don't have anything else to say."

His expletive bounced off the walls, and she braced herself for what was to follow.

"You're lying."

She stared him down. "You can't prove that."

"I can and I will. And don't think for a minute that just because we fucked I'm going to cut you any slack, because I'm not."

"Get out," she snarled, choking on her own rage.

"With pleasure." Ryker turned and strode out.

Blythe was still trying to gather her wits about her a few minutes later when Susan breezed into her office. "What was that all about?"

"Trust me, you don't want to know."

"He looked mad enough to kill."

"He was."

"At you?"

Blythe nodded, while Susan whistled. "Want to talk about it?"

"I can't, not right now."

And she couldn't. Nothing Ryker had told her made sense. But she had to try to sort it out. Alone.

Sinking down into her desk chair, Blythe placed her forehead on her desk. She didn't know how long Susan stood there before she quietly left the room.

"Delaney, you know I've never liked you or your attitude."

"Don't tell me you've changed your mind?" Ryker said drolly, eying his chief. He'd been called into Foley's office unexpectedly, something that created a sour taste in his mouth.

"Not just no, but hell no."

"Damn." Ryker snapped his fingers. "Here I was thinking you were going to suggest we kiss and make up."

Foley's face turned ashen, then a high red. For a second Ryker actually felt a pinch of concern, afraid the chief might have a stroke.

"I oughta go after your balls," Foley said instead.

Ryker shrugged. "That's always an option. And your call."

"Does anything ever shake you up? Does that ice in your veins ever thaw?"

Yeah, when I was screwing Blythe Lambert, who's tops on my suspect list. He wished he had the guts to say that. What a hoot it would be to get Price's reaction to that one. Even that wasn't worth it. Ryker wasn't proud of his conduct; he would just as soon keep that sin to himself.

"I'm assuming this discussion is leading up to the Lambert case." His voice sounded dull and tired.

"Yeah. The D.A.'s office is crawling all over me. What's the status of the investigation?"

"We're making headway."

"You damn sure better be. Now get outta here."

Twenty minutes later, Ryker was nursing his frustration, sitting in his car across the street from Blythe's office. He had men to do this kind of thing, but he chose to do it himself, knowing he was nuts. Still, he couldn't seem to help himself.

That romp in the hay with Blythe had him pussy-whipped and longing for more. He jammed the palm of his hand against the steering wheel and cursed. But all was not lost. His personal fixation with her aside, he hadn't lied to his superior. She still remained tops in the suspect spotlight.

Yet guilt gnawed at his gut, especially since he'd sent Mike out alone on a case that called for the two of them. Mike hadn't said anything; he'd just raised his eyebrows and given him a knowing look.

"You're a head case, for sure, Delaney," he told himself now, only to suddenly straighten.

Blythe had walked out of the building and was getting into her car. He cranked his engine and pulled into the street behind her. After several turns, he knew where she was headed—to the nursing facility where her grandmother lived.

Nothing incriminating there, he told himself, feeling dejected. Hell, he didn't know what he'd expected, but it wasn't this. And then it happened.

A truck with tinted windows appeared out of nowhere and bashed into the side of Blythe's car, sending it hurtling toward the ditch.

"Shit!"

Thirty-one

Ryker was sick with terror.

What if she was dead? He prayed that she was wearing her seat belt and her air bag worked. It seemed an interminable length of time until he reached Blythe's Lexus, which was now on the shoulder of the road, having been stopped by a limp-looking oak tree.

As he'd slammed on his brakes and screeched his wheels to a halt, the cop in him had taken over and he'd called in the accident. Dammit, though, he hadn't been able to get the license plate. Reason? The truck hadn't had one.

Frustrated to the max, Ryker cursed. He hadn't seen who had been driving the other vehicle, either. Too bad. Right now his concern was for Blythe. Soon the place would be overrun with fellow officers, along with an ambulance. He winced at that thought even as he lunged from behind the wheel and raced toward Blythe.

Was she conscious? He could see that her air bag had deployed, thank God. And she indeed had her seat belt on. Another good sign was that she wasn't leaning forward on the air bag but back against the seat.

Still. She was so still. His heart sank. She was dead. No. As if he'd willed her to, she moved. Relief made him weak, yet he wasted no time in jerking open the door.

"Blythe?" His voice came out sounding like a croaking bullfrog.

She raised her eyes, and though they seemed filled with stark confusion, he didn't see any visible signs of serious injury. At least, there wasn't any blood on her face or body.

"Are you all right?" he demanded, his voice still hoarse.

Before she had a chance to answer, he gently urged her over so that he could slide behind the wheel. He could feel her eyes on him before he faced her again.

"I...think so."

"Let's make sure."

Without asking permission, he ran his hands over her upper body, ignoring her vague moans of protest. His instincts had paid off. No limbs seemed to be broken; she was one lucky lady. Hell, she didn't even have a scratch on her.

"What...what happened?" she asked, her lower lip trembling.

His gut twisted. Had he been wrong? Had she received a blow that had given her amnesia?

"You mean you don't know?"

When she didn't answer him right off, his stomach tightened with renewed fear. "Did you hit your head?"

"I...I don't think so."

"Do you know who I am?"

"Of course."

"Say my name. Out loud."

"It's Ryker."

She sounded annoyed, which was a better sign. But he still wasn't satisfied that she was one hundred percent herself.

"What's your name?"

She told him.

"So far, so good. Now, take your time and tell me your version of what happened."

She frowned. "I'm not...sure I can. My head hurts too badly."

"It's because you're upset. I'm pretty sure the air bag and seat belt saved you from hitting your head against the windshield."

"Everything happened so fast."

"So you do remember?"

"Someone ran me off the road."

"That goddamn truck came out of nowhere."

"Did you see who was driving?"

It wasn't so much what she said but the way she said it that kicked his cop instincts into overdrive. She knew something.

"Hell, no. It had tinted windows and no rear plate."

Blythe started to shake then, and while he wanted to hold her, he suddenly wanted to throttle her more. "But you know who it was, don't you?"

"I...of course not."

"Let's cut the bullshit, okay?"

"I don't know what you're talking about," she responded in a weary voice. But he noticed she made a point of not looking at him.

"Yes, you do, dammit!"

Blythe's shaking worsened, but he wasn't about to cut her any slack. Enough was enough. His thin thread of patience had finally snapped. He was determined to get some answers.

"I can't tell you," she said, her eyes dark with fear.

"You have no choice."

"Yes, I do."

His fury factor went off the charts. "Look, don't you

goddamn get it? Whoever ran you off the road, broke into your house and left a snake on your bed means business. They're not playing games. Nor is the person who plunged that knife into that man's belly in the motel room! Do I make myself clear?"

"Very," she whispered in a small voice.

"That's a start. Now, it's my guess that one person's behind all this, and you know who that one person is."

Blythe flinched visibly at that last statement. Good. He hoped he'd scared her shitless.

"What do you think's going on?" she asked.

"I know you're stalling, which is all right now that we're no longer alone." As expected, his cohorts had arrived. "But just so you know, I *am* going to get the answers to my questions."

Blythe felt better. Not great, but better. After she'd given her official statement, Ryker had driven her home, where she had immediately taken two muscle relaxants.

Now, as she sat on the sofa, she stared up at Ryker while he lounged against the fireplace. His eyes, fixed on her, seemed to peel away her thoughts like an onion, removing layer after layer until she had no secrets left.

He had dug his heels in and wasn't about to let her off the hook. Even if he hadn't already warned her, his fierce expression and his seemingly immovable body drove home that point.

"Let's have it."

"Then will you go?"

"Depends."

"On what?"

"Don't push your luck, that's what."

She squared her shoulders and shot him a hard look,

despite the added pain to her head. "I won't tell you one thing unless you promise you'll leave."

"You win. I'll leave. Now talk."

Although he was cavalier with his promise, she didn't dare argue. It was that deadly tone that finally convinced her she had indeed pushed her luck to the limit. Anyway, the sooner she told him what he wanted to know, the sooner she would be alone in a hot shower.

She was counting on that shower to remove both the fear and the cobwebs from her brain so she could think. At the moment, it felt like she had two heads and neither one was working properly.

"The French Canadian, Jacques Dawson, is the one who broke into my house and who most likely left the snake."

"I'm listening." Ryker's voice was low and tense.

She told him everything, including the threat against her beloved grandmother.

"That's quite a tale."

Her tongue felt like a big ball of cotton in her mouth, but she was still able to get around that and ask, "You believe me, don't you?"

"No one could make up a story like that."

"Somehow I don't find that comforting."

"You should. I'm not arresting you."

She stood. "I'm going to take a shower. Lock the door behind you."

"You're not afraid to stay here alone?"

I'm much more afraid of you. "No. So, are you leaving?"

"Yes, ma'am."

Ignoring his mocking sarcasm, Blythe repeated, "Please, lock the door behind you."

Then, turning her back, she made her way to the bedroom, where she peeled off her clothes. She then stepped into the shower, certain she heard the door slam.

A while later, she was out and in the process of drying off when she realized she'd been mistaken. Using the reflection in the long floor-to-ceiling mirror in front of her, her eyes went to the doorway.

"You!"

Ryker's eyes blazed a trail up and down her body as he lounged against the door frame.

"You...you told me you were leaving."

"I lied," he said thickly.

She swallowed, unable to take her eyes off him as he walked slowly toward her. "No, don't." Even to her own ears, those words sounded lame, insincere.

"Don't what?" he asked, stopping so close that she could feel the heat of his body, even as he reached out and thumbed a nipple.

His touch was so unexpected, so erotic, that her legs almost gave way beneath her. She didn't have to worry; he held on to her at the same time that he jerked the towel out of her hand and threw it down.

"Ryker?"

"Go on, say it."

Her eyes were wild and her mouth dry. "Say what?"

"That you want me."

"I...can't."

"Yes, you can. After watching you, I couldn't keep this in my pants one second longer." To prove that point, he unzipped his fly. Taking hold of her hand, he placed it on him.

"I can never look at you without wanting you. Now you can feel for yourself just how much."

Even as he spoke in that low, husky voice, he was backing her up against the mirror, nudging both her lips and her legs apart. Before she could so much as whimper, he was inside her, hot, hard and thrusting.

The orgasm came hard and quick, and she cried out. Then more orgasms, as they turned and watched themselves in the mirror.

Her brain told her that this was madness in its highest form, something she was bound to pay dearly for. But her body thought she was brilliant.

Following the final shattering climax, she leaned her head against his chest, so drained she couldn't speak. It was as if her mind had disconnected itself from her body, yet she was still on an incredible high. But when she snapped back, she looked up at him and burst into tears.

He held her.

"This is madness," she whispered, voicing her thoughts of a moment earlier.

"I know. Like before."

She didn't respond. She simply didn't know how.

"It was bound to happen again." She peered up at him. "When I'm around you, I go berserk. I can't think straight."

"Me, either."

"We're in trouble."

"In more ways than one." Blythe paused. "What are we going to do?" she asked.

"I know what I *want* to do."

Her voice wavered. "What?"

"Make love to you."

"Again?"

He took her hand and placed it on him. "Think *it* doesn't have a mind of its own?"

"I won't argue," she whispered against his lips, taking his penis in her hand and massaging it until the end was lathered with his own juices.

"If you don't stop, I'm going to come in your hand."

"I'd rather it was my mouth."

His eyes burned into hers. "Are you sure?"

She didn't answer. Instead she slipped to her knees, his moans caressing her ears.

Somehow they ended up back on the bed, too spent to do anything except sleep. Blythe was the first to awaken to a partially lit room. Crushing the panic that seized her by the throat, she eased her eyes toward the clock on the bedside table.

Eight-thirty.

She couldn't believe it. They had slept for hours. In fact, Ryker was still asleep. Or so she thought.

"I was playing possum," he said, facing her.

"Why didn't you wake me up?" Her voice was raspy.

"Why?"

She perused her lips. "You know why."

"I enjoyed watching you sleep. Among other things."

She flushed and turned away.

"Don't you think we're slightly past that stage?"

Her color deepened.

He turned her head back around and smiled, which took away the rest of her breath. He looked like a different person—a human being with real emotions.

"You really ought to make a practice of that."

"What?"

"Smiling."

"I've almost forgotten how."

"Did the smiles stop when you lost your...wife?"

She felt him stiffen, but he didn't move away. "Guess so. How'd you know about that?"

"You're not the only one who did their homework."

"Ah, so you checked me out?"

"I read the articles about the bomb."

"One of the worst days of my life."

"No doubt."

"I loved her, but—"

"But what?" She hated the flash of jealousy that went through her.

"We had a lot of problems. She wasn't suited to be a cop's wife, but that didn't stop me from trying to make her one. If she hadn't gotten killed, she would have left me."

"I'm sorry."

"Me, too, for more reasons than one. If she had bailed, then maybe she would still be alive, married to some boring accountant with three point two children."

"Life has a habit of kicking us when we least expect it."

"Why didn't you leave Lambert?"

"The path of least resistance, I'm sorry to say."

"*He* was sorry."

"How do you think Mark used the business?" she asked suddenly, venturing into another dangerous area.

"I'm not sure."

"Is that the truth?"

"Yes. When I know, you'll know."

"You think he was involved with Dawson in stealing jewelry, don't you?" she pressed.

"Yes."

"That's why you think we had something to do with your niece's—"

"Shh, I don't want to talk about that now."

"Normally that's all you want to talk about."

"Right now, things are far from normal. All I can think about is fucking you again."

She winced.

"Sorry, didn't mean to offend you. Unfortunately, that sort of language comes with the job. When it comes to you, it's meant as a compliment."

"That's good."

"*We're* good. Together."

"Show me."

He did.

"I have to go," Ryker said much later, regret hardening his tone.

"I know."

"I don't want to."

"I know that, too."

She watched as he swung off the bed and reached for his clothes. Once he was dressed, his eyes met hers, and they simply stared at each other.

"Do you still think I'm guilty?"

She hadn't planned on asking that question. It had just slipped out, and now she was mortified with fear that he would respond in an equally blunt manner.

Ryker's features contorted. "I hope the hell you're not." He leaned over and kissed her hard on the mouth. "For both our sakes."

Thirty-two

"How are things at the office?"

Eleanor stared at her mother, noticing that time had finally added wrinkles to Cynthia's patrician features. Or was it tragedy? The tragedy of losing a child?

She suspected it was mostly the latter. Jealousy pricked at Eleanor; her mother wouldn't grieve over her daughter's passing. She would probably be glad. Because that thought made her feel worse, Eleanor dismissed it.

"Eleanor?"

"Sorry, Mother. My mind's wandering."

"You seem dazed. You okay?"

"No, as a matter of fact, I'm not. And to answer your question, things are not going well."

"Between you and Frank, or at the office?"

"Both. Right now, my life's pretty shitty, actually."

She watched her mother wince at the use of such gritty language, but then, that was why she'd said it. Sometimes it did her heart good to shake up Cynthia. Today was one of those days.

They had finished lunch in the solarium, a rarity for both. Eleanor had been wanting to talk to her mother but hadn't had the courage to approach her. Cynthia had ended up making the overture, but so far, all they had done was make small talk.

"What's going on?" Cynthia asked.

"Do you really care?"

Cynthia's lightly colored lips tightened. "You're not happy unless you're stirring up trouble. I've never understood that."

Eleanor pursed her mouth, then wished she'd kept it shut. Now was not the time to antagonize her mother, but she couldn't seem to help herself. Maybe it stemmed from the fact that Cynthia had never understood her, that Mark, even in death, remained the fair-haired child.

To point that out to Cynthia would be an effort in futility, especially now. Her mother had never recognized, much less admitted, the flaw in herself that made her love one child more than the other.

"Designs is in trouble," Eleanor said instead.

"I know."

Eleanor's jaw went slack. "You know?"

"Unfortunately."

"I don't have to guess who told you. Blythe, right?"

"Yes."

Eleanor laughed unpleasantly. "Bitch!"

"Please, there's no need for name calling."

"I bet she blamed me."

"You and Mark, actually," Cynthia admitted.

Eleanor laughed again.

"This isn't a laughing matter."

"You're telling me." Eleanor's tone was biting. "I bet she hit you up for money."

"She did."

"I hope you didn't give her any."

Cynthia shook her head. "I didn't."

"Thank God."

"Is Blythe to blame for any of the company's downfall?"

"Not to hear her tell it. She's making everyone else out to be the bad guys, especially Mark, saying he bled the company dry on account of his gambling."

Cynthia placed a hand against her heart, but Eleanor didn't get disturbed. She suspected that Cynthia used her condition to her advantage at times like now, when she didn't want to discuss things that were unpleasant.

"Can she prove that?" Cynthia asked.

"Says she can. Moody Bowers is backing her up."

"Oh my, what an embarrassment."

"Is that all you have to say?" Eleanor demanded. "Is that all you care about—the reputation of this goddamn family?"

"How dare you swear in front of me!"

"Jeez, Mother, you're something else."

"You've never understood me." Cynthia's voice trembled. "Mark was—"

"Save it. I didn't join you for lunch to hear you slobber about how wonderful Mark was."

"Then why did you join me?"

"To let you know about the company and—" She broke off.

"And what?" Cynthia prodded coldly.

"To ask for your support in ousting Blythe."

"And money?"

Eleanor averted her gaze. "Would that be such a crime?"

Her mother didn't respond, which made her see red, but she kept her anger to herself. For now. "Also, I've made a decision concerning Frank."

"You really should have done something about him a long time ago. *His* gambling's gotten completely out of hand as well."

"So are you saying I have your permission to divorce

him?'' When her mother didn't answer, she went on. ''I figured you'd have a cow if I even mentioned that word.'' She paused. ''The only other alternative is to kill him.''

Cynthia gave her an incredulous look. ''How can you joke about such a thing after what happened to your brother?''

''That's another reason why I wanted us to talk.''

''Mark? You know something about his death that I don't know?''

''Sure do.''

''What?''

''You'll know soon enough. I just wanted to prepare you for some fireworks.''

''It concerns Blythe, doesn't it?''

''Yep. She's pissed me off one time too many.''

''I hope you haven't done something that will air our dirty laundry in public. You know how I feel about holding on to our good name.''

Eleanor threw her mother a vicious look. She had wanted Cynthia's support, but she should have known she wouldn't get it. Her mother was as self-centered as her brother had been.

The family name was everything. Well, screw the family.

This family unit, such as it was, was about to be blown to smithereens. Personally, Eleanor couldn't wait. That bitch of a sister-in-law couldn't take her to task without paying for it.

''Eleanor, did you hear what I said?''

''Oh, I heard you, all right.''

''Then you'll be careful?''

Ignoring the plea in Cynthia's tone, Eleanor wiped her mouth one last time, tossed down the napkin, then stood.

"I'm tired of being careful. From now on, it's blood-drawing time."

"I can't believe you live like such a slob. And a drunken one, at that."

Ryker stared at his sister out of red, bleary eyes. "I don't recall asking for your presence or your opinion."

"Don't be a jerk, Ryker."

"Dammit, Marcy, I'm not in the mood—" He stopped short and rubbed his eyes, trying not to say something he would be sorry for later. After all, it wasn't his sister's fault that he'd gotten himself in a jam he couldn't get out of.

"Just what *are* you in the mood for, pray tell?"

Ignoring her question, Ryker got up off the sofa and muttered, "Getting dressed and going to work. Look, if it'll make you feel better, straighten up my place, then go on about your business."

"God, you're acting like a jerk."

"I've had two lousy days."

"You didn't get fired, did you?"

The corners of Ryker's mouth turned down. "Not yet."

"Oh, Ryker, what am I going to do with you?"

"Disowning me sounds like a good idea."

She grinned. "It's too late for that. Is something going on that you're not telling me?"

"No," he lied.

"Well, something's going on with me. Actually, I came over to buy you breakfast and tell you about it."

The thought of food hitting his stomach made Ryker physically ill. His expression must have communicated that to Marcy.

"Not a good idea, huh? The food, I mean?"

"Not unless you want me to embarrass you."

"I'll pass."

"But feel free to tell me what's on your mind."

"Why don't you take a shower first, okay?"

He forced a smile. "Do I stink that bad?"

"Yes, you do."

Ryker smiled again ruefully. "Thanks, sis, for not giving up on me."

"You're welcome. Now hurry. I haven't got all day."

"Neither do I."

Ten minutes later, he strolled back into the room. Just as he thought, Marcy had the den back to its uncorrupted state.

"So, lay it on me."

"I'm getting married." She cocked her head. "And I just might be pregnant."

"Whoa!"

"Does that translate into congratulations?"

"You betcha it does. Come here and give big brother a hug. Then I want all the details."

Marcy giggled. "You wish."

Ten minutes later, Ryker shut the door behind her, trying to be more excited than envious. The envy won, much to his chagrin.

He wished the hell it were him wearing that happy face. Instead, he was wallowing in the pits of hell, all because he couldn't stop thinking about a woman he *shouldn't* want and *couldn't* have.

What was there about her that could turn him inside out?

At first it had been her cool outer aloofness that attracted him. She had offered a challenge, which he hadn't been able to pass up. He'd always referred to that bullheadedness as another glitch in his personality.

Now Blythe Lambert was much more than a cool challenge; she had turned into a hot obsession. And he was more confused than he'd ever been in his life. He wanted to love her, yet he wanted her to be guilty of murder so that he could punish her.

What a fucking nightmare.

Quickly shutting down those thoughts, Ryker picked up his gun and shoved it into his holster, then strode out the door and headed for the station.

When he arrived, Mike was waiting for him.

"Where the hell have you been?" his partner demanded.

"Sobering up."

Ryker's blunt answer seemed to take him by surprise. "You sure picked a helluva time to tie one on. I've been trying to get hold of you."

Ryker shrugged, already having lost interest in the conversation. He didn't have to justify himself to anyone, least of all his green partner.

"You've got company."

"Blythe?"

Mike's eyes narrowed into an odd look. "Blythe? Mmm, when did you get on a first-name basis with her?"

"None of your business?"

"When you want to, you can be a real bastard."

"What else is new?" Ryker asked in a controlled tone. "So who's waiting for me?"

"See for yourself," Mike said, stalking off.

Cursing, Ryker stomped into his office.

Eleanor Brodrick stood to greet him. "Afternoon, Detective. I think it's past time you and I had a talk."

* * *

"Mr. Farmer's busy at the moment. May I take a message?"

"Yes," Blythe said, almost choking on her frustration. "Please let him know that Blythe Lambert called. Again."

"I'll tell him."

Blythe was tempted to slam down the receiver, but she refrained. Pitching a temper tantrum wouldn't solve one thing. Besides, it wasn't Farmer that had her in such a snit, although she was panicked at the thought of not getting the contract.

She had to believe she still had a chance, however slim. To date he hadn't given the bid to another company. Time, however, was a luxury she had run out of. She couldn't hold off much longer.

The certificate of deposit she'd cashed in was gone. Money from the small jobs was barely keeping the company's head above water. Soon her only alternative would be to declare bankruptcy.

Right now, if Mark weren't already dead, she would have been tempted to strangle him herself, especially since his so-called partner was still on the loose. She had no idea when he would strike again, although Ryker had placed a twenty-four-hour guard around her place, as well as the nursing home. She hadn't asked him how he'd managed to pull that off, considering she was a suspect herself.

But then, she hadn't seen him to ask.

Since that night of hot sex, he hadn't been around, nor had he called. But out of sight was not necessarily out of mind. Far from it, she thought with a tightness in her chest.

Since they had made love, she'd thought of little else, which was what was making her crazy.

She and Ryker had no future. Yet she wanted one with him. She had fallen in love with the grim-faced detective. To add insult to injury, she could be pregnant.

That thought forced her to sit down and grab her stomach. God, what had she done? Even if he hadn't thought she could be guilty of murder, their personalities were totally incompatible.

When she married again, she wanted a true soul mate. She wanted someone who shared her interests, someone who was a homebody, something Mark certainly hadn't been. Ryker would never fit into that mold, either; his job wouldn't permit it.

Still, when he touched her, accidentally or otherwise, every nerve in her body reacted and nothing else mattered.

A knock on the door jolted her out of her thoughts. "Come in."

It was Susan. "Detective Delaney and his partner are here."

Blythe stood, while her heart fluttered. "Send them in."

Seconds later, both men walked across the threshold, but it was Ryker who spoke.

"Blythe Lambert, I'm here to place you under arrest for the murder of your husband."

Thirty-three

Ryker watched her sway visibly from shock. For a second he was tempted to say to hell with it, throw caution to the wind and jerk Blythe into his arms.

Instead, he kept his eyes on her, while an expletive died on his lips.

"Rushmore, read Mrs. Lambert her rights."

Mike cleared his throat and did as he was told.

"I'm not budging," Blythe said.

A stunned silence penetrated the room.

"Excuse me?" Ryker's tone was cold and low.

"You heard me."

Though her voice quivered, Blythe's shoulders were stiff and her stance rigid.

Mike glanced at Ryker, a "what do we do next" question in his eyes. Susan, on the other hand, loudly sucked in her breath and held it.

Ryker knew Blythe meant what she'd said. If he wanted her to leave this room, he would have to carry her, which was something he could certainly do, had done to other suspects on occasion. Little as she weighed, lifting her would be a piece of cake.

But he wasn't about to do that, not unless he had to. Suddenly his eyes met hers again. For a moment it seemed that only he and Blythe were in the room, on stage, acting out a play that had nothing to do with reality. But cold reality was the order of the day, and nothing could change that.

Ignoring the continuing drumbeat of silence, Ryker withdrew his cuffs from his back pocket. Still, he didn't make a move toward her. Her next words stopped him.

"I have the right to know on what grounds I'm being arrested."

"God, Blythe," Susan put in, "don't make things worse than they already are." Her tone was pleading, and her eyes were wide and tear-filled.

"It's okay, Susan," Blythe said, without looking her way. "Just go back to your desk, please. I'll handle this."

"Handle what?"

They all turned and stared at Curt, who was standing in the doorway, his face grave.

Ryker knew why. The assistant's eyes were on the handcuffs.

"What in heaven's name is going on?" Curt's eyes bounced like a Ping-Pong from one to the other.

"Detective Delaney and his partner have come to arrest me," Blythe told him.

His curse echoed off the wall.

Ryker's temper snapped. "Out! Both of you. Now!"

Susan didn't argue, but neither did she immediately follow Ryker's order. Instead, he felt her stare at him with daggers before finally huffing toward the door.

Curt, on the other hand, stepped forward, his hostile gaze on Ryker, one hand clenching and unclenching. Ryker sensed that he would like nothing better than to take a swing at him.

Not a smart idea.

"Don't even think about it," Ryker muttered under

his breath. "I'd hate to send you to the hospital, then to jail."

Curt stopped dead, but his expression didn't change. Hatred discolored his eyes. "You're making a big mistake."

"Please, Curt," Blythe injected before Ryker could make a suitable comeback. "Let it go. I can take care of myself."

"I'll call your lawyer."

"No," Blythe said, "I'll take care of that later. You and Susan just hold the fort down."

"That goes without saying." Curt pivoted and joined Susan at the door. They went out together.

Ryker focused his attention on Mike. "It's your turn. Leave us alone."

Mike's eyebrows shot up. "I don't think—"

"Do it!"

"Don't say I didn't warn you," Mike muttered, before stomping out the door and slamming it behind him.

Moments later, Blythe and Ryker found themselves alone, staring at each other. Although Blythe's face was colorless, her lips remained a creamy coral, which accentuated her pallor. But she hadn't lowered her chin one iota.

"So, what's your damning evidence?" she demanded, her head remaining high.

She wasn't going down without a fight, Ryker decided, not sure if that trait was to her credit or not, though he admired her for it, among other things. But his opinion no longer mattered; regardless, the beat went on.

"Well, to start with, there's the matter of the insurance policy left to the mistress, the episode with the wine bottle, the laborer with the knife in his gut, and last, but certainly not least, the matter of a divorce."

"Divorce?"

"Yeah, does that word ring a bell, by chance?"

Blythe's increasing pallor was the only visible sign that he'd struck a home run.

"I'm waiting."

"Who told you about that?"

"I think you know."

"If I did, I wouldn't have asked."

Ryker decided to humor her. This way he could keep her to himself a while longer. God, he hated being pulled in so many different directions. She was so beautiful and brave in her confusion and anger.

And so damn desirable. Even now, he would like to— Forget that, he told himself. "Your sister-in-law," he said gruffly, desperate to get past this. "That's who told me."

"But—"

"You're not denying it, are you?"

"No."

"No! Is that it?"

"What do you want me to say?"

"I want the *truth,* dammit!"

"All right, Mark did ask me for a divorce."

"Were you naive enough to think that was just your little secret?"

"I—"

Ryker didn't let her finish the sentence. "I gave you credit for having more sense than that."

"Apparently Mark told Eleanor," Blythe said, with what Ryker interpreted as resigned indifference.

"And she's been holding that trump card until just the right time."

''Is that what she said?''

''More or less.''

''Just because Mark asked me for a divorce doesn't mean I killed him.''

''People have murdered for much less.''

''Not me.''

''Well, from the law's standpoint, it's a strong motive, especially when you add it to the other evidence.''

''I assume you're referring to Mark's extracurricular activities.'' Her tone was bitter.

''Those, too.''

''If you really think he was involved in stealing jewelry, then you're dead wrong to think I had anything to do with that.''

''Apparently his partner thinks so.''

''Where do you think I'm hiding the goods, under my bed?'' Bitterness seeped into her voice.

For his own sake, he had to ignore that bitterness and the pain he heard underneath, and keep a stiff upper lip. Dammit, he'd known this arrest was going to be hard, but not this hard. If only she'd gone with him peacefully. This long, drawn-out mess was ripping him to pieces.

Besides that, he wasn't exactly following policy. ''If you *are* hiding anything, we'll find it.''

''You stay out of my house, damn you!''

''I'll do whatever it takes. You should know that by now.''

''Then why haven't you found that Dawson person and brought him in for questioning?''

''That's in the works.''

Blythe's lips formed a smiling sneer. ''He's outsmarted you, hasn't he. You haven't been able to find him.''

Her on-target accusation hit a sore spot. Ryker squirmed inwardly. ''We'll find him.''

''Meanwhile, you're still content to get your revenge by tormenting me.'' She laughed a humorless laugh. ''My, but this must be a grand day of celebration for you.''

''Dammit, do you think I—''

''Yes, I do,'' she fired back. ''I think this moment is what you've lived for. If you can just find a way to tack on your niece's murder, then you'll really have it made. Maybe even get to be chief.''

Ryker opened his mouth to return fire, only to stop himself cold. If she only knew the real truth hidden under his icy demeanor. He knew now and had known for some time that Blythe was no murderer; his gut instinct had told him that, only he'd been too pigheaded to admit it, even to himself.

Now it was too late. His gut instinct would hardly hold up in court. Besides, his superior had issued orders for her arrest, and under those circumstances, he didn't have a choice. But he damn well didn't have to like it.

''Anything else, Detective?'' she asked, derailing his train of thought.

The venom he heard in her voice was far removed from the husky moans she'd made when he'd sucked her nipples while deep inside her.... Clearing his throat and his mind, he said, ''You attended a party at the home of a Carolyn and Ned Grimes. Remember that?''

''Vaguely.''

''Maybe this will jog your memory.''

She waited with her arms crossed over her breasts, breasts that he had... Shit! He'd veered off again. If he didn't get hold of himself, both this arrest and his job were likely to get flushed down the toilet.

"She also heard you and Mark arguing."

"So what?"

"Carolyn heard *you* make this comment to your husband—'I'll see you dead first.' Was that when he told you he was going to divorce you?"

"I don't know."

"Or you're just not saying?"

"You made love to me, you bastard, knowing you were going to arrest me."

Her sudden and unexpected accusation kicked his breath from his lungs. "Making love to you wasn't part of the plan."

Blythe rolled her eyes. "Spare me, please. It *was* the plan."

He closed the gap between them. "That's not true!"

She stepped back. "Stay away from me, you hear? I don't want you near me ever again."

This time her words hit him in the belly with the force of a heavyweight's fist. "I wish that were possible, but it's not."

She didn't respond. She merely looked at him with those big accusing eyes, which further scrambled his insides. Christ!

Things were *not* supposed to have worked out this way. He wasn't supposed to care what she thought. She was right; he should have been rejoicing that someone in this family was getting some comeuppance.

So why the hell wasn't he? Why *wasn't* this a grand day?

"Let's go," he said in a harsh tone. "We're wasting time."

She held out her hands at the same time that the door opened and Mike walked in, his face looking like a thundercloud.

"Dammit, Ryker, we gotta go!"

Without looking at Blythe or his partner, Ryker snapped the cuffs around her wrists.

"I know, Mother. I've already heard."

Eleanor listened to the drone of Cynthia's voice with the receiver nestled between her shoulder and her ear.

"Look, I'll talk to you more about it later, okay?"

With that, Eleanor put the phone back on the hook and turned to her companion, who was sprawled naked beside her on the bed. Perry Miller was watching her.

"Is she upset?"

"Of course, but not for the reason you think."

"You mean she doesn't think Blythe's guilty?"

"She hasn't ever said, and I've never asked her."

"So why do you think she's upset, then?"

Miller's voice was lower as he began toying with her navel, a distraction that was annoying.

"Because her arrest puts a blight on the family name."

"That's a joke."

"That's *Mother.* She lives in her own world, fooling herself with the illusion that we have no skeletons in our family closet."

His probing into her navel deepened. She fought the urge to slap his head away. She would let him get his jollies one more time, then burst his bubble.

When his tongue reached the apex of her thighs, however, she grabbed a handful of his hair and yanked.

"Ouch!" he yelled, looking up and glaring at her.

"You know how I feel about *that.* It's disgusting."

"After all I've done for you, I thought—"

"Well, you thought wrong."

Perry's face turned purple, but he didn't say anything

else. Eleanor smiled to herself. She often thought Perry was a bit afraid of her, which made her feel that much more powerful.

"But you can fuck me again, if you like," she finally said.

His features took on a new color, and for the next few minutes there were sounds of quick grunts and groans. When he'd rolled off her, Eleanor got up and smiled back down at him.

"You're one lucky lady."

"Luck has nothing to do with it." Eleanor smiled a cruel smile. "It's called strategy."

"Think the arrest will stick?"

"Oh, she'll get out on bail, but the damage is done. Even if she's found not guilty, no one will ever let her on their property again."

"So what next?"

"What I intended all along. I'm going to take over the company."

"What about Frank?"

"I'm going to boot him out."

"Great. Then we can finally tie that old knot."

She didn't dare tell him that that was *not* going to happen. When she pulled off this coup with Blythe, Perry would also be history. She didn't intend to let another man touch her ever again.

Until that mission was accomplished, however, she would have to put up with Perry's groping hands and mouth. She still needed him in her camp.

"Right now, we're going to have a small bonfire."

Perry chuckled, then swung off the bed. By the time he joined her at the dressing table, she had the copy of Mark's will in one hand and a match in the other.

"Go ahead, light it."

"With pleasure."

Thirty-four

He looked as if he should be sitting atop a horse, riding the range, pausing along the way to brand a few cattle. If the situation hadn't been so serious, Blythe would have chuckled at the sight. But the situation *was* serious, and she couldn't even muster up a smile.

Still, Clayton Carrell was the consummate Texas bigwig criminal attorney, up there on the same pedestal as Percy Foreman and Richard "Racehorse" Haynes. And she was glad to have him in her legal pasture, pun intended.

The attorney's tall and lanky build, magnified by a hat, a mustache and a pair of tall boots, added to that know-it-all, in-charge attitude that helped give her confidence, which had heretofore deserted her.

All Clayton needed to complete his high-profile persona was a six-shooter strapped to his thigh. She figured he probably had one of those tucked away somewhere.

In many respects, he reminded her of Ryker in looks and in personality, except that Clayton Carrell was older, in his sixties, with an abundance of gray hair and twinkling green eyes. Contrary to Ryker, smiles were his forte.

Don't think about *him,* she told herself. It only made her furious to the point of tears, an indulgence she couldn't afford, especially now, when she was fighting for both her sanity and her life.

Blythe shuddered.

"Everything's going to be all right."

"I wish I could believe that, Mr. Carrell."

"Darlin', you'd best call me Clayton," he drawled, "'cause we're gonna be as snug as two bugs in a rug."

"All right, Clayton," she responded with a slight smile.

Blythe didn't know as yet how she was going to afford his fees, but he didn't seem to be worried, touting this as a high-profile case, the kind he loved to sink his teeth into.

Tony Upshaw had called in Carrell, a long-time cohort and buddy of his. But it had been Upshaw who had come to the station and helped her get released by signing a personal recognizance bond for her.

Now, as she faced Clayton Carrell across her desk a day later, the horror of what she'd endured, and was about to endure, didn't bear thinking about. But she had to think, to stay on top of the situation.

It was her life she was fighting for.

"I'll have to give you credit, Mrs. Lambert," Clayton said in his raspy drawl, at the same time removing his Stetson and tossing it onto an empty chair, "you've got spunk."

"Thanks," she said in a skeptical but soft voice, so as not to disturb the pain that raged behind her eyes. "However, I don't see it that way."

"Trust me. Behind that fear is someone who's willing to fight."

"You're right about that. If that's what you mean by spunk, then I do have it."

"Atta girl."

"You haven't asked me if I'm guilty."

"Frankly, my dear, I don't give a damn." Clayton grinned cheekily at his use of Rhett's remark to Scarlett.

Her lips broke into a real smile.

"Ah, now we're getting somewhere, darlin'. You're a knockout when you smile. Did anyone ever tell you that?"

"Thanks," Blythe said again, feeling her face turn red, but not because she thought he was flirting with her. She knew better. He was a happily married man, having already shown her pictures of his wife and four children, expounding on how perfect each was.

"On a few occasions," she finally added, beginning to feel better. This man was just the kind of tonic she needed. Since she'd been hauled to the police station by Ryker, she'd been so down on herself that she wasn't sure she could ever get up.

"Another smile. I like that."

"Don't get used to them. Lately, I haven't had much to smile about. And until this murder charge is resolved, I..." Blythe's voice faded as she felt her throat jam.

"You stop worrying, you hear?"

"I can't."

"Yes, you can." Gone was the soft charm; in its place was the sound of hard steel. "That's what you've got me for."

"I still want to know what you think," Blythe said.

"About your innocence or guilt?"

"Yes. That's important to me. You have to believe in me or I don't see how we can pull this off."

He shrugged. "Believe me, we—*I*—can pull this off, but if my opinion's important to you, then the answer is that I think you're as innocent as fresh driven snow."

"Are you serious?"

"When I'm not, you'll know it."

"Fair enough."

"Now, why don't you tell me everything there is to tell, from the moment that skirt-chasing husband of yours got himself killed and that jackass detective appeared on the scene."

Colorful words from a colorful man. "Are you always this direct?"

"I don't see any reason to pussyfoot around. Do you?" His green eyes were as piercing as his words.

"No, not if frank talk will get me out of this mess."

"That's exactly what I aim to do—clean up this mess without so much as a spot left on you anywhere."

"That would be wonderful. My life's been turned upside down for so long now, I'm thinking it's never going to change."

"Do you trust me?"

"Do I have a choice?"

"No."

"Then I trust you."

"So let's get down to the nitty-gritty."

"Do the police have a sound case against me?" Blythe asked.

"They don't have shit. More to the point, they're full of it, especially if they think their weak charges will stand up in court."

"Ryker has those witnesses."

"Hell, witnesses can be bought. What they have is based on circumstantial evidence and hearsay."

"I pray you're right."

"Well, you go ahead and pray, darlin', but I'm gonna kick butt."

"For the first time since Mark was killed, I can see a glimmer of light in all this darkness."

"Good, so let's scrape the bottom of that nasty barrel. I have to know what's rotten as well as what's fresh."

Blythe bent her head and rubbed her fingers across her forehead, unable to meet that direct look. How was she going to tell him about her torrid affair with Ryker? She couldn't. She would choke on the words. Besides, she hadn't sorted it all out in her own mind, hadn't come to terms with having fallen in love with a man who had arrested her for murder.

She would have to be careful, though. She sensed that Clayton Carrell would see through her; he had the same kind of nose and instinct that Ryker did. Both men were so much alike it was uncanny.

Right now, though, one was her enemy and one was her friend. She'd best keep in mind who was who.

"You're stalling," Clayton said bluntly. "Why?"

"I'm trying to get my thoughts together."

"Is there something going on between you and that detective I ought to know about?"

Blythe's breathing faltered. "Like what?"

Clayton snorted, giving her a direct look. "Oh, I think you know like what. If he hasn't already gotten between your sheets, he sure as hell wants to."

Her face went from scarlet to white. "That's—"

"Don't lie to me, Mrs. Lambert." He got up and came to her desk, where he leaned toward her. "That's the first rule. I have to know the whole truth and nothing but the truth."

"So help you God."

"No, darlin'. So help *you* Clayton Carrell."

Blythe sighed. "I get the picture."

"Good. So let's be about gettin' you free of this bogus murder charge."

Blythe, when she began talking, didn't even recognize her own voice.

"Hello, Mrs. Lambert."

Blythe nodded at the R.N. behind the nurses' station. This was her grandmother's primary caregiver, which meant that Blythe knew her better than anyone else there. "It's nice to see you, Nancy."

"Uh, thanks. Look, we all want you to know how sorry we are about—"

"I appreciate your concern," Blythe said, cutting her off, though with as much gentleness as possible. She shouldn't have been surprised that something was said, considering the headlines in the paper.

Everyone in town knew about her arrest. Probably everyone in the entire state knew. Yet she forced herself to take no offense at Nancy's comment, though being on public display smarted, just as it had when Mark's murder became public knowledge.

Right now, all she wanted was the comfort of her grandmother's arms and sweet voice.

"If there's anything we can do—"

Again Blythe cut her off. "You're sweet, but there's nothing anyone can do. My fate's in the hands of my attorney."

"I hope he's a good one."

"He's the best," Blythe said, upping her pace down the hall.

And she was convinced of that, too, especially following her marathon session with Clayton, which had ended only a short while ago. If anyone could get her off, it was him.

He was planning to go for the prosecuting attorney's jugular, which further strengthened her confidence in

Clayton. Still, there was Ryker. And while Clayton had done his best to get her to admit Ryker was more than her nemesis, she hadn't. Some things were too personal and too painful to talk about.

She suspected her secret was safe. She didn't think Ryker would be disclosing the fact that they had made love, either. He had too much on the line, too.

Suddenly Blythe stopped and leaned against the wall, hating herself for the emptiness and longing she felt. Where was her pride, for God's sake? But the heat waves kept on coming as she relived the way she felt when he was inside her....

Stop it, Blythe Lambert! Have you no shame?

He had betrayed her in the worst possible way. She had to forget him.

Only after she was nearly to Honey's room did she breathe. She knew her respite would be short-lived. Once she left here, she was due at the mansion, another unpleasant excursion, but one that was necessary.

Designs was all she had left.

Anyway, Cynthia was demanding her presence, which was both good and bad. She knew what Cynthia wanted, to know if Blythe was guilty as charged. But she also had her own agenda with her mother-in-law. She was looking forward to getting that visit behind her.

The door to her grandmother's room was partially open. She peered inside.

''Hi, Honey,'' she whispered around the lump clogging her throat.

''Hello, sweetheart,'' her grandmother responded in a surprisingly strong voice, holding out her arms.

Blythe dove into them. At length she pulled back and sat down in the chair beside the bed, clasping Honey's hand in hers.

"I'm so glad to see you."

"Me, too."

"You're in trouble, aren't you?"

"Oh, Honey, I never could keep anything from you."

"What's wrong?"

"Too much to talk about today."

"I have something to tell you."

"What?"

"I had a visitor, a nice man."

"A man?"

Blythe frowned, her mind splintering in all different directions.

"Uh-huh."

"Who was he?"

"He didn't tell me his name."

"Oh."

"But he was real nice."

"Honey—"

"He said he knew you and hoped to see you the next time he came."

Blythe's body broke out in a cold sweat. Ryker? He was her first thought. Had he been there? If so, why?

"What did he look like?"

Her grandmother hesitated, a confused expression on her face.

That was when Blythe saw it, on the table next to the window. A glass of water was sitting in the middle, the sunlight framing it. A muted sound almost strangled Blythe.

A cigar butt was floating in that water.

Thirty-five

Somehow Blythe made it to the Lambert mansion. Now that she looked back, she didn't know how she'd accomplished that feat. She was sick to her stomach; her clothes were damp, her heart racing.

Panic.

She was in the dark throes of panic. Determined to fight off a full-blown attack, she took slow, deep breaths, trying desperately to put things in perspective. Honey *hadn't* been harmed. He hadn't so much as touched her. Still, the thought of that man having stolen into her grandmother's room sent Blythe's blood pressure skyrocketing.

Don't, Blythe told herself. Don't get yourself so overwrought you can't think. If only she knew what that sicko wanted, she would gladly give it to him. Why couldn't he grasp that fact?

In light of the failure of the scare tactics he'd already used, it should have struck him that she hadn't been a party to his and Mark's side venture. Or maybe he would never get it. Maybe he was so amoral that he thought the love of money took precedence over everything.

He'd best think again; she would do anything to protect her beloved grandmother from harm. If she ever came into contact with that bastard again, she would be tempted to do more than knee him in the balls.

Why hadn't Ryker found this guy? How did Dawson keep one step ahead of the law? If she hadn't seen him herself, she would think he had been a figment of her imagination. He seemed to appear on the scene when he felt like it, then slink away with the same ease, which infuriated her.

She blamed Ryker and shoddy police work.

Yet after she'd recovered from the paralyzing fear of seeing that gross cigar butt swimming in the water, she'd lunged toward the phone to call Ryker, until the memory of Dawson's threat had stopped her cold.

Besides, Ryker had let her down in more ways than one. Where had his detective been? If he'd been doing his job, Dawson would never have gotten past him to Honey's room.

That had been her first question to herself and to the nursing facility.

"I assumed he was still here," the director stammered, a small, mousy-looking man who looked as if he might wet himself at any moment. Blythe suspected the word *lawsuit* was flashing through his mind.

"Well, you assumed wrong," Blythe said, so furious she could barely talk.

"Ma'am—" he began, his feet doing a tap dance on the carpet.

"Don't 'ma'am' me." Blythe got in his face. "When it comes down to it, this facility is responsible for my grandmother's care."

"But I thought the cops were—"

"They were," Blythe interrupted, her fury rising. "And I intend to find out what happened there."

And she intended to deal with Mike Rushmore to do it. She couldn't face Ryker again—not now, not so soon after her arrest.

Another thought along that line slam-dunked Blythe. Since her arrest, had Ryker removed the plainclothesman from her grandmother's room, thinking the threat was no longer in force?

Right now, though, she had to get through this time with Cynthia.

When she was shown into the parlor, her mother-in-law was alone. Blythe went weak with relief. She had hoped she wouldn't have Eleanor to contend with. After that jaw-biting episode at the nursing home, her sister-in-law would have made this visit impossible.

"I'm surprised you wanted to see me," Blythe said, sitting on the edge of the sofa and staring into Cynthia's suddenly lined face.

"Did you kill my son?"

Although Blythe was surprised by Cynthia's straightforwardness, she was glad to clear the air. "No."

Cynthia took a shuddering breath. "That's all I wanted to hear."

"Do you believe me?"

"Yes."

"Thank you," Blythe muttered.

"But my opinion hardly counts."

"Yes, it does. I'm going to need all the moral support I can get."

"I never thought anything like this would happen to our family."

"Me, either, and I'm so sorry that it has."

"What about Designs?" Cynthia asked, sounding tired, the tension obviously having taken its toll.

"It's headed for bankruptcy." Blythe paused. "Unless—" She broke off, hating to say what was on her mind.

"Unless I bail you out. Was that what you were about to say?"

"Yes."

"The last time we spoke, you hinted at that."

"And you never gave me a direct answer," Blythe said, trying to trap the old woman's gaze.

She couldn't; Cynthia seemed to concentrate on something in the room as if she were alone. Blythe waited, but not patiently, feeling as though her insides had been scraped raw.

"I'm afraid I can't help you."

Blythe's features clouded. "Can't?"

"That's right."

Silence.

"Why not?" Blythe pressed, feeling as if she was pulling eyeteeth to get the information out of Cynthia.

"Because I don't have the money."

"You don't have the money," Blythe repeated like a foolish parrot.

"That's right. I'm...I'm almost broke. In fact, I *am* broke."

Blythe blinked, unable to grasp what Cynthia had said. How could that be? When she'd married into the Lambert family, they had been millionaires, or so she'd thought. What had gone wrong? Had she been wrong? Or had Mark led her down another primrose path?

"But how...I mean..." She simply couldn't find the words to go on.

"Mark."

"What about Mark?" Even though she asked the question, Blythe knew the answer. And though she wanted to cover her ears to avoid having her worst fears confirmed, she couldn't. She would take this on the chin just as she had everything else that had been thrown at her.

"Mark bled me dry."

"With his gambling," Blythe said, more to herself than to Cynthia.

"He...he said they'd hurt...him." Cynthia's voice broke.

"Who are they?"

"I...I don't know. He just kept coming to me for money, saying that if he didn't pay his gambling debts, something worse than death would happen to him."

"Oh, God," Blythe whispered. "I'm so sorry."

"Me, too, especially since I—since the money wasn't able to save his life."

"Don't worry about Designs. It's my responsibility. I'll find a way to salvage the company. What's important now is finding out who murdered Mark."

"We all know who that is."

On hearing Eleanor's words, Blythe sat unmoving, though inwardly she cringed. But rather than let her sister-in-law have the satisfaction of knowing she'd unnerved her, Blythe swung around. "Hello, Eleanor."

"Don't you dare 'hello' me." Then, to her mother, "What the hell is she doing here?"

"I invited her."

"Are you crazy?" Eleanor's raucous voice rose to a high pitch.

Cynthia glared at her daughter before speaking in a calm but cold tone. "That's the least of my problems."

"I don't want her here."

"Despite what you think, this is still my house," Cynthia declared. "And you will show respect."

Blythe's admiration for her mother-in-law jumped by

leaps and bounds, though the words were lost on Eleanor.

"For heaven's sake, Mother, give it a rest. Your days of holding court are long over."

It was all Blythe could do not to lunge out of her chair and slap her sister-in-law, a slap that was long overdue. But she didn't. Cynthia seemed more than able to take care of herself, though her face lost what little color it had in it.

"As long as I'm alive, I'll hold court any time I please."

"Even if it means holding court with a murderer?"

Cynthia's pupils dilated.

Blythe was barely aware of that; she was too busy scrambling to her feet. "I didn't kill your brother."

"Save it for the jury."

"Eleanor, I'm warning you," Cynthia began, her voice shaking audibly now. "Get control of yourself or get out."

"Mother, what on earth's wrong with you?"

"I told you, absolutely nothing."

"You came here with your hand out, didn't you?" Eleanor's eyes bounced off her mother to Blythe, then back again. "You told her you weren't going to give her any money, right?"

"Yes, because there's none to give."

Eleanor pitched back her head and laughed. "That's good. That's real good."

"No, it's not good," Cynthia said in a small voice, "but it's the truth. You have your brother to thank for that."

"I don't believe a word of that." Eleanor's tone sounded desperate. "You're just saying that for Blythe's benefit."

Although Cynthia stared at her daughter with pity, her face was ashen and her hands were shaking.

Blythe's concern deepened. If Eleanor didn't stop pushing, Cynthia could have a heart attack on the spot. Maybe that was something Eleanor would have liked to see happen, though then she would find out for certain that there was no money for her to inherit.

If anyone deserved those just desserts, it was Eleanor, but not at Cynthia's expense, Blythe reminded herself.

"Dammit, Mother, tell me you're lying!"

Cynthia moved toward her daughter. "Eleanor, don't do this to me or yourself."

Eleanor faced Blythe. "Damn you! This is all your fault."

"What's going on in here?"

This time it was Frank who strode into the parlor unannounced, ending the verbal skirmish between mother and daughter. Blythe stiffened, knowing now that she'd definitely overstayed her welcome. While she disliked Eleanor, she despised Frank. She would as soon be in a room with a box of live snakes.

Almost.

"I could hear y'all upstairs, especially you, Eleanor."

"So what?" Eleanor flung at him, breathing hard.

Shrugging, Frank turned to Blythe. "Well, well, look who's graced us with her presence."

"Not for long," Blythe said, staring at him with all the loathing she could muster. "I was just on my way out."

"Don't go on my account," Frank responded in his oily voice.

"Get the fuck out of here," Eleanor said to Blythe, her eyes filled with venom.

Cynthia blanched. "Eleanor, I'm warning you. I won't have you talking like that."

"Your mother's right," Frank said with a mocking sneer. "You do have a nasty mouth and should apologize. First, though, have you by chance seen a button, the one that goes on this coat? I'm going out, and I just noticed it's missing."

He held out a sleeve that was definitely minus a button.

"Button?" Eleanor screeched. "I don't have the slightest idea where your goddamn button is. And furthermore, I don't care. I'm not your maid."

Blythe paid little attention to Eleanor's tirade. She was too busy staring at the blazer. *I know where that button is.* The words almost slipped unheeded out of her mouth. Thank God she caught them in time.

Still, Blythe's mind spun, and if she hadn't been close enough to the sofa to grab the arm, she might have crumpled to the floor.

That button Frank had so causally mentioned was at home. Unimportant and forgotten, or so she'd thought.

Though her blood was now pumping hard and fast, Blythe schooled herself to show no emotion, but the implication of the brass button was staggering.

She hadn't realized she had moved toward the door until she heard Cynthia's voice. "We'll talk later."

Blythe pulled up short but didn't turn around. "I'll...I'll call you."

"Don't call and don't come back here!"

Ignoring Eleanor's parting shot, Blythe walked outside, only to lean heavily against her car.

Frank had been on the yacht that fateful day. The button proved that.

Had *he* murdered Mark?

Thirty-six

"Do you know yet who...who killed my Ted?"

Ryker exchanged glances with Mike, who was clearly uncomfortable with the situation. But then, so was he. The situation was pitiful, starting with a house full of kids, no husband and no money. Ryker knew they were existing on food stamps and other government handouts.

"No, Mrs. Armstrong, but we're working on it."

She sniffled, then wiped the back of her hand across her nose. Ryker flinched and didn't dare look at Mike. "I...don't understand why anyone would want to...to hurt my Teddy."

"That's why we've come back. We want to make sure you haven't found anything or thought of something that might lead us to his killer."

After they had first identified the dead laborer, he and Mike had come here and told Irma Armstrong her husband was dead. She had gone berserk.

To this day, they still hadn't gotten anything out of her that made sense. She'd been too devastated over the loss of her husband.

Ryker had never heard anyone who could wail and carry on like this woman. Now, as they questioned her again, he was optimistic that time had tempered her grief and she would be more coherent. They needed her help.

"Nope," she said into the growing silence. "Ted just told me he was gonna make us rich."

"How?" Ryker asked.

Irma shrugged. "Dunno. Said he was gonna meet some foreign man."

Ryker's head came up. "What did you say?"

Irma repeated her statement, then went on. "I wasn't sure what he was talking about, and he didn't tell me." She paused and once more wiped at her wet nose with the back of her hand. "Do you know?"

"We have an idea," Mike said.

Ryker backed away. "Thanks for your help. We'll be in touch."

"When you find the guy who hurt my Teddy, I hope you cut his balls off. He didn't deserve to die that way."

"You're right, he didn't," Ryker said grimly. "We'll do our best to catch him."

When he and Mike were back in the car, Ryker expelled a pent-up breath. "That damn Dawson again."

"Yep."

"Do you think he killed Armstrong?"

"I'm betting on it. How 'bout you?"

"But why?"

"Blackmail. I'm guessing our guy overheard Lambert and Dawson on one of their jobs and wanted a piece of their action."

"Works for me."

"What I can't get is how that slippery bastard keeps outsmarting us."

Using the composite drawing of Jacques Dawson made from Blythe's description of the man, one of the undercover cops had located his temporary home—a sleazy motel. The problem was, he hadn't shown up for them to arrest him.

But he would. Ryker was confident of that, though time was running out and so was his patience.

"You thinking what I'm thinking?" Mike asked as Ryker pulled away from the curb.

"That Dawson might also have killed Mark? Yeah, that's crossed my mind."

"So where does that leave Blythe Lambert?" Mike asked, giving his partner a searching look.

Ryker kept his face on the road. "That'll have to shake out along with the rest of this crap."

"Our asses are going to be in trouble if we don't hurry and tie up some of that crap."

Ryker took his eyes off the road for a moment. "Do you think I care?"

"Well, I damn sure do. Foley's gonna be on us like ants on sugar."

"Fuck Foley."

Mike grinned. "Thanks, but no thanks. I'll leave that to you."

"You're turning into a real comedian."

"Thanks."

"Shut up, Rushmore. You're starting to get on my nerves."

Blythe was impatient, and it showed. She didn't care. Dear Lord, Ryker's office was the last place she wanted to be. But here she was, pacing the floor, her insides a tangled mess.

She had to talk to him, though. She had no choice, despite the fact that she might be wasting her time. She had to try, even if walking into his office was one of the hardest things she'd ever done.

She was still in love with a man who thought she could take another human life. All the psychology books said she should hate him, that her love should have turned into hate.

Maybe it had. Maybe when Ryker came through the door only loathing would surge through her. One could always hope.

"Who did you say was here?"

Blythe froze, along with the saliva in her mouth. She didn't have to turn around to know that Ryker had just walked into the station. His voice had a timbre like no other.

"Mrs. Lambert, sir."

"In my office?"

He sounded incredulous. Blythe wished she couldn't hear the exchange in the adjacent room, but she could. She fought off the urge to get up and run out of the building, murder charge hanging over her head or not.

At that moment, she would almost rather go to prison than face Ryker.

While her thoughts were raging, he walked in and shut the door. Silence drummed between them as he simply slouched against the door and pierced her with his eyes.

She forced her gaze to meet his, hoping her face showed none of the turbulence going on inside her. "This is official business," she said stiffly.

"You didn't have to tell me that."

Another silence fell, during which their eyes held. Blythe tried not to notice the heat that simmered in his. Damn him. She shifted her gaze and swallowed.

He cleared his throat. "What's up?"

"Dawson was back at the nursing home."

Ryker spat an expletive. "Did he harm your grandmother?"

"No, thank God."

"Did you see him?"

"No, but he left his calling card."

"Which is?"

"A cigar butt. It was floating in a glass of water."

Ryker stalked to his desk, shoving a hard hand through his hair. "How the hell did he get in there?"

"That's what I'd like to know. I assumed you'd pulled your man off."

"Well, you assumed wrong. He was probably taking a goddamn leak."

Blythe flushed, then turned away as he picked up the phone and punched out a number. She could only hear Ryker's end of the conversation, but that was enough. His harsh tone and words stripped the constable's hide off his body.

"Just as I thought," he muttered, slamming the receiver down.

"But he's back on the job now?"

"Oh, yes." Ryker killed a second, then asked, "You still don't have a clue as to what he wants from you?"

"No, dammit. The idea that he's willing to hurt Honey for something he thinks I have is tearing me up."

"He apparently doesn't just think it. He's convinced of it."

"Whatever."

Ryker didn't comment, which brought on another silence, a silence in which they intentionally kept their eyes off each other.

Finally Blythe said, "There's something else you have to know."

"Shoot."

She told him about Frank and the button.

"That doesn't prove your brother-in-law murdered Lambert."

Blythe's eyes blazed. "It doesn't prove he didn't, either."

"You're right."

"So what are you going to do about it?"

"Hey, I'm in charge here."

"Well, so far your tactics stink."

"Dammit, Blythe, don't—"

She stood. "Don't tell you how to do your job?"

His response was to clench his jaw.

"Frank was on Mark's cruiser." She flattened the button on his desk. "This proves it."

"I told you, it doesn't prove he killed your husband."

"It does prove Frank lied."

"Right, and I intend to find out why."

"He's every bit as much a liar and gambler as Mark was."

"But is he a murderer? That's still the unanswered question."

"I'm not sure about anything anymore," Blythe said in a down-in-the-mouth tone of voice. "But still—"

"I'll haul him in, and we'll go from there. With the threat of prison hanging over his head, maybe he'll spill his guts."

"Let us pray."

Now that their business was concluded, a different kind of quietness settled over the room. Blythe suddenly felt as if the walls were closing in on her. She had to get out.

As if he sensed her quandary, he trapped her gaze once again, and her heart faltered. She didn't want to feel anything for him. His steady look shouldn't snatch her breath or send a flush of heat through her. After what he'd done to her, it wasn't fair.

"So how have you been?" he asked in a low, raspy voice.

"Why do you care?"

"You know why I care," he shot back. "These last few days have been hell."

And he looked like he'd been to hell and back, too. She hardened her heart. She hoped he was miserable.

"Save the violin music for someone who cares. I sure as hell don't."

"You're not making this easy."

She laughed. "All you care about is yourself and your needs. Well, screw that. *Screw you.*"

Before she burst into tears, Blythe made her way out of the room. Only after she got to her car did she realize that her face was already drenched.

"We're not going to bust your chops yet," Mike said.

"I was thinking more in terms of your balls," Ryker added.

Frank whimpered, throwing Ryker a sick, scared look. "You're crazy!"

"You're history," Ryker retaliated in a voice hard with indifference.

Frank pulled back as far as he could without falling out of the chair. "Don't...don't you dare lay a hand on me."

Ryker slammed his hand down on the table in front of Frank. Frank jumped as if he'd been shot, then cried out.

"Listen, you sick SOB," Ryker hammered, "I'll do anything I damn well please. I'm running this show, not you."

Although Frank didn't cower, Ryker knew he'd gotten his point over. Frank's fear was so acute, he actually had a stench. Ryker could swear he smelled it. And spittle had gathered in the corners of Frank's mouth. This wormy weasel was guilty of something; he just didn't know what yet.

But he would find out.

"You'd best be telling everything you know," Mike was saying. "Or else I might just have to leave the room and let Ryker here do his thing."

Frank's eyes widened, and the spittle thickened. "No, don't...don't do that."

"Then start chirping like a happy canary," Mike said in a nonchalant tone.

Ryker propped a booted foot on the chair next to Frank and purposefully stared down at him, then reached out and casually fingered the knot in his tie.

Frank's Adam's apple convulsed. "That...that bitch told you, didn't she?"

"Now, just what bitch would that be?" Ryker's tone was so smooth and low that it was barely audible, a clue that Frank should have picked up on, but didn't.

"Blythe Lambert."

Frank was hauled out of the chair and slammed against the wall.

"Let go of me, you bastard!" Frank cried, gasping for breath.

Ryker squeezed tighter. "You're lucky I don't break your neck."

"Please," he begged, "put me down. I didn't mean—"

Ryker dropped him like a box of hot rocks, then peered at Frank, his face twisted. "Get up."

Frank scrambled back into his chair. "So I lied about having been on Mark's boat, but I didn't kill him. Swear to God I didn't. But I know who did."

"Who?"

"Jacques Dawson."

Ryker got in his face. "This had better be the truth and nothing but the truth, so help *you* God."

"I...know what Mark and Dawson were into."

Ryker patted Frank on the head. "Good boy. You're doing fine. Just keep on talking."

Thirty-seven

The day was hot but gorgeous, perfect for being outdoors.

"When can we swim in the pool, Daddy?"

Walter Steed peered up at the sun, shading his eyes from its harsh glare. Then he looked down at the top of his son's corn-colored head, tousling his silky curls. "Soon."

"When's soon?"

Walter laughed as his wife walked onto the deck, all smiles. "What's going on out here?"

Every time Walter looked at her, he sort of melted inside. They had been married for ten years, and not one day had he ever regretted that, especially when they had finally created their son, Todd, who was now four years old.

What more could a man want?

A swimming pool for that wonderful family, he thought with an inward smile, proud because he was able to make that dream come true. They had built this house in the country club subdivision several years ago, once his salary jumped sky-high from a design he'd patented.

He'd been so successful that he and Beverly had chosen the best landscape people in town—Designs by Lambert. Blythe and Mark Lambert had been an awesome team. Together they had made this yard into a showplace, planting flowers, trees and shrubs that were now breathtaking in their beauty.

Too bad part of that beauty was the backyard and had to be destroyed. But Todd and Beverly wanted a pool, and as long as he could give them what they wanted, he would.

"Do you think this mess will ever end?" Beverly asked, slipping her fingers through his as they watched the bulldozer continue to dig deep into the dirt of their once perfectly manicured yard.

"You sound like our son."

"I know, but I can't wait."

"Me, neither, Mommy."

She smiled down at Todd, who was creeping close to the deepening hole. "Be careful. That man doesn't want you in his way."

"Can I go down there?" Todd asked, squatting and watching the dozer as it continued to lift and toss dirt.

"No. Absolutely not. He might scoop you up in that thing."

"He's got something in it now."

"It's only a wad of dirt, silly." She tweaked his ear.

"No, it's somepin' else, Mommy. It's a sack."

Walter shaded his eyes once again and concentrated on the scooper. "I'll be doggone, Bev. It does appear to be something besides roots and leaves."

Beverly also squinted against the sun, although she had on her sunglasses. "I can't tell what it is, actually."

"Maybe it's a treasure, Daddy."

He grinned. "You've been watching too much TV, son."

Todd jerked on his hand. "Let's look."

"Yeah, sweetheart," Beverly chimed in. "Let's see."

Having always indulged his family, Walter didn't see any reason to stop now.

"All right, but it's nothing, I'm telling you."

Before the machine operator unloaded his catch onto the mounting pile of dirt, Walter waved his arms. The man halted his worked immediately.

"What's up?" the burly driver shouted.

"Dump what's in the scooper off by itself, okay?"

"No problem."

When the task had been done, the family hurried over to the spot. "I told you it was somepin'," Todd said.

Walter knelt and fingered what at a distance had indeed looked like a grocery sack. However, on closer observation, the object wasn't a sack at all, but a large, heavy plastic pouch.

"What is it?" Todd asked, his large eyes glued to it.

"Don't know, son," Walter said, even as he reached over and picked it up.

"Oh, goody!" Todd cried. "It *is* a treasure."

"Hey, hold your horses," Beverly said, her gaze locking on Walter, who was frowning.

"Aren't you going to open it?" she asked, scooting closer, as did Todd.

"Not until I get out of this boiling sun. Let's take it to the table on the deck."

Moments later, Walter plopped the pouch down and began to untie the cord wrapped around the neck of the pouch.

"Hurry, Daddy."

"Down, boy," Walter said with a grin, actually warming to the game of suspense. Then Beverly slapped his hand away. He stared at her in amazement.

"I'm like Todd," she said, grinning. "You're taking too long."

Walter grinned back, then shoved the bag toward her. "Be my guest."

Without wasting another second, Beverly untied the string and emptied out the contents.

Their breath gushed out simultaneously, and their eyes widened. Spread in front of them were numerous pieces of jewelry, running the spectrum from rings to necklaces to earrings.

Diamonds. Rubies. Emeralds. Sapphires.

"What the h—" Walter began; then, remembering his son was present, he swallowed the rest of the sentence.

"Oh, my goodness," Beverly wheezed, staring up at him with startled eyes.

"Told you it was a treasure," Todd said, jumping up and down before fingering the stones.

"No," Walter said with more harshness than he intended.

Todd stuck out his lower lip. "Why can't I play with 'em?"

"Because they're not ours," Beverly said in an awed tone. Then, gazing at her husband, she asked, "Are they real?"

"These days, you can't be sure. But if they aren't, I'll be surprised."

"What do we do? I mean, they're not ours."

Despite the shock, he gave her an indulgent smile. "That's for sure, sweetheart. If they are the real thing, then I'd have to rob Fort Knox to buy these."

"What are we going to do?"

"Keep 'em, Mommy," Todd said.

"'Fraid not."

"Ah, shucks, Daddy," Todd muttered under his breath.

Hiding a smile at his son's mutiny, Walter reached for the cell phone on the table.

"What are you doing?" Beverly asked.

Walter's handsome face was grim. "Calling the police."

"I'm sorry, but Mr. Farmer's not seeing anyone."

"Is he in?" Blythe asked, having planted herself in front of the secretary's desk, refusing to budge.

"Yes, he is, but I have my orders."

Blythe's mind worked like a beehive. Only twenty minutes ago she had left the office after meeting with Susan, Curt and Moody. It hadn't been a pleasant session, with Designs hovering on the brink of locking the doors. The only saving grace had been Eleanor's absence.

That, too, would be short-lived, Blythe suspected. With a murder charge hanging over her, it seemed Eleanor held all the cards, certainly the winning hand. But she wouldn't dwell on that now. She had another agenda, one that, if she pulled it off, would certainly save Designs.

She would deal with Eleanor later.

"Is there something else I can do for you, Ms.—" The gray-haired woman was staring at her with a question in her now hostile eyes.

"It's Lambert. Blythe Lambert."

"Ah, Mrs. Lambert," she said in a prim voice, laced with uneasiness. "We've spoken on the phone."

"Several times."

The woman flushed. "Well, Mr. Farmer's still unavailable."

"I don't think so," Blythe said, giving in to the impulse that suddenly sent her past the desk to the boss's door.

"You...you can't go in there," the woman sputtered, standing with such abruptness that her chair spun.

Blythe ignored her, twisting the knob on the door and barging in. A short, wiry-looking man had his back to her. A file drawer was open, and he had one hand in it. He didn't bother to turn around.

"What, Rachel?" His voice sounded strained with irritation. "I told you that I didn't want to be disturbed."

"It's not her fault."

At the sound of the strange voice, Cecil Farmer swung around, thick gray eyebrows failing to hide piercing blue eyes, eyes that were vivid reminders of Ryker's. Her face bunched in pain.

"It most certainly isn't, sir," the secretary said, pushing past Blythe. "This woman took it upon herself to—"

"It's all right, Rachel. I can handle things from now on."

"But, sir—"

"Close the door behind you, please."

Clearly not happy with the turn of events, the woman glared at Blythe, then strode quickly out the door.

"Long time no see, Mrs. Lambert. What's so urgent now?"

"What I have to say."

A twinkle appeared in those previously cold eyes. "Is that a fact?"

"That's a fact."

"Well, I can say right off the bat that I'm never too old to listen to a beautiful woman."

"Thank you."

"You're welcome."

A beat of silence.

His lips twitched. "Now that we've established that, maybe we can get down to the heart of the matter."

"You mean I can stay?" Blythe gave him her most dazzling smile.

"Do I have a choice?"

His eyebrows shot up again, and a closed expression shuttered his features. "So, are you still a suspect in your husband's death?"

Blythe's heart skipped a beat. Uh-oh, she had underestimated herself and him. He intended to boot her out. "Yes, I am."

"Did you kill him?"

"No, I did not."

"How many times a day do you tell people that?"

"Too many to count," Blythe admitted ruefully, though secretly rejoicing that she was still in the room.

"Okay, tell me what's on your mind?"

"My ideas."

"As I recall, I liked them."

"That's why I'm here."

That twinkle again. "To reiterate that."

"Yes, and to convince you that Designs is the company you need to hire for your projects."

"Sit down, Mrs. Lambert."

Blythe almost *fell* down, she was so relieved.

"So start convincing."

She did, for the next two hours.

Finally, Farmer pulled back from the drawings spread out on the table and simply stared at her. "You've got more balls than anyone I know."

Trying not to show her shock, Blythe smiled, then said inanely, "Women don't have balls, sir."

"You do."

"Should I take that as a compliment?"

"Damn right."

"Good, then do we have a deal?"

"We have a deal."

Blythe hid her excitement behind a shield of cool professionalism. But it was hard, when she wanted to do a tap dance on top of his desk. "Thank you, Mr. Farmer."

He stared at her hard for a long moment.

"You won't regret this," she said hastily, afraid he was about to change his mind.

"I'd better not. I'm going out on a limb with my stockholders. If you screw up—"

"That's not going to happen."

His chuckle followed her out the door.

Everything sparkled.

At least in the house, Blythe reminded herself. Although she had pulled off the coup with Farmer, she hadn't been able to do the same with her emotions. Her heart was a shambles.

Because she'd had her nose to the grindstone for days trying to keep her heartbreak at bay, Blythe had neglected her house. Cleaning had always been one of her best stress outlets.

Today was no exception. She'd opted to remain home and clean, but not without an ulterior motive. The will. She had hoped that her diligence would prove productive on that front.

It hadn't.

The copy of Mark's new will had disappeared as if it had never existed. But dammit, she knew that it had. And she would find it. Eleanor was *not* going to get Designs, especially now that she had Farmer's name on the dotted line. Without Ryker, work was all she had.

She couldn't think about *him*, either.

What she would think about was replanting that large ficus plant in the den, which had begun to show signs of neglect. In fact, it was dying.

"So stop stalling," Blythe murmured, "and get to it."

Blythe strode into the den, fell to her knees and began digging. At first, she thought she'd hit a large root, but when she jerked on it, the object turned loose, knocking her backward.

She sat up and stared down at her hand. In it was a small, plastic-wrapped box. With her heart palpitating out of control, she opened it, only to drop it as if it were another snake.

"Oh, my God," she whispered.

Jewelry.

Rare and precious jewelry. She would bet her life on both. But that wasn't all the pouch held; once the bounty was scattered on the carpet, out came a piece of paper.

Somehow she managed to pick it up, though her hands were shaking so hard that even that small feat was difficult. Printed in black ink were four names; two had been crossed off. In addition to the paper, there was a key with a note taped to it.

Blythe sat dumbfounded for the longest time, her mind splintering in a million directions, only to home in on one explanation.

"Oh, Mark, Mark, Mark," she moaned out loud, while rocking back and forth. "What have you done?"

Jewelry. *Hard Candy.* One and the same.

That was what Mark's death had been about. Cold sweat, mixed with hot tears, ran down Blythe's face.

Thirty-eight

What should she do?

For the time being, Blythe was too stunned, too confused, to move. She could only stare at the millions of dollars' worth of jewelry in front of her through glazed eyes.

Should she call Ryker? No. Yes. No, she finally decided. He would figure out a way to turn this unexpected twist against her. She couldn't take the chance of further incriminating herself.

Her attorney. Clayton Carrell. She would call him. *He* could call Ryker. Carrell would know how to deal with the detective. Meanwhile, maybe she should call Curt or Susan for emotional support. She was so shaken and so afraid that she didn't want to be by herself. Besides, she hadn't told either one of them about Cecil Farmer.

God, how could she think of Designs when her life was turned upside down? Because the company was her escape. If she didn't think about something else, she might indeed lose her mind.

Finding this jewelry could definitely be detrimental to her health if the wrong person knew she'd found it—Jacques Dawson, to be specific. She could die before she even went to trial.

That morbid thought shot Blythe into action. Scooping

up the loot, she placed it back in the pouch, her thoughts going haywire as she looked for somewhere to hide it.

The wall safe.

Scrambling to her feet, Blythe ran to the mantel above the fireplace, where a small picture hung. She removed the painting and placed the bag in the vault. She had just slammed the door shut when she heard a noise behind her.

She stood motionless with her heart in her throat.

Ryker shook Walter Steed's extended hand. "Thank you for coming in."

"I don't think I had a choice."

"Sure you did," Ryker said, smiling perfunctorily. "You and your family could've taken the goods and flown off into the sunset."

"Yeah, I guess we could have at that."

"But you didn't," Mike put in, "and that's what counts."

"No, sir, we didn't." Steed paused and rubbed his clean-shaven jaw. "Do you have any idea what this is all about?"

"We do," Ryker admitted, "and when we can, we'll let you in on it."

"Fair enough," Steed said. "Until then, good luck."

Once he was gone, Mike whistled. "Man alive, look at all those colored rocks."

"Don't you mean hard candy?"

"Whatever."

"Well, look all you want, then go log 'em."

Mike groaned as he gave the stones another wistful look. "You figured out what's going on?"

"Yep. Have you?"

"Think so."

"Lambert's accomplice stole from homes where the Design crew wasn't working, then buried the treasures on the grounds where they *were* working."

"They almost got away with that bizarre plan."

"Sooner or later, even the best laid plans go awry."

"You think Mrs. Lambert was in on it?"

"No."

"You sound sure."

"I am."

Mike didn't argue.

"Delaney, line one."

Ryker tried to maintain a stiff upper lip, but his insides felt like they were in a gravel grinder. Maybe it was Blythe.

Moments later, his letdown was almost sickening. Still, all wasn't lost. He looked at Mike and said, "Jacques Dawson's been picked up."

"All right!"

"It's time we built a fire under *his* butt."

Mike stood. "What if he's got a fireproof butt?"

"Then we'll find a big stick of dynamite to put under it."

Mike grinned. "You coming?"

"In a minute. You go and light the match."

Once he was alone, he checked his gun. Things were starting to pop. Soon, thank God, Blythe would be in the clear. What then? She would be out of his life forever. His mood soured even more.

He wished she would stop consuming his thoughts. But that wasn't going to happen. Blythe haunted him day and night. He'd picked up the phone to call her a thousand times, only to slam down the receiver, too chickenshit to follow through.

He still was.

Somehow, though, he had to right so many wrongs. He had to tell her he'd fucked up and that he loved her.

He almost laughed out loud. What did he think would come of that? He would have liked to think she would tell him all was forgiven and that they could live happily ever after, but that was *not* going to happen.

He had lost her, and he knew it. Because of that dark need for revenge festering inside, he'd thrown away the best thing in his life.

Well, that revenge would be laid to rest just as soon as he got his run at Dawson.

An hour later Ryker was on an emotional high. Regardless of his insecurities, he had to see Blythe, especially now. He hoped she was at home, since he was headed there. If not, he would try her office. He would do whatever it took to find her.

He had so much to tell her.

He noticed her car in the drive right off, then noted that she had a visitor. When he recognized the other vehicle, he frowned, then cursed.

With his heart hammering inside his chest with the force of a jackhammer, Ryker made his way to the door. It was unlocked. Only after he'd quietly opened it and walked inside did he hear voices.

Rather than barge into the room the way he wanted to, he stopped and removed his pistol from the holster. Lifting it in firing position, he waited in the shadows.

"Whatcha hiding in that safe, sweetheart?"

Though vexed, Blythe relaxed, then swung around. "I'm not your sweetheart, Frank, and I'm not hiding anything that concerns you."

His grin said, "Liar," which further infuriated her.

"What are you doing here? More to the point, how dare you just stroll in here unannounced?"

Of all people to have to contend with—her no-good brother-in-law. His presence made a volatile situation that much more so, especially if his wolfish look was anything to judge by. Was he drunk? She didn't think so, but with Frank, one never knew. Drunk or sober, she had to get rid of him.

Now.

Using her old standby scare tactic, she asked, "Does Eleanor know you're here?"

Frank leaned against the door frame. "Nope."

"She wouldn't be happy."

"Who gives a fuck?"

"I do, for one."

Frank pushed his stocky frame away from the door, his eyes bypassing her to the vault. "Forget about my wife."

"Get out of here, Frank."

"Bet I know what's in there."

"In where?" Blythe asked, playing dumb.

He grinned. "In that bag you just put in the safe."

"I bet you don't. Anyway, it's none of your business."

"Ah, come on, sweetheart, let's cut to the chase."

Irritated beyond words, not only at his annoying presence but at his nosiness, as well, Blythe tightened her lips, then folded her arms across her chest. Just sharing the same space with him gave her the willies. She just wished he would leave, though she didn't even know why he was there.

But she did know she didn't trust him.

"Look, Frank, I don't want to get ugly, so I'm asking

you in a nice way to go. It doesn't matter why you came, just go."

"Not on your life, sweetheart. Not until I get what I came *for.*"

It wasn't so much what he said, though that was spooky enough, but rather the way he said it, that set off the alarm bells inside Blythe's head. Had she missed something somewhere?

"And just what is that?"

"What you just put in the safe."

For a millisecond Blythe was at a loss for words. How did Frank know for sure what she'd put in the safe? Why did he care? Something definitely was not quite right here, even though she still couldn't put a finger on the pulse of her uneasiness.

"That's no concern of yours."

"Wrong."

"Excuse me?"

"Don't play fucking head games with me."

"Frank, you're talking crazy. Now get out of my face and out of my house."

"No can do, sweetheart."

"Do I have to call Eleanor?"

"You go anywhere near that phone and I'll break your fingers."

"Are you nuts?" Her voice was a tightly coiled whisper. "You can't talk to me like that."

"Reach for that phone and see what I can do."

A frisson of fear went through Blythe. Still, her eyes cut in that direction. The phone was definitely within reach. Should she call his bluff?

As if he could read her thoughts, Frank grinned again, only this time that grin was maniacal in nature. Blythe tried to swallow her burgeoning fear.

"I'm glad you're not going to do anything stupid," Frank said, moving toward her.

She backed up. "You're the one who's stupid. I don't know what kind of game you think you're playing, but—"

"You think this is a game?" He spat the words, his eyes narrowing to slits. "Well, think again, bitch!"

Blythe forced down her mounting panic, still convinced he was full of hot air, and that if she remained cool and calm, she could get rid of him.

"Look, what I put in the safe has nothing to do with you," she said. "It's nothing you'd want."

Frank pitched back his head and laughed. "You think it's yours, huh?"

"What?"

"That innocent act won't work. I know about the jewels, or rather, the hard candy." He grinned again, then winked.

Oh, Lord.

"How?" Blythe barely pushed the tiny word through her stiff lips.

"That's not important. What *is* important is getting my hands on the goods and the list."

"How did you know—" The rest of her sentence froze on her tongue as the truth struck her. She stared at him in muted horror.

His grin widened. "Ah, you finally get the picture."

"*You* killed Mark."

"Sure did, sweetheart."

"Oh, my God!" Blythe cried.

"You better pray there's a God and that he's on your side." Frank reached behind him and pulled out a gun. "Because if you don't open that safe and part with the loot, I'm going to kill you."

Blythe clutched the back of the chair, terror robbing her of speech and the ability to function.

"'*Comprende?*"

When she still didn't respond, Frank clicked the hammer on the gun and placed it against her temple.

"Please...please don't," she pleaded.

"Then open the goddamn safe."

"No...problem. Just put the gun away."

"No way, not until I get what I came for."

Despite her fumbling fingers, Blythe managed to open the safe and retrieve the bag. She turned then and placed it in Frank's outstretched hand.

"You done good."

"Why, Frank?" She hadn't meant to prolong this nightmare, but the words tumbled out before she could stop them. "Why did you kill Mark?"

"I'm in debt up to my eyeballs with the loan sharks, the same as your old man. Eleanor won't bail me out, and I'm tired of getting beat on because I can't pay 'em back."

"Where did those jewels come from?"

"You really don't know, do you?"

"No, I don't!"

"Mark and Dawson had a racket going, a damn clever one, too. While Mark supervised the landscaping at those ritzy-titsy homes, Dawson would break into someone else's home and steal the family jewels."

"Then what?" Blythe said in a voice she didn't recognize as her own.

"Old Mark would then plant them on the grounds where he was working. When the heat was off, he'd retrieve the goods and split them with Dawson."

Blythe fell onto the couch and clutched her stomach. "How...did you find out?"

"Overheard Mark and Dawson talking."

"So you decided to cut yourself in."

"Right, but your husband didn't think much of that." Frank paused and waved the gun. "Truth is, I didn't mean to kill him. His death was a freakin' accident. I hit him, and he slipped on the deck and knocked the crap out of his head."

Blythe's loud groan interrupted his confession.

"Couldn't help it. Anyway, when I realized the bastard was dead, I shoved him overboard."

"So now that you have what you came for, please go." Blythe staggered to her feet.

"Sorry, can't do that."

"But you said—"

"I lied. Despite that damn button you found, no one can prove I was on that boat *that* night."

"So you're a free man."

"Not as long as you're breathing." He lifted the gun and pointed it at her heart.

"No, Frank!" she cried, bending her head and covering her ears with her hands.

The sound of gunfire exploded in the room.

Thirty-nine

"Is...is he dead?"

Later, Blythe didn't know how she was coherent enough to utter one word, much less make a complete sentence. But she couldn't just stand there and shake, not with Frank lying facedown on the carpet, his blood creating a bizarre halo around his head.

"Are you all right?"

Ryker's face looked cast in iron, but his voice was soft and low. When she didn't answer, he strode to her, then reached out a hand. Coming to her senses, Blythe instinctively jumped back and stared at him.

"Don't...don't touch me."

His eyes turned to slits at the same time that his face turned a deathly white. "I..." His voice faded into a muttered expletive.

"Is...is Frank dead?" Her voice was fragile, battered, and she couldn't bear to look at her brother-in-law.

"No. My bullet just grazed his head, though he *is* out cold."

Blythe's shakes increased. "But there's...there's so much blood."

"That happens with a scalp wound. Look, would you please sit down? Any minute I expect to pick you up off the floor." He paused. "And since you don't want me to touch you, I suggest you do as you're told."

For once Blythe didn't argue. Ryker was right. She couldn't stand up much longer. The shock of his shooting Frank before Frank shot her was just now hitting her. In cadence with her shaking body, her teeth chattered. They were banging together, making a music all their own.

In the distance, Blythe could hear the screeching sound of an ambulance, and she knew it was headed to her house. The house would soon be filled with cops, followed by questions galore, a drumbeat that seemed to have no end.

"How...how long were you outside the door?"

"Long enough," Ryker expressed tersely.

"Then you know he...killed Mark."

Ryker stopped his pacing and stared at her; his eyes actually bored into hers. "I suspected as much."

"When did you suspect?" She didn't know where the stamina to pursue this line of questioning came from. However, something told her she had to talk, to try to make sense out of the madness, or she would collapse.

"We picked up Dawson."

"Thank the Lord for that," she whispered, then trapped her bottom lip between her teeth to try to hold it steady.

"When we put pressure on him, he squealed like a pig. Then he listed all his sins on paper, which included killing my niece."

"You know how sorry I am about that," Blythe said in a sad, quiet tone.

"So am I," Ryker muttered. "The sonofabitch also stuck that knife in Ted Armstrong."

"But why him?" Blythe asked. "I know why he killed Stacey. She caught him in the act of stealing. But what did Armstrong do to Dawson?"

"Like Frankie here, he overheard Lambert and Dawson talking on one of the jobs and wanted in on the action."

"Greed again."

"Right, only Dawson didn't want to share, so he waxed him."

Blythe felt her flesh crawl. "Such a waste of life in the name of money and greed."

"It happens every day."

"I was afraid Eleanor might have killed him." The thought was almost too repugnant to voice. "Even though I have no love for Eleanor, I don't think I could have coped with her killing Mark. And I know that would have finished Cynthia."

"What about you? Are you going to be okay?"

She turned away, fighting back tears and cursing silently at the injustice of it all.

"Blythe?"

It was the husky undertone of his voice that pulled her back around, despite her efforts to remain strong. Yet she dared not look at him again for fear she would be tempted to leap into his strong arms. How she needed them. How she needed *him*.

That need would never be assuaged. He had betrayed her with his heart and with his mind. How could she love someone who thought she was capable of murder?

"Blythe," he repeated in that same tone.

"What?" she whispered, keeping her face averted.

"Please, look at me."

"No."

"Dammit—" He was once again pacing the floor like a crazed man.

"It's no use."

He stopped. "What's no use?"

"You saying anything, trying to make amends."

"Even if I told you I was sorry? That I made a mistake?"

She whipped around, and this time their eyes met. "It's...it's not that simple."

"It could be."

"No, it can't."

"What if I told you that I—"

Suddenly noise from outside intruded, and the room was suddenly jammed with people.

"This conversation's not over," he said, bending over her, his words and breath caressing her ear.

Blythe forced herself to remain as rigid as a block of ice, though inside she was melting. But he would never know that. There was too much muddy water under the proverbial bridge for her to capitulate now.

She loved Ryker, but he had broken her heart and her trust. Two unforgivables.

"Get him out of here," Ryker told the paramedics.

"He's still breathing."

"Only because I chose not to kill him."

"Yes, sir," one of the young men said as he lifted Frank onto the gurney, throwing Ryker a strange look.

"Hey, boss," Mike said, walking up to him, "what the hell went down?"

"The bastard was going to kill Blythe."

Mike muttered an expletive, then peered at Blythe. "Are you okay?"

"No, she's not okay," Ryker spoke for her. "Call her friend Susan—" He broke off.

She gave him the name and number, thinking Susan's presence would be a godsend indeed. She couldn't bear to be alone, not after what she'd been through.

When Ryker had pulled that trigger and Frank had

fallen to the floor... No! She wouldn't think about that now. Instead she would think about getting Ryker and all of these people out of the house so she could regain her sanity.

"I'll be in touch," Ryker said. "You'll have to come down to the station and give a statement."

"Fine."

He looked at her for a moment longer. "Dammit, I hate to leave you."

"I don't want you here."

Cursing, he followed the others out the door. Blythe wasted no time sinking back onto the sofa, curling into a fetal position, making sure she couldn't see the wet spot on the floor that had once been a pool of blood. Frank's blood.

If it hadn't been for Ryker, it could have been hers. Sick to her stomach, she ran to the bathroom.

She had just walked back into the living room when Susan walked in the front door. Taking one look at Blythe, she whispered, "You poor baby, tell me all about it."

Blythe hurried into her outstretched arms. "It's a long story."

"Well, I have all the time in the world," Susan said, hugging her back.

To her credit, Blythe jerked herself upright by her bootstraps and kept busy, instead of wallowing in self-pity the way she wanted to. She had made up her mind to pick up the fragmented pieces and get on with her life.

Though she had seen Ryker later at the station when she'd given her statement, no personal exchange had taken place. Still, she'd felt his smoldering eyes follow her and known he wanted to trap her gaze and hold it.

Nothing doing.

Where he was concerned, she didn't trust herself. She was much too vulnerable. She had crossed him out of her life, convinced that what he felt for her wasn't love but lust. He had wanted her physically, and he'd taken her. And she had let him. She would have to live with that. What *he* had to live with was his problem, and she hoped he was choking on it.

If only she didn't still love him.

Now, as she arrived at her destination, sheer willpower and the fear of breaking down again were what enabled her to jerk her thoughts off Ryker and back to reality. Although reality wasn't all that great, either.

Actually, she was beginning to feel like an idiot, but she wasn't going to back down. Besides, she was desperate in more ways than one. But first things first, she told herself, staring at the modest but nice brick home in one of the better neighborhoods in Tyler.

Amy Britton's home. Her husband's mistress.

For a moment Blythe was tempted to crank the engine and drive off. But she couldn't afford the luxury of giving in to the despair that stuck like a knife in her stomach.

She had stopped loving Mark a long time ago. In fact, she had never loved Mark, not the way she loved... No! She wouldn't think about Ryker again or his betrayal of her. That pain was too raw, too unbearable.

Before she lost her courage, Blythe got out of the car and made her way to the front door, praying all the while that no one would be home.

Luck was against her.

A young woman came to the door, a lovely young

woman with dark brown hair and dark eyes. Blythe couldn't seem to tear her gaze away, waiting for something akin to jealousy to hit her. It didn't. She couldn't have cared less that Mark had made love to this woman, who was staring at her with a puzzled, then shocked expression on her face.

"Aren't you…?"

"Yes," Blythe said, a catch in her own voice. "I am."

"What do you want?" Amy's tone was cold and taut.

"May I come in? I…I want to talk to you."

"I don't think that's a good idea."

"Please." Blythe stopped short of begging. "I didn't come to make trouble."

"Then why did you come?"

"If you'll let me in, I'll tell you."

Amy stood aside, albeit grudgingly, and gestured with her hand for Blythe to precede her. The living room was tastefully decorated and smelled of rose potpourri.

"If you're here about the insurance policy, then—"

Blythe held up her hand, interrupting her. "No, that's not why I'm here at all."

"Are you saying you're not going to fight me on that?"

"Look, I won't pretend that I'm overjoyed about you and Mark, but not because I'm jealous. It's the fact that he didn't tell me he had someone else he cared about."

Amy's stare was skeptical. "You mean you would've divorced him?"

"In a heartbeat."

"He…he told me you refused."

Blythe's heart went out to this innocent woman who, like herself, had been taken in by someone with no morals or integrity. "Well, he lied."

Amy covered her chest with her arms and averted her gaze.

"Oh, we definitely had words over the matter," Blythe said. "But I would never have held him against his will if he'd told me there was someone else."

"Okay, so if you're not going to fight me over the money, then why have you come?"

"I was hoping he might have left something here."

"Like what?" Amy's tone was still suspicious and chilly.

"Papers, a briefcase, maybe."

Blythe knew she must sound desperate. Why not? She was. She had to find the copy of that will. If she didn't, then her success with Farmer would be for naught. Eleanor would get the company.

Dammit, that will had to be somewhere. Since it wasn't at home or at the office, she had thought of the next best place. Here.

"Did you kill him?"

For a second Amy's quietly spoken words failed to register. Then their impact hit their target—her stomach. It rebelled. "No," Blythe croaked.

God, where had this woman been? Hadn't she read the papers or listened to the news? How could she not know what was going on?

"Somehow I never thought you did," Amy was saying.

Though still befuddled by Amy's lack of knowledge, and curious to boot, Blythe blurted out, "Why is that?"

"I know Mark was involved in something, something dangerous, something that didn't involve you."

"He was, only it did involve me—in the worst way. His shady dealings almost got me killed."

"What...are you talking about?"

"Look, have you been gone or something?"

"Actually, I have. Out of the country."

"That explains it, then."

"Explains what?"

"Mark's killer is in custody."

Amy's mouth gaped, but nothing came out.

Blythe took pity on her and filled her in on what had taken place.

"Oh," she said, clutching her chest.

"It's been a terrible ordeal."

"But it's over, right?"

"Unfortunately, no. There's still some unfinished business."

"Is that why you want his briefcase?"

Blythe's hope rekindled. "So it *is* here?"

As if Amy realized she'd given herself away, she tried to backtrack. "I didn't say that."

"Yes, you did. Please, let me have it, or at least let me look through it."

"I guess it can't hurt."

"I promise I'm not out to hurt you in any way."

"I'll be right back."

Blythe released her breath and waited.

Forty

She knew she looked her best, having chosen to wear a stylish Christian Dior suit. Being dressed to the hilt acted as the extra armor she needed to face the Lamberts.

Her mother-in-law had called and asked her to tea. Blythe wanted to smile at that thought. God, the hypocritical nature of this family never failed to amaze her.

Never mind that Mark, the fair-haired son, had gambled away the family fortune, stolen from others and lost his life in an act of violence. Never mind that Frank, the son-in-law, had also gambled, then murdered his own brother-in-law for money. And though he wasn't dead, he might as well have been, since he was in a mental institution.

Talk about family skeletons flying out of the closet. Blythe shook her head. And through it all and beyond, Cynthia had remained insulated in her make-believe world, sure that family breeding and name would triumph.

Blythe fought the urge to throw up even as she rang the doorbell.

"I'm so glad to see you," Cynthia said, joining her a few minutes later in the solarium.

Blythe leaned over and kissed her on the cheek. "Are you feeling better?"

"Yes, how about yourself?"

"I'm making it. But you didn't ask me here to make small talk, did you?"

"No. I wanted to thank you for saving Designs and not shutting us—me out of your life."

Blythe sat down on the settee and took the cup of tea Cynthia handed her. "You don't have to thank me for anything. I'll always see you, and Designs—well, it's all I have left."

"I'm glad you brought that up."

Blythe swung her head to her left, realizing for the first time that Eleanor was in the room. She had sort of disappeared into the shadows, whether purposefully or unintentionally, Blythe didn't know.

"Hello, Eleanor," Blythe said. "I'm glad to see you're doing better."

Eleanor stiffened, as though she didn't like being reminded of how she had gone berserk when she'd learned what Frank had done. She had just gotten out of the hospital herself.

"I'm planning to return to the office in a few days."

Blythe's eyebrows rose. "Oh?"

"I know how you must feel about me." Eleanor's tone was defensive.

"You don't have the slightest idea," Blythe said.

Eleanor clenched her jaw. "Like Mother, I'm appreciative of what you've done for Designs, but nothing's changed on that score."

"Eleanor, for heaven's sake," Cynthia said. "I told you not to—"

"It's all right, Cynthia." Blythe deliberately sat her teacup down. "I'm glad she brought the subject up. We need to get this matter settled once and for all."

"There's nothing to settle." Eleanor moved toward

Blythe. "The injunction time ran out, and without the other will, Designs is mine."

Blythe didn't say anything. Instead, she reached for her purse, opened it and pulled out a document. "I don't think so." She held an envelope out to her sister-in-law.

Eleanor recoiled. "What's that?"

"You know, but I'll tell you, anyway. It's Mark's copy of his new will."

"You're lying."

"Go on, read it. See for yourself."

The room fell quiet as Eleanor did just that.

Finally she looked up, her face devoid of color. "Wait'll I get my hands on—"

"Perry Miller?"

Her eyes widened. "How—"

"I'm not stupid, Eleanor. I knew you and Perry were in cahoots against me all along."

"Is that true, Eleanor?" Cynthia asked, sounding horrified.

"Of course it's true," Blythe said. "I'm just curious as to how you convinced Perry to go along with you. Did you promise to marry him?"

"You're way off base," Eleanor hissed.

Blythe knew better. Her sister-in-law was wearing a telltale flush if there ever was one. "I know how lazy Perry is and how much he wants to live the good life without earning it."

"You don't know anything. You're just fishing in a dry pond, hoping to get lucky."

"I did get lucky. Mark had Perry's secretary make a copy of the original will without Perry's knowledge." Blythe grinned with a shrug. "Just one of those fluky little things. I knew it was there somewhere, but he didn't.

"Anyway," Blythe continued, that grin still in place, "it doesn't matter. I understand the State Bar is after Perry on another violation, so he'll get his just rewards. It's only a matter of time."

Eleanor glared at Blythe. "You think you're smart, that you have this all figured out."

"You're right, I do. And I just needed this will to prove it."

"So what are you going to do? Kick me out?"

"That's what you would've done to me, right?"

Eleanor didn't respond, but her answer was obvious in the obstinate set of her shoulders.

"Eleanor, how could you?" Cynthia cried.

"It's all right, Cynthia. Eleanor can work for Designs."

Eleanor was clearly taken aback. "I can?"

"Yes, but only because I don't want to bring any more pain to your mother."

"But there's a catch, right?" Eleanor asked, her tone resigned for once.

"You're damn right. You'll keep your place and take orders from *me,* like everyone else." Blythe paused. "If you have a problem with that, then you can clean out your desk and hit the road."

"I wish you'd do something, even if it's wrong."

Ryker threw his sister a nasty look. "You're talking gibberish."

"But you know what it means. You're a fuck-up."

"Why, Marcy Montgomery, I oughta wash your mouth out with soap, especially since you're with child."

Marcy rolled her eyes. "Only I'm *not* 'with child,' as you so eloquently put it."

"Oh, false alarm, then?"

"For now." She grinned cheekily.

They were in the new house that Marcy's husband had bought her two days after they married. Ryker had left the station and stopped by, unable to go home to his empty apartment.

"I know what you're up to," Marcy went on. "You want to change the subject, but it won't work. Just admit your trespasses, brother dear, and you'll feel better."

"You sound like Rushmore."

"Well, Mike's right."

"Okay, so I'm fucked-up. Feel better now?"

"It's you who needs to feel better."

Ryker was quiet as he glanced down at the bottom of his cup. "I'd kind of like that myself, only it isn't going to happen."

"Go to her."

Ryker jerked his head up. "Who?"

"Blythe, that's who. You know good and well who I was talking about."

A scowl covered his face. "She'd only kick me in the balls."

"No harder than you're kicking yourself, so what have you got to lose?"

Ryker rubbed the back of his neck. "I don't know, sis."

"Do you love her?"

"Yes."

"Then tell her."

"I'd like to," he said in a tormented voice. "Hell, I've thought about nothing else. But it isn't that easy."

"Yes, it is."

"No, it isn't."

"Convince me."

"For starters, I kept throwing it in her face that she, along with that scumbag she was married to, had something to do with Stacey's death."

"That was your job."

"No, it wasn't. That was my lust for vengeance."

"I disagree. You thought you were right about her. Now you know you weren't."

"You think that'll cut any ice with her?"

"I haven't the foggiest. But you won't know till you ask her."

Ryker made an impatient gesture. "Ah, you're too naive."

"If I'm too naive, then you're too jaded. To live," she muttered under her breath.

He half grinned. "Think so?"

"I know so."

"Maybe I will call her."

"I wouldn't."

Ryker shook his head to clear it. "But you just said—"

"Go see her in person, you idiot. You don't tell someone you love them over the phone."

His gut twisted. "I'm not sure I can face her."

"Sure you can. Don't think about it. Just go, okay?"

"Just like that?"

Marcy smiled. "Just like that."

"All right, you win," Ryker grumbled under his breath, then strode out the door.

Blythe was proud of herself.

She had accomplished what she had set out to do. Both her goals had been met—she had saved Designs, and she had beaten the murder charge. More important, she had learned a valuable lesson. She no longer had anything to prove to anyone. She was a whole person, capable of leading a rewarding life no matter what the circumstances.

So why wasn't she happy?

She knew, but she hated to admit the reason. What she hadn't planned on was missing Ryker, coping with the gaping hole he'd left. She missed him. It was that simple and that complicated. For so long he'd been a constant shadow, almost an extension of herself.

Maybe she should go to him, tell him how she felt. That day he had shot Frank, she'd known he wanted her. But did he love her? Now that her mind had cleared somewhat, something told her that was possible.

Which meant what? She didn't know. She just knew she was miserable and lonely. Would both of those unwanted emotions ever disappear? Would that gaping hole inside her ever be filled?

When the doorbell rang, she jumped up, glad of the interruption. She didn't care who was on the other side. Anyone, even an insurance salesman, would be preferable to her own company.

She jerked it open. Ryker stood in front of her.

"Before you slam the door in my face—"

"I'm not."

"If you'll just give me a chance—"

"Okay."

As if it just dawned on him what she'd said, the panic disappeared from his eyes and the color returned to his face. "You're…not? You…will?"

She smiled. "No and yes."

Ryker swallowed with obvious difficulty before stammering, "Can…can I come in?"

"I wouldn't have it any other way."

Groaning, he jerked her into his arms.

Epilogue

Six months later

"I don't want this to end."

Ryker's voice was a raspy whisper as Blythe sat atop him, smiling into his moist face. "We can do it again, you know."

He propped himself on his elbows, then circled a nipple with his lips and tugged it deeper into his mouth.

"Oh, Ryker," she cried, thinking the top of her head might come off as another orgasm rippled through her.

Moaning himself, he lay back down and clutched her hips, moving them frantically until they were both spent once again.

"One of these days, that's going to kill me."

"You wish," she teased, rolling off him.

"And what a way to go, is all I can say." Ryker tweaked her nose before pulling her close to him again.

"Since we've been married, it seems we've spent more time in bed than out."

He chuckled. "Making up for lost time, the way I see it."

"You're insatiable."

"It's lust, my darling. Pure and simple."

She grabbed a handful of the hair on his chest and yanked.

"You little wench!"

She grabbed another load of hair. "What about love?"

Although she knew the answer to that question, Blythe never got tired of hearing him say those magical words, knowing that he meant them. The changes that love had brought to both their lives was a miracle in itself.

Three days after he showed up on her doorstep, they had gone to a small chapel and gotten married. Still, at times, Blythe had to remind herself that Ryker was a permanent part of her life.

So far, it had been a good life, despite the fact that the past and its consequences were never far from their minds. There were moments when Blythe couldn't believe all she had gone through and survived.

Because of Mark and his greed, three people were dead—Stacey, Ted Armstrong and Mark himself. For what? Greed. Jacques Dawson's love of money had bought him a life sentence. If and when Frank became competent to stand trial, he would share that same fate.

"What are you thinking about?" Ryker asked, interrupting her mental wanderings.

"Wasted lives."

"Stacey's the one I think about." Horror still lurked in his eyes.

"Well, at least you have Dawson where he belongs, in prison for life without parole."

"That certainly gives Marcy and me both some comfort."

"And then there's Frank."

Ryker let go of a few choice curses under his breath.

"If I had my way, that bastard would be underground instead of in an institution."

"Now, honey, where's your compassion?"

Ryker snorted. "You don't want to know. After what he almost did to you, he's lucky he's still breathing, not to mention having his balls intact."

"You're not the big tough guy you pretend to be," she mused with a smile. "You could've killed him and didn't."

"Don't think I didn't consider it."

"Well, from what the doctors say, he'll never be able to function in society again. He's gone totally nuts."

"What about his wife?"

Blythe chuckled, almost smelling the sour taste that even speaking of her created in his mouth.

"Eleanor's actually groveling to make amends."

"As long as she's not the one who's making you throw up."

Blythe cut him a sly look. "So you noticed?"

"Love, I notice everything about you."

She snuggled closer. "Mmm, that's nice, especially since—"

"Especially since you're going to be the wife of the next captain and assistant chief," he said, cutting in.

"You're right about that."

And she was. Foley had retired, and Ryker's lifelong dream had become a reality. She couldn't be prouder.

"Only that wasn't what I was going to say."

"Well, don't keep me in suspense."

"Eleanor isn't who's keeping my tummy upset."

"Uh-oh, don't tell me all hell's broken loose on the Farmer project?"

"It certainly has its moments, I won't lie about that. But it's coming along great, and so is Designs."

"I never doubted you'd pull that out of the fire."

"Thanks for that vote of confidence."

"But that wasn't what you were going to tell me, right?"

Blythe nodded.

"So out with it, woman."

"You still don't get it?"

"Guess not."

"I'm pregnant!"

The look on Ryker's face was indescribable. Shock, surprise, glee, all those emotions seemed rolled into one. Then he laughed out loud. "Boy, did I do good!"

"You! How—"

He kissed her soundly. "I guess you can have some of the credit."

She caressed his cheek, her features sobering. "You're not upset?"

"Upset? Are you nuts?"

"It's so soon, and your job—"

"Hey, nothing's more important than you and our child—certainly no job."

"So, do you want to celebrate?"

Ryker kissed her soundly. "For life, my love, for life."

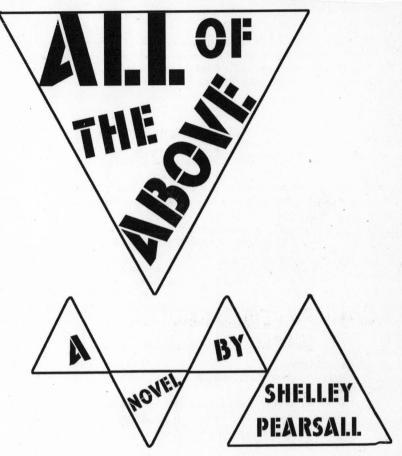

ALL OF THE ABOVE

A NOVEL BY

SHELLEY PEARSALL

Illustrations by Javaka Steptoe

LITTLE, BROWN AND COMPANY
New York Boston

Little, Brown and Company

Hachette Book Group
237 Park Avenue, New York, NY 10017
Visit our website at www.lb-kids.com

Little, Brown and Company is a division of Hachette Book Group, Inc. The Little, Brown name and logo are trademarks of Hachette Book Group, Inc.

First Paperback Edition: January 2008
First published in hardcover in 2006 by Little, Brown and Company

Cover photos clockwise from top, © Photodisc/Veer, © Digital Vision/Veer, © Rubberball/Getty Images, © Corbis/Veer.

Library of Congress Cataloging-in-Publication Data

Pearsall, Shelley.
All of the above / by Shelley Pearsall. — 1st ed.
p. cm.
Summary: Four urban middle school students, their teacher, and other community members relate how a school project to build the world's largest tetrahedron affects the lives of everyone involved.
ISBN: 978-0-316-11524-7 (hc)
ISBN: 978-0-316-11526-1 (pb)
[1. Interpersonal relations — Fiction. 2. Self-confidence — Fiction. 3. Family problems — Fiction. 4. City and town life — Fiction. 5. Geometry — Fiction. 6. Schools — Fiction.] I. Title.
PZ7.P3166All 2006
[Fic] — dc22 2005033109

10 9 8 7 6 5 4

RRD-C

Printed in the United States of America

The text was set in ITC Korrina, and the display type is Campaign.

for the 2002 tetrahedron team members

and their teachers

ALL OF THE ABOVE

If you follow Washington Boulevard past the smoky good smells of Willy Q's Barbecue, past the Style R Us hair salon, where they do nails like nobody's business, past the eye-popping red doors of the Sanctuary Baptist Church, you'll finally come to a dead end.

That's where our school sits. Right at the dead end of Washington Boulevard. We know there's a lot of people out there who think our school is a dead end. And that all the kids inside it are dead ends, too.

They drive past our school, roll up their car windows, and lock their doors. Let's get out of this bad neighborhood, they say. Fast.

But they've got it all wrong. Because inside our crumbling, peeling-paint, broken-window school, we are gonna build something big. Something that will make all of them sit up and take notice, even the people with their big, fancy cars and rolled-up windows. Something that hasn't been built in the history of the world. By anybody.

JUST YOU WAIT AND SEE. . . .

MR. COLLINS

Before this story begins, there are a few facts you should know. This is not for a quiz, but if it was, I would tell you to write the following facts *neatly* in your math notebook:

1. Tetrahedrons are geometric solids with four faces. All four faces are equilateral triangles.

2. Small tetrahedrons can be joined together to make larger ones.

3. The largest tetrahedron ever constructed was approximately seven feet tall, and it was made of 4,096 smaller tetrahedrons.

4. It was built by students at a private school in California. They had plenty of time and money.

5. I teach at a city school in Cleveland, Ohio, where I have been a middle school math teacher for the past twenty years.

6. We don't have much time or money.

7. The idea for the tetrahedron project began with one of my worst classes in twenty years of teaching.

8. It happened on a Friday.

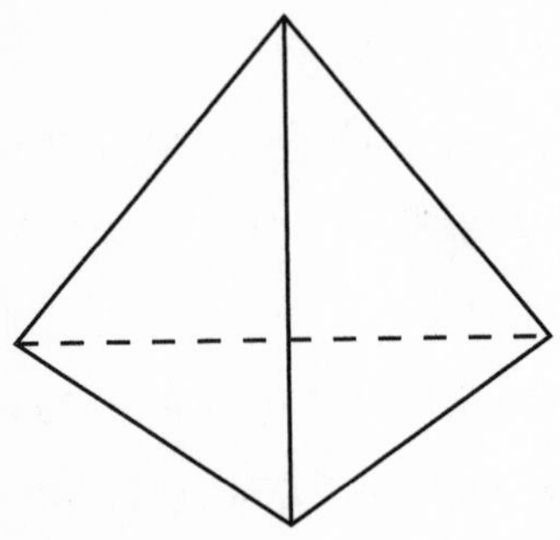

JAMES HARRIS III

I don't listen to nothing in Collins' math class. Only thing I listen for is the bell. That bell at the end of class is just about the sweetest sound in the world. The whole class, I sit there waiting on that bell and watching the hands of the clock jump from one little black mark to the next. You ever notice how school clocks do that? How they don't move like other clocks do; they jump ahead like bugs?

I even saw one move backward once. I swear the hands went five minutes back right before lunch. I told the teacher that the clock was cheating us out of recess and got a detention just for saying that.

Mr. Collins teaches seventh grade math and I'm telling you, straight up, he's one of the worst teachers you can get at Washington Middle School. My older brother, DJ, had him for math two years ago. He told me Collins would do nothing but talk and write on the board for the whole period, and the hardest part of his class was not falling asleep. And forget his tests; don't even bother to try.

Every Friday, me and Terrell and three of the other guys who can keep their big mouths shut take bets on which tie Collins will have on when he walks in. He's been wearing the same ones for forever. DJ's class did the same thing. Everybody put in a quarter and whoever guessed right on the day they were betting got all the money.

It gonna be pea green, puke orange, red stripe, yellow diamond, or dirt brown, today, huh?

I've won three bucks so far this year, and it's only September.

But then one Friday, Collins did something crazy. Like cracked. I was sitting there in class that afternoon staring at the jumping clock like usual, and Collins' voice was going on and on about how important geometry was. Yeah, right. His voice was talking to itself, while his hand drew on the board.

This is a cylinder, class. This is a cube.

Nobody was paying attention to a word he was saying.

This is a cold Pepsi can, my mind said. This is a box with a big, juicy Big Mac inside. No mustard. Extra ketchup.

And then Collins suddenly stops his hand in midair, whips around, and stares at us. "Is anybody listening to me?" He waves his arms and yells. You know, it was almost funny. You could see the little veins in his forehead popping out and his neck starting to turn beet red.

All week he'd been giving us this same line. How nobody in our class was listening to him. What's there to listen to? That's what I kept wanting to ask. Only four people turned in their homework on Tuesday and almost everybody failed his quiz on Wednesday, and you shoulda seen him losing it about that —

But this time he completely flips out. He throws his piece of yellow chalk onto the stack of papers sitting on his desk, goes over to the side of the room, and stands there staring out the windows with his arms crossed. While he's doing that, the piece of chalk rolls off the papers, hits the floor, and shatters into a thousand little pieces. That makes everybody crack up. But Collins, he doesn't even turn around to look. He just keeps standing there at the window, not saying a word.

I swear he doesn't move for about a half hour. You shoulda seen the looks the whole class was giving behind Collins' back while he stood there. Everybody rolling their eyes at each other and pretending to cough and shaking their heads. Like nobody knows what to think.

When Collins finally does turn around, he's got his serious face on. You know the one I'm talking about. Like we are about to get another big long lecture. Maybe because me and Terrell are in the row right next to where he's standing, Collins starts in on us first. I slouch down in my chair, figuring he'll get a clue and move somewhere else. But he doesn't.

"James," he says, "what would make you care about being here?"

"Where?" I ask, trying to give the least answer I can.

"Right here. Math class, room 307, Washington Middle School, Cleveland, Ohio." Collins motions toward the windows. "What would make you want to be right here, in room 307, James?"

"Nothing. I hate math," I say to Collins, and the whole class starts laughing.

"I'm sorry to hear that," the teacher answers in a strange voice once the class gets quiet again. He moves on to Terrell next. "You, Terrell? What about you?"

Behind me, Terrell's answer is too low to hear. I mean I hear it because that's the way me and Terrell talk all the time in class, but Collins doesn't. He comes walking closer to him. "I didn't hear exactly what you answered," he warns.

"Maybe some kinda contest," Terrell mumbles.

I swear under my breath. *You tell him about the ties and you're a dead man, Terrell.* DJ and the others would never let me forget it if Collins found out. I could hear my brother already — "Figures you'd be the fools who'd go and give away the whole thing. Been doing this for years and your class had to be the one that snitched."

"A contest . . ." Collins repeats Terrell's words like he always does with whatever you answer. "What kind of contest?"

I can hear Terrell shifting around in his seat behind me. "Just a contest," he mumbles again, "or something like that."

For about a minute, the teacher stands there staring into space like he's thinking about Terrell's answer or waiting to hear something more. Then he goes back up to the chalkboard, erases the whole thing, and starts drawing these big crazy lines. The chalk goes *screak, screak, screak,* like fingernails scraping, he draws so hard. He slashes one diagonal chalk line from the top of the board to the bottom, then a straight line top to bottom, then another diagonal one, then a few more at the bottom until there is something that looks like a big pyramid on the board.

"Anybody know what this is?" he says loudly, rapping his knuckles on the board.

Nobody says a word. I think everybody believes Collins has lost his mind.

"T-E-T-R-A-H-E-D-R-O-N" the teacher writes in big crooked letters across the whole board. Then, he whips around and shouts, "WHY AREN'T ANY OF YOU WRITING THIS DOWN?"

I yank Terrell's pencil out of his hand and tell him

he had better keep his fat mouth shut for the rest of class. On the inside cover of one of my notebooks, I copy the word from the board. TETRA HEED RON. That's what I put down.

While Collins is writing the definition, I draw a guy standing on a tall, pointy mountain with the words "Help me, help me! I'm Tetra Heed Ron" coming out of the guy's mouth. That cracks me up. I turn around to show it to Terrell and a shadow falls across my desk.

"I'll take that notebook," Collins says. The little metal spirals make a zipping sound as he pulls it right out of my hand and tosses it onto his desk. *Man*, another detention. I slam my chair back so hard it hits Terrell's desk behind me.

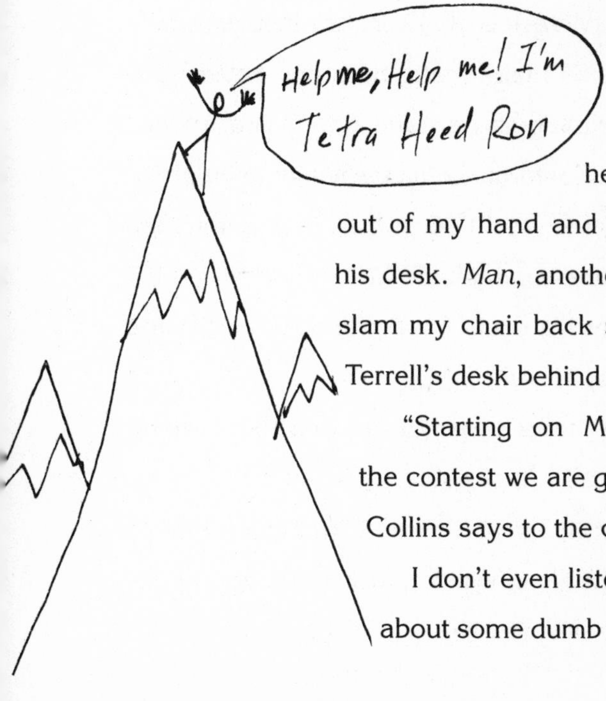

"Starting on Monday, here's the contest we are going to have," Collins says to the class.

I don't even listen. Who cares about some dumb math contest?

"We are going to have a contest to build one of these." Collins smacks his palm on the chalkboard pyramid and chalk dust flies up in the air. "A tetrahedron. Nobody has ever made one larger than six levels before. That's the record. So, our school is going to build a bigger one." Collins looks around the classroom like he is expecting us to be excited about his crazy idea. "So what do you think? Who wants to give this a try?"

Not one single person raises their hand, because what kind of contest is that? Building a pyramid? How's that gonna make math class any better? But the teacher keeps going on and on. Telling us how some school in California holds the world record. How their six-level one had 4,096 pieces. How our school could get into the *Guinness Book of World Records* if we do this. How we could be on the news across the country.

Yeah, right. I just keep my eyes on the jumping clock.

"How about it, Terrell? It was your idea to have a contest," Collins says, walking around trying to convince people. "Donte — how about you? Or Sharice? Rhondell?"

The teacher looks over at me again. "James — you have art talent. You could do this. Don't you want to be in the *Guinness Book of World Records* for something? Don't you want to see your name right there on its own page" — he draws a page in the air with his hands — "James Harris III?"

No. *Wish you would just get away from me, fool, that's what I wish.*

Sharice, who's always kissing up to the teachers, says maybe. And Rhondell Jeffries, who's got brains but is nothing to look at, says she'll think about it, too. Nobody else agrees to help, except for Marcel.

He waves his hand in the air and says if they need somebody to sign autographs and take pictures with all the ladies, he'll be there. Marcel always thinks he's something, just because everybody in town knows his daddy owns Willy Q's Barbecue.

I could pound Marcel's face into barbecue with one hand if I wanted to.

"All right," Collins says, just as the bell rings.

"Anybody who wants to be part of this project, be here after school on Monday." As I'm sliding out the door in the middle of the other kids, Collins holds up my notebook and calls out, "Detention on Monday or here, James. Your choice."

Yeah, right.

Like I got any choice.

RHONDELL

All the way home on the bus in the rain, I roll the word *tetrahedron* around in my mouth. I keep my face turned toward the steamed-up bus window, and I let my lips try the word over and over without using my voice. *Tetrahedron.*

I wonder if this is one of those words that might get me into college someday. It sounds as if it could. Inside my mind, I keep a whole collection of college words for someday. Words like *epiphany, quiescent, metamorphosis . . .*

My mom says it's okay to have dreams about going to college, but a person must face reality, too. Reality is that nobody we know has ever gone to college, and we don't have any money to go with, and you have to be very, very smart or very lucky to get in.

Sometimes I imagine college as a big wooden door where you have to knock and say the right password to get in. Only people who know big words like *metamorphosis* and *epiphany* are allowed inside. So, I think I try to save all the words I can because maybe deep down, I believe they will somehow get me inside college without money or luck.

But around here, if you talk and act like you have dreams, or as if you think you are better than everybody else, it only causes trouble. So, I keep most of my college words locked up in my head, and I try to make it through each day by saying as few words as possible. "She's quiet" is the way most people describe me, and I figure being quiet is just fine because it means you won't be bothered.

As the bus rattles down Washington Boulevard with everybody shouting and shoving past my seat because I'm one of the last to be dropped off, I draw a little tetrahedron in the window steam with my finger, and I try to decide if being in Mr. Collins' contest will get me a step closer to my dream or not.

MR. COLLINS

When I am asked why I started the tetrahedron project, I usually — but not always — give one of the following answers:

1. I don't know exactly why.

2. I had been reading an article about the California school and their math record.

3. I was frustrated with my teaching, my school, my students, myself.

4. I was approaching my limit — or in mathematical terms, convergence.

5. All of the above.

Sometimes I also admit that although starting the project was my idea, I never really expected any of my students to show up — and I didn't have a plan when they did.

SHARICE

Six people are already in the math room when I get there on Monday. This kinda surprises me a little. I take a look around the doorway first 'cause if it's only me and Mr. Collins, I don't plan on sticking around. But then I see Ashlee and Deandra from math class. They are hanging all over Terrell (how desperate can you be?) and passing a bag of chips back and forth.

Marcel is there, too, acting like his usual self. He's sitting on the edge of Mr. Collins' metal desk, banging a rhythm on the side of it with his shoes. And James is in the corner near the windows not paying attention to anybody, with his head down on his desk and the hood of his gray sweatshirt pulled up.

Since I'm not crazy about Marcel (and definitely

not James), I slide into the desk next to Rhondell and thunk my backpack on the floor.

"Hey, girl," I say, trying to be friendly even though Rhondell is a real hard person to figure out. She's plain-looking, but not in an ugly way, and she's smart, but not in a lord-it-over-your-head way, and she's friendly, but not in a real friendly way.

"Hi, Sharice," she says, glancing up quick from the book she's reading and then back again. To tell you the truth, it kinda surprises me that she actually knows my name, because Rhondell is one of those people who seem like they wouldn't be bothered with knowing people's names at all because they have too many other important things to think about.

I take a stick of gum out of my purse and unwrap it slowly. Mr. Collins' math room isn't much to look at. First of all, it's on the third floor and the ceiling leaks, so there's always a couple of garbage cans in the middle of the room with the words DO NOT MOVE written on them in permanent marker. And the blank walls drive me crazy whenever I'm sitting in class. If it was up to me, I'd fix the ceiling and hang up something (anything!) and that would be a big improvement.

I can't decide if coming to the math room is going to be any better than hanging around the Washington Boulevard Public Library day after day with the librarians giving me their usual over-the-nose stares and asking me if I have some school stuff I should be working on.

You see, foster non-parent #5 (Jolynn) doesn't allow anybody at home when she isn't there, and since she isn't there most of the time, I'm not allowed to be there either. Which is why I mostly end up sitting in the blue plastic library chairs or in the mall food court, or riding around on the city bus (or wherever I can find a seat without too many weirdos or drunks around).

After I pop my gum into my mouth, Mr. Collins comes into the room. His face doesn't look real thrilled to see us. He goes straight to his desk and starts shuffling through his stack of papers and books like he always does before he starts teaching. This better not be a rerun of math class, I think to myself.

Finally, he looks up, clears his throat, and says, "So all of you are here to build a tetrahedron, right?"

"No," a muffled voice calls out from the corner of the room. "Don't want to be here at all. Don't care about no stupid geometry."

Mr. Collins doesn't answer James, but I notice his face gets a shade more red.

"Well, this is the first time I've tried something like this, so all of us are going to learn this as we go along," Mr. Collins continues in a not very confident-sounding voice. "I'm going to put a chart up on the board and we'll get started." Then he turns toward the chalkboard and takes about ten minutes to draw a big chart, using a yardstick to make every line perfectly straight and erasing any place where they cross over.

Mr. Collins is one of those white teachers who looks like he never gets out in the sun much. He's soft-looking in terms of muscles and kinda thin and his light brownish hair is always parted too far to one side in my opinion.

He writes the words "TETRAHEDRON TEAM" at the top of the chalkboard, and puts each of our names, first and last, on the chart. Of course, he spells my name with an *E* — Sherice, the same as he always does. I just shake my head and think Sh-A-rice. AAAAAAA. How come you can teach math and you can't remember a simple thing like that?

As Mr. Collins fills in his chart, I get the feeling that he doesn't have a clue about how to run after-school clubs. I've been in just about every club there is, because being in one means you don't need after-school daycare, and if you don't need after-school daycare, it means your foster non-parents can keep more of the money they get for you.

So, I've been in a spelling club, a cheerleading club, Brownies (foster non-parent #2 was Head Brownie), dramatics club, and even a hairstyle club. I'm almost an expert on clubs, you know.

When the teacher finishes our names, I put up my hand. "You gonna elect a Secretary and a President next?" I say. "Because I'm good at being Secretary."

Mr. Collins rubs his nose and says, "Sure, all right, let's do that," and he writes "Secretary" next to my name without even taking a vote. Marcel says he'll be President, and Terrell wants to be Vice President.

"And I want to be Vice President to the Vice President," says Smart Mouth from the corner of the room. The teacher doesn't even argue with James. He just writes "V.P. II" next to James' name.

I keep trying to help Mr. Collins, even though I don't know why.

"Maybe we should make a list of supplies for the project," I suggest, "and I can write them down." Since I don't know the first thing about building tetrahedrons, I get out a sheet of paper and wait for the teacher to tell us what we'll need.

"Glue," he says.

I look up. "What kind — Elmer's glue? Rubber cement? Or glue sticks?"

"I don't know. We'll have to see," Mr. Collins answers in an uncertain voice. I don't think he does crafts very much.

"What else?" I ask, writing a neat number two on my list. I'm a very neat person because most foster non-parents don't like messy kids. So I keep my clothes folded in the drawers and my bed always made. (Hey, at least it gives them one nice thing to say about me.)

“A pattern. Some type of tetrahedron pattern.”

“From where?” I ask.

Mr. Collins rubs his eyes. “I don’t know. I’ll have to find one.”

All right, number three.

“Scissors,” Mr. Collins says. “And heavy paper.”

I write “scissors” and “paper” carefully on my list. “What color paper?” I ask.

Deandra shouts out, “Red, red, red!” like it’s the last color on earth. White’s cheaper than colored paper, I try to say, because I know a lot about how to get along on not much. For instance, nobody would notice that my shirt is about two years old and a hand-me-down from one of my old foster non-sisters. I always iron my shirts with Jolynn’s iron so they will look almost new.

“What do we care about money?” Deandra shoots back at me. “If we’re gonna be famous, who cares?”

From the back of the room comes James’ voice again. “Rainbow-colored,” he says, just being a smart mouth. “Why don’t we get rainbow-colored paper?”

“All in favor of using rainbow-colored paper,” I say. (Because it isn’t that bad of an idea, you know —

why not use all different colors if money doesn't matter?) And everybody votes in favor except James, who doesn't vote at all. He tugs his hood tighter over his head and mumbles that we are a bunch of losers. Marcel tries to tell him to chill, but he gets a punch in the arm for being dumb enough to say that to James Harris. Mr. Collins shuffles through his papers and pretends not to see any of it.

Even with James Harris in the club and Mr. Collins not knowing much about running one, I have a good feeling about it as we get up to leave. I figure that working on something (even math) has got to be better than sitting in the mall or the Washington Boulevard Library, day after day, waiting on Jolynn. You never know — maybe I would turn out to like the math club so much, foster non-parent #5 would have to come looking for *me*.

Now wouldn't that be a real change?

MARCEL

Marcel the Magnificent, that's me. After our math club meeting, I head on over to the Barbecue. Slap a big slab of ribs on a plate. Take fifteen orders at the same time.

"How you want your ribs done, ma'am, heat or no heat? Hot sauce or mild?"

"We got Blast Off to Outer Space Hot, Melt the Roof of Your Mouth Hot, Tar in the Summertime Hot, Red Heels Hot, Mama Thornton Sings the Blues Hot, and Just Plain Ol' Hot. Which you want? Yes, ma'am. Two Singing the Blues coming up. Napkins and forks on the right side. Fire hose on the left. We aim to please at Willy Q's Barbecue. You have a good day, too, ma'am." I slam the order window shut.

Ahhh. Feet up. Butt down.

My daddy, who everybody calls Willy Q, looks over from the grill, where he is sweating and melting like tar in the summertime. He mops his face with a towel. “Who said you could take a break?”

“Homework,” I say, pointing. “I got English. History. And a whole lot of math. Going for a world record in math.”

My daddy thunks the grill lid down and wipes his hands on his old blue apron. “Willy Q’s Barbecue is going for the world record, too,” he says. “Three hundred dollars in sales today. Willy Q’s Barbecue is hot, hot, hot. You sell two more Singing the Blues, Marcel, and we are set for the night. We can go home and eat a pizza.”

He points at the school stuff beside my chair. “Why you got so much homework? Ain’t you been doing your work in school? And why you so late getting here to work today? You in some kind of trouble?”

On the back of an order pad, I do a quick sketch. “We got a new math club at school,” I tell Willy Q. “Trying to break a world record. They elected me Prez. Gonna take different colors of paper and make them into little shapes that look like this." I hold up my drawing. "See?"

"That's a pyramid," my daddy says.

"No." I show him. "Tetrahedron. All triangles, see?"

My daddy smacks my arm. "Don't you get too smart for Willy Q's Barbecue," he tells me. "'Cause we don't need smart, we need sales."

He crosses his arms and squints at me. "How long this club gonna last, Marcel? You got a job to do — hope you ain't forgetting that."

I give him Marcel's special Turn-on-the-Charm-and-Give-Them-the-Big-Pearly-Whites smile. Same smile I use for when the grill's too slow or we got too many people waiting in line. "Ain't gonna last very long, teacher says. Not that long."

Willy Q don't fall for that smile, though.

"Better not," he warns, getting up and going back to the grill. "Break's over. Get back to work, Marcel."

Singing the Blues Barbecue Sauce

¼ cup brown sugar

½ cup ketchup

⅓ cup white vinegar

4 tablespoons olive oil

¼ cup water

2 tablespoons Worcestershire sauce

½ teaspoon salt

¼ cup molasses

2 tablespoons lemon juice

2 tablespoons sweet hot mustard

Combine all ingredients and bring to a boil. Simmer 15 minutes, stirring occasionally until sauce is sweet and singing the blues.

MR. COLLINS

Math problem to solve:

Each level of a tetrahedron increases by a factor of four. So, in order to build a bigger tetrahedron, the students at Washington Middle School will need to add a new level and make four times as many pieces. If the California tetrahedron had 4,096 pieces, how many pieces will the Washington Middle School students need to make?

JAMES HARRIS III

Forget this. That's what I feel like telling Collins. We're sitting in the guidance office and Collins says that I'm going to fail math for the first grading period because I'm not passing his tests or turning in any of the homework. He shows me all the empty boxes in his grade book.

Like I care about those empty boxes.

"I'm very concerned about you," he tells me. He puts on that sad-eyed look that teachers use to show they're concerned when they're really not. They're just worrying about handing out too many F's and looking like bad teachers.

I stare at the window behind Collins and think about how good it would feel to jump out that window and send all that glass flying into the air like one of those jagged comic book pictures with the word *CRASH* written above it. Get out of school, Collins' class, all the other dumb teachers' classes — and never come back.

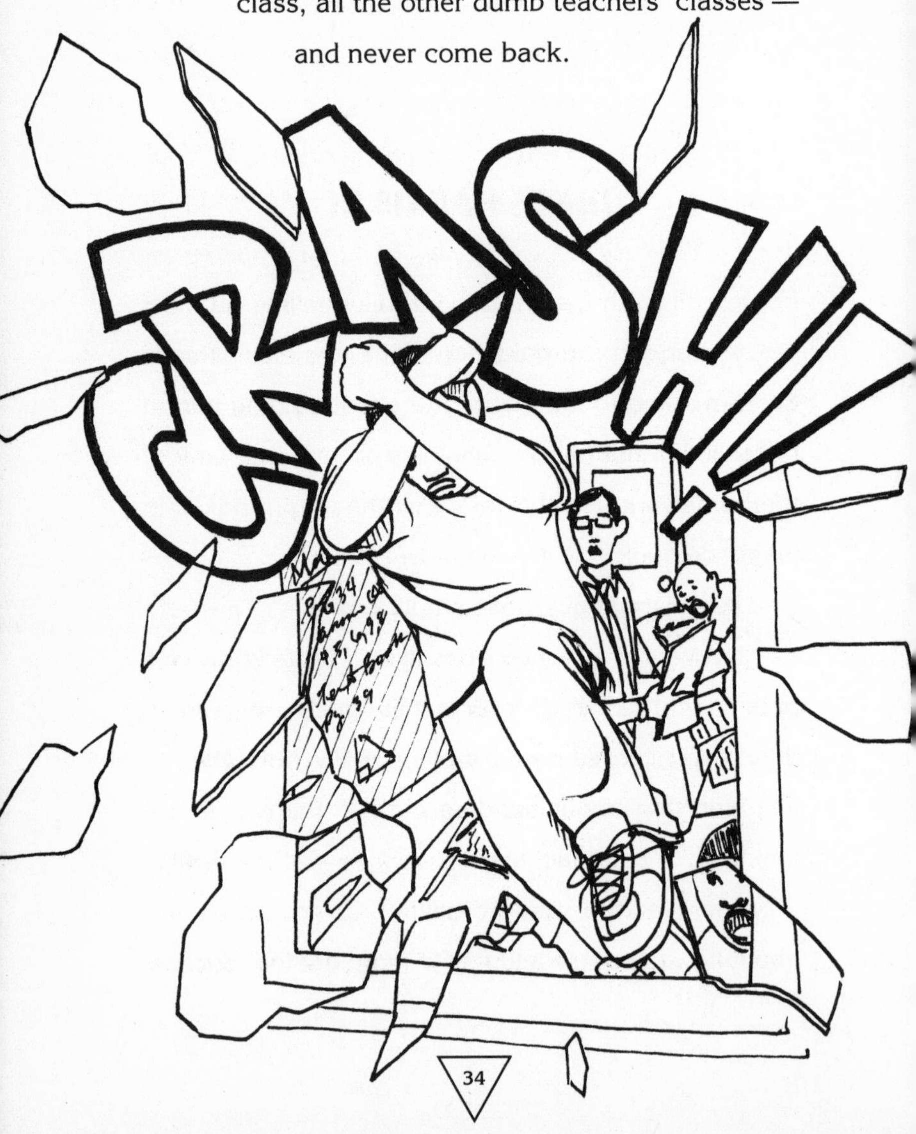

Collins says if I start coming more often to his math club after school, he might let me pass the first grading period with a D. "We need a lot more help with the project," he says, leaning back in his chair and waiting for me to answer. "So, James, what do you think? Would you consider doing that or not?"

I think about telling Collins — gimme an F. That I'd rather fail. That I don't feel like doing his dumb math homework or making his dumb pyramid, either. Most days, I got better things to do after school than sit with a bunch of losers. Even Terrell says he's thinking of dropping out because the girls are nothing special to look at.

But I decide to play Collins' little game. "How many days a week do I have to keep coming to the club to pass math?"

The teacher's eyes waver, like he hadn't thought of being asked this question. "Every day you don't turn in your math homework," he answers finally.

"And how long I gotta stay?"

"Well . . ." Collins' eyes glance toward the clock. "Four o'clock, how about that?"

"Ain't staying past 3:45," I reply, staring out the

window again. "I got a life, you know, and it ain't here in school."

Collins shakes his head and gives me the sad-eyes look again. He starts into a long speech about how he wishes he could make me see that my life would be so much different if I realized that school was a way out.

"You've got such a talent for art," he says. "Don't you see that? You could go to college someday, or art school. . . ."

I've heard this speech from teachers so many times I could give it myself. What they don't get is, I don't like school, and I'm already good in art and there's nothing else I feel like learning about it. They should see the wall of drawings I got at my uncle's place if they think I need to learn something.

I snooze and count sheep in my head until Collins finishes.

"Can't stay until four," I repeat again when he's done talking. "Gotta be home by four. I got rules."

That rules excuse was just a lie, of course. I didn't have no rules. Not one. Me and my brother, DJ, lived with our uncle, who didn't care what we did. The real reason that I had to be back by four was that DJ and his friends always showed up at my uncle's place around then and sometimes they'd let me hang out with them, if they didn't have plans — plans meaning something they didn't want me being a part of.

Most of my brother's friends were the kind of people you wouldn't want to mess with if you saw them on the street, especially Markese. He'd been kicked out of school already for the stuff he'd done. Wouldn't that be nice, right? But the others were cool to me. When they saw me in the hall at school, they'd slam into my shoulder and say "Hey, little brother — wake up, what's happening?" Two more years and I'd be the one slamming into shoulders just like DJ and the others. The hallway would move apart to let me pass —

Collins closes his grade book with a thump, which brings me back to where we were at. "All right, James," he says with a sigh. "If you keep coming to the math club and stay until 3:45 — not 3:30, or 3:35, or 3:42 and a half — I'll give you a passing homework grade. But just for this marking period. And you have to show up every day the club meets, do you understand that?"

"Ain't coming on Saturday and Sunday," I say. "No way."

Collins gives me a look. "You know what I meant."

As I walk out the door, I can't help grinning to myself and jumping up to high-five the top of the door frame. "See ya later, Mr. Collins," I call out. "You have a good weekend now."

See, Collins may be a math teacher, but he ain't very smart. All I said was that I would show up from 3:00 to 3:45. Didn't agree to do nothing for the club. So I could waste forty-five minutes drawing comics in the back of the classroom, and he'd still have to let me pass math. Man — DJ and his friends would say — you a genius.

And I was.

MR. COLLINS

Another math problem to solve:

If seven students and their math teacher worked on building the giant tetrahedron from 3:00 to 4:00, Monday through Friday, and each person made about 30 small tetrahedrons an hour, how long would it be until they reached their goal of 16,384? Extra credit: What if it is not that easy?

WILLY Q

Nothing gets past Sergeant Willy Q. Williams.

I'm a Vietnam vet, so I seen it all, you know what I mean? I was in the Army for fourteen years. So I know a thing or two about kids. Seen kids not much older than my son go to war, get shot up, and die. That's what I'm always telling Marcel. He may think he's smarter than me. He may think he can pull the wool over my eyes — but nothing gets by Willy Q. Williams.

When I see Marcel coming in late to work again — the third time in a week — I pick up the phone we use for taking orders and call his school. I ain't gonna listen to another smooth excuse about why he's late. I know the streets and I know everybody in this neighborhood, good and bad, and I'll find out where he's been and what he's been up to, and he'll think twice before lying to me again. And if he's doing drugs or hanging out with the wrong crowd, he'll be sweating over the grill at Willy Q's Barbecue for the rest of his life.

A lady answers at the school.

"Good afternoon," I say, "this is Marcel Williams' father, Willy Q. There a math class meeting there?"

The lady says no, not that she knows about. There's basketball practice and cheerleading; that's all.

I start counting on my fingers. One lie.

"There a Mr. Collins there? A math teacher?"

I wait for her to say no, there's nobody named Collins either. But she says hold on, she'll page him on the loudspeaker. A customer walks up to the take-out window, but I tell him to hang on and I stay on the line waiting. When Mr. Collins finally picks up the phone, I can tell right away that he's a white guy. About forty or fifty years old maybe. Least that's what he sounds like.

I tell him I'm calling to check if my son is in an after-school math club of his, because that's what he's telling me, and I want to find out if that's true or not. And I have to admit that it surprises me a little to hear the teacher answer yes, it's true.

"What's the purpose of this club?" I ask. "Does Marcel need extra help in math? He failing or something?"

Mr. Collins says no.

"This for some kind of test that kids need to graduate?"

Mr. Collins says no.

"This just some kind of self-esteem club like they're always pushing these days, to make black kids feel good about themselves?"

Mr. Collins says no, the kids are learning geometry and trying to break a math record set by a school in California.

Same story Marcel gave me.

"Now, maybe some kids have time to stay after school and break math records, but my son doesn't." I say this in a respectful tone of voice, though. I tell Mr. Collins that if it wasn't for our barbecue place, me and my son wouldn't have a roof over our heads or food in our mouths. I can't run the place alone, I explain, not with how much business we get. I need my son here every day, helping me after school. I expect that you can understand that.

Mr. Collins tries to make me change my mind. He wants me to let Marcel stay for the club once or twice a week. "Maybe you have some days that are slower than others," he tries to argue. "Marcel is a big part of the team, and we'd hate to lose him."

I tell the teacher that I'm a Vietnam vet and being a soldier taught me that responsibility always comes first. Marcel's responsibility is to work at the Barbecue. When you're a soldier, you learn to do what you have to do, not what you want to do, and that's the way I'm trying to raise my son, I say.

"Now" — I glance over at the customer who is getting impatient — "what time is school dismissed every day, Mr. Collins?" After he answers 3:25, I thank him for speaking to me and tell him to be sure that Marcel leaves school at that exact time each afternoon. "I'll be waiting right here for him," I finish.

MARCEL

I got Slow Burn Sauce cooking inside me. The kind of sauce that gets hotter after you swallow it. Hotter and hotter. Like flames licking up the inside of a house.

We don't aim to please nobody at Willy Q's Barbecue, ma'am. We got the worst food in the whole state of Ohio. Maybe the entire world. No hot sauce. No mild sauce. Nothing. You have a terrible day, too, ma'am, and don't you ever come back.

That's what I'd like to say.

Instead I smack some ribs over on the grill and slop sauce on them. Won't look at Willy Q. Won't talk to him neither. Let him disappear in a puff of smoke. Wouldn't care.

Ain't spending the rest of my life working at Willy

Q's Barbecue. Saying sweet things to customers who don't deserve sweet. Smiling like I care about selling rib bones and chicken wings and pig meat.

Ain't joining the Army either, like my daddy thinks. Won't salute nobody. Least of all, him.

I'm gonna be a comedian. Or a Hollywood actor. Here comes Marcel Williams. The movie star. Can't you hear them saying that? Big black stretch limo. Hot girls on each arm. Ain't he something? they'll say.

Willy Q doesn't want me staying for the math group anymore. He says I gotta be at work every day by 3:30. Mr. Collins bent the truth about what time school lets out, just to get my daddy to believe that. "But at least you can stay with us for twenty minutes or so after school," Mr. Collins said, trying to make me feel good.

Twenty minutes.

The Slow Burn Sauce starts bubbling inside me again. I can feel the heat rising. Maybe I'll work harder in those twenty minutes, Willy Q, than in all the hours I'm working and sweating for you —

Willy Q hollers at me. "We got a customer, Marcel. Over at the window. You watching out or not?"

I open the order window real slowly and give my best I-Don't-Really-Care-What-You-Want-to-Order smile.

Good afternoon, ma'am, I say inside my head. You better order real fast because Marcel Williams ain't gonna be here too long, no matter what his daddy thinks. He's gonna leave this place and be a star. . . .

"We got Blast Off to Outer Space Hot, Melt the Roof of Your Mouth Hot, Tar in the Summertime Hot . . ."

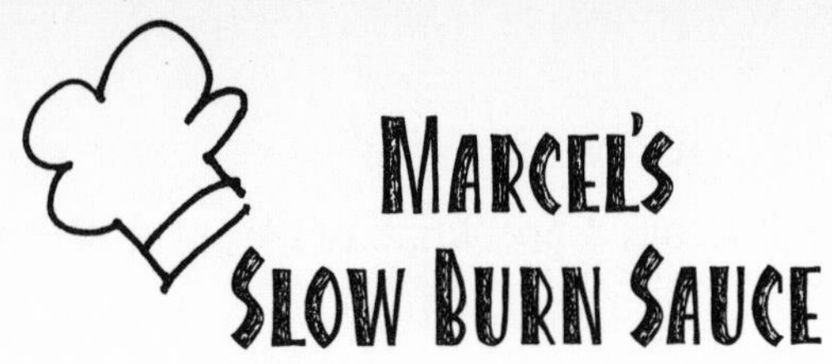

Marcel's Slow Burn Sauce

½ cup ketchup

¼ cup water

1 tablespoon brown sugar

½ tablespoon lemon juice

1 tablespoon vegetable oil

½ teaspoon cayenne pepper (or more for hotter taste)

1 tablespoon Worcestershire sauce

½ teaspoon dry mustard

¼ cup white vinegar

¼ teaspoon red pepper flakes

Combine all ingredients, bring to a boil, and simmer for about 15 minutes. Makes about 1 cup of sauce. When served, this sauce will be very hot with a slow burn that takes its time cooling down.

SHARICE

Mr. Collins' club is falling apart right in front of his eyes, and he acts like everything's fine. Hey, Mr. Collins, I want to wave my arms and say, this club is getting smaller and smaller, or haven't you noticed? Like pretty soon it's just gonna be me, Rhondell, and you, if you don't do something about it.

"You should try bringing snacks," I tell him one afternoon when nobody else shows up except me and Rhondell. "It's too long to wait from lunch until we get home and the school lunch is usually some kind of mystery meat, so half the time we don't eat it anyway. That's why most clubs have snacks."

After that, Mr. Collins starts to bring in bags of chips and popcorn. Sometimes his wife sends in something sweet like homemade chocolate chip cookies or fudge brownies — just like my mom probably would have made for me every day after school if she was around. I don't think foster non-parent #5 has made a cookie in her entire life, so I'm always trying to slip an extra one or two into my purse to eat later. (You know, pretend my mom or Gram made it for me.)

Even though foster non-parent #5 is causing me more and more problems, I don't talk about them with anybody. (LIKE, I DON'T HAVE TO SHARE EVERYTHING THAT IS MESSED UP IN MY LIFE.) I just keep on acting like my smiling, friendly old self.

At least kids start showing up for the first half of the club now, before the snacks run out. We stand around Mr. Collins' desk eating our handfuls of pretzels or potato chips, and drinking the cans of pop that Mr. Collins lets us sneak from the pop machine in the teachers' lounge, if we've got quarters — or he gives out loans if you don't.

We can usually count on Marcel and James and sometimes Terrell and Deandra being there. Ashlee doesn't come anymore now that she finally woke up and got herself a new boyfriend. Me and Rhondell are always there, of course. Mr. Collins calls us the Dynamic Duo. I don't like the name much, but I think he is trying hard (too hard, if you ask me) to act like a more friendly teacher to us, and so I let it go.

Mr. Collins says he still remembers how quiet everybody was on the first couple of days we worked together. Me and Rhondell were hunched over our desks, trying to get the pieces to fold on the lines and stay glued. Which was impossible. About halfway through the second day, I remember looking over at Rhondell and she had blobs of glue all over her desk and one of her pieces had just come unstuck again and the two of us almost fell over we were laughing so hard — like it was the funniest thing to see that orange piece she'd been holding for about twenty minutes suddenly come flying apart. That's when I knew we'd get along okay.

We're faster now, of course, but we're still not making much progress on building the giant pyramid. Like no progress. "If we were Egyptians, we would have been fired, girl" — that's what I tell Rhondell. In my opinion, most of it is Marcel's fault because he's the president of the club and he hasn't been sticking to his job. He eats the snack and leaves halfway through the club — what kinda president is that?

So, I decide it's time to tell Marcel that even though I like him a lot (not like as in LIKE, like as in — he's ALL RIGHT to be around), we need somebody new for president. If people are going to come to the club and eat snacks, they have to do the work, too, I say. And if the president can't stay for the whole time and help build, then somebody else should take over, or we're never gonna break the world record. (It's already the beginning of November.) I tell Marcel that I'm willing to volunteer to fill in for him.

But I think everybody just about choked on their pretzels when James jumped into our conversation and said he wanted to be the president instead. We were standing around Mr. Collins' desk and he came strolling over to us with that sly, sneaky grin of his and announced, "I'm already Vice Prez, right? So I'm the next in line to be Prez before any of you except Terrell, who's not here, so that means I should be the new Prez, doesn't it?"

We tried to argue with James that he hadn't done any work, so how could he possibly take over everything. But he said we were all wrong about him.

"I got more talent than any of you," he said. "Way more talent."

I couldn't believe it when Mr. Collins took his side and agreed to give James a chance. See, Mr. Collins doesn't have a clue about kids. That's his problem as a teacher. Other teachers would have seen right through James. They would have known he was trying to pick a fight with Marcel like he picks fights with everybody. James is just plain mean and I don't know why Mr. Collins couldn't see that. He just lets him butt on in and take over.

"Girl, this whole club is gonna fall apart now," I say to Rhondell as we walk down the hall after school. "You mark my words. He'll ruin the whole thing. Why would Mr. Collins *do* something like that?"

Rhondell is silent. I figure she doesn't want to tell me that it was really my fault for opening my mouth about us needing a new president. See, she's smart and I'm not. She knows when to keep her mouth shut and I don't. (WHY CAN'T I EVER LEARN THAT?)

I should have just left things the way they were. See, that was always my mistake. I was always trying to fix things — like trying to make my foster non-parents be nicer people or trying to act better so they would like me more. One time, I had a foster non-parent who used to lock up every room in her house at night because she was afraid of foster kids stealing from her, so I told her it would save her a lot of trouble if she waited to see if I was honest first instead of wasting her time locking everything up. Just suggesting that idea got me into trouble with her.

And if I had left things the way they were years and years ago, maybe I wouldn't even be living with foster non-parents in the first place, because maybe my Gram would still be alive. In fact, you could probably say that if I hadn't been born when I was, things could have been different. Maybe my mom wouldn't have gotten into that car to get away from her screaming, throwing-up baby (me). . . .

As Rhondell pushes open the front door of the school and we step outside, the first snow of the year is falling. Actually, it isn't really snow, but more like round spitballs zinging out of a freezing gray sky.

"Look at that, Sharice," Rhondell says, squinting up at the sky. But I'm so mad at myself, I just duck out into the snow without saying good-bye to Rhondell or even stopping to pull on the sweatshirt I've got in my backpack. I head down the street toward the library, letting the spitball snow sting my arms.

JAMES HARRIS III

"This pyramid's gonna have STYLE now that I'm working on it." That's what I tell the group on the first day I'm Prez. "And everybody better do exactly what I say now that I'm Prez, too. Or else you gonna get a beating from me."

"James —" Collins raises his eyebrows and gives me the teacher look, but I just pretend to ignore it. I stroll on over to the big pyramid that Marcel and Collins have been starting to glue together, and I show them how they don't have a clue about what they're building.

"Why you gluing the colors like that?" I point to a section where little purple and green and yellow tetrahedrons have been all mixed together. "You should be gluing the same colors next to each other — you know, make one big section of purple, then blue, then green" — I show them with my hands — "so the whole pyramid looks like a rainbow when it's done. That would make more sense than this mess —" I wave my arm at the pyramid.

See, I've been sitting back there in my corner drawing my comics and watching them try to build this pyramid for about a month now — and it's been cracking me up because Collins can't build and Marcel doesn't know what he's doing when it comes to art. Just look at his daddy's barbecue signs. I could have given them about fifty ideas for how to make the pyramid look better, but they didn't ask me for help, did they?

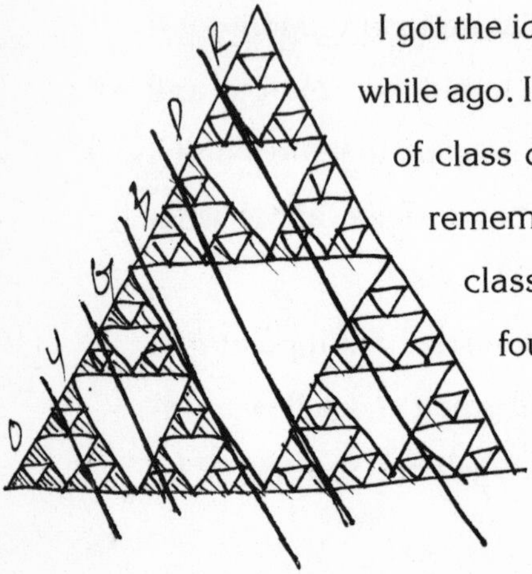

I got the idea for making the rainbow a while ago. I was sitting there in the back of class doing nothing one day and I remembered something I did in art class when I was in third or fourth grade. The art teacher, who was this cool guy who sometimes played music

in class, had us soak this heavy piece of white paper with water and then paint big stripes of different colors. The water on the paper made the colors blend together like a rainbow, and once the paper dried, we did pen and ink drawings on top of it. Mine was a bald eagle with its wings out. It was one of the best things I had ever done, and I wished I still had it, but I didn't. Who knows where all that stuff went?

But I figured if the tetrahedrons were glued together by color, they would blend into a rainbow just like that painting did. Even though nobody else looks like they agree, Collins says he likes my idea, and since the pieces are only attached at the points, it wouldn't be too hard to pull apart the glued ones and rearrange them. We haven't gotten too far on building anyway, he says — and that's the truth.

So that's how I start turning the project around. Trust me, Barbecue Face Williams never would have thought of this rainbow idea, if he was still being Prez.

Every day, I stay later and later at school, trying to keep everybody doing what they're supposed to do and not messing up the colors. Afterwards, I ride home on the bus, still trying to peel the dried glue off my fingers. Sometimes I don't get back to my uncle's apartment until way past 4:00. Come dragging in, half-starved, and find DJ and his friends hanging out in the living room, with their cans and cigarette butts lying around everywhere. Don't know why they can't pick up nothing.

"Hey, Math Boy," they call out, "go out and find us something to eat."

I'm not sure what's up with DJ these days, but he's getting a real attitude. Like he's turning into somebody I don't even know. We always used to look out for each other. When we first came to our uncle's, I remember the two of us sitting on the beds in the apartment and my brother saying that even though it was just the two of us now, I could always count on him as my family. He was serious, too, which he almost never is. Then he told me the story for the hundredth time about how he was the one who carried me up three flights of stairs by himself when I was about four or five and fell on the sidewalk outside the apartment where we lived back then and cut open my forehead.

These days, I figure he'd probably just leave me facedown on the cement.

I think that's why I keep spending more and more time with the math club. Because DJ isn't acting like anybody I'd call family — or anybody I'd even call related to me — and I'm tired of getting ordered around by him and all his friends.

Or maybe I just like being Prez and telling everybody else what to do.

RHONDELL

Quiescent. I saved that word from a poem we read in English class, and although it was used to describe caterpillars curled up in their cocoons, I liked it. I sometimes feel like a caterpillar hidden inside a cocoon, even though my Aunt Asia often tells me I need to consider changing how I am around people. Aunt Asia is my mom's younger sister. She works as a stylist at the Style R Us hair salon, and she's the kind of person who doesn't mind talking to anybody and everybody. I think she probably wishes my mom and I were more like her, but I believe that being quiet and hidden means you sometimes notice things that other people don't.

One of the things I've noticed after coming to Mr.

Collins' math club since the end of September is how people are different than they seemed at first. For instance, I've worked with Sharice since the first day, but I've learned that she is somebody who has some very odd beliefs and superstitions about things, which you don't realize until you spend time with her.

"Purple — now that's my good luck color," she always says when we're working together, folding and gluing the little tetrahedrons. "Hand me all the purple." The first time she said it, I asked her why purple was her good luck color and she gave me an annoyed look and said, "What's wrong with having a favorite color, Rhondell? Don't you?"

There are other colors she won't touch. I have to fold all of the yellow and blue, for example. "Get that paper away from me, Rhondell," she'll tell me, pushing a stack across the desk. "Those colors are bad luck for me. Real bad luck. Don't even let me look at them."

But how could certain colors be good luck or bad luck to somebody? I wonder. And why?

Marcel is different than I expected, too. Even though everybody always thinks he's good-looking and smooth, if you really watch him, you'll notice that he acts like he's nervous deep down. His brown eyes flicker around the room when he's talking to you, and his foot taps up and down, and he never sits anywhere too long — he perches like a jumpy bird on the heater, or on the teacher's desk, or on the edge of a chair.

He and Mr. Collins are usually the ones who take our little pieces as we finish them and join them together to make the larger tetrahedron. It takes steady hands to glue the pieces together point to point. Maybe because his whole body seems like it is always moving and balancing on the edge of something, Marcel is better than anybody at doing this.

But *metamorphosis* is the college word I'd pick for James. For weeks, he showed up after school and wouldn't help with any part of the project. He sat in the corner near the windows, with his big feet propped on the chair in front of him, and drew in his notebook or spun quarters on his desk until they flew across the room and hit the walls or the front of the metal heater, making all of us jump. My mom would have called him trouble with a capital *T*.

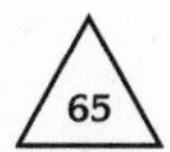

And then overnight, he turned into somebody else. Once he became president, he started bringing in his sketches of how the tetrahedron should be built and where all the colors would go. His idea was to make the pyramid look like a rainbow. Even though everybody thought he wasn't being serious at first, that he was trying to be rude to Marcel by making him take apart everything that had been done, now I can see what he meant — how the colors are supposed to blend into each other.

But sometimes I wonder if James Harris has really changed, or if underneath his pretending to care about the math club and being president is the same person. He still calls Marcel "Barbecue Face," and me "Ron Dull," no matter how many times Mr. Collins warns him about not using those names. And Sharice told me she heard that James' father is in jail for drugs and he lives with his older brother, who has been in trouble for drugs, too. They're bad news, she says.

Could someone who is bad news really change that much? For a math project? Was it a metamorphosis or something else?

SHARICE

I'm the one who comes up with the idea for the Christmas party.

Sometimes when we're working, this silence will come over the room when all you can hear is the buzzing of the fluorescent lights or the clanking of the old heating pipes, and if it goes on for too long, it kinda makes me crazy, you know?

Maybe it reminds me too much of the Washington Boulevard Library, or of sitting in the hospital room next to my Gram, when she was sick. So I'm the one who always tries to keep the conversation going. When it gets too quiet, I just pull a question out of thin air — whatever pops into my head, whatever I want to know right at that moment. Why do fluorescent lights buzz? Is the new English teacher gay? Why does it get dark so fast in the winter?

"I got a question, Mr. Collins," I'll say in the silence, making my voice a little louder on purpose, and everybody will crack up, except for Rhondell, who usually just bites her bottom lip to keep from smiling too much and looks the other way.

"Yes, Sharice," Mr. Collins will answer from somewhere on the other side of the big tetrahedron, where he's working. "What's on your mind?"

"What about a Christmas party?" I ask one afternoon.

The snow's coming down like pillowcase stuffing outside the math room windows and maybe that's what gives me the idea. Or maybe it's the Christmas music I've been listening to every day in the mall, that won't get out of my head now. ("Have a holly jolly Christmas" . . . you know, what does that really mean anyway???)

"Don't you think having a Christmas party's a good idea, Rhondell?" I kick her chair leg with my foot, trying to get her to agree. Rhondell glances around in her usual way before she says sure in a non-sure voice.

Marcel jumps in. "I can bring all the food," he tells us. "Whatever you want. Ribs. Wings. Sandwiches. My daddy's got the best barbecue in the whole state of Ohio —"

"Yeah, right," James snorts, even though everybody pretends not to hear him.

"Sure, okay, why not?" Mr. Collins answers, breaking into a big smile (which you don't see very often from him in class). "Let's have a Christmas party."

So we start planning who will bring what — the food, the dessert, the decorations, the plastic plates and cups, the drinks, the music. James is the only one who doesn't offer to bring anything, because he says he isn't coming. We try to convince him that the president has to be there, but he says a Prez doesn't have to do anything he doesn't want to do. A Prez has got better ways to spend his time than going to girlie Christmas parties, he says.

The rest of the day, I can't keep my mind from thinking about the party. I plan about a hundred different ones in my mind. The last real party I remember being at was one that my Gram had for me when I was six or seven. She brought home a cake from the grocery store. It was a Snoopy cake because I loved Snoopy back then, and she gave me the silver necklace with the little cross that I still have (way too small to wear now), and some of the kids from her church came.

That night, as I'm riding around and around on the city bus waiting for Jolynn to get home, I spend so much time thinking about the party that I almost forget to get off the bus when it passes by our stop for the fifth time at about eight o'clock, and I have to jump up and tell the bus driver to let me off at the next stop. Walking back to Jolynn's house in the slushy snow and the pitch-black winter darkness, I've still got "Holly Jolly Christmas" playing in my head.

MARCEL

I wait until Willy Q's in a good mood to tell him about the Christmas party. The Lots-of-Orders-Making-Us-Lots-of-Money good mood. This time of year, that's Friday and Saturday nights. I wait until after he's counted up our money and he's cleaning up the kitchen.

"My class is having a Christmas party after school next week," I say real smooth. Don't mention a word about the math club being the reason.

Willy Q doesn't look up. "What's that got to do with me?" he says. Like he knows exactly what I'm gonna ask next.

Maybe I shoulda waited for the Saturday good mood.

“They were wondering if Willy Q’s Barbecue could send over something. Just for the party. Something little to try.”

“Ain’t a charity,” Willy Q answers, scrubbing the pans harder.

I give Willy Q my best Turn-on-the-Charm-and-Big-Pearly-Whites smile. “They heard we got the best barbecue in the whole city,” I say.

“We does.” Willy Q shrugs. “So what?”

The Slow Burn Sauce starts bubbling inside me again. I think about answering, so what would you do if I told you I ain’t working for you anymore? Or what if nobody ordered your tasteless old barbecue — not on Friday night or Saturday night or any other night?

Instead I say, “So maybe we should show them we do.”

Willy Q crosses his arms and turns toward me. “Bet they haven’t tried some of our new barbecue wings, now have they? Or some of that good Southern cornbread I’ve been making?”

I don’t tell Willy Q that his cornbread ain’t all that good. Cannonball Cornbread, that’s what I call it. Too heavy. Shoot it out of a cannon and a chunk of

Willy Q's cornbread could wipe out half the city of Cleveland.

Willy Q reaches for one of the order pads. "How much food you need and when?"

Even though I tell Willy Q that the party's only for about five or six people, he says he'll go ahead and send food for ten. When the math club sees all the food Marcel the Magnificent is lugging to the party, they ain't gonna believe their eyes. Cornbread. Wings. Short ribs. Cake —

"Don't want folks to think we're stingy," Willy Q insists.

Take my advice. Don't try to figure out Willy Q. Just grab what he gives you and run. That's what I do.

Willy Q's Cannonball Cornbread

1¼ cups flour

¾ cup yellow cornmeal

2 tablespoons sugar

½ teaspoon salt

1 tablespoon baking powder

½ teaspoon dry mustard

dash of nutmeg

1 cup milk

1 egg, beaten

¼ cup margarine, melted

¼ cup onion, finely chopped

1 cup canned white shoepeg corn, drained

Preheat oven to 425 degrees. Grease 9-inch square pan. In medium-sized bowl, combine flour, cornmeal, sugar, salt, baking powder, dry mustard, and nutmeg. Mix well. Stir in milk, egg, and melted margarine. Lightly mix in onion and corn. Spoon batter into greased pan. Bake at 425 degrees for 20 to 25 minutes or until toothpick inserted in center comes out clean. Serve warm. Cover and refrigerate leftovers. Trust me, there will be a lot.

JAMES HARRIS III

Maybe I'll come to the party and maybe I won't. I don't make my decision until I'm walking past the classroom at the end of the day, already wearing my coat to leave. I shove my hands in my coat pockets and slow way down to listen to what's happening before I get to the doorway. I ain't staying to sing with any karaoke machine or play any stupid party games, if that's what's going on. That ain't me.

But the only thing I can hear coming out of the room is whining country music. I stick my head in the doorway just to call out, "Who's listening to that sicko country music?" And then Collins comes over wearing a party hat that has a turtle on it. He looks like a complete fool. The hat says HAPPY 10TH BIRTHDAY, even though this is a Christmas party and Collins isn't ten. "Come in and join us, James." He waves his arm at me.

"Ain't listening to that music," I answer, shoving my hands deeper in my coat pockets and leaning against the doorway, staying right where I am.

"Well then, find some music you like, James," Collins answers in the same happy white voice, pointing toward the boom box. "Just come in and have something to eat." Then he heads back over to the table where the food is set up.

If it was up to me, I'd rather sit on the other side of the room and work on the project. We're only about halfway to the top, and we got a bunch of blue pieces waiting to be glued together. But working on the tetrahedron doesn't seem to matter to nobody but me. Sharice and Rhondell are laughing themselves silly and taping Christmas streamers everywhere — stringing them around Collins' desk and across the top of the chalkboard. Marcel and Collins are leaning against the heater, stuffing their faces with barbecue. Terrell and Deandra squeeze past me, carrying two heaping plates of food in front of them. "Sorry we can't stay.

Gotta go catch the bus." Terrell waves to Barbecue Face. "Thanks for all the good food, man."

Still not making up my mind about staying, I walk over and check out what's left to eat. Marcel pushes a plastic plate into my hands as if I'm standing at his daddy's barbecue window or something. "Try some of our wings." He buzzes around me like a fly that needs swatting.

"And the ribs." He points. "If you like hot sauce, try the ribs. Tar in the Summertime Hot, that's what me and Willy Q call them —"

I give Marcel a hard stare. "Get outta my face, fool. I can pick out my own food."

But I gotta admit that after all the fast food and pizzas and boxes of cereal we eat at my uncle's, maybe I forgot how good real food tastes. I take four big pieces of chicken. Ribs. Wings. Pile them on my plate like a barbecue mountain. When I pick up the ribs with my fingers, I can feel my fingertips burning, I swear. And by the time I've eaten about half the food on my plate, my whole body is breathing heat. I have to open my mouth to let out the smoke.

"Stuff's pretty good, man," I hear myself saying to Marcel.

Maybe it's all the food, or Collins getting rid of the country music on the boom box and playing some rap, but I stay longer than I planned. I been to worse parties; let's just say that. We stand around the food table, talking about all kinds of things. Sports. Music. Movies. Collins is up-to-date on his movies, even though he doesn't have a clue about basketball. Doesn't even know who plays center for Cleveland. How could you not know that?

But when Sharice starts running her mouth about how our math club is like its own little family, I have to get up and leave. We're all sitting around eating Marcel's chocolate cake when Sharice looks up. "We're kinda like a little family, aren't we?" she says, smiling and licking frosting off her fork. "Mr. Collins is like the head of the family. And the four of us — me, Rhondell, Marcel, and James — are like the kids. And Terrell and Deandra are the second or third cousins who show up out of the blue every once in a while, right?"

Makes my skin crawl to listen to her. Who would

picture our math club as a family? What's this girl thinking? That's what goes through my mind.

"You crazy," I say, pulling my coat off the back of the chair and putting it on, because I'm not sticking around any longer for this kind of talk. "Gotta get going," I say. "Bye." And then I'm out the door.

I sprint past all the empty classrooms, locked up for the night. The only sound you can hear is my shoes slapping on the tiles. In my mind, I draw a picture of big footprints disappearing over a hill like they show in cartoons. The farther away I get from Sharice's idea of a Christmas party, the better I feel.

SHARICE

After James leaves, nobody speaks at first. I'm feeling real embarrassed for saying what I did (WHY DON'T I EVER LEARN?), but then Marcel jumps up and says, "Maybe the Prez don't want to be family with us, but here's the real question — who wants to be family with him?" And that makes everybody start laughing. Marcel reaches for the plastic cake knife and twirls it between his fingers. "Anybody want more cake to eat, because I do. . . ."

While we're stuffing ourselves with second pieces of cake, I ask Mr. Collins to tell us more about his family. "How old are your kids?" I ask him, through a mouthful of cake.

He takes out his wallet and shows us their pictures.

“Here’s Emma.” He points to a picture of a little girl with curly blond hair and a round pie face. “And that’s Max,” he says. The boy in the next photograph is older, maybe ten or eleven, and has Mr. Collins’ thin face, brown hair, and serious look, no doubt about it.

“Is he good in math?”

“Terrible.” Mr. Collins smiles and shakes his head. “He’s like his mother, more into music and computers and that sort of thing.”

“And what was that first picture in your wallet?” I ask.

Rhondell gives me one of her stop-being-so-nosy looks. But I can’t keep from being curious about people, you know. As Mr. Collins was turning to his kids’ pictures, I couldn’t help seeing the black-and-white picture of somebody’s face in the front. All I wanted to know was who it was.

Before Mr. Collins turns back to the picture in his wallet, I hear him take a deep breath and let it out slowly (like maybe I shouldn’t have asked to see any more). But then he holds up the picture and everybody leans closer to get a look at it. It’s a small photograph of a teenager in a military uniform. His face is serious, but he's good-looking, you can tell.

"That's my brother Jerry," Mr. Collins continues in a quiet voice. "He was a soldier in Vietnam." And just the way he says that sentence makes your stomach suddenly turn over and you don't even have to ask the question to know that his brother is dead.

"He doesn't look that old," I say, feeling uncomfortable. "How old was he in that picture?"

Mr. Collins closes up the photographs carefully and puts his wallet away. "Nineteen," he answers in a soft voice. "Old enough to die in Vietnam. At least the people who sent him to war thought he was."

"My daddy is a Vietnam vet," Marcel adds, acting prouder than he should, I think, especially after somebody has told you that their brother died in the same war.

But Mr. Collins just replies, "Well then, you've heard a lot about it."

"Willy Q wants me to go into the military just like him." Marcel shakes his head. "Ain't doing that, though. No way. I'm gonna be a movie star. Or a comedian."

I try to change the conversation to something else. I pull another question out of the air. "Did you always want to be a math teacher?" I ask Mr. Collins.

He stands up and brushes the cake crumbs off his shirt. "After my brother died, I did," he replies.

When Marcel asks him why, Mr. Collins says it was because math had answers when life didn't. "In math you can solve problems and find solutions," he explains. "There are rules and patterns. Like the tetrahedron." Mr. Collins points in the direction of our half-finished one. "But when your older brother dies in a war and you're only twelve years old, there aren't any solutions to find. Somebody dying when he's nineteen years old on May fourteenth in 1969 on a hill called 937 in South Vietnam — those numbers in life don't have answers, they don't make sense, no matter how hard you try to understand them."

There's a long, uneasy silence after he finishes talking until Marcel jumps up nervously and shouts, "Why we talking about this serious stuff, all of a sudden? Making me DE-pressed. I thought this was a CHRISTMAS party!"

"Yes, you're right, it is." Mr. Collins puts on a big smile and walks over to the boom box. "Let's get some Christmas music on and talk about something else."

But later, when we're loading up Mr. Collins' car with leftover food and party stuff, I can't keep my voice from starting to tell him the story of my mom and Gram. (Maybe Marcel doesn't understand what he meant, but I do.)

"I lost my mom when she was nineteen, too," I say as we're walking down the hallway and the other two are way back of us. "So I know what you mean about math and life."

Then, before I can stop it, I hear my voice pouring out the whole story. How my mom went out riding in a shiny blue sports car the night she died. How I'd been sick and colicky, my Gram said, and I'd spent two solid days and nights screaming and crying until nobody wanted me anymore, least of all my mom, who was still young and not ready for a baby at all, especially not wrinkly-faced, screaming me. "Just going out for a drive with some friends and getting something to eat," she told my Gram. "I'll be home before eight."

But she never came home. The cops knocked on Gram's door about nine that night and asked if she had a daughter who had gone out riding with two friends in a dark blue car. When Gram said yes, they told her that the car had been racing down the road, lost control, hit a pole, and all of them were killed. All three people. Every time Gram told this story, I always blamed my mom's death on the blue car. I don't know why. (Maybe it was easier to hate a car than people.)

I tell Mr. Collins that Gram raised me until her heart began to act up. That was the phrase she always used — "act up." It started with trouble catching her breath. I remember how I would fly up the dark wooden steps in her house, taking them two at a time, and I'd stand at the top waiting and she would go up three or four steps and have to stop to rest. "You and your young legs," she would say, trying to smile in between coughing and fanning her face with her hand. "Not sure I can make it all the way up there to tuck you into bed tonight, honey pie."

And then, it wasn't long before she couldn't even go up the steps. She slept on the couch in the living room wrapped in the bright-colored crocheted afghans she liked to make, and I was the only one who lived in the upstairs rooms. When I was seven years old, she had to be put in a hospital, and she died in that same hospital just about a month later.

But I leave out the other part of the story — which is the fact that I was the one who called for the ambulance that took her to the hospital in the first place. If I hadn't done that, maybe everything would have just continued on like always — me running around the upstairs rooms, playing magic castle and building forts, and Gram sleeping under her crocheted quilts downstairs.

I also don't mention the bouquet of yellow flowers either. When the nurse sat down next to me in the waiting room one morning and told me that Gram had left for heaven during the night, I was holding a bouquet of yellow daisy flowers I had planned on giving to her that day. I remember staring at those yellow flowers and hating them with all my might, because it seemed to me those flowers must have known Gram was gone and just let me go ahead and buy them anyway.

Yellow and blue had been my bad luck colors ever since.

After the whole story pours out of me like a river that can't be stopped, I feel afraid right away. I had never told anybody about my Gram and my mom before. (What is my problem?) But Mr. Collins seems to understand some of what I'm saying, I think. "That's a hard way to go through life, I know, Sharice," he says, quickly patting one hand on my shoulder like an uncomfortable father. "I felt the same way about my brother, very much the same way. It isn't easy — still isn't easy."

I know this sounds like a strange Christmas party, but to tell you the truth, it was a really good time. When I walked down the street to the bus stop after the party was over, I felt lighter. My mind was full of Christmas songs, and chocolate cake, and red and green streamers. And for the first time I had told somebody the story of my mom and Gram, and I felt better about that, too.

(I should have known that the feeling wouldn't last long.)

MARCEL

Nobody eats barbecue in January. That's the truth.

It's teeth-chattering, spit-freezing weather. Me and Willy Q huddle in the back room. Try not to freeze to death from cold and boredom. Parking lot covered in about a foot of snow. Order window jammed shut. If anybody comes up to order — which almost nobody does — I gotta put on my coat, push my shoulder into the side door to get it to open against the snowdrifts, go around the building, and take their order. I always give them my What-Kind-of-Crazy-Person-Would-Want-Barbecue-When-It's-Ten-Below look.

You poor kid, they usually say. Does your boss make you come out here and take orders without any hat or gloves? Yep, I always nod, while my fingers turn into blue icicles writing down their order. Maybe they won't come back again, I figure. Child abuse, you know.

Willy Q spends most of the day hunched over on his stool, squinting at the little black-and-white TV on the counter. He watches all the talk shows and worries about how much money we aren't making. "Pack your bags, Marcel," he'll tell me about every half hour. "I hear them coming to evict us." Worst month in all the years he's been doing business, he says.

Always been the worst month. Every January. Don't say that to Willy Q, though. Ever since that conversation in math club about Mr. Collins' brother dying in Vietnam, I've been trying to be nicer around him. That conversation in math club got me thinking: No Willy Q. No me.

Maybe I'm trying to show him I'm glad he kept himself alive in Vietnam, so I could be alive, too. I don't know.

"How about making up a new sauce?" I say on one no-customer afternoon.

Willy Q's eyes flicker from the TV to me. "What's wrong with the sauces we got?"

I shrug my shoulders. "Just trying to think of something new," I tell him.

Willy Q snorts. "We don't need new, we need sales."

He goes back to watching TV and I go back to doing a half-finished crossword from an old newspaper I found sitting on top of the meat freezer.

But it isn't long before Willy Q turns toward me again. "What kinda sauce were you thinking of?"

I tell him we need a winter flavor. Nobody wants Tar in the Summertime in January. Can't even see tar. Or blacktop. Or anything but snow in January.

Willy Q snaps his fingers. "Snow in January Sauce. That's it."

The rest of the afternoon, me and Willy Q make a mess of the back kitchen, trying to cook up a winter barbecue sauce that's white. We pull out just about every bowl in the place and mix together all kinds of crazy ingredients. Willy Q starts pulling stuff off the shelves and out of the refrigerator, left and right. Mayonnaise. White vinegar. Milk. Cream of tartar. Even a handful of snow.

Man, that's awful, we laugh and choke and cough,

trying a taste of everything. A few times we nearly fall over, laughing so hard. When I spit tartar and mayo sauce all over my shirt, Willy Q has to stop for air and wipe the tears out of his eyes.

We never do get a good Snow in January Sauce made. But like Willy Q says, it don't matter. Least it keeps us from freezing to death. Or going crazy.

RHONDELL

Maybe I notice things about Sharice that no one else sees. Nobody else seems to realize how different she is after coming back from Christmas vacation. Before vacation, she asked unstoppable questions and talked more than anybody else except my Aunt Asia. She organized the Christmas party, and we did all the decorating together. But after coming back, she is mostly silent and lost somewhere inside herself. She is like one of the small tetrahedrons after they are folded up and glued together. *Withdrawn* is the college word I'd use for her.

I wonder if there is something wrong in her family. Maybe somebody who has let the devil take hold, as my mom says about families who fall into drinking or drugs. But then I realize that even though I've told her all about my mom and how she is a religious person who directs the Sanctuary Baptist Church choir on Sundays, and I've talked about my dad who left when I was two years old, and I've even told her about my Aunt Asia (who wears gold nail polish and has different hair every time you see her), Sharice has kept herself a mystery the entire time.

I don't even know what kind of family Sharice has. I can't remember whether she ever talked about a mom or a dad or even other brothers and sisters. In fact, the only thing I know about her family is the street where they live — Fifteenth Street, because she takes the number 209 bus with me sometimes and I see her turn the corner there when she gets off at the stop.

"Is there anything bothering you?" I try to ask her one afternoon at math club when we are sitting down to work. The words come out of my mouth nervously.

"No. Why?" she answers, and I can't think of what to reply except to say that she seems different all of a sudden. Her eyes flash me a look of suspicion. "What's wrong with different?" she asks.

A day or so later, while we are riding on the school bus, I try to find out more about her family. I choose a question carefully and ask it while I'm talking about my mom's job at the downtown hospital and all of the hours she works. "Where does your mom work?" I inquire, as if it is just an ordinary question. But Sharice turns her face toward the bus window and tells me that she doesn't like talking about her mom.

There are other things I notice, too, and I feel embarrassed for noticing them — as if I'm being prying, and I don't think that's a good word to be. But I can't help noticing how Sharice's face is too ashy-looking and dry and her eyes are shadowy and tired, as if she's staying up way too late. Her hair isn't kept up the way it used to be, either. It straggles out of its twists in fuzzy wisps that she's always reaching up and trying to smooth down with her hands.

In math club, she acts strangely now whenever we are ready to leave. After we walk outside, she is always forgetting something in the building and asking Mr. Collins if she can run back to get it — her purse, her homework, her keys, her gloves. . . . "Don't wait for me," she'll tell us.

Each time, Mr. Collins sighs and shakes his head. "You need to be more organized, Sharice. I shouldn't let you back in the building if I'm not there." But she'll always duck inside the door fast, before he can say any more. "I'll remember next time," she always promises. Only she never does.

Sometimes I have the feeling that Sharice is hiding more secrets than any of us really knows.

MR. COLLINS

An important fact to remember about tetrahedrons:

Although the large tetrahedron appears strong and stable, it should be noted that its pieces are joined together only at the smallest of points. The edges and faces remain largely separate and unconnected.

JAMES HARRIS III

My brother's friends start in on me the minute I walk through the door one afternoon. I check out the living room but there's no sign of my brother DJ. Course that's nothing unusual with DJ these days. Three of his friends — Anthony, Markese, and Leon — lounge on the floor with CDs and burger wrappers scattered all around them.

"Where you been, little brother? You late," Markese says, grinning and looking at me with his sharp switchblade eyes. He is half-crazy on drugs most of the time. You don't mess with Markese because you never know.

"Nowhere, man," I answer, trying to slip past them into the kitchen, without looking like I'm slipping past.

Anthony throws a wadded-up hamburger wrapper at my back. "Hey, you still working on that math thing with Collins? That why you late all the time?"

"Why?" I answer, cutting my eyes back at him.

Another burger wrapper nails my back. "Hey, just asking. Chill."

But the switchblade eyes are curious now. Markese sits up and leans back against the couch. He folds his arms across his chest. "What math thing?" he says in a slow voice.

I can feel my stomach tighten up exactly like it does before a fight or when you think somebody is about to come after you. Last thing I want to be doing is talking about a school math project with Markese.

"Nothing," I answer, trying to duck out.

But Anthony, who's in eighth grade at Washington because he flunked a year, jumps in and gives Markese all the details. He tells him how Collins' classroom is building something that looks like a pyramid. "It's different colors, and they're trying to break some world record, that's what I heard," he says.

Markese's eyes slide over to me. "That true about

the pyramid?" he asks, with a curious smile spreading across his face.

I shrug. "Maybe. Who knows?"

Markese's eyes sharpen. "Can anybody go and see it?"

"Yeah, whatever . . . ," I answer, trying to say as little as I can, but still saying too much, I feel like. Like I said before, you don't want to mess with Markese.

"Hey, if you wanna see it sometime, I'll get you into the school." Anthony grins, looking over at Markese. "You know me. I'm up for anything —"

Even after I go into the kitchen, the three of them keep on talking and laughing behind me. The warning feeling stays in the pit of my stomach. I pour a big bowl of cereal that I don't feel like eating and tuck a can of Pepsi under my arm.

In the room that me and DJ share, I shut the door, put on my headphones, and turn up the music as loud as it will go. Stretching out across my bed, I smack open one of my notebooks and start drawing whatever comes into my head. I do a whole page of clenched fists — ones that are getting ready to slam into somebody's face if they get too close. I'm good at drawing hands. Half of my notebooks are filled with them. But no matter how many fists I draw slamming into windows and walls and faces, I still can't get rid of the bad feeling I have about Markese.

SHARICE

I get tired of always finding excuses for staying later, so finally I ask Mr. Collins if I can work extra on the tetrahedron, after the math club leaves. I make up a big story and tell him how my foster mom's hours at work have suddenly changed and nobody's home until five or six. "My neighborhood's real dangerous with break-ins and all," I say. "It's safer here."

The truth is that Jolynn isn't coming home until midnight or later some nights because she's out with her new man. "Better stay with some of your school friends tonight, Sharice," she'll holler from the bathroom while she's doing her hair in the morning. "I'll be out late again."

"I'll just come home when you get back," I always insist.

"It'll be awfully late, honey," she'll answer. "Sure you don't want to stay overnight at your friend's house if you're already there?"

What friend's house?

I don't know what Jolynn thinks I'm supposed to do. I have friends at school, but not the kind I want knowing all my business. For instance, what would Rhondell think if I turned to her and said, "Girl, would your mom mind if I stayed over your house this week because foster non-parent #5 isn't coming home?" So I try to stay at school as late as I can, and then I usually find another place to sit for the rest of the time.

Mr. Collins says if I'm going to stay later, I have to be out of the building when the basketball team leaves at six. And it's my responsibility (he stretches out this word to emphasize how important it is) to turn off the lights and pull the classroom door shut when I do. "Twist the knob and make sure it's locked." Mr. Collins shows me.

But I never leave anywhere close to six o'clock.

Usually it's seven or eight. A few times, even nine o'clock. The custodians don't come upstairs to clean until way after eight. I know because I asked one of them, "What time do you get to cleaning the third floor?"

The old custodian, Mr. Joe, covered his mouth with his hand and whispered, "Girl, with all there is to do in the place, sometimes we don't ever get up to the third floor." (Which you could tell by looking around, I guess. Same chocolate bar wrapper stuck in the same water fountain for a week sometimes.)

I've got my own little way of doing things, once everybody in math club leaves. I turn off the first two rows of lights and ease the door shut. Mr. Collins' door has a shade, so I pull that down, too. No one can tell I'm sitting inside the room because I've stood in the hallway and checked.

After that, I take my supper out of my backpack and set it neatly on a white paper napkin as if I'm sitting in a fancy restaurant. Usually supper is half of whatever I had for lunch (a squashed cheese sandwich, or tater tots wrapped up in a napkin — something like that), a soda pop, and a candy bar from the vending

machine. I prop my feet up on one of the desk chairs and eat slowly to make it last.

After I'm done with dinner, I try to work on my homework a little to keep my Gram happy in heaven (because you know she's probably watching). Although there are always some nights when I can't make myself care, and I take out my homework, look at it, and slide it back in my bag without doing a thing.

After that, I fold the little tetrahedrons and listen to music on my headset the rest of the time. It's the only part of the day I like, to tell you the truth. When I'm sitting by myself in the math room and my fingers are flying (folding, gluing, folding, gluing) and music is playing in my ears, I can't worry about all of the things that are going wrong in my life, so maybe that's why I like it.

The tetrahedron is getting closer to the top every day — mainly with all my extra work. We're only a few thousand pieces away from finishing. Everybody's always asking me how I get so many done, and I have to bite my tongue to keep from telling them if they were at school until eight or nine, they'd get a lot done, too.

I like looking at the big tetrahedron at night when nobody's around. I walk around it, squinting at the colors and spaces from different angles, fixing places that have come unstuck here and there. At night, the colors seem to glow more than they do during the day — shimmering purple, red, orange, yellow — one color blending into the next, like James said they would.

Sometimes I turn out all the lights and perch on the top of the heater, tilting my head from one side to the other, studying the pyramid. With the streetlights shining through the iced-up classroom windows behind it, the tetrahedron changes from paper triangles into something that looks more like lace. It reminds me of the point of a big snowflake, the way it looks so delicate and fragile in the darkness.

If I stare at it long enough, sometimes I can kinda pull myself inside that tetrahedron snowflake, and imagine all the starry edges and points floating in the air around me. I can drift through the night sky just like one of the tumbling snowflakes outside, thinking about my mom and my Gram who died, and everything I don't let myself think about during the day usually. (Good thoughts, not bad ones.)

And maybe that's what happened on the last night of January when I drifted out of the room without remembering what Mr. Collins told me to never forget. I left for home at about seven o'clock, and I never turned back to check the door.

MR. COLLINS

In random number sequences, it is impossible to predict the number that will come next. There is no pattern. What happened to my students' math project was random and patternless in the same way. It was early on a Wednesday morning when Joe Hill, our school custodian, stopped me at my classroom door. He told me that something had happened during the night. That someone had broken into the math room and vandalized our project. Nothing of the tetrahedron — not a single piece, he said softly — was left standing.

RHONDELL

There are no words — college words or any words — for what I feel when I see the empty space where the rainbow tetrahedron used to be, and look at the crumpled pieces of paper covering the entire floor, and remember how hard we worked to make those pieces every afternoon for months. It is as if everything shrivels up inside me, like a caterpillar turning to dust inside its cocoon. I stand in the middle of the room, still holding on to my books, trying to understand how it could be gone.

Next to me, Sharice is silent. Even Marcel, who is always teasing and joking, has a frozen look on his face.

Mr. Collins tries to talk to us about what happened. "I know all of us worked hard on this project and this is very difficult —" His voice catches in his throat and he has to pause. "Very difficult to understand . . ."

He looks around the room helplessly. Everything is covered with shreds of colored paper. Even some of the textbooks have been torn apart and trampled. "I don't know why somebody would do this. . . . I just can't explain why anybody would be so cruel as to come in and wreck a project like this, when all of us were just trying . . . to do something good."

James can't handle hearing any more than that. Out of the corner of my eye, I see him suddenly turn while Mr. Collins is talking, pick up one of the desks, and slam it into the others. Another desk tips over and crashes to the floor, making us all jump. Then, without a word, he runs out of the room, punching his fists into the lockers, all the way down the hall.

Mr. Collins tries calling out for him to stop. He goes into the hall and tries to order him to come back, so we can sit down together and talk over our feelings and figure out what to do. Doors all along the hallway open as teachers and kids look out to see what is happening — but nothing stops James. Even the security guard in the hallway doesn't dare to get in the way of James' out-of-control self.

As James' punches echo down the hall, Sharice crouches down to the floor and begins to carefully gather up the torn pieces. I watch as she scoops up handfuls of purple and yellow and green pieces and puts them into her backpack. What is she thinking? I wonder.

"Why you doing that, Sharice?" Marcel snaps. "Just forget it. Just throw all those pieces out." He moves toward the door, kicking at the piles of torn paper. "Just throw the whole thing out."

Tears are flowing down her cheeks and her nose is running, but Sharice just keeps wiping her nose on her sleeve and scooping up piles of paper and dumping them into her backpack, as if she believes she will be able to put them back together.

I pick up a handful and try to convince her it won't work. Maybe Mr. Collins will start the project over again next year, I tell her, and you and I and Marcel can work on it again. But she just shakes her head and orders me to get away from her. "Leave me alone, Rhondell," she says. "You don't know anything about what happened."

Mr. Collins can't get her to listen either.

"I'm gonna rebuild it," she tells him stubbornly. She just keeps repeating the same four words — I'm gonna rebuild it. She doesn't stop until her whole backpack is full of colored paper. Then she zips it closed and slips it over her shoulder. "I'm going back to my English class now," she tells Mr. Collins, even though I don't think she does, because we have English class together at the other end of the hall, and I hear her feet go down the steps instead.

After Marcel and Sharice leave, I help Mr. Collins and the custodian sweep up the rest of the room. We fill up four garbage bags of dreams.

SHARICE

Sitting on the back steps of Jolynn's house, leaning against the screen door, I watch the snow fall like torn paper out of the gray sky. The snowflakes land on the legs of my jeans and melt, land and melt, until the tops of my jeans are soaked clear through, and I don't care at all.

Nobody else knows what I did, but I do. I'm the reason our project was torn to pieces. I'm the one who was in the math room when I wasn't supposed to be there, and I'm the one who didn't lock the door. And if you want to go way back again, I'm the reason why my mom died in a car crash and I'm the reason why my Gram went to the hospital and died, too.

Rhondell was right. Nothing's gonna fix those

torn pieces, you know. Not all the glue in the world. I pull out a handful from my backpack and look at all the colors jumbled up together. I think about how close we were to finishing. Maybe only two or three weeks or so. I remember how that tetrahedron looked in the darkness. Just like lace and all. A big tower of lace.

Opening my fingers, I let the handful of paper scatter onto the snow. Little flecks of red, blue, green, and purple fall around my feet. I reach down and pick out a crumpled lavender piece that lands near my shoe. Opening it up and smoothing it on my knee, I can still see the triangle shapes we folded over and over.

The purple paper always reminded me of my mom's dress. In my bedroom upstairs in Jolynn's house, I keep a small silver-framed photograph of my mom wearing a purple dress. It's a little out of focus, but you can still see it's a nice summer dress with thin straps over the shoulders. My mom was a pretty woman — stick-thin, but pretty, Gram always said. The picture was taken at the Methodist church picnic, and it's the last one I have of her. She's wearing dark sunglasses and sitting between Gram and one of Gram's old friends, with her chin resting on her hand, like she's looking at something far away. I'm in a baby carrier half in and half out of the picture.

I watch the snowflakes fall on the lavender paper, watch it melt into a piece of soft lavender fabric in my hand, just like my mom's summer dress. I curl my bare fingers around that fabric, holding on.

It's snowing heavier now, and everything in Jolynn's backyard is getting covered — the empty doghouse, the crab apple tree, and the rusty refrigerator leaning against the garage. Won't be long before the snow covers me up, too.

Closing my eyes, I lean back against the door of Jolynn's house. I'm not going anywhere — not to the bus station, or the library, or the school. Not anymore.

AUNT ASIA

Rhondell's mom is my sister, but we are about as alike as hot peppers and sweet potatoes, or lemons and honey — if you know what I mean. Don't get me wrong, I love my sister to death, but we are not the same people. She walks around with the weight of the world on her shoulders, and probably the rest of the planets, too. I just take things as they come. Easier that way, you know?

Anyway, I'm just finishing up my last client at the Style R Us salon — old Mrs. Jenkins, who has hair as coarse and dry as a wire brush — when Rhondell calls. Now, since my sister works at the downtown hospital and taking care of sick folks isn't as simple as rescheduling haircuts, I've always been kinda like a second mom to Rhondell. If she needs to be picked up from school or gets locked out of her house — which Rhondell almost never does, of course, being as smart as she is — she's supposed to call me at the salon. "You just give me a ring, honey," I'm always telling her. "Any time of day. It don't matter. Poor folks' hair can wait, but my only living niece can't."

I'm always pestering her to do something with her hair whenever she calls, too. Rhondell's plain-looking, but that doesn't mean something can't be done to plain. Come on in and let me fix up your hair for you, I try and beg her. We could put it up, or press and curl it — whatever you want, hon. Everybody needs a new look.

But like mother, like daughter, I guess. Rhondell's been wearing the same pulled-back, head-hugging hair as long as I've known her. Still, hope springs eternal. I pick up the phone, thinking maybe this time, maybe she's gonna start growing up and caring about her looks.

"What can I help you with today, Miz Rhondell?" I say, balancing the phone on my shoulder and holding up one finger to tell Mrs. Jenkins to wait just one minute.

"Are you busy?" Rhondell asks in a soft, serious voice, just like her mother. "If you're busy, Aunt Asia, I can call back some other time."

I squint out the salon window at the falling snow. "You stuck at school? Once I'm done with Mrs. Jenkins, I can come on up there and give you a ride home, hon. You don't need to be wandering around catching cold in this kind of weather."

But Rhondell says no, she doesn't need a ride, she's calling for advice about a friend of hers. I almost drop the phone, to tell you the truth, because in all the years I've known Rhondell, she has never once called me about any friends, at least none that I can recall. Although I've asked her about friends so many times, I finally gave up and decided to save my breath.

I told my sister that Rhondell's shyness was something she should look into, and my sister said she had enough to do, and shyness was better than some things she could name. Like mother, like daughter, again.

"What kinda advice you looking for, hon?" I say, trying not to sound too pleased at being asked, while giving Mrs. Jenkins another glance.

"Something happened at school today, to a project we were working on . . . ," Rhondell says. The story comes out slowly, with a lot of hesitations and pauses, and I don't follow a lot of it, but I don't push her for more.

"A girl who works with me left the school right after it happened," Rhondell continues. "But even before this, there was something wrong with her, I think. I don't know exactly what, but I was wondering, well —," her voice hesitates, "maybe what to do now."

This is more words than Rhondell ever says usually, so I'm jumping for joy inside my head at the same time that I'm trying to decide what to answer.

I tell Rhondell that if it was me, and if the girl was my friend, I would give her a call first. "I had lots of girlfriends in school, Rhondell — and we called each other all the time. About big things, little things. We were always there for each other, you know what I mean?"

But, knowing Rhondell like I do, it doesn't surprise me at all when she says she doesn't even have the girl's phone number.

"Where's she live? Near your street?" I ask. "Maybe you could try stopping by her house. You know, just go on over and ask how she's doing."

Rhondell says she thinks the girl lives on Fifteenth Street, but she doesn't feel right stopping by. "I'll just wait until she comes back to school to talk to her. Thanks, Aunt Asia. I'm sorry for bothering you at work —"

"Hold on now —," I call out. Old Mrs. Jenkins reaches up and pats the uncombed side of her wet hair, giving me a tight-lipped, impatient look. "After I finish with Miz Jenkins here, I'll drive you over to the girl's house to check on her; how about that?" I say.

"No, that's all right —"

"I'll come around about five. No trouble at all. Drive right past Fifteenth on my way home. Gotta go now, hon, see you soon."

Sometimes the hot peppers have to tell the slow sweet potatoes what to do, I tell myself as I hang

up the phone. If somebody doesn't start pushing Rhondell, she's never gonna have a soul in this world except me and her mom, and what a pair we are, you know what I mean?

Next thing I'm gonna insist on changing is her hair.

RHONDELL

Even though it is snowing hard enough to be a blizzard and Aunt Asia is wearing heels and a dress, she still insists on driving me down Fifteenth Street to find Sharice's house. I watch her gold-painted fingernails tighten on the steering wheel as the car wheels slip and slide in the snow.

The college word for Aunt Asia is *determined.*

"We should turn around and go back," I try to tell her. "I'll just talk to Sharice next week."

"Don't be silly," she answers, leaning closer to the windshield. "We're having fun, aren't we?"

The windshield keeps filling up with snow even with the wipers going full speed, so Aunt Asia rolls down her window to try and see the house numbers on Fifteenth. She calls them out as we pass: 345, 347, no number, can't see, 365 . . .

I keep hoping that we don't find the number I told her, the one I got by calling the school, because I haven't even thought about what to say to Sharice if we do find her house. What will she think when she opens the door and sees somebody from math club standing there?

But then Aunt Asia shouts, "There it is!" and our car slides into the driveway with a soft crunch of snow. I'm not sure we'll ever get out of the driveway again, by the way the car sounded. Aunt Asia cuts off the engine and we peer through the windshield at the house. It's a worn-looking two-story brick house with an old front porch in need of painting. All the windows of the house are dark. "Nobody's home," I say, hopefully.

"You can't ever tell," Aunt Asia answers. "Maybe their electricity is out. Maybe they don't keep up with their bills. Could be that's one of your friend's problems. Maybe her family's fallen on hard times. Families do, this time of the year. Don't I know it." She rolls her eyes. “Half the business I usually get — gone, this time of the year.”

Aunt Asia fiddles with the heater. “I’m gonna sit right here keeping warm, and you go up there and check if she’s home. Come and get me if you need me, Rhondell.” She smiles at me and pats my arm. “You’ll do fine, hon. All you have to be is a good listener.”

I want to sit in the warm car with Aunt Asia and not go anywhere. I stare at the house number on the paper in my hands and try to decide what to say to Sharice, if she answers the door. Just checking to see if you’re okay. . . . Everybody was worried after you left, so I said I’d stop and see about you. . . . Mr. Collins told me to come by. . . .

Looking up at that house with no lights and the snow swirling around it, I feel as if the house has a big sign saying GO AWAY. KEEP OUT. CLOSED.

“Don’t forget to check the back door, too,” Aunt Asia calls as I slide slowly out of the car. “Some people don’t answer their front doors, you know.”

On the front porch, a big pile of rolled-up yellow

newspapers and junk mail fills the space between the screen door and the front door. It looks as if nobody has used the door in months, and the only footprints I can see on the porch are cat prints in the thin layer of snow. I reach my hand behind the broken screen door and try knocking on the inside door, but nobody answers.

As I walk around to the back, I can feel the snow drifting into my shoes and soaking my socks. The yellow headlights from Aunt Asia's car shine ahead of me like two flashlights. With the swirling snow and the darkness of the house and yard, I don't know what makes me notice the bits of colored paper on the snow beside the house. Perhaps the headlights from Aunt Asia's car catch a few of them. But when I see the torn pieces scattered across the snow, a jolt goes through me. My heart begins pounding watch out, watch out, watch out, on its own, as if it knows something is wrong with those pieces being in the yard.

I come around the side of the house with my heart pounding watch out, and that's when I see the dark shape of somebody sitting on the back porch steps. The shape is huddled over, curled up, on the steps. I don't even check to see who the somebody is; I just go slipping, running, flying down the driveway to get Aunt Asia.

MARCEL

"What's up with you?" Willy Q asks me.

"Nothing."

He crosses his arms and gives me the five-minute Willy Q Army stare. "Don't lie to me. Something's wrong," he says. "I can read your face like a book."

"Nothing's wrong."

"Fights? Grades? School? Girl trouble? What's up?"

"Nothing."

"We'll see about that," Willy Q says. He walks over to the counter where we keep the cakes and pies. Goes right to the chocolate cake in the middle. Lifts the round plastic cover. Cuts a slab the size of a sidewalk, plops it on a plate, and pushes it in front of me. Sets a fork next to my hand. "Have some cake," he tells me.

I know better than to eat Willy Q's Chocolate Truth Cake. *Sweet enough to make tongues start talking* — that's what it says on the menu. Willy Q always insists if he coulda made his Chocolate Truth Cake in Vietnam, even the enemy would have talked.

You can see the look in people's faces after they take the first bite. They try the first mouthful of cake kinda fast, and then everything goes into slow motion. Their eyes close. They lick the sweet frosting and cake off one side of their fork. Then, they turn it over and get every last crumb and speck on the other side. "My, that is good. That is REAL good," they say.

And then they start talking.

They tell us about their family. Where they grew up. Who made the best cake, and who didn't. What's going wrong in their life now. Money problems. Health problems. No job. But how a bite of this good cake has made them feel better. Sugar does wonders, they declare. Me and Willy Q just nod our heads. Chocolate Truth Cake, we say, works wonders every time.

But it ain't gonna work for me. I push the cake to the side. Go back to thinking about what happened at school again. How it felt to see all that work torn apart. How it meant that none of us would have a chance at getting our names in the news. Probably be working at Willy Q's Barbecue the rest of my life. Giving folks my big I-Shoulda-Been-in-Hollywood-But-Instead-I'm-Working-Here smile.

Willy Q pushes the cake back in front of me.

"Talked to my friend Joe at your school today," he says slowly. "You remember Joe, right? The one who was in Vietnam with me?"

I nod.

Willy Q leans closer, giving me his Army-interrogator look. "Joe told me some vandals broke into your school and ruined a big project some of the seventh grade kids were working on with their math teacher. He said it was a real sad sight. Don't suppose you know anything about that project, do you, Marcel?"

I shake my head no. Not much, I say.

Willy Q points his finger about two inches from my face. "Don't you keep secrets from Sergeant Willy Q. Williams. I know everything that goes on around here, Marcel. I got eyes and ears in places you don't even know about. That was the project you were working on with those kids, wasn't it?"

“Don’t matter now, does it?” I answer.

Willy Q goes over to the Chocolate Truth Cake and cuts another sidewalk slab for himself. He slides it onto the counter and sits down next to me.

“Joe told me you were staying after school and working on that project with those other kids,” he says, taking a big bite of cake. “Don’t think I didn’t know what you were doing. Joe checked it out for me a while ago. . . .”

Willy Q points at my plate.

“Keep eating cake,” he says. “Then we’ll talk.”

Willy Q's Chocolate Truth Cake

1 cup all-purpose flour

1 cup sugar

¼ cup unsweetened cocoa powder

1 teaspoon baking powder

¼ teaspoon baking soda

¼ teaspoon salt

dash of cinnamon

¾ cup milk

¼ cup shortening

1 egg

½ teaspoon vanilla

¼ cup chocolate chips

Preheat oven to 350 degrees. In a bowl, combine flour, sugar, cocoa powder, baking powder, baking soda, salt, and cinnamon. Add milk, shortening, egg, and vanilla. Mix with an electric mixer (medium speed) for about two minutes or until well-mixed. Pour batter into 9" x 1½" round baking pan that has been greased and floured. Sprinkle chocolate chips on top of the batter. Bake at 350 degrees for 30 to 35 minutes, or until toothpick inserted in center comes out clean. Allow to cool for 10 minutes, then remove cake from pan and cool thoroughly on a baking rack. Frost with a thick layer of sweet chocolate frosting and wait for the truth to come out.

RHONDELL

I won't repeat all of the biblical names that Aunt Asia uses as she jumps out of the car and runs toward the back of the house to help the huddled shape I saw on the steps. She follows me, running through the snow in her stockinged feet, with her arms holding her red wool coat tight around her.

When we reach the backyard, Aunt Asia starts screaming, "Wake up, wake up!" at the shape before we even get there, and I am filled with relief when the huddled shape moves and begins to sit up slowly. A head covered by a striped yarn hat lifts slowly and scatters off its layer of snow, and then I can see for certain that the face belongs to Sharice.

"What in the name of Jesus are you doing out

here, sweetie?" Aunt Asia yells, almost nose to nose with Sharice, rubbing her shoulders up and down with her hands. "You gonna freeze to death, don't you know that?" She yanks Sharice up from the steps. "Come on back to our car now. We gotta get you to a hospital or a doctor or something."

With one arm and half of her red coat tucked around Sharice, Aunt Asia runs back to the car with her. Once we get inside, she huddles us together on the front seat and turns the heater on high. Hot air comes pouring out like an oven at the three of us. Going through another list of biblical names, Aunt Asia rubs her feet and stomps them on the car mats, trying to warm them up.

"Get that girl's shoes off," she says to me. "We gotta see if she has frostbite."

But Sharice shakes her head and finally says a word or two. She tells Aunt Asia her feet are fine and she doesn't need to go to any hospital.

"Well, we'll let my sister, Thea — Rhondell's mom — decide that," Aunt Asia insists. She pushes her foot down hard on the accelerator and barrels the car back down the driveway, with the tires spinning and squealing in the snow. "I'm gonna go to your house first, Rhondell, and see if your mom's home from work yet."

When we get to the house, the lights are on and my mom opens the door. She doesn't ask any questions at first, even though you can tell by the look she gives Aunt Asia that she isn't too pleased with her. All Aunt Asia says is, "This is Rhondell's friend, Sharice, and she's just about froze to the bone."

Mom sends me upstairs for a blanket or two while she and Aunt Asia try to pry some answers out of Sharice. Even from upstairs, I can hear them asking questions about where her mom is and what family she has in Cleveland. When I come back down the steps, my mom is settling Sharice into her recliner, with her feet in a pan of warm water and eucalyptus oil, just like she does to her own tired feet after work every day.

"Just keep your feet in there while I make something warm to drink," my mom is saying. Her eyes move over to me. "You keep her company, all right, Rhondell?"

After that, Mom and Aunt Asia disappear into the kitchen and I can hear them talking softly. I imagine

they are trying to decide who to call about Sharice, and I can hear Aunt Asia's heels tapping back and forth on the linoleum, pacing while they talk.

I don't know what's polite to ask Sharice. Sitting with my knees pulled up to my chin, I look down at my shoes and weave the ends of the laces back and forth through each other. Is it polite to ask why she was sitting outside in the snow? Whether she's upset about what happened at school — or something else? Should I ask if she wants to talk? Or perhaps she would rather that nobody bothered her and just left her alone.

The smell of toasting bread comes drifting from the kitchen and Aunt Asia returns balancing a tray in her hands. "My old waitressing days coming back to haunt me," she says in a loud, extra-cheerful voice. "Brought you girls some bread and jam and hot chocolate, how about that?" She sets the tray on the end table.

Settling down on the sofa, Aunt Asia stretches one of my mom's flannel blankets over her legs and reaches into her purse to pull out a big pink nail file.

"Did Rhondell tell you that I'm her aunt?" she chatters to Sharice as if she is talking to one of her clients, and I wonder if she's trying to cover up the sound of my mom in the kitchen talking on the phone to somebody.

"I work at the Style R Us hair salon on Washington Boulevard. Did Rhondell tell you that?" Aunt Asia holds her hand at arm's length, studying her nails, and then goes back to filing. "And I keep telling her" — she points the file at me — "girl, you gotta DO something with that hair."

Sharice smiles a little and Aunt Asia keeps going. "Now you have beautiful hair, Sharice, honey. I can tell that, just by looking at you. And I can tell you CARE about your hair, unlike that one." The nail file points again.

Somehow, talking about hair and nail polish makes the difference. Sharice's expression turns from closed up to half-interested. Before long, Aunt Asia is heading upstairs to dig through my mom's old dried-up nail polish collection. She brings back a color called champagne silver, and she and Sharice start painting their nails a silver-white color on my mom's coffee table. I don't say a word about that, even though I know my mom will.

After talking on the phone for a long time, it's my mom who decides that Sharice will stay at our house for the night. She comes into the living room and announces that it's too bitter cold to go outside again, so Sharice will stay over in my bedroom. My room used to be Mom and Aunt Asia's room when they were growing up, so I have their old twin beds. "And Asia," my mom adds emphatically, in the same sentence about Sharice staying at our house, "that's my good table."

It feels strange to have somebody from school staying in my room. After we climb into our beds, I can't fall asleep. I stare at the light from the half-open door and listen to Sharice moving and fidgeting. Each time she rolls from one side to the other, the bed creaks as if it's not used to having anybody sleeping in it, which it probably isn't since it's usually covered with my reading books and school papers.

Just when I think Sharice is asleep because she hasn't moved or stirred for a while, she talks to me.

“You ’wake, Rhondell?” she says softly.

“Yes.”

“I was the one who ruined the tetrahedron,” she says, her voice sounding half-muffled by her pillow. Her voice pauses, as if she’s waiting for me to say something, but I don’t know what to answer. I’m startled, I guess. And shocked. And bewildered. Those are the college words for what I feel.

“I forgot to lock the door,” she continues. “I was working late in the math room, and I never locked the door. That’s how they got in, you know. They didn’t break into the room, they just walked right in.”

Now I start to understand — a few things, but not everything. I try to tell Sharice that leaving the door open wasn’t what wrecked the project. “The people who came through that door were the ones who wrecked the project,” I explain to her. “Not the door being open.”

“But if the door hadn’t been left open, they wouldn’t have gotten in.”

“They would have found a way.”

Sharice seems to think about that for a while. “Maybe you’re right,” she says finally. “Maybe they would have." Then there's another long pause and she adds, "Thanks, Rhondell, for coming to get me, too."

"Sure," I answer, feeling uncomfortable, even in the darkness.

"How did you know where I lived?" her voice continues.

"I called the school and asked."

"You are so smart, Rhondell," she says. "I never would have thought of that."

"It's not that smart."

"I think it is."

And then it's quiet for a long time, so I guess that Sharice has finally fallen asleep. I continue staring at the ceiling and thinking to myself. The light coming from the hallway makes a skinny triangle shape, like one side of a tetrahedron, on the ceiling of my bedroom — and that reminds me again of how much I'm going to miss the math club.

Although I told Sharice it didn't matter about leaving the door unlocked, I have to admit that it does matter — deep down at least, it does. I know she didn't mean to cause any harm. And I know it wasn't Sharice who tore the project down, it was vandals. But I can't keep my mind from considering the same question over and over: would things have been different if she had just remembered that one little thing?

MR. COLLINS

Four questions of mine that still don't have answers:

1. Who destroyed our tetrahedron project?

2. Why did they destroy it?

3. Should the tetrahedron be rebuilt?

4. And who will do that?

JAMES HARRIS III

I draw eyes all over the back of my notebook — staring sideways at me, staring down at me. Feel like everybody's eyes are on me all the time — Mr. Collins, Marcel, other kids, other teachers, as if they know I've got information I'm not sharing. But I'm not telling nothing. Not even about Markese.

Principal called me into his office and tried to find out what I knew. "Other people here at Washington may trust you, James," he said, leaning across his desk to stare at me. "They may think you've mended your ways. But I know better. You come from a rough crowd, and it wouldn't surprise me if you had some hand in this."

How's telling people like you what happened gonna

help me, fool? That's what I'd like to say to Principal. You gonna snap your fat white fingers and make everything better? Why don't you step into my shoes for a while? I got a brother who's no brother, an apartment with no food, my brother's friends who are just looking for a reason to come after me . . . and that's only the beginning of all my problems. Why'd I be stupid enough to cause more trouble and spill my guts to you?

So I tell Principal I don't know nothing, even though I do.

They try all kinds of bribes and threats to get other kids to talk — all-school detention, canceling a Friday basketball game, offering a $100 reward — but nobody confesses anything because I'm the only one who knows that it was Markese and his friends who wrecked the project, and even though I'd like to see them have to glue the whole thing back together piece by piece for the next fifty years, I still keep my mouth shut.

But in English class, while Clueless Sub is reviewing what we know about clauses, I start thinking about how long it would really take to rebuild. Eight months? Six months?

"James, tell us one thing you know about clauses," Clueless Sub says.

"Santa Claus. That's all I know, man," I answer.

And Clueless Sub says, "Get out in the hall, young man, and don't come back until you're ready to respect my authority."

Yeah, right . . .

So I sit in the hall and try to figure out how many days we would need if we started the project again. I tear off part of a sheet of notebook paper that's sticking out of somebody's locker and pick up a chewed-up pencil that's sitting under the water fountain. It takes me about half an hour to figure out all the dividing and carrying to do. Math ain't my thing, so I don't know why I'm even trying. Nothing else to do in the hall, though, and I'm not going back to Clueless Sub.

My figuring says if we could make 150 pieces a day, divided into 16,384 — the number of pieces needed for the record — it would take us about 110 days. Meaning, if we started now and worked five days a week, we could probably be done sometime in July. Which doesn't seem that impossible as long as you don't look outside and realize it's only the beginning

of February, and there's a blizzard outside, and half the winter is still left to go.

At lunchtime, I go and find Mr. Collins. He's eating lunch at his desk.

"This right?" I say, pushing my paper in front of him.

"What were you trying to figure out?" he asks, squinting at my scrawled numbers.

"How long would it take to rebuild? Is a hundred and ten days right or not?"

Collins gives me a strange look, like he's surprised at something, but I don't know what.

He folds the paper in half and hands it back to me. "Think about how hard it would be to start all over again," he says, beginning to clean up his lunch. "Is that what you really want to do, James?"

He crumples his sandwich bag and sweeps up the crumbs from his desk with his hands. "But you're right," he continues. "If we had the time and made a hundred and fifty pieces a day, it would probably take about one hundred and ten days."

"What if I get the other people to come back?" I ask.

Collins shakes his head and says it's too much work.

"I don't care, I'm gonna try. You give me some paper and I'll start on the new pieces tonight," I insist.

I walk toward the cupboard where he keeps the stacks of colored paper. "I'll make one hundred and fifty by myself tonight, you just wait and see."

"James . . ."

Collins tries to get me to give up, but I won't. All those eyes that are watching me are raising their eyebrows and looking sideways at each other, not sure what I'm gonna do next. Keep it that way.

110

150 per Day

Approx 110 Days

22 weeks

approx 5 months

109.2266

150 | 16384

150 × 10 = 1500

150 × 9 = 1350

5 | 110 = 22

4 | 22 = 5.5

Feb March, April, May, June, July
1 2 3 4 5

WILLY Q

Don't know what's wrong with kids these days. They're soft. When times are tough, they melt like butter in the hot sun.

A couple of days after talking to my friend Joe at the school, I ask Marcel when he's gonna rebuild that project, and he tells me he's not.

That's what I mean. Soft.

When I was growing up, kids were tougher. Had to be. We were getting married at eighteen or nineteen and getting sent off to war. It wasn't no picnic.

"You just gonna let the people who ruined your project win?" I turn to look at Marcel, who is standing by the counter while I'm shredding some pork for barbecue sandwiches.

Marcel gives me that shrug of his that I don't allow.

I get in his face because I won't stand for that attitude. "You better abandon that rude habit of yours and show me some respect," I warn him, still holding the knife in one hand. "Willy Q's son don't act that way. You disagree with me, you say it to my face. You don't shrug your shoulders at me, you understand?"

Marcel says he does, but I can tell it won't last. I repeat my question. "You gonna let the people who ruined your project win?"

Marcel answers as slow as he can, still being disrespectful, in my opinion.

"Maybe," he says.

He's playing with the coffee stirrers on the counter, making squares and triangles. Doesn't even try to look at me while he's talking.

I give Marcel the list of all the times I could have given up. I count them one by one on my fingers: when my daddy died when I was eight years old, when we lost everything we had in a fire and we had to live in a shelter for three months, when I got drafted, when three of my buddies were killed in Vietnam, when I had to turn my drinking habits around, when the first barbecue place I owned got burnt to the ground and I lost all my money. . . .

"But I never let the enemy win," I say to Marcel. "Death, fire, booze, the Viet Cong, none of them could beat this man" — I point at my chest — "Willy Q. Williams."

"And you ain't gonna give up either," I tell him. "Ain't gonna stand for having no son like that. Williams people don't give up. Your granddaddy didn't give up, I didn't give up, and you ain't going to either." I can feel myself getting emotional, thinking about my own daddy and all, so I try to finish up talking before I do.

"So you just head on back to school tomorrow and start working, all right?" I say, thumping another slab of pork onto the counter. "Whatever time it takes, that's what it takes. I'll look after the Barbecue until you get here. And in between times, you bring me some of that math project because I'm gonna help with making those triangles, too."

I see Marcel's doubting eyes glance at my rough working hands.

"I know they ain't things of beauty, but in the Army, they could sew buttons on a shirt faster than anybody. My buddies called me the Button Man."

Marcel arches his eyebrows. "The Button Man?"

"What? You think all I can do is barbecue?" I give Marcel a smack on the shoulder. "Don't you go doubting the talents of Sergeant Willy Q. Williams."

RHONDELL

My mom says Sharice is someone who has been through a lot. The house on Fifteenth Street wasn't her family's house, it was a foster house. She was being neglected, my mom tells me. I try to imagine what it must feel like to be neglected, how it would feel to live with strangers who didn't care about you.

My mom's anger is fierce when she talks about how Sharice slept on buses and in doorways. "Who would treat a child like that?" she asks. "What kind of world do we live in?"

I wonder why Sharice didn't tell anybody.

My mom says maybe fear, maybe shame, maybe she just didn't know who to tell. "It's not our place to ask questions," my mom warns, "not when we don't know the whole story, not when we haven't walked in her shoes."

The social service agency could have taken Sharice somewhere else, to another temporary place, but Sharice is allowed to stay with us while the agency decides what to do with her. I think this was arranged because of somebody my mom knows at the hospital, even though I don't think it's something my mom wanted to do. I hear her complaining to Aunt Asia, "I take care of people all day, and then I come home and take care of more." With my mom, there are always two sides, the soft side that feels obligated to help everybody and the sharp side that resents always being asked.

Since Sharice is staying with us, I have to loan her some of my clothes, and even a pair of pajamas, because nobody from her old house has cared enough to bring her any clothes. The second night, Aunt Asia drops by with a plastic bag filled with shampoo, conditioner, hair gels, styling creams, toothbrushes, deodorant, combs — things that Sharice doesn't have either.

My mom gives Aunt Asia a disapproving look about some of the things — makeup and nail polish, for instance — but Aunt Asia just laughs at her and says girls will be girls.

Later, I notice how Sharice takes all of Aunt Asia's gifts and arranges them carefully on the little white table next to her bed, as if they are a display in a store. While I'm lying across my bed reading our new book for English, she opens all of the bottles of creams and lotions and oils and tries dabs of each one of them. The whole room starts to smell like grapefruit and oranges and cocoa butter.

"This lipstick tastes just like chocolate chip cookies," she says, smacking her lips together loudly, after trying one of Aunt Asia's lipsticks. "When I lived with my Gram, I remember she used to make the best chocolate chip cookies. . . ." Sharice is quiet for a minute, as if she's waiting for me to say something or look up. "You want to hear about my Gram or are you busy, Rhondell?" she asks softly.

I put down the book I'm holding because this is the first time Sharice has mentioned a word about her

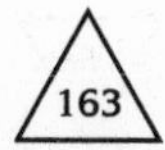

family in the two days she's been with us. "If you want to talk about her," I answer carefully. "But you don't have to."

Sharice smiles with her extra-shiny lips. "My Gram was great. . . ." And that night is when the story of her life starts coming out. I don't say much. I just listen.

SHARICE

You ever have the experience of sitting in the comfy stylist's chair at the hair salon, closing your eyes, letting your shoulders down, and just forgetting who you are for a minute?

That's what happens to me on the Friday afternoon that Rhondell's aunt tells us to stop by for a free appointment at the Style R Us salon, where she works. Me and Rhondell both come by after school, even though Rhondell says she'll read magazines and wait, because she doesn't want anything done to her hair.

"Not even a little something?" I try to convince her, but she just shakes her head and tells me her hair is exactly the way she likes it.

It feels strange to walk into the salon and tell them I have an appointment with Asia Taylor. Only a few of the chairs have any customers and they are all moms and grams, with their hair in foil and big plastic clips. (Like some kind of electrical experiment — that's what they look like, you know.) I can feel all of the eyes glancing in the mirrors when I come in. Who's that? the eyes are saying.

Aunt Asia (she says to call her that) keeps stopping and introducing me at each chair as if I am a famous guest. "This is my niece's best friend from school, Sharice Walker." Even though everybody is friendly to me — smiling and shaking my hand, saying how are you, dear — I can see that they can hardly wait to ask a million questions about me later on.

I'd like to be able to tell them it's none of their business that the Sanctuary Baptist Church T-shirt and too-short jeans I'm wearing aren't mine (on loan from Rhondell), or that my appointment is a free gift because I'm poor, or that I'm a foster kid who's had five different non-homes since my Gram died (soon to be six, probably).

But I just smile and act like my friendly old self

and hope Rhondell's aunt won't tell the real story about my whole life after I leave, with all the details that make people pity me. Or if she does, maybe they won't believe a word of it after seeing how happy and confident I looked. (No way that could be true about her, they'll whisper and shake their heads. She looked just like your normal, average girl.)

Once we reach Miss Asia's chair, it feels good to sink into the black leather seat and have the beauty salon cape float down over my head and hide the clothes that aren't mine.

I don't even remember which non-parent took me to the salon, but I think I've only been to one once or twice before. Gram always did my hair herself. She liked to put my hair in braids with those big round beads on the end that look like white gum balls.

Aunt Asia smiles at me in the mirror, and her hand reaches up to smooth one part of her caramel-colored hair, which is arranged in tight little curls all over her head. If Rhondell's mom is plain and simple-looking, Rhondell's aunt is like a fancy frosted cake. Her rows of silver and gold bracelets clank and jangle next to my ear. "Now, I know you are ready to be beautiful,

Miss Sharice," she says, starting to snip the rubber bands out of my hair. "Am I right?"

I nod, thinking how this is probably the only time I'll ever have a chance like this. (Girl, you better savor every minute.) After Aunt Asia finishes conditioning my hair at the sink and brings me back to her chair, I close my eyes and listen to all the voices talking around me. I try to remember the smoky smells drifting from the curling irons and oils and hot combs, and how it feels to sit in the chair like a queen.

While Aunt Asia works on combing out my hair, my mind kinda drifts back a little, and I remember Gram's old hands tugging at my hair when I was little, and how I would sit sideways on one of the chairs in her kitchen, howling and squirming.

You hush now, child, she'd keep on saying. You're gonna wake the dead.

And that always made me wonder, if I screamed loud enough, if my mom would jump up from the grave and come running for me.

I remember doing that once, you know — standing in the middle of Gram's backyard and screaming at the top of my lungs. My poor Gram came flying out the door thinking that I had split open my head, but when she found out why I was screaming, I remember her pulling me against her big chest and saying, Oh honey, the dead are a long, long way away.

And while Rhondell's aunt is tugging at my hair, I start thinking about Gram and my mom and everybody being a long, long way away (and getting farther away), and how Rhondell's aunt is nearby. How she's standing right behind my chair, with her jangling bracelets and her caramel hair, trying to make me look beautiful. How she bought me a shampoo that smelled like sweet grapefruit, and Pink Sunrise nail polish, like my mom or my Gram would have.

And I think I just forget who I am for a minute because I suddenly hear my voice blurting out, "Do you ever think about having somebody stay with you?"

(WHY CAN'T I EVER LEARN TO KEEP MY MOUTH SHUT?)

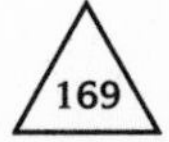

RHONDELL

About a week after our math club project ends, I see James in the hallway. He's standing by a locker and he turns around quickly when he sees me. "Rhondell," he calls out. "Hey, wait up, I gotta talk to you."

I hug my books tighter and glance around to see who else is in the hallway. I try to pretend I haven't heard anybody call my name. I walk faster, but not so fast that it looks like I am. James catches up. I hear his shoes coming behind me.

"Hey," he says, giving me a hard push. "Hold up."

When I stop walking and look back at him, I'm surprised by what he asks.

He wants to know if I would work on the math project again. "Same group," he says. "You, me, Sharice,

Marcel, Collins, and whoever else shows up. What do you think?" I glance up at his smooth face to see if it's a joke, to see if he's just trying to convince me to answer yes so he can start laughing.

I tell him that I can't work on it. I have other things I have to do at home now.

"What things?" he replies, glaring at me, and I start to wonder if maybe he really means what he's asking, because of how serious he looks.

Just things, I tell him.

What I don't tell him is the real reason I'm saying no. The real reason is that when you have a dream and you see it broken right in front of your eyes, it makes you think that maybe you never should have dreamed it in the first place. It makes you feel like not taking any risks or dreaming any dreams that are too big for yourself again, because you can't tell which ones to trust or what to believe in. And how could anybody say for certain that the people who ruined our first project wouldn't ruin the next one, and the next?

That's what I would like to say to James. Instead I tell him I'm going to be late for class and I can't talk any longer.

But later on, something happens that changes my mind.

In the afternoon, Sharice and I are using the library computer at school. Although we're supposed to be online researching the Romans for history class, Sharice types in the word *tetrahedron* — just to see what appears, she insists.

What comes up is a page about a math professor who studied tetrahedrons years ago. There's a small black-and-white picture of him, wearing thick glasses and a suit and tie, and below the picture, it says his name is Waclaw Sierpinski.

"What kinda name is Waclaw?" Sharice grins, leaning closer to the computer screen. "And how would you say that last name?" She taps her pen on the monitor. "You try saying it first, Rhondell, because you're smarter than me."

But when I try pronouncing it, the name comes out sounding like something a knight in medieval times would be called, Sir Pinski, and Sharice starts getting overcome with laughter, so that even the librarian who is usually nice gives us a sharp look.

Trying not to get us into any more trouble, I duck

my head down behind the monitor to read a little more, and that's where I see the part of the story that changes my mind about working on the tetrahedron again. *Epiphany* would be the college word I'd use for what I find on the page.

Below the picture, the article starts talking about "Sir Pinski" and how he was a math professor from Poland who was known for writing a lot of important math papers and theories. But during World War II, Sir Pinski lost his house and his entire library of mathematical books and research when the Nazis burned them to the ground.

My breath catches in my chest and my eyes blink after I get to those words: "burned to the ground."

All those words and numbers — years and years of work — turned to nothing but ashes? I remember my own college words, only a handful of words, not books and books filled with them. How would it feel to see your own library, a whole lifetime of words and work, lost just like that? In one day?

For the rest of the afternoon, I can't keep my mind from thinking about the mathematician with the name of a knight who saw his library burned to the ground and refused to give up. In a way, the story makes me feel ashamed. We only worked about four months on a simple paper pyramid, just folding paper into triangles, and when the project was ruined, we went our own separate ways and gave up. What if it had been a lifetime of work? A library of words? What then?

That afternoon, I stop by the math classroom and ask Mr. Collins about the possibility of beginning the project again. I tell him I've had a sudden change of mind. An *epiphany*.

AUNT ASIA

"You, raising a kid?"

My sister, Thea, shakes her head.

"You're crazy, Asia. You're just about the least likely foster mom I could imagine," she says. "Think about it. You have to be R-E-S-P-O-N-S-I-B-L-E." (She spells it out.) "You've never been responsible in your entire life, not from day one. I grew up with you, and I know what you're like."

My sister arches her responsible eyebrows and points to herself. "I'm the responsible one," she says. "Working two jobs, raising Rhondell, sending money to half my relatives to keep them on their feet, leading the church choir every Sunday — *that's* responsible."

Both of us reach for another glazed doughnut

from the box in the middle of the table. It's Saturday morning, and Sharice and Rhondell are at the video store getting a movie. The two of us are sitting in the kitchen, drinking coffee and eating doughnuts.

"And what do you know about raising kids, Asia?" my sister continues, taking a bite out of her doughnut. "Rhondell and Sharice are almost high schoolers, and then you've got a whole laundry list of things to worry about," she says. "You gotta watch teenagers, especially girls, like a hawk, you know. You ready to do that?"

I try to tell Thea that she trusts me to help with Rhondell and I've always been there for her. "Name one time I haven't," I say.

My sister counts my other problems on her fingers. "And you've had men trouble, and money trouble, and you don't go to church regular like you should, and you live in a place that doesn't have enough room for a kid, let alone you, and you don't keep your place clean enough for my standards."

She gets up to pour another cup of coffee.

"Don't know why you're even thinking about this, Asia." My sister stands at the counter with the coffeepot in her hand. "You're just being influenced by what that girl told you."

"You didn't hear how she asked if she could stay with me," I argue. "It would have made you cry — I know it would have — the way she asked it."

My sister shakes her head.

I keep on talking.

"And her hair was a mess," I try to explain. "Like nobody had cared about her in years. It was like —" I search for the right words. "It was like her hair was tangled up with all the mess of her life," I say finally. "Like you could almost feel how sad and lonely it must have been for her."

"Sure it was." My sister sits down, still shaking her head. "How do you know that the girl doesn't have mental things wrong with her?" she says, looking at me. "That girl's been in foster care and social services most of her life; think about all the burdens she could be carrying. You ready to deal with all those things?"

"Maybe," I answer, standing up and sticking the box of doughnuts under my arm. "Maybe I am."

MR. COLLINS

A math problem to solve:

If four students and their math teacher begin the tetrahedron project again in February and they work five days a week, making and adding 150 pieces a day to their structure, how many weeks will it take to rebuild the tetrahedron with 16,384 pieces? Extra credit: What if four hairstylists, one Vietnam vet, and a custodian named Mr. Joe also take part?

MARCEL

"Nothing hard about making those little pyramids," Willy Q says, once I show him how you fold the three triangles up to a point, glue the sides together, and hold the sides for about a minute until they stick, and you're done.

Willy Q insists he could do a hundred fifty pieces by himself. One hand tied behind his back. Blindfolded.

When business is slow, me and Willy Q sometimes have races at making the pieces. We don't bet money. We bet who has to clean the public bathroom that's outside the Barbecue, or who has to scrub the greasy cooking pans, or who is gonna mop the kitchen floor.

I win, you clean the bathroom. You win, I clean. That's the way we bet.

Or — you win, I wash all the greasy pans. I win, you gotta mop the kitchen floor. On your hands and knees. Twice.

We race making ten at a time. Or twenty. Tetrahedrons go flying across the counter and floor. Willy Q is fast. His fingers don't look fast, but they can move. Sometimes we gotta crawl across the floor and gather up the ones that have flown all over the place.

I win more often than Willy Q. But not much.

Most of the time we have to glue our pieces all over again, or take them apart and refold the sides. "Fast don't always mean good," Willy Q says. "That's a lesson to keep in mind for life — and for working here, too," he adds, giving me a look.

A few days into March we get a warm spell. One of those Pretending-It's-Spring-But-Then-Hit-You-With-a-Blizzard warm spells. Business starts picking up again because people think it's spring even though it isn't. We gotta make tetrahedrons in between ribs and barbecue sandwiches and Singing the Blues wings.

Some people see the bowl of shapes on the

counter and ask, What's that? Some kinda new barbecue sauce packet?

Then Willy Q tells them how they are called tetrahedrons and how my math class is trying to get in the *Guinness Book of World Records.*

For real? they answer, wide-eyed.

Me and Willy Q start handing out pieces for other people to make. Help Washington Middle School get in the records book, Willy Q tells them.

You can always figure out the ones that come from the barbecue. Hold them up to your nose and you can smell the charcoal and wood smoke and barbecue sauce. Better watch your fingers with these, I tell the math club when I bring them in. They're hot, hot, hot.

All the pieces have little *Q*'s written on them, too. "Why you always drawing a little Q on every tetrahedron we make?" I ask Willy Q one afternoon.

He squints at me. "How long you been my son?"

"Thirteen years."

"And all that time, you haven't noticed my name is Willy — Q?"

I grin and pour one of the little sugar packs into my hand. "Stands for Quincy, right?"

Willy Q smacks my arm. "Don't you go telling nobody my real name, unless you want to be scrubbing the public toilet with a toothbrush till you're twenty-one — and stop messing with the sugar packs."

"But why put a Q on the tetrahedrons?" I ask.

"Advertising." Willy Q grins. "For the Barbecue. Willy Q. Williams don't do nothing for free."

JAMES HARRIS III

Way back in elementary school, when my brother DJ was in third or fourth grade, he won a basketball jersey signed by four pro players. Half of them don't even play no more, but it's the one thing he's got that means something to him. He always keeps it folded up in a shoebox, taped shut, in the back of the closet underneath a pile of clothes. Nobody's allowed in.

But all rules are off these days with DJ.

One morning, I slip that box out from under the clothes pile, shove it in my backpack, and take it somewhere else. I wait about a week to tell DJ. He's lying on the couch, flipping through channels one night, with a bag of chips sitting on his chest.

"You missing something," I start by saying, and he

flies off the couch like he can read my mind. His hand slams into my chest while he's going past.

"You better not have touched nothing of mine," he swears.

I'm waiting for him when he gets back. "You keep Markese and the others away from our project this time," I tell him.

He gets up in my face. "You gimme that shirt back," he yells.

We keep on repeating the same words over and over, like a CD that's stuck, until my uncle comes slamming out of the bedroom where he was sleeping and tells us both to get out of the apartment, or he's calling the cops.

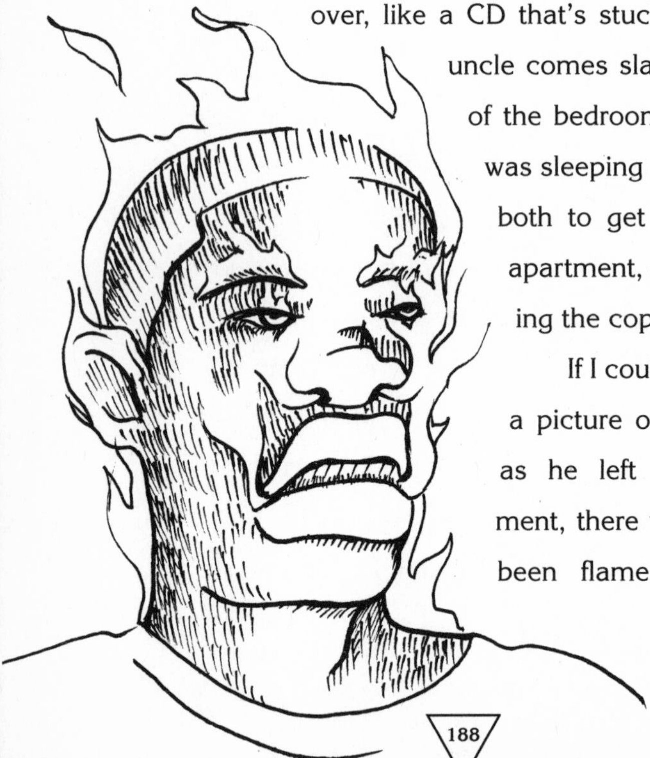

If I could've drawn a picture of DJ's face as he left the apartment, there would have been flames shooting out of his eyes and smoke coming out of his nose and mouth.

But I'm not gonna take any chances this time, not even with my own brother. I lean over the railing of the stairwell and shout that he'll get his jersey back in one piece when the tetrahedron is done. "As long as it stays in one piece — you know what I mean?" I holler. A door slamming is all the answer I get.

SHARICE

I decide it's time to take a chance. I tell Rhondell that she can hand me the yellow or the blue pieces one afternoon when we're working after school, folding and gluing the little tetrahedrons like usual.

Rhondell gives me a quick look. "You sure?" she says. "Because I've got plenty of purple if you want them." She pushes a stack of purple shapes toward me.

"No, I'll take the yellow," I insist. "I'm okay with yellow."

See, I've been trying to change some of the beliefs I have about things (such as the colors blue and yellow). All blue cars don't cause what happened to my mom. For instance, Aunt Asia drives a blue car, and it's about fifteen years old with 174,300 miles and a lot of rust — and nothing has happened to it yet. People are always honking when I'm riding in the car with her because she drives it so slow. You want to scrunch down in your seat sometimes, when people honk their horns and go zooming past, like you're a big blue turtle holding up the whole road.

And when Aunt Asia took me to see her third-floor apartment (at the top of a house) for the first time, to talk about how I might feel about living there, all I could see was yellow when she opened the door. The walls were the yellowest yellow you could imagine. "Isn't that the color of sunshine?" Aunt Asia said, clasping her hands behind her back and happily studying the walls. "That's why I picked it. If I couldn't have an apartment with lots of windows, at least I'd have sunshine, that's what I figured.

"And it won't hurt my feelings if you don't want to stay here after seeing my small place, so don't you worry about that," she told me, twisting her bracelets nervously on her arm and giving me an uncertain look. "It's just me and this little place, and I know it isn't much to offer. Other homes they'd put you in would probably be a whole lot nicer than this."

While she showed me all the things that were wrong with her place — the leaky refrigerator with the towel underneath, and the stove with only one burner that worked, and the rusted bathtub, and the bathroom sink that only ran cold — I thought about how all the things that were wrong with her place were still better than the few things that were right in the other places.

During the tour, I didn't say a word about the yellow walls, either, or tell her how it was my bad luck color. I just said that everything looked fine with me, and I wouldn't mind staying there someday if she didn't mind having me there. (I tried not to sound too hopeful, you know, because hope will get you nowhere.) Aunt Asia gave me a surprised look and said she hadn't made up her mind just yet — that there was still a lot of paperwork to do. . . .

But maybe yellow was my good luck color after all, because Aunt Asia didn't wait very long (like one or two days) before she decided to go ahead with applying to be my foster mom.

And when I thought about those yellow walls later, and how Aunt Asia loved looking at them, I wondered

if maybe my Gram was trying to tell me something. Maybe by sending me to a place that was the same color as the flowers I brought to the hospital when she died, she was finally saying thank you to me and telling me it was time to move on.

AUNT ASIA

We talk all the time at the Style R Us hair salon. You know how it is with women. The other stylists are always asking me about Sharice and how she's doing since coming to stay with me at the beginning of May. She into boys yet? they ask. She talk about her past life at all? She adjusting okay to being with you?

I keep a snapshot of her and Rhondell taped in the corner of my mirror. "Those two are my girls," I tell my clients. "That's Miss Rhondell, my sister's girl," I say pointing at Rhondell, who's looking serious in the picture, as usual. "And that's Miss Sharice," I say, pointing at the girl with her hair done up fancy and a wide smile on her face.

I'm not saying we're nosy people at the salon, but

once the other stylists hear how the girls are trying to break a math record with their class at school, they all want to help. Especially after finding out what happened to their first project.

But I have to confess that we have our own sense of style here and we each like to do our own creative things. So after Sharice and Rhondell show us how to make the little pyramids, we can't help giving them a few special touches, like painting them with sparkle nail polish, or giving them purple stripes and gold dots and silver zigzags, or gluing on some rhinestone nail art — just extra little things like that. Sharice says the president of her math club probably won't appreciate our originality. We just laugh and tell her that's all right — most people don't.

My clients are always noticing the pyramids on my counter and asking if they are Christmas tree ornaments. Every time they ask, I have to look at the little piece of paper where Sharice has carefully printed the math word for what they are.

"Tetrahedrons," I explain. "It's something that the kids are studying in math now." Then I bring over

Kyra, our nail tech, and show them how she's painted little gold pyramids on her nails, in honor of the kids.

My clients always shake their heads and say, "Math sure has changed. We never learned words like that when I was in school. Your girl must be real smart, if she's already learning words like that —"

And whenever they talk that way about Sharice, I always feel proud for one quick minute, as if she's my own daughter. And then I remember who I am and I answer, "I don't know where she gets all her math talents from, to tell you the truth. But she's a real hard worker, just like her cousin Rhondell."

Sometimes when Sharice is at school and I'm at home, I slip into her room and look at the photograph of the pretty woman in the lavender dress that she keeps on the little table beside her bed. Sitting there on her bed, I wonder to myself what her mom might have been like and if I'm doing a good job in her eyes.

MR. COLLINS

An important fact to remember about tetrahedrons:

As the tetrahedron structure grows larger and larger, the empty spaces within the tetrahedron grow larger and larger, too.

JAMES HARRIS III

I'm seeing tetrahedrons in my sleep. One thousand eight hundred left to make. The way I figure it, we still got about two more weeks until we're done.

Unless we die of heatstroke first.

"Whose idea was it to sit in a sweaty math room in June working on this project?" I ask. I go over to the windows and point at the neighborhood below us. "Look out there. Everybody else is smart. They're hanging out in the air-conditioning or going to the mall or the movies or wherever. We need some air-conditioning or something in here," I say to Mr. Collins.

Collins is standing on a chair, working on the upper half of the pyramid. He's wearing shorts and a faded green T-shirt that says "Running Man," but you can tell his legs have never run anywhere. They are about as pale and skinny as a chicken's. We started calling him Chicken Legs the first time he wore shorts to math club, and he just smiled and said in the summertime we could call him whatever.

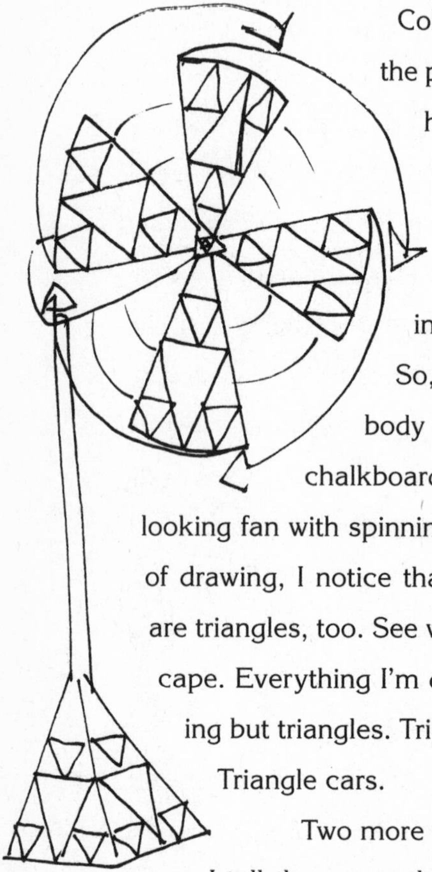

Collins looks around the side of the pyramid. "Air-conditioning?" he repeats, raising his eyebrows. "Maybe you could draw us a big electric fan, James — and then point it in our direction, okay?"

So, I do. Just to make everybody laugh. I go over to the chalkboard and draw a big scary-looking fan with spinning blades. But in the middle of drawing, I notice that the blades I'm sketching are triangles, too. See what I mean? There's no escape. Everything I'm drawing these days is nothing but triangles. Triangle fans. Triangle people. Triangle cars.

Two more weeks . . .

I tell the group that I, for one, don't care if I

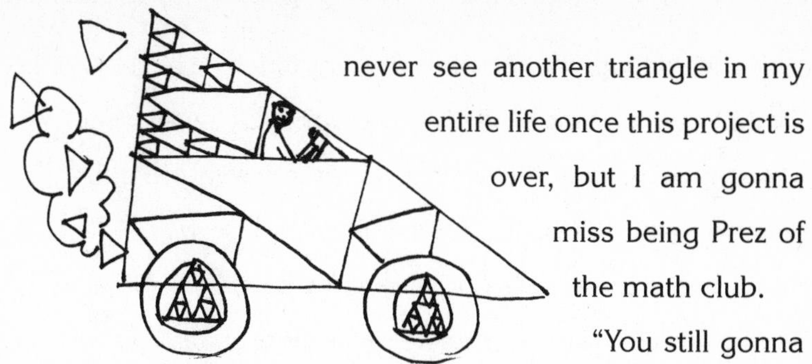

never see another triangle in my entire life once this project is over, but I am gonna miss being Prez of the math club.

"You still gonna call me Prez after this is over?" I ask the group while we're working and sweating. "Because if it wasn't for me, you all woulda quit, I bet. Or you wouldn't have even started on this project again in the first place."

Sharice sends a yellow tetrahedron flying in my direction. "Wasn't for us making nine hundred thousand nine hundred ninety-nine tetrahedrons, you wouldn't have anything to be Prez of," she says.

"Wasn't for me bringing barbecue to eat, you all would have starved," Marcel adds.

Collins tells us if we don't stop wasting time talking and arguing, we're still gonna be here in August. And who wants that?

When he looks away, I whip the tetrahedron piece back at Sharice and

hit Rhondell's arm instead. She just glances over her shoulder and gives me the scared-rabbit look she always does. I let out a loud sigh. That girl needs to get more guts or attitude or something.

Maybe because I was spending every day in June at school, gluing little triangles together, that's how I missed what I should have seen coming at my uncle's place. I don't know. I think I was just working so hard on the project at school, trying to be a good Prez and all — eight hours a day some days — that everything at home just went sailing right over my head. Like the tetrahedron flying past Sharice.

But I don't know how I could've missed the big pile of cardboard boxes sitting in the living room of my uncle's apartment, or the official letters stacking up on the kitchen table, or the phone and cable going out and never coming back on.

Or maybe if I noticed those things — why couldn't I have figured out sooner what they meant? Or maybe if, deep down, I knew what they meant, why couldn't it have waited a few more weeks to happen?

MARCEL

Me and Willy Q get a Dog-Days-of-August-and-Everybody-Wants-to-Order-Barbecue customer line in June. Goes all the way out to the parking lot and along the side of somebody's shiny BMW.

"You see that car?" Willy Q hollers from the grill. "We are hot, hot, hot tonight."

Me, I'm wearing my special Sorry-You-Had-to-Wait-For-an-Hour-But-That's-the-Way-It-Goes smile. Taking orders as fast as my hand can write.

"What can I get for you tonight, sir?"

"How can I help you, ma'am?"

"We got Blast Off to Outer Space Hot, Melt the Roof of Your Mouth Hot, Wait in Line for Ten Years Hot. . . ."

One whole family of white folks wants everything

mild. Why'd you come to a barbecue in the first place? I want to ask. Why not just sit at home and eat plain bread and water?

"You got fried green tomatoes?" one old hunch-backed black lady with a Southern accent asks me.

"Nope."

"Black-eyed peas?"

"Nope."

"Why'd I wait forever in this line, then, young man?"

A black man in a fine-looking suit and red tie asks me, "What's Tar in the Summertime Hot? And how's that different than Plain Ol' Hot?"

I lean on the counter and give him one of my You-Better-Not-Ask-Me-Any-More-Questions-Because-There-Are-Fifty-People-Behind-You-In-Line-or-Haven't-You-Noticed smiles. "One's hotter than the other," I tell him.

It's almost dark when James comes up to the window. Turn back to the counter to take another order and see him standing there. Moths and bugs flitting around his head like halos. "Hey," I say, forgetting all my customer speeches. "How's it going, Prez?" Reach my hand through the order window so he can smack it.

Willy Q looks over from the grill. "We got lots of people still waiting," he says. "Ain't time for socializing with your friends, Marcel. Ask him to come back later."

"He's ordering," I call out to Willy Q. Then I tell the Prez that I'll give him Marcel's special No-Charge Discount. Ask Willy Q to fix up two Singing the Blues, a side of cornbread, and one homemade lemonade for him.

James slips an envelope through the window. "Give this to Collins tomorrow," he says. "It's a note for him."

"Why can't you?" I ask.

"Things to do," he answers.

I slip the Prez's food out through the window. Two boxes of wings, one bag of cornbread, and a cup of cold lemonade with lotsa ice rattling in the cup. "That'll be twelve fifty-seven, thank you very much," I say loudly, opening and closing the window like he's just paid me for the food.

"You crazy, Marcel," the Prez says, grinning.

Willy Q shouts behind me, "Get busy, Marcel."

"Don't forget to give Collins that letter," the Prez finishes, talking fast. "And make sure he does what it

says." He points at me. "I'm counting on you, Marcel." And then he slips away into the darkness.

I only remember that last part later. Me and Willy Q are cleaning up the place, and suddenly Marcel the Magnificent's mind stops and thinks — what's he counting on me for?

MR. COLLINS

Dear Mr. Collins,

It's Friday night and I'm writing you this letter to tell you and everybody that I won't be back at math club. My uncle is moving tonight and he doesn't know where but I won't be there when the tetrahedron is finished and I did a lot of work on it, but everything isn't easy is it? I wrote out some things for everybody to do and they better do them right.

Here they are:

1. Don't forget the top part should be almost all red with a few orange. Don't make any more blue, green, or purple ones - there's enough already!

2. Make sure that everything is glued right, especially at the top.

3. Don't forget my name when you're talking to the Guinness World Records people. I want it spelled James Harris III ok? (Don't forget the III.)

4. Mr. Collins - remember to call the newspapers and TVs and maybe the National Enquirer, too.

5. DON'T GIVE UP!!!!!

6. Marcel - you can be the Prez now instead of me as long as you don't mess up.

I would work on the tetrahedron some more if I could but I'm proud of it anyway. Remember everyone - DON'T GIVE UP (or I'll kick your butt)!!!!!

Bye for now,

James Harris III

P.S. It was fun while it lasted

RHONDELL

Nobody says a word after Mr. Collins finishes reading the letter to us. I can hear the smack of a basketball on the street outside and the sound of locusts whirring in the trees and a car alarm going off somewhere, but inside the math room, the four of us are silent.

"Are you sure this letter came from him?" Mr. Collins asks Marcel.

Marcel nods.

Sharice leans forward. "Did he look sad or upset or anything?"

Marcel shrugs his shoulders and keeps his eyes on the floor. "Not that I saw."

I can hear Mr. Collins sigh as he's folding up the letter. He leaves it sitting on his chair as he stands up and walks over to the open windows that face the streets. His hands are in his pockets, and his head shakes back and forth. I know he's seeing a whole neighborhood of run-down, poor houses with people like James' family, who never stick around, but I want to tell him that's not true of everybody. My mother's family has always lived in the neighborhood, and Marcel's father has, too. My grandma sang in the Sanctuary Baptist Church Choir when she was a girl, and one of my uncles helped to build the gymnasium of Washington Middle School years ago. *Permanence* is the college word for us.

Sharice reaches for the letter on Mr. Collins' chair. "Didn't he leave an address or phone number or anything?" she says, unfolding the letter to read it again. But I guess there isn't anything else written there because Sharice quietly puts the letter back where it was.

I don't know how I feel about James leaving. How should I feel? I wonder.

I look over at the big tetrahedron and see all the colors he made us assemble by following the exact order of a rainbow. It looks beautiful, that's a fact. Next to the tetrahedron is a big poster he was starting to color with Magic Marker. It says "THE RAINBOW TETRAHEDRON PROJECT."

But I remember the first day of math club, too, when he was sitting in the corner of the room with his sweatshirt pulled over his head, spinning quarters on his desktop. I remember how he always called my name Ron Dull, no matter how many times Sharice and Mr. Collins told him to stop it.

In a way, he was like the tetrahedrons we made, I think to myself. He started out being just a plain old flat sheet of paper — angry and mean paper, most of the time. And then, slowly, he began to turn into someone else, with different sides and angles to who he was, and some of those sides were okay. He was a talented artist and mostly a good Prez, but other parts stayed the same —

Marcel smacks his hands together, making all of us jump out of our sad thoughts. "Why you sitting here doing nothing?" he says, trying to copy James' tough expression and voice. "We got a hundred and fifty pieces to do today. That's the rule. Get up and get busy, girl." He pretends to tug on Sharice's reluctant arm. "I'm the new Prez now and you better do what I sez."

That gets all of us laughing. Even Mr. Collins turns away from the window, smiling a little. Although we can't stand looking at the blinding color red all day, we make one hundred and eighty-one red pieces, a new record. The Prez would be proud of us, Marcel says.

SHARICE

As we get closer to finishing, I start having dreams about what's gonna happen when we do. In most of my dreams, there is this big flash of light when we finish the tetrahedron, and our school isn't a crumbling, peeling-paint building anymore. It's rainbow-colored. (I know this sounds kinda weird.) And our giant pyramid sits on top of the school roof shooting out colors all over the neighborhood, like spotlights. Houses turn shades of red and orange and blue. And people stop their cars and roll down their windows, to take pictures of the sight.

Rhondell just shakes her head when I tell her about my dreams. We're walking home from math club, eating chocolate ice-cream cones from the Super Scoop Ice Cream Shop. It must be about 100 degrees.

"I don't think it will be anything like that," she says.

"How do you know? Nobody's ever finished one before."

Rhondell rolls her eyes. "Sharice . . ."

But it was true — when we put the last piece on the top, none of us knew what would happen after that.

MARCEL

Hope nobody wants a Melt the Roof of Your Mouth barbecue sandwich on Monday at noon, because Willy Q's Open-Every-Day-of-the-Year-Except-Christmas Barbecue is closed. Willy Q says he wouldn't miss the tetrahedron celebration for all the customers in the world.

"You kidding?" I ask him when he tells me on Sunday that he's closing the grill.

"You think I'm lying, Marcel?" He gives me one of his Army stares. Then, a smile splits across his face and he drapes his arm across my shoulders.

"You didn't let the name Williams down and I'm real proud of you for that," he says, squeezing my shoulders hard. "I thought maybe you would, but you didn't, and so we're gonna celebrate the first Williams in the *Guinness Book of World Records.* Who woulda thought it'd be in math?"

"And now" — he snaps his fingers — "do I have a surprise for you. Wait there. Watch the ribs on the top rack."

While I'm keeping an eye on the ribs, he wipes his hands on his apron and goes into the back room. Comes out holding a new suit and tie. Shiny dark gray suit with a metallic silver tie.

"Man, that is sharp," I say. "That for me?"

Willy Q nods. "Cost me a mint."

"It's like being in the Academy Awards or something."

Willy Q laughs. "Not much different," he says.

Then he goes in the back room again. Comes out holding a black T-shirt with the words "Willy Q's BBQ, Cleveland, Ohio" on the front in huge white letters. Phone number just below the name. "This is what I'm wearing," he says. "What do you think?" He squints at the shirt. "Will folks on national TV be able to read our phone number?"

You just gotta admire Willy Q sometimes.

"One more thing I've been working on," he says, going over to one of the metal warming pans. He picks up a barbecue wing, puts it on a paper plate, and brings it over to me. "Try this new sauce."

I pick up the wing with the end of my fingers. Try to cool it off by blowing on it.

"Stop being a baby," Willy Q says. "Just eat it."

The sauce is sweet and kinda spicy, too. Willy Q points to a pan on the counter. "That's my new sauce. Guess what it's called?"

I give up after about ten guesses.

Willy Q smacks his hands together. "Willy Q's Tangy Tetrahedron Barbecue Sauce. A little brown sugar, a little lemon juice, some ketchup, some green celery — you know, a sauce with some *color* to it —

"And of course," he adds with a grin, "a few secret ingredients we won't tell nobody. Because in barbecue you always gotta have a secret or two."

Tangy Tetrahedron Barbecue Sauce

2 tablespoons butter or margarine

3 tablespoons chopped onion

½ cup chopped green celery

2 tablespoons brown sugar

1 tablespoon Worcestershire sauce

2 tablespoons malt vinegar

¼ cup lemon juice

1 teaspoon dry mustard

1 cup red ketchup

Melt butter in a small skillet. Sauté onions and celery in butter until tender. Combine remaining ingredients in a saucepan. Add sautéed onions and celery from the skillet, and bring sauce to a boil. Simmer over low heat for about 10 to 15 minutes, stirring to blend the sweet and tangy colors and flavors.

MR. COLLINS

A few last facts you should know:

1. The tetrahedron project was completed at the end of the first week in July.

2. It took about twenty-one weeks, more than three thousand sheets of paper, and hundreds of glue sticks to finish.

3. The final tetrahedron was close to nine feet tall with 16,383 pieces.

4. The students at Washington Middle School beat the California record by 12,287 pieces — or more if you include the first tetrahedron.

5. But one piece was still missing. . . .

SHARICE

Early on Monday morning (and I mean early), we meet at the school. I think all of us are kinda nervous, you know. Mr. Collins says the media's coming at noon. We stand on the front steps of the school rubbing our goose-bumpy arms, even though it's July and it isn't even cold. As Mr. Collins unlocks the door, Marcel tries to make everybody crack up by saying we're way too early for school in September, but nobody laughs.

We walk down the empty hallway and up the steps, with our shoes echoing loudly on the tiles. To tell you the truth, we look like we're going to church, the way we're all dressed up. Marcel and Mr. Collins are wearing suits. (Marcel looks kinda good, but you didn't hear that from me.) I've got a red skirt and a new blouse that Aunt Asia just bought for me, and I'm wearing a pair of her nice red shoes with Kleenex stuffed in the toes to make them fit.

Me and Aunt Asia even talked Rhondell into doing a little something with her hair, so it is pulled back with a nice puff of curls. She's wearing one of her church dresses, but her mom said no earrings or lipstick. Her mom is strict.

When we get up to the third floor where the math room is, we see the shadow of something near the math room door at the other end of the dark hall. I don't know about anybody else, but my heart starts to thump in my chest, because I remember what happened before (don't even think about it, girl . . .).

But as we get closer, I can see that the shadow is a person sitting in a folding chair next to the door. The person is Mr. Joe, the custodian.

He has a plaid blanket across his lap, and beside him is a classroom desk with a clock, a silver thermos, and a little radio on the top. A baseball bat is leaning against the other side of the desk, I notice, too.

"Have you been here all night?" Mr. Collins asks in a surprised voice.

"Yes sir," Mr. Joe says. He gestures with his thumb at the closed door behind him. "Just makng sure nobody was getting in again. No way." He points to the baseball bat and grins. "Not if I had anything to say about it."

Standing up slowly, the custodian starts folding up the blanket and packing up his things. "Wish I could stay for all the news and pub-licity. I hear there's gonna be a lot," he tells us. "But I'm not much for all that, and I need something to eat, that's what I need. And a bed." He turns to give us one last look before he shuffles down the steps. "You all sure do look nice, though," he says, holding on to the railing and looking back up. "Like grown-ups overnight."

After the custodian leaves, Mr. Collins unlocks the door to the math room and opens it. We don't even turn on the lights at first. We just take in the sight of that huge pyramid shimmering in the dusty morning sunlight coming through the old windows. In the shadowy room, the colors look like they're glowing — purples and blues and greens — as if they aren't paper anymore, but something else. (Not spotlights, but close.)

We walk around the tetrahedron, trying to see it from different angles. The top almost touches the ceiling tiles. With all of the open spaces letting in the light, the triangle pieces look as if they're floating in the air. Glancing through the open spaces, you can see parts of the room and flickers of sunlight and other people's blinking eyes looking back at you.

Nobody says a word for a while because all we want to do is walk around and admire our work, I guess. I get the feeling that everybody is seeing something different, though, as they're walking around. Me, I'm seeing that very first day when I decided to come to the club to get out of sitting in the blue plastic library chairs. (Wasn't my life sure a mess then?) I see James sitting in the corner, and Mr. Collins not having a clue about what he was doing, and Rhondell with her nose in a book not even knowing that she would become my half-cousin, or foster cousin, or whatever it is we are now.

Mr. Collins flips on the overhead lights, making us all squint. "Time to get ready," he says, "before the guests arrive."

RHONDELL

The math room is filled, wall-to-wall, with people. My mom is there, and Aunt Asia is standing in the front with the beauty-shop ladies on their lunch break, and the pastor of the Sanctuary Baptist Church is somewhere in the crowd. Marcel said his daddy even closed the barbecue, just so he could come.

It is hot, even with the windows wide open and bees buzzing in. As I walk up to the front to stand next to the tetrahedron, my heart is pounding and my legs feel like they are trembling enough for everybody to be able to notice them.

Take a deep breath, Rhondell, I hear my mom whispering inside my head. Pretend you are in church, standing up to sing with the choir.

I'm giving the part of the presentation about the math facts we learned. I hear my voice explaining about tetrahedrons and telling the story of Waclaw Sierpinski and what happened to his library. My voice is shaky at first and I keep looking down at the notes on my paper, but then the college words that I've been saving for years start pouring out. *Epiphany. Metamorphosis. Estimation. Determined . . .*

I see Mr. Collins nodding and nodding, so I know I'm doing all right, and I don't look in the direction of the TV cameras at all. I just keep my eyes on the math club and think about those college doors swinging open to let Rhondell Jeffries inside. When I finish, everybody claps and Mr. Collins says, "You can see why we think this young lady is one of our best and brightest," and everybody claps again.

One of the reporters asks us if we had any favorite colors when we were working on the project. The three of us — Mr. Collins, Marcel, and I — look in the direction of Sharice. She waves her hand in the air and says, "Okay, okay, I'm the one who kinda liked purple."

A woman reporter with blond hair and silver

glasses asks us why we decided to participate in the project in the first place. We look at each other, trying to decide who will reply first, and I'm surprised when my voice answers before anybody else and tells the reporter that I hope to go to college someday, and that's why I joined the math club.

"What particular college would you like to attend?" the reporter wants to know, and my heart begins pounding in my chest. Everybody stares at me, waiting for an answer, and I realize that I never saw a name printed on those college doors in my mind. They were just fancy wooden doors with iron hinges and ivy plants trailing along the sides.

"She's planning on going to Harvard," my Aunt Asia calls out in the silence. "Right, Rhondell?" And I can see my mom give her a poke with her elbow to hush up.

"Harvard — or wherever it wouldn't cost too much," I answer quickly, and everybody laughs.

After that, Mr. Collins and Marcel pull a stepladder over to the tetrahedron to add the final piece at the very top, for the cameras. The room is as silent as a church prayer. With the afternoon sun coming through

the windows and Marcel standing on the top of the ladder in his fancy gray suit and silver tie, I have to admit that he looks almost like a movie star.

"I don't know how his daddy afforded to buy a suit like that," Sharice whispers to me.

I can see Marcel's father standing near the doorway of the classroom looking proud, as all of the cameras get ready to show Marcel putting the last red tetrahedron on the top. Mr. Collins helps him add the glue to the piece, he reaches toward the top, and then his hand freezes in midair.

"Just a minute," he says, relaxing his arm and giving his movie-star smile for all the cameras. "I'm not quite ready."

After a minute or so, he raises his arm again, turns to smile at the cameras, and puts the last tetrahedron, number 16,384, at the top. "This one's for James Harris III," he says, and all the cameras flash like spotlights.

JAMES HARRIS III

What's taking them so long? Every day for two weeks, I walk down to the convenience store on the corner, buy a paper, open it up, and look for a picture, and then feel like a fool when nothing is there.

"You looking for somebody you know?" the old store manager asks me.

"Some friends," I tell him, and each day, he waits until I page through the whole paper piece by piece, even the sports section, before he says, "Not there today?"

"Nope."

"Maybe tomorrow," he always answers, and then he pushes a peppermint candy or a piece of chocolate or something across the counter toward me.

"Here — consolation prize," he says, and after two weeks, I get the feeling that he's starting to think I'm just coming in the store for the consolation prize. When I walk through the door, I can see his head shake back and forth a little.

"You know," he tells me one evening when I stop by, "I've heard that getting in the newspaper isn't all that easy. Too much news to cover these days, and so the reporters have to pick and choose. . . ."

I tell him that they'll be in the paper.

The old man's head shakes back and forth again.

And then, one Tuesday night, I open up the newspaper and there it is.

"No way," I say out loud, and the old man slams the cash drawer shut and comes hurrying over from behind the counter to see what I'm looking at. He pulls a paper off the stack and turns to the same page I'm on.

A photograph fills almost half the page. Page 4A. "Students Break Math Record!" the headline says. The photo shows Marcel, who doesn't even look like Marcel, wearing a sharp-looking suit and tie like he's a big star or something. He's standing on a ladder, grinning like a fool, as he's getting ready to put the last tetrahedron on the top.

I squint at the picture, trying to tell if the tetrahedron is red or not. Better be red, Marcel. At the side of the picture, Mr. Collins and Rhondell and Sharice are standing there, watching. Only person missing is me.

But then I see the first sentence at the beginning of the article: "'This one's for James,' seventh grader Marcel Williams says, as he proudly puts the final touches on the 16,384-piece tetrahedron built by a group of inner-city kids in Cleveland, Ohio."

"I'm the James he's talking about here," I tell the store manager. "Look at that first sentence." I point at the words. "That's me."

The store manager's eyes go from the newspaper to me and back again. "You're a math champion?" he asks, like he doesn't quite believe I'm telling the truth.

"That's right." I nod. "My name is gonna be in the *Guinness Book of World Records* someday."

The old man sticks out his hand. "Well, let me shake your hand, son," he says in a formal voice. "I've never met anybody who had a world record before."

And then he lays the paper on the store counter and carefully cuts out the article and the photograph. "This is a real accomplishment," he says while he's cutting. "You should be real proud of yourself." He asks me to put my autograph on the article so when I'm famous someday, he can show people my name and say he met me in his store.

I sign my name across the bottom of the article in big scrawling artist letters. But before the manager tapes the article to the front of the counter where everybody can see it, I add one more thing.

I add a drawing of myself standing next to Sharice and Rhondell and Mr. Collins, with an arrow pointing to my head. I write my name above the arrow: James Harris III.

Just so everybody knows I was there.

MR. COLLINS

One final fact to remember about tetrahedrons:

Because of its repeating pattern, the tetrahedron structure can expand to infinity. So, in theory, you can keep adding more and more tetrahedrons forever. . . .

Our math teacher Mr. Collins says that next year Washington Middle School is gonna build something even bigger, something even more amazing.

So if you are driving down Washington Boulevard someday, past the smoky good smells of Willy Q's Barbecue, past the Style R Us hair salon where they do nails like nobody's business, past the eye-popping red doors of the Sanctuary Baptist Church, and you get to a dead end — LOOK UP!

You just might see a forty-foot-tall silver and gold tetrahedron on the roof of our school building spinning to rap music.

Mr. Collins says nothing is impossible.

You want to fold silver or gold?

AUTHOR'S NOTE

In 2002, a group of students at Alexander Hamilton School, an urban middle school in Cleveland, Ohio, completed what is called a "Stage 7" Sierpinski tetrahedron. They were one of two schools in Cleveland to attempt to build a structure of this record-breaking size and complexity.

The Alexander Hamilton team named their tetrahedron "The Rainbow Connection" because of the eye-catching and intricate rainbow-color pattern they created. The students worked at home, through their summer vacation, and after school to assemble the 16,384 smaller tetrahedrons needed to build the larger structure.

During the original project, the team used an Ellison paper-cutting machine with a custom-made die to cut out the small tetrahedron shapes. Although this saved one step in the laborious process, each one of the 16,384 pieces still had to be individually folded, glued, and joined together by hand, just as the characters describe. Hot-glue guns, which are often used for model-building and craft projects, proved to be the best tool for gluing the pieces and sections together, and the team assembled the large tetrahedron in stages.

During the writing of *All of the Above,* I read everything I could find about tetrahedrons — and also polished up some of my long-dormant math skills. I was often amazed by the connections between math and life. Mr. Collins' facts about tetrahedrons are based on the actual properties of the structure — and yes, the tetrahedron really can be expanded to infinity. But I'm not planning to try that anytime soon!

One mathematical note from Mr. Collins: Although some of the characters in the story use the terms "pyramid" and "tetrahedron" interchangeably, keep in mind that a tetrahedron is a special type of pyramid with a triangular base. Other types of pyramids with bases of different shapes would not be tetrahedrons.

Professor Waclaw Sierpinski, who is mentioned in the novel, is the person who first studied the properties of the tetrahedron as a flat, plane figure called a "gasket." As Rhondell learns, he was a renowned math professor in Warsaw, Poland, during the early part of the twentieth century. Even though his house and personal library were destroyed by the Nazis during the Warsaw uprising of 1944, he went on to publish more than 700 research papers and fifty books in his lifetime.

The other characters, places, and events in this novel are fictional; however, I tried to capture the spirit and determination of the students who were part of the record-breaking 2002 team, and give readers a glimpse into the urban community where they live. The California school that built the “Stage 6” tetrahedron is not based on a particular school; however, several schools in the United States have built Stage 6 tetrahedrons of various heights.

I first saw the stunning rainbow tetrahedron during a visit to Alexander Hamilton School in late 2002. The magical sight caught my imagination. Later, I had the chance to talk to some of the past and present team members. At that time, the students were already hard at work on a new construction — an inverted Stage 6 tetrahedron, designed to spin on one of its points and match the colors of the Ohio flag for the state's bicentennial year.

However, Alexander Hamilton Middle School closed its old and well-worn doors three years later, and the school's tetrahedron projects ended. Its former students are now enrolled in other schools throughout Cleveland. The Alexander Hamilton team did submit their record to Guinness World Records for consideration. Although they did not receive a reply, the team and their teachers still believe that their 2002 tetrahedron set a math record. But as one student told me — it was just fun to be part of something.

— *Shelley Pearsall*

ACKNOWLEDGMENTS

I would like to gratefully acknowledge my editor, Jennifer Hunt, for bringing this story and its characters to life. A special thanks to Principal Hiawatha Shivers, and to the former tetrahedron team at Alexander Hamilton School and their always gracious teachers, James Wallace and Dianne Marsh, who answered my tetrahedron questions and shared their expertise with me. Thank you to math teachers Laura and Richard Little, as well as local students Cameron Granger and Artia Gunn, for reading early drafts of *All of the Above.* And finally, I can't forget to mention Bill and Sandi Pearsall, and my husband, Mike. Without their culinary advice and assistance in preparing (and tasting!) the recipes for this book, Willy Q and I would both be singing the blues.

HOW TO BUILD A TETRAHEDRON

A tetrahedron is a type of pyramid, made up of four triangles of equal size. Make a copy of this tetrahedron model. Color it, cut it out, and glue or tape it together to make your own tetrahedron.

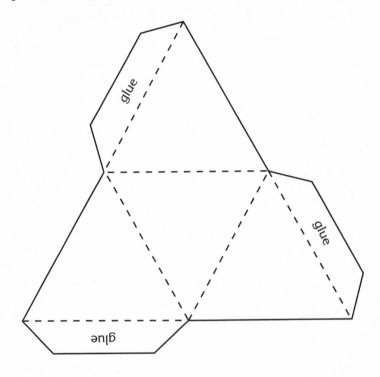

Next, tape your tetrahedrons together in sets of four to form larger tetrahedrons. These can be combined to form even larger tetrahedrons, if desired.

READER'S GUIDE

1. James Harris III dislikes school and anything connected with it. How does James's home life affect his attitude toward school? How does Mr. Collins's approach to James pull him into the project? How does James's attitude toward himself change as he becomes involved in the project? How do others' opinions of James change?

2. Although Mr. Collins has the idea for the tetrahedron project, he doesn't really expect that any of his students will want to participate (page 18). What is the motivation for each of the students to become involved in the project? How does Mr. Collins's lack of expertise in running a club help unite the students to work toward a common goal?

3. James and Sharice both feel responsible for the destruction of the project. How does that guilt affect them? What actions do they take as a result of their feelings of responsibility? How do their guilt and shame affect the group and the completion of the project?

4. What contributions, both positive and negative, do the adults make in the lives of James, Rhondell, Marcel, and Sharice? How do the actions of the adults affect the lives of the teens?

5. Rhondell and her aunt Asia are the ones who find Sharice after her emotional breakdown. How does this one event alter the course of many lives?

6. The author reveals that the role of each of the four students in the group mirror a tetrahedron in some way. Discuss the role each character plays in the group. How do each character's personality traits determine how he or she is like a tetrahedron? Reread Mr. Collins's words about tetrahedrons on pages 3, 99, 199, and 237 to gain some insight.

7. In the end, how does the project change Rhondell, Marcel, James, Sharice, and Mr. Collins? Predict what the future may hold for these characters.

What's the Meaning of Life? Find out inside this book...

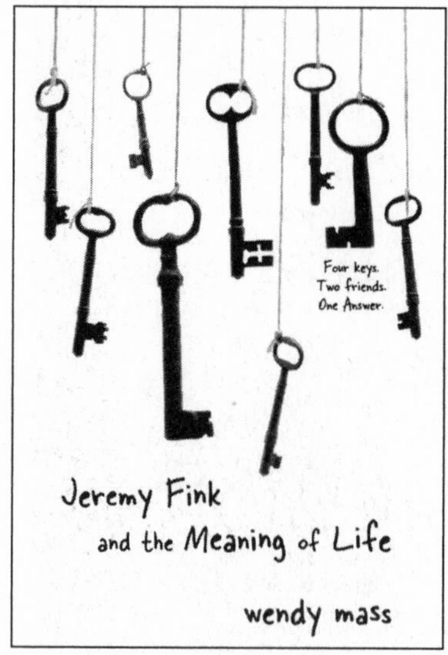

Jeremy Fink and the Meaning of Life

by Wendy Mass

Join Jeremy Fink and his friend Lizzy as they set out on incredible adventures in search of keys that unlock a box that just might contain the meaning of life.

www.lb-kids.com

Available wherever books are sold.

Hachette Book Group USA

The Harlem Renaissance seen through the eyes of a bold young girl

Celeste's Harlem Renaissance

by Eleanora E. Tate

Celeste is not thrilled to trade in her home in North Carolina for big-city life with a famous actress—her Aunt Valentina. While experiencing the magic of the Harlem Renaissance, Celeste soon learns that it is as much grit as glamour. A passionate writer, talented violinist, and an aspiring doctor, Celeste eventually faces a choice between ambition and loyalty that will change her forever.

www.lb-kids.com

Available wherever books are sold.

Hachette Book Group USA

• Little, Brown Books for Young Readers • Little, Brown Books for Young Readers •

• Little, Brown Books for Young Readers • Little, Brown Books for Young Readers •

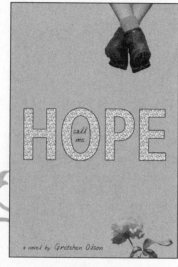